Helen Hunt Jackson

Nelly's Silver Mine - A Story of Colorado Life

Helen Hunt Jackson

Nelly's Silver Mine - A Story of Colorado Life

ISBN/EAN: 9783744791212

Printed in Europe, USA, Canada, Australia, Japan

Cover: Foto ©Andreas Hilbeck / pixelio.de

More available books at **www.hansebooks.com**

ROB AND NELLY.

A STORY OF COLORADO LIFE.

By H. H.,

AUTHOR OF "BITS OF TRAVEL," "BITS OF TRAVEL AT HOME,"
"BITS OF TALK ABOUT HOME MATTERS," "BITS OF
TALK FOR YOUNG FOLKS," "VERSES."

———oo⫶⚬⫶oo———

BOSTON:

ROBERTS BROTHERS.

1878.

CONTENTS.

NELLY'S SILVER MINE.

CHAPTER I.

CHRISTMAS-DAY IN NELLY'S NEW-ENGLAND HOME.

IT was Christmas morning; and Nelly March and her brother Rob were lying wide awake in their beds, wondering if it would do for them to get up and look in their stockings to see what Santa Claus had brought them. Nelly and Rob were twins; but you would never have thought so, when you looked at them, for Nelly was half a head taller than Rob, and a good deal heavier. She had always been well; but Rob had always been a delicate child. He was ill now with a bad sore throat, and had been shut up in the house for ten days. This was the reason that he and Nelly were in bed at six o'clock this Christmas morning, instead of scampering all about the house, and waking everybody up with their shouts of delight over their presents. When they went to bed the night before, Mrs. March had said: " Now, Rob, you must promise me not to get out of bed till it is broad daylight, and the house is thoroughly warm. You will certainly take cold, if you get up in the cold room."

" Mamma," said Nelly, " I needn't stay in bed just because Rob has to, need I? I can take his presents out of the stocking, and carry them to him."

"You shan't, either," said Rob, fretfully. "I want to take them out myself; and you're real mean not to wait for me, Nell. 'Tisn't half so much fun for just one. Shan't she stay in bed too, mamma, as long as I have to?"

Mrs. March looked at Nelly, and smiled. She knew Nelly had not thought Rob would care any thing about her getting up first, or she would never have proposed it. Nelly was always ready to give up to Rob, much more so than was for his good.

"Nelly can do as she pleases, Rob," she answered. "I don't think it would be fair for me to compel her to stay in bed because you have a sore throat: do you?"

But Rob did not answer. He was not a very generous boy, and all he was thinking of now was his own pleasure.

"Say, Nell," he cried, "you won't get up, will you, till I can? Don't: I'll think you're real unkind if you do."

"No, no, Rob," said Nelly. "Indeed I won't. I don't care. It will be all the longer to think about it, and that's almost the best part of it." And Nelly threw her arms around Rob's neck and kissed him.

."It's too bad, you darling," she said, "you have to be sick on Christmas-day. I won't have any pudding, either, if you don't want me to."

Mrs. March was an Englishwoman, and had lived in England till she was married, and she always had on Christmas-day a real English plum-pudding with brandy turned over it, and set on fire just before the pudding was brought to the table, so that when it came in the blue and red and yellow flames were all blazing up high over it, and the waitress had to turn her head away not to breathe the heat from the flames.

You would have thought it would have made Rob ashamed to have Nelly propose to go without pudding because he could not eat any, but I don't think it did. All he said was, —

"Don't be a goose, Nell. That's quite different."

Just before they went to sleep, Sarah, the cook, went past their door, and Nelly called to her : —

"Sarah, mamma says we mustn't get up to-morrow morning till the house is very warm. Couldn't you get up very early and start the furnace fire ?"

"Why, yes, Miss Nelly, I can do that easy enough, sure ; but where'll you be sleeping ?"

"Just where we always do, Sarah," replied Nelly, much surprised at this question.

"Well, miss, I'll be up long before light and get the house as warm as toast by the time you can see to tell the toes from the heels of your stockings," said Sarah. "Good-night, Miss Nelly. Good-night, Master Rob."

"What could she have meant asking where we'd be sleeping?" said Rob.

"I'm sure I don't know," said Nelly; "it's very queer. We've never slept anywhere but in these two beds since we were babies. I don't know what's got into her head. It's the queerest thing I ever knew. I guess she was sleepy," and in a few moments both the children were fast asleep.

Rob was the first to wake up. It was not much past midnight.

"Nelly," he whispered. No answer.

Twice he called: still no answer. There was not a sound to be heard except the loud ticking of the high clock at the head of the stairs. Presently there came a rustle and quick low steps, and his mother stood by his bed.

"What do you want, my dear little boy?" she said. "Is your throat worse?"

"No; isn't it time to get up?" said Rob. "Hasn't Sarah made the fire?"

"Oh, mercy!" exclaimed Mrs. March. "Is that all? Why Rob! it isn't anywhere near morning. You must go to sleep again, child; it is a terribly cold night," and she tucked the bed-clothes tight around him, and ran back to her own room.

"I don't care," said Rob. "I'll just stay awake. I don't believe it'll be very long;" but before he knew it he was fast asleep again. The next time he waked, it had begun to be light, or rather a little less dark. He could see the outline of the window at the foot of his bed, and he could see Nelly's bedstead, which was on the opposite side of the room.

"Nelly," he called again.

"I'm awake," said Nelly.

"Why didn't you speak?" said Rob.

"I was thinking," replied Nelly. "Sarah hasn't gone down yet."

"Pshaw," said Rob, "she must have. She said she'd go long before light. She went before you were awake."

"It's awful cold," whispered Nelly; "I can't keep even my hands out of bed. I'm going to jump up and see if any hot air comes in at the register." So saying, she jumped out of bed, ran to the register, and held her hands above it.

"Cold as Greenland, Rob," she said, "Sarah can't have made the fire. I don't believe she is up."

"Oh, dear," said Rob, "every thing all goes wrong when I'm sick. I think it's too mean I have to be the sick one just because we're twins. I heard a lady say once to mamma, — she didn't think I heard but I did, — 'Weren't you very sorry, Mrs. March, to have twins? You know they can't ever both be strong. Your Rob, now, he looks very sickly.' Civil, that was, to mamma, wasn't it? I was so mad I could have flung my ball at her old wise head. But I think it must be true, because mamma answered her real gentle, but with her voice all trembly, and she said, 'Yes, I know that is usually said to be so; but we hope to prove the contrary. Rob grows stronger every year, and he and his sister take so much comfort together, I can never regret that they were born twins.' But I do: I think it's a shame to make a fellow sick all his life that way. I say, Nell, I don't believe you'd mind it half as much as I do. Girls are different from boys. I think it would have been better for you to be the sick one than me. Don't you? Say, Nell!"

This was a hard question for poor Nelly.

"Oh, Rob!" she said, "I don't want to be selfish about it. I'd be willing to take turns and be sick half the times; or some more than half, — I guess three-quarters: but I think you ought to have a little."

"But don't you see, Nell, it can't be that way," interrupted Rob; "it can't be that way with twins. It's got to be one sick one and one strong one. That's what that lady said, and mamma said she'd heard so too; and I think it's just as mean as any thing. They might have let us be born as much as three days apart, or a week: that wouldn't have made any difference in the fun; we could have played just as well, and, besides, we'd have had two birthdays to keep then, don't you see?"

"I don't think that would be so nice, Rob," said Nelly, "as to have one together. That would be like my getting up now, before you do, and having my stocking all to myself, and you didn't want me to do that."

"Pshaw, Nell," replied Rob, impatiently as before: "that's quite different; but girls never see things."

Nelly laughed out loud. "I don't know why: we have as many eyes as boys have. I see lots more things in the woods than you do, always."

"Oh, not that sort of things," answered Rob; "not that kind of seeing; not with your eyes: I mean to see with your — well, I don't know what it is you see with, the kind I mean; but don't you know mamma often says to papa about something that's got to be done, 'don't you see? don't you see?' and she doesn't mean that he is to look with his eyes: that's the kind I mean. Now where is that Sarah?" he exclaimed suddenly, sitting bolt upright in bed in his excitement. "It's as cold as out-doors here, and there isn't a creature stirring in the house, and it's broad daylight."

"Oh, Rob, do lie down and cover yourself up," cried Nelly. "You're a naughty boy, and you'll have another sore throat as sure's you're alive. It isn't broad daylight nor any thing like it. I can't but just see the stockings"

"Can't but just see them!" said Rob. "Didn't I tell you girls couldn't see any thing? Why I can see them just as plain, just as plain as if I was in 'em! Ain't they big, Nell? I know what's in yours, for one thing."

"Oh, Rob! do you? Tell me!" exclaimed Nell.

"I can't," replied Rob. "I promised mamma I wouldn't. But it's something you've wanted awfully."

"A doll, Rob! oh, is it a doll with eyes that can shut? oh, say, Rob!" pleaded Nelly. "It's long past the time I ought to have had it, if you hadn't been sick: you might tell me. I'll tell you what one of your things is if you will."

"I don't want to know, Nell," replied Rob, "and you needn't tease me, for I'll never tell you: not if they lie abed in this house all day. Dear me! where can Sarah be? I'm going to call mamma."

"You can't make her hear, Rob," answered Nelly. "They shut the doors ever so long ago. They were talking about something they didn't want us to hear."

"How do you know?" said Rob.

"Because I heard some of what they said, and I coughed so that they might know I was awake," replied Nelly. "Oh, Rob, it is awful!" and Nelly began to sob.

"What's awful? what is it, Nell? Tell me, can't you?" said Rob, in an excited tone.

"No, Rob, I'm not going to tell you any thing about it," replied Nelly. "It wouldn't be fair, because they didn't want us to know. It'll be time enough when it comes."

"When what comes?" shouted Rob, thoroughly

roused now. " I do say, Nell March, you 're enough
to try a saint. What did you tell me any thing about
it for? I 'll tell mamma the minute she comes in, and
tell her you listened. Oh, shame, shame, shame on a
listener ! "

" Rob, you 're just as mean as you can be," cried
Nelly. " I didn't listen, and mamma knows very well
I wouldn't do such a thing. Of course I couldn't help
hearing when both doors were open, and I coughed out
loud as soon as I thought about it that most likely they
didn't mean we should know any thing about it. I
heard papa say something about the children, and
mamma said, ' we won't tell them till it is all settled,'
and then I gave a great big cough, and she got up and
shut both the doors ; so now, Rob, you see I wasn't a
listener. I wouldn't listen for any thing : mamma said
once it was the very meanest kind of a lie in the whole
world ! Mamma knows I wouldn't do it, and you can
just tell her what you like, you old hateful boy."

This was a very unhappy sort of talk for Christmas
morning, was it not? But both Rob and Nelly were
tired and cold, and their patience was all worn out. It
really was a hard trial for two children only twelve
years old to have to lie still in bed, hour after hour,
Christmas morning, waiting for their presents ; it grew
slowly lighter and lighter ; each moment they could see
the big stockings plainer and plainer ; they hung on the
outside of the closet door on two big hooks, where were
usually hung the children's school hats. One stocking
was gray, and one was white. I must tell you about
these stockings, for they were very droll. They were
larger than the largest boots you ever saw, and would

reach the whole length of a man's leg, way above his knee, as far up as they could go. They belonged to the children's grandfather March. He was one of the queerest old gentlemen that ever was known, I think. He lived in a city a great many miles away from the village where Mr. and Mrs. March lived, but he used to spend his winters with them. About six weeks before he arrived, big boxes used to begin to come. There was no railroad to this village: every thing had to come on coaches or big luggage wagons. Early in November, old Mr. March's boxes always began to arrive at his son's house. When Rob and Nelly saw Mr. Earle's big express wagon drive up to the back gate, they always exclaimed, " Oh, there are grandpa's things coming!" and they would run out to see them unloaded. You would have thought that old Mr. March supposed there was nothing to eat in all the village, to see what quantities of food he sent up. But the most peculiar thing about it was that he sent such queer things. He was as queer about his food as he was about every thing else, and he did not eat the things other people ate. For instance, he never ate butter; he ate fresh olive oil on every thing; and he had a notion that no olive oil was brought to this country to sell which was fit to eat. He had an intimate friend who was an old sea captain, and used to sail to Smyrna; this sea captain used to bring over for him large boxes of bottles of olive oil every spring and autumn; and two or three of these boxes he would use up in the course of the winter. He never used more than half of the oil in a bottle: after it had been opened a few days, he did not like it; he would smell it very carefully each day, and, by the third or fourth day, he would shove the bottle from him, and say, "Bah! throw the stuff away! throw it away! it isn't fit to eat!" Mrs. March had great trouble in disposing of these half bottles of oil; everybody in the neighborhood took them, and very glad people were to get them too, for the oil was delicious; but there were enough for two or three villages of the size of Mayfield. These sweet-oil boxes had curious letters on them in scarlet and blue, and the bottles were all rolled up in a sort of shining silver paper, which Rob and Nelly used to keep to cover boxes with. It was very pretty, so they were always glad when they saw a big pile of the olive-oil boxes. Then there were also boxes full of bottles of pepper-sauce; this came in big black bottles, and the little peppers showed red through the glass; the smallest drop of this pepper-sauce made your mouth burn like fire, but this queer old gentleman used to pour it over every thing he ate. The big bottle of pepper-sauce and the big bottle of olive oil were always put by his plate, and he poured first from one and then from the other, until the food on his plate was nearly swimming in the strange mixture. Salt fish was another of his favorite dishes, and he brought up every autumn huge piles of them. They came in flat packages, tied up with coarse cord; when Mr. Earle threw them down to the ground from the top of his wagon a strong and disagreeable odor rose in the air, and Rob and Nelly used to exclaim, "Groans for the salt fish! groans for the salt fish! Why didn't you lose it off the wagon, Mr. Earle?"

"It wouldn't have made any odds, miss," Mr. Earle

used to reply. "The old gentleman 'd have made me go back for more." Besides the salt fish, there were little kegs full of what are called "tongues and sounds," put up in salt brine; these are the tongues and the intestines of fish; there were also jars of oysters and of clams, and a barrel of the sort of bread sailors eat at sea, which is called hard-tack. Now, after hearing about the extraordinary food this old gentleman used to bring for his own use, you will be prepared to believe what I have to tell you about his big stockings. He had just as queer notions about his bed and all his arrangements for sleeping, as he had about his food. No woman was ever allowed to make his bed. He always made it himself. Except in the very hottest weather, he would not have any sheets on it, only the very finest of flannel blankets; a great many of them; and he never wore any night-gown; he believed they were very unwholesome things.

"Why don't animals put on night-gowns to sleep in?" he used to say; one might very well have replied to him, "Animals don't crawl in between blankets either, and if you are going to be simply an animal, you must go without any clothes day and night both." However, he was a very irritable old gentleman, and nobody ever argued with him about any thing. Mr. and Mrs. March let him do in all ways exactly as he liked, and never contradicted him, for he loved them very much, in his way, and was very good to them.

Of all his queer ways and queer things, I think these big stockings were the queerest. As I said, he never wore any night-gown in bed, but he was over seventy years old, and, in spite of all his theories, his feet and legs would sometimes get cold: so he went to a tailor and got an exact pattern of a tight-fitting leg to a pair of trousers; then he took this to a woman who knit stockings to sell, and he unrolled his leg pattern before her, and said: —

"Do you see that leg, ma'am? Can you knit a stocking leg that shape and length?"

The woman did not know what to make of him

"Why sir," said she, "you'd never want a stocking-leg that long?"

"I didn't ask you what I wanted, ma'am," growled the old gentleman, "I asked you what you could do. Can you knit a stocking-leg that length and shape?"

"Why, yes, sir, I suppose I can," she replied, much cowed by his fierce manner.

"Well, then, knit me six pairs, three gray and three white. There's the pattern for the foot," and he threw down an old sock of his on the table, and was striding away.

The woman followed him.

"But, sir," she said timidly, "I couldn't knit these for the price of ordinary stockings. I'm afraid you wouldn't be willing to pay what they would cost. It would be like knitting a pair of pantaloons, sir, — indeed it would."

Old Mr. March always carried a big gold-headed cane; and, when he was angry, he lifted it from the ground and shook the gold knob as fast as he could right in people's faces. He lifted it now, and shook the gold knob so close in the woman's face, that she retreated rapidly toward the door.

"I didn't say any thing about money: did I, ma'am?

Knit those stockings : I don't care what they cost," he cried.

"But I thought," she interrupted.

"I didn't ask you to think, did I?" said Mr. March, speaking louder and louder. "You'll never earn any money thinking. Knit those stockings, ma'am, and the sooner the better," and the old gentleman walked out of the house muttering.

"Dear me, what a very hasty old gentleman!" said the woman to herself. "I'll go over and ask Mrs. March, and make sure it's all right." So the next day she went to see Mrs. March, who explained to her all the old gentleman's whims about sleeping, and that he was quite willing and able to pay whatever the queer stockings would cost. In a very few weeks, the stockings were all done ; and the old gentleman was so pleased with them that he gave the woman an extra five-dollar bill, besides the sum she had charged for knitting them. And this was the way that there came to be hanging up in Nelly's and Rob's chamber two such huge stockings on this Christmas morning of which I am telling you. They were splendid stockings for Christmas stockings ! It did really seem as if you never would get to the bottom of them. The children used to lay them down on the floor, and run around them, and pull out thing after thing. Mrs. March sometimes wished they were not quite so large ; it took a great deal to fill them : but, after having once used them, she had not the heart to go back to the ordinary-sized stocking, for it would have been such a disappointment to the children. She used them, first, one Christmas when Nelly's chief present was a big doll about two feet and a half tall, which wore real baby clothes like a live baby. This was so big it could not go into a common stocking, and Mrs. March happened then to think of her father's. The old gentleman was delighted to have them used for the purpose, and stood by laughing hard, while Mrs. March put the things in.

"Ha! ha!" he said, "the old stockings are good for more than one thing: aren't they?"

But we are leaving Nelly and Rob a long time in bed waiting for their Christmas presents. It grew lighter and lighter, and still there was no sound in the house, and the room grew no warmer. Rob was so thoroughly cross that he lay back on his pillow, with his eyes shut and his lips pouting out, and would not speak a word. In vain Nelly tried to comfort him, or to interest him. He would not speak. Even Nelly's patience was nearly worn out. At last the door of their mother's room opened, and she came out in her warm red wrapper.

"Why, you dear patient little children!" she exclaimed; "are you in bed yet? this is too bad. What does make your room so cold!" "Why, bless me!" she exclaimed, going to the register, "no heat is coming up here; what does this mean?"

"I don't think Sarah has gone down yet: I've been awake a long time, mamma," said Nelly.

"A thousand years, it is," exclaimed Rob, "or more, that we've been lying awake here waiting: Sarah's the meanest girl alive."

"Hush, hush, Rob!" said Mrs. March. "Don't speak so. Perhaps she is ill. I will go and see. But you may have your presents on the bed;" and, going to the closet, she took down first the gray stocking, which was for Rob, and carried it and laid it on his bed. Then she carried the white one, and laid it on Nelly's bed.

"Oh, goody, goody!" they both cried at once. "You're real good mamma;" and in one second more all four of the little arms were plunging into the depths of the big stockings.

"You've earned your presents this time," said Mrs. March, as she pinned warm blankets round the children's shoulders. "I think you are really very brave little children to be quiet so many hours. It is after eight o'clock. I am afraid Sarah is ill."

Then she went upstairs and the children heard her knocking at Sarah's door, and calling, "Sarah! Sarah!" Presently she came down very quickly, and went into her room; in a few minutes, she went back again, and Mr. March went with her. Then the children heard more knocking, and their papa calling very loud, "Sarah! Sarah! open the door this moment." Then came a loud crash.

"Papa's smashed the door in," said Rob. "Good enough for her, lazy old thing, to sleep so Christmas morning! I hope mamma won't give her any present." Nelly did not speak. She had scarcely heard the knocking or the calls: she was so absorbed in looking at her new doll, — a wax doll with eyes that could open and shut. To have such a doll as this had been the great desire of Nelly's heart for years. There was also a beautiful little leather trunk full of clothes for the doll, and four little band-boxes, each with a hat or bonnet in it. There was a bedstead for her to sleep in, and a pretty red arm-chair for her to sit in, and a play piano, which could make a little real music. Then there were four beautiful new books, and ever so many pretty little paper boxes with different sorts of candy in them: all white candy; Mrs. March never gave her children any colored candies.

Rob had a beautiful kaleidoscope, mounted with a handle to turn it round by; it was about as long as Nelly's doll, and as he drew it out he couldn't imagine what it was. Then he had a geographical globe, and a paint-box, and four new volumes of Mayne Reid's stories, and the same number of boxes of candy which Nelly had.

You never saw two happier children than Rob and Nelly were for the next half-hour. They forgot all about the cold, about Sarah, and about having had to wait so long. For half an hour, all that was to be heard in the room were exclamations from one to the other, such as: —

"Oh, Nell! see this picture!"

"Oh, Rob! look at this lovely bonnet!"

"Nell, this is the splendidest one of all."

"This doll is bigger than Mary Pratt's: I know it is. Oh, Rob! don't you suppose it must have cost a lot of money?"

At last Mrs. March came back into their room, looking very much annoyed.

"Well, children," she said, "we're going to have a droll sort of Christmas. Sarah is so fast asleep we can't wake her up, and your papa thinks she must be drunk. We shall have to cook our Christmas dinner ourselves. How will you like that?"

"Oh, splendid, mamma, splendid! Let us get **right up** now," cried both the children, eagerly laying down their playthings.

"**No,**" said Mrs. March. "Rob must not **get up yet: it** is too cold; but you may get up, Nell, and help me **get** breakfast. Can you **leave** your new dolly?"

"Oh, yes, mamma!" cried Nelly, "indeed I can." **And** laying the dolly carefully between the bed-clothes with her head on the pillow, she kissed her, and said, "Good-by, dear Josephine Harriet: you won't be very long alone. I will come back soon."

Rob burst out laughing. "What a name!" he said, mimicking Nelly. "Josephine Harriet! whoever heard such a name?"

"I think it's a real pretty name, Rob," replied Nelly. "Boys don't know any thing about dolls' names. **Be-**sides, she is named for two people: **Josephine is** for that poor, dear, beautiful Empress that mamma told us **about; I**'ve always thought since then if ever I had a doll handsome enough, **I'd** name her after her. And Harriet is after Hatty Pratt. I love Hatty dearly, **and** she's named two dolls after **me.**"   .

"Well, **I** shall **call** the doll the Empress, then," **said** Rob, in a tone intended **to be** very sarcastic.

"Yes; **so shall I,**" replied Nelly: "I thought of that. It will sound very nice."

Rob **looked** a little disappointed. He thought it **would tease Nelly** to have her doll called "**The Em-**press."

"**No:** I think I'll call her Mrs. Napoleon," said he.

"Well," said Nelly, "I suppose that would **do,**" — Nelly had not the least idea that Rob was **making fun**

of her, — "but I don't believe they ever called the real
Empress so. I don't remember it in the story. I'll
ask mamma. I think Mrs. Napoleon is a beautiful
name: don't you, Rob?"

By this time Rob was too deep in the "Cliff Climbers"—one of his new books—to answer; and Nelly
was all dressed ready to go downstairs. As she left
the room, Rob called out: —

"I say, Nell, tell mamma I don't want any breakfast. I'd rather stay in bed and read this story."

It was a very droll Christmas-day, but the children
always said it was one of the very pleasantest they ever
spent. It turned out that the cook was really in a
heavy drunken sleep. She had been partly under the
influence of liquor when she went to bed the night before. That was the reason she had asked Nelly where
they would be sleeping in the morning. She did not
know what she was saying when she said that. Mr.
March went and brought a doctor to look at her in her
sleep, for they were afraid it might be apoplexy; but
the doctor only laughed, and said: —

"Pshaw! The woman's drunk. Let her alone.
She'll wake up by noon."

Mr. and Mrs. March felt very unhappy about this,
for Sarah had lived with them two years, and had never
done such a thing before. She did not wake up by
noon, as the doctor had said. She did not wake up till
nearly night; and, when she went downstairs, there
were Mrs. March and Nelly and Rob in the kitchen,
all at work. Mrs. March and Nelly were washing
the dishes, and Rob was cleaning the knives. They
had cooked the dinner and eaten it, and cleared every

thing away. Sarah dropped into a chair, and looked from one to the other without speaking.

"Hullo!" said Rob, "you cooked us a nice Christmas dinner: didn't you? We'd have never had any if we'd waited for you."

"Do you feel sick now, Sarah?" said good-hearted little Nelly.

Sarah did not speak. Her brain was not yet clear. She looked helplessly from Mrs. March to the children, and from the children to Mrs. March. Then she rose and walked unsteadily to the table, and tried to take the towel out of Nelly's hands.

"Lit me wipe the dishes," she said: "my head's better now."

"No, Sarah," said Mrs. March, sternly. "Go back to your room. You're not yet fit to be on your feet."

The children wondered very much that their mamma, who was usually so kind, should speak so sternly to Sarah; but they asked no questions. They were too full of the excitement of doing all the work, and looking at their presents, and talking about them. The hours flew by so quickly that it was dark before they knew it; and, when they went to bed, they both exclaimed together: —

"Oh, Nell!" and "Oh, Rob! hasn't it been a splendid Christmas!"

They remembered it for a great many years, for it was the last Christmas they spent in their pleasant home at Mayfield.

CHAPTER II.

A TALK ABOUT LEAVING MAYFIELD.

THE next day a big snow fell. It was one of those snows which fall so thick and fast and fine, that when you look out of the windows it seems as if great white sheets were being let down from the skies. When Rob first waked and saw this snow falling, he exclaimed : —

"Hurrah! here's a bully snow-storm! Now we'll get some snow-balling. Say, Nell, won't you help me build a real big snow-fort with high walls that we can stand behind, and fire snow-balls at the boys?"

"Oh, Rob!" said Nelly, "I'm afraid mamma won't let you play in the snow yet: your throat isn't well enough; but by next week I think it will be. We'll have snow right along now all winter."

"Oh, dear!" said Rob, fretfully: "there it is again. I can't ever do any thing I want to."

"Why, Rob," replied Nelly, "aren't you ashamed of yourself, with that lovely kaleidoscope and all those books? I shouldn't think you'd want to go out to-day. I'm sure I don't. I'd rather stay at home with Mrs. Napoleon and the rest of my dolls all day than go anywhere, — that is, unless it was to take a sleigh-ride.

Mamma said perhaps, if it **stopped snowing,** papa might take us on a sleigh-ride **this afternoon.**"

"Did she?" exclaimed Rob; "oh, bully!" "But then I suppose I can't go," he added, in a quite altered tone.

"Oh, yes! you can," answered Nelly, "**mamma** said so. I heard her tell papa it would do **you good to go** well wrapped up."

"I hate to be bundled up so," said **Rob.** "It's as hot as fury; and, besides, it makes the boys laugh; last time I went out so, Ned Saunders he stood on his father's **store** steps, when we stopped there, — mamma wanted to buy a broom, — and Ned called out, ' By-by, baby bunting, where's your little rabbit skin?' I shan't **go** if mamma makes me wear that red shawl, so!" and Rob's face was the picture of misery.

Nelly's cheeks flushed at the thought of the insulting **taunt to Rob** which was conveyed **in** that quotation **from** Mother Goose: but she was a very wise and clear-headed little girl, as you have no doubt discovered before **this** time, and she knew much better than to **let** Rob **think** she felt as he did about it; so all she said was, "I don't care: I shouldn't **mind. If Ned** Saunders had the sore throat, he'd have to be wrapped **up** just the same way. Boys are a great deal hatefuller than **girls.** No girl would ever say such a thing as that to **a girl** if she was sick, or to a boy either."

"No, I don't suppose they would," said Rob, reflectively. "**Girls are nicer than** boys some ways: that's a fact."

In the excitement of the Christmas presents, and the getting of the Christmas dinner, and all the housework which had to be done afterward, Nelly had forgotten about the conversation which she had overheard in the night between her father and mother. But in the quiet of this stormy morning it all came back to her. She and Rob were spending the forenoon in the place which they liked best in all the house, their mother's room. It was a beautiful sunny chamber, with two big bay-windows in it, — one looking to the south, and one to the west; the south window looked out on the garden, and the west window looked out on a great pine grove which was only a few rods away from the house; on the east side of the room was the fire-place with a low grate set in it; the fire burned better in this fire-place than in any other in the house, the children thought. That was because they had a nice time every night, sitting down a while in front of this fire and talking with their mother. This was the time when they told her things they didn't quite like to tell in the daytime; and this was the time she always took to tell them things she was anxious they should remember. They associated all their talks with the bright open fire; and, whenever they saw the flames of soft coal leaping up and shining, they remembered a great many things their mother had said to them.

There was a large old-fashioned mahogany table on one side of this room, which Mrs. March used for cutting out work, and which the children liked better than any thing in the room. It had droll twisted legs which ended in knobs and castors, and it had big leaves fastened on with brass hinges which opened and shut; when these leaves were open the table was so big that both Rob and Nelly could be up on it at once, and have plenty of room for their things. This morning their mother had **let them open it** out **to its** full size, and **push it** close up **in** one corner of the room, so that **the** walls made a fine back for them to lean against. Nelly **sat** on one **side, with** all her dolls ranged in a **row** against the wall, Mrs. Napoleon at the **head.** In front **of** her, she had all their clothes in one great pile, and was sorting and arranging them in the little bureau and trunk and boxes in which she kept them. Rob sat **opposite her with his feet on** a blanket shawl, so that **they** would not scratch the mahogany; he was reading the "Cliff Climbers," and every few minutes he would break out with : —

"This is the most splendid story of all yet."

"Nell, **look at this** picture of them going up over the cliff by ropes. Oh, don't I just wish I could go to some such place!"

After a while, Nelly leaned her head back against the wall, and stopped playing with her dolls. She looked at the snow-storm **outside,** and the bright fire in the grate, and exclaimed, "Oh, mamma! isn't it nice here?"

There was something in Nelly's tone which made **her** mother **look** up surprised.

"Why, **yes, dear; of course** it is nice here; it is always nice here; what made you think of it just now?"

Nelly March was one of the honestest little girls that ever lived. Nothing seemed to her so dreadful as a lie; but she came very near telling one now.

"I don't **know,** mamma," she said; but, almost before **fore the** words were out of her mouth, she added : —

"Yes, I do **know**, too; I meant **I didn't** want to tell."

"**Why not?** my little daughter," said Mrs. March, looking **much** puzzled. "Surely it cannot be any thing you do not want mamma to **know**."

"Oh, no, mamma! it is something you didn't want me to **know**," said Nelly hastily, turning very red.

"**Something I didn't** want you to know, Nell," she said. "**What do you mean?** And how did you know it then?"

"**She** listened, she listened," cried Rob, throwing down his book, "**and she** wouldn't tell me a thing either, and she was real mean."

The tears came into Nelly's eyes, and Mrs. March looked very sternly at Rob.

"Rob," she said, "telling tales is as mean as listening: I'm ashamed **of you.** Nell, what does he mean?"

Poor Nelly was almost crying.

"Indeed, mamma," she exclaimed, "I didn't **listen;** and I told Rob then **I didn't;** he's told a lie, a wicked lie, and he ought to be **punished, mamma; he knows** it's a lie."

"It ain't either," shouted Rob, "**if** you didn't listen how'd **you hear? She did listen,** mamma, and **now** she's told a lie too."

Mrs. March threw **down** her **sewing, and** walked quickly across **the room to the table where the** children were sitting. She **put** one hand on Nelly's head, and one on Rob's.

"My **dear** children," she said, "you shock me. **Do** think what you are saying: this is a **bad** beginning for the new year."

"'Tain't New Year yet for a week," muttered Rob. "This needn't count."

Mrs. March laughed in spite of herself.

"Every thing counts, Rob, which we do, whether it is the beginning of a New Year or not. Mamma ought not to have spoken as if that made any odds. But you must not accuse each other of lying. That is a most dreadful thing. I know neither of you would tell a lie."

"Course we wouldn't," cried both the children.

"Neither would Nelly listen, Rob, in any such sense as you meant," continued Mrs. March. "Sometimes we overhear things when we do not mean to."

"That's just the way it was, mamma," interrupted Nelly eagerly; "and I told Rob so: it was in the night, night before last, and you and papa were talking, and I was awake, and I could not help hearing, and I coughed as loud as I could for you to hear."

"Oh," said Mrs. March, "that is it, is it? I remember you coughed, and I shut the door. I did not think you were awake, but I was afraid we should waken you. We were talking about going away from this place."

"Yes, mamma," said Nelly, in a sad tone.

"Going away! Oh, mamma, are we really going away? oh, where? say where, mamma, say quick!" cried Rob, throwing down his "Cliff Climbers," and springing from the table to the floor at one bound.

"Gently, gently, wild boy," said Mrs. March, catching Rob by one arm and drawing him into her lap. In spite of all Rob's ill temper and selfishness, I think Mrs. March loved him a little better than she loved Nelly. Neither Nelly nor Rob dreamed of this, and perhaps Mrs. March never was conscious of it herself; but other people could see it.

"Why, Rob," she said, "would you be glad to go away from this house, and the grove, and the pond, and from all your friends, and go to live in a strange place where you didn't know anybody?"

Rob's face sobered.

"To stay, mamma?" he said, "to stay always?"

Nelly did not speak. She knew more about this matter than Rob did. She watched her mother's face very earnestly and sadly, and tears filled her eyes when Mrs. March answered: —

"I am afraid so, Rob: if we go I do not believe we shall ever come back. I didn't mean to let you know any thing about it till it was all settled. But, since you have heard something about it, I will tell you all I know myself. Come here, Nelly; both of you sit down now at my feet, and I will talk to you about it."

Nelly and Rob sat down on two low crickets by their mother's knee, and looked up in her face without speaking. They felt that something very serious was coming. Before Mrs. March began to speak, she kissed them both several times, then she said: —

"There is one thing I am very sure of: both my little children will be brave and good, if hard times come."

"Oh, mamma! tell us quick; don't bother," interrupted impatient Rob, "let's know what it is quick, mamma. Are we going to be awful poor, like the people in story books? I don't care if we are, if that's all. Let's have it over."

Mrs. March laughed again: one reason she loved

Rob so much was that his temper was so much like her own. It had been very hard for her herself to learn to be patient, and to be sufficiently moderate in her speech; and even now there was nothing in the world she disliked so much as suspense of any kind. She could make up her mind to endure almost any thing, if only it were fixed and settled. So when Rob burst out with impatient speeches like this one, she knew exactly how he felt. And sometimes when Nelly took things quietly and calmly, and was so deliberate in all her movements, Mrs. March misunderstood her, and thought she did not really care about any thing half as much as Rob did. But the truth was, Nelly really cared a great deal more about almost every thing, than he did. He forgot things in a day, or an hour even; sad things, pleasant things, all alike: they blew away from Rob's memory and Rob's heart like leaves in a great wind, and he never thought much more about any thing than just whether he liked it or disliked it at the moment. The phrase he used to his mother just now was very often on his lips, " Oh, don't bother!" Especially he used to say this to Nelly whenever she tried to reason with him about something which she thought not quite right or not quite safe. You would have thought to hear them talk that Nelly was at least five years older than he: she talked to him like a little mother. At this moment, when Rob was hurrying his mother so impatiently, Nelly exclaimed, " Oh, hush, Rob! do let mamma tell it as she wants to;" and Nelly drew up close to her mother's side, and laid her cheek down on her mother's hand. Nelly's heart was as full as it could be of sympathy: she knew that her mother felt very unhappy about going away, and Nelly's way of showing her sympathy was to be very loving and tender and quiet; but, strange as it may seém, this did not comfort and help Mrs. March so much as Rob's off-hand and impatient way.

"Well, but she's so slow: ain't you slow, mamma? And it's horrid to wait," replied Rob.

"Yes, Rob," laughed Mrs. March. "I am rather slow, and it is horrid to wait; but I won't be slow any longer: this is what papa and I were talking about the other night, — about going out to Colorado to live."

"Colorado! where's that? Is it anywhere near the Himalayas?" cried Rob. "If it is, I'd like to go; oh, I'd like to go ever so much."

Mrs. March laughed out loud. "Oh you droll Rob," she said. "No, it's nowhere near the Himalayas; but there are mountains there about as high as the Himalayas, — higher than any other mountains in America."

"Are there elephants?" said Rob. "I wouldn't mind about any thing if there are only elephants."

"Rob, how can you!" burst out Nelly, with a vehemence very unusual in her. "How can you! It's because papa's sick that we are going."

"Why, what's the matter with papa?" said Rob, wonderingly.

Mr. March had been a sufferer from asthma for so many years that no one any longer thought of him as an invalid. He was very rarely confined to the house, and, except in the summer, his asthma did not give him a great deal of trouble; but in the summer it was so bad that for weeks he was not able to preach at all: I believe I have forgotten all this time to tell you that he was a minister. I have been so busy talking about Nelly and Rob, that I have hardly told you any thing about their papa and mamma.

Mr. March had been settled in this village of Mayfield for fifteen years, and the people loved him so much that they would not hear of having any other minister. When his asthma was so bad that he could not preach, they hired some one else; always in the summer they gave him a two-months' vacation; and, whenever any stranger said any thing unkind about his asthmatic voice, they always replied, "If Mr. March couldn't preach in any thing more than a whisper, we 'd rather hear him than any other man living." The truth was, that they had grown so accustomed to the asthmatic, wheezy tone, that they did not notice it. It really was very unpleasant to a stranger's ear, and everybody wondered how a whole congregation of people could endure it. But it is wonderful how much love can do to reconcile us to disagreeable things in the people we love; and not only to reconcile us to them, but to make us forget them entirely. Nelly and Rob never thought but that their father's voice was as pleasant as anybody's: when his breath came very short and quick, they knew he was suffering, but at other times they did not remember any thing about his having asthma; this was the reason that Rob said so wonderingly now: —

"Why, what is the matter with papa?"

Mrs. March's voice was very sad as she replied: —

"Only his asthma, dear, which he has had so many years, but it is growing much worse; and we have seen a gentleman lately who has just come from Colorado, and he says that people never have asthma at all there, and the doctor says if papa does not go to some such climate to live, he will get worse and worse, so that he will not be able to do any thing. You don't know how much poor papa suffers, even here. He has not been able to lie down in bed for almost a year now; ever since early last summer."

"Not lie down!" exclaimed Nelly, "why, what does he do, mamma? How does he sleep?"

"He sleeps propped up with pillows, dear, almost as straight as he would be in a chair," replied **Mrs. March.**

"Oh, dear," cried Rob, "isn't that awful! Why didn't you ever tell us, mamma? Isn't he awful tired? What makes people not have asthma in Colorado, anyhow?"

"Which question first, Rob?" said Mrs. March. "I haven't told you, because papa dislikes very much to have any thing said about it. Yes: he is very tired all the time. He never feels rested in the morning as you do. I don't know why people never have asthma in Colorado; but I think it must be because the air is so very dry there. They never have any rain there from October to April, and the country is very high; some of the towns where people live are twice as high as the highest mountains you ever saw."

"Mamma!" exclaimed Rob, with so loud and earnest a voice that both Mrs. March and Nelly gave a little jump. "Mamma, if it's the being so high up that does the good, why couldn't we go to the Himalayas instead? Oh, it's perfectly splendid there! just let me read you about it," and Rob ran back to the table for his "Cliff

Climbers," and was about to begin to read aloud from it. Mrs. March could not help laughing : and Nelly laughed too ; for Nelly, although she was no older than Rob, was very much ahead of him in her studies at school, and she knew very well where the Himalaya mountains were, and that there would be no way of living there comfortably even if it were not quite too far to go.

"But, Rob, — " began Mrs. March.

"You just wait till I read you, mamma," interrupted Rob ; "you haven't read the 'Cliff Climbers,' and you don't know any thing about it. Perhaps the doctors don't know how many good things grow there ; and the mountains are five miles high, some of them. I 'm sure papa couldn't have the asthma as high up as that : could he?"

"My dear little boy," said Mrs. March, putting her hand on the book and shutting it up, "you are always too hasty : you must stop and listen. Nobody could live five miles up in the air. That would be as much too high as this is too low ; and things which sound very fine to read about would be very inconvenient in "real life."

"Yes ;" interrupted Rob, "an elephant tore down their cabin one night, — just tramped right over it, and smashed it all flat as we would an ant-hill. That wouldn't be very nice : but we needn't live where the elephants come ; we could just go out to hunt them in the summer."

Rob's eyes were dark blue, and when he was eager and excited they seemed to turn black, and to be twice their usual size. He was so eager now that his eyes were fairly dancing in his head. He was possessed of this idea about going to live in the Himalaya mountains, and nothing could stop him.

" They 're all heathen there too, mamma, and wouldn't papa like that? He could preach to them don't you know? Oh, it would be splendid! and I could collect seeds just like these cliff climbers. and stuff birds, and make lots of money sending them back to this country."

" Oh, Rob!" exclaimed Nelly, at last; " do stop talking, and let mamma talk: she hasn't half told us yet. It 's all nonsense about the Himalayas. We couldn't go there; nobody goes there. I 'll just show you on your new globe where it is, and you can see for yourself." So saying, Nelly ran for the globe, and was proceeding to show Rob what a long journey round the world it would be to reach the Himalayas; but Rob pushed the globe away.

" I don't care any thing about the old globe," he said; " people do go there, for Mayne Reid's books are all true; he says they are, and it isn't all nonsense about the Himalayas; is it, mamma? Couldn't we go there?"

Rob was fast growing angry.

" No, Rob," said Mrs. March: " we cannot go to the Himalayas to live; that is very certain. One of these days, when you 're a man, I hope you will be able to go all about the world and see all these countries you are so fond of reading about: you will have to wait till then for the Himalayas. If we go away from home at all, we must go to Colorado. That is quite far enough: it will take us four whole days and five nights, going just as fast as the cars can go, to get there."

" I don't care where we go, if we can't go to the Himalayas," said Rob, sulkily. " I think it 's real mean if we 've got to go away not to go there. I know it would be real good for papa."

Mrs. March laughed again very heartily.

" Rob," she said, " you are a very queer little boy. Mamma can't understand how you get so excited over things in such a short time. A few minutes ago you had never thought of such a thing as going to the Himalayas ; and here you are already sure that it would be good for papa to go there. Why, even the doctors are not sure what would be good for papa ! It is very hard to tell."

" Does it really take four whole days and five nights to get to Colorado ? " asked Rob. He had already given up the idea of the Himalayas, and was beginning to think about Colorado. Rob's mind moved from one thing to another as quickly as a weathercock when the wind is shifting.

" Yes : four whole days and five nights," said Mrs. March ; " or else four nights and five days, according to the time you start."

" Five days ! days ! Let 's start so as to make it come five days ; so as to see all we can," exclaimed Rob. " That 's splendid ! When will we start, mamma ? "

" It isn't really sure, is it, mamma, that we are to go," asked Nelly, who had hardly had a chance yet to speak a word : Rob had been talking so fast. " Does papa want to go ? "

You see how much more thoughtful Nelly was for other people than for herself. All Rob was thinking of was what good times might come of this journey ; but Nelly was thinking how hard it was for her papa and

mamma to break up their pleasant home, and how
sad it might be for all of them to go to live among
strangers.

"No, dear," said Mrs. March. "Papa does not want
to go at all. It is very hard for him to make up his
mind to do it. And I do not want to go either, except
on papa's account: but we would go anywhere in the
world that would make papa well; wouldn't we?"

"Yes, indeed," said Nelly, earnestly.

"Why doesn't papa want to go?" cried Rob.
"There 'll be plenty of people there to preach to: won't
there? And that's all papa cares for."

"Papa doesn't like to leave all these people here that
he has preached to for so many years: he loves them
all very much," replied Mrs. March; "and he does not
expect to preach any more if he goes to Colorado.
There are not a great many villages there; it is chiefly
a wild new country: people live on great farms and
keep large herds of sheep or of cows; and the doctor
wants papa to be a farmer and work out of doors, and
not live in his study among his books any more."

"Be a farmer like Uncle Alonzo?" exclaimed Nelly.
"Oh, mamma, wouldn't that be nice? and wouldn't papa
like that? He always has a good time when he goes to
Uncle Alonzo's. He says it makes him feel as if he was
a boy again. And oh, mamma, the cows are beautiful.
Don't you like cows, mamma?"

Nelly was now almost as excited as Rob. She had
been several times to make a visit at her Uncle Alonzo's
house. He was a rich farmer, and had big barns, and
fields full of raspberries and huckleberries, and a beautiful pine grove close to the house; and he had nearly

a hundred cows, and used to make butter and cheese to sell, and both Nelly and Rob thought there was nothing so delightful in the whole world as to stay at Uncle Alonzo's.

"No, dear," said Mrs. March. "I can't honestly say I do like cows. I am so silly as to be afraid of them. But I like your Uncle Alonzo's farm very much."

"Oh, mamma, how can you be afraid of a cow!" cried Rob. "They never hurt you."

"I suppose it's because I am a coward, Rob," answered Mrs. March; "but I can't help it. I was chased by a bull once when I was a girl; and, ever since then, I have been afraid of any thing which has horns on its head."

"Is that what the word coward comes from, mamma?" asked Rob: "does it mean to be afraid of a cow?"

"I guess not, Rob," said Mrs. March, laughing. "Don't begin to make puns, Rob: it is a bad habit."

"Puns!" said Rob, much surprised: "what is a pun?"

Then Mrs. March tried to explain to Rob what a pun was, but it was very hard work; and I don't think Rob understood, after all her explanations, so I shall not try to explain it to you here; but I dare say a great many of you understand what a pun is, and, if you do, you will see that Rob had accidentally made rather a good pun, for a little boy only twelve years old, when he asked if a coward was a person afraid of a cow.

Presently the dinner-bell rang.

"Why, mamma," exclaimed both the children, "it isn't dinner-time, is it?"

"Yes, it really is," said Mrs. March, looking at her watch: "I had no idea it was so late. Where has the morning gone to?"

"Gone to Colorado," exclaimed Rob, running down-stairs, "gone to Colorado! Hurrah for Colorado."

"By way of the Himalayas," said Nelly behind him, as they ran downstairs.

"Be still, Nell, can't you," said Rob, half vexed, half laughing. "I haven't been in Geography half so long as you have. We haven't come to the Himalayas yet."

Mr. March was just coming in at the front-door. He was so covered with snow that he looked like a snow-man; and as he stamped his feet on the door-mat, and shook off the snow from his overcoat and hat and beard, there seemed to be quite a snow-storm in the hall.

"Hurrah for Colorado," he repeated. "What does that mean? Who is going to Colorado?"

"All of us, papa; all of us, papa," cried Rob. "Mamma's told us all about it, so you can't keep it a secret any longer."

Mr. March looked up inquiringly at Mrs. March, who was coming down the stairs behind Nelly and Rob.

"Yes," she said, in answer to his inquiring look. "Yes. I have told the children all about it, and they are both wild to go, though Rob thinks the Himalayas would be a better place for you."

Mr. March burst into a loud laugh.

"The Himalayas!" he exclaimed. "Why, what do you know about the Himalayas, my boy?"

It was rather too bad to laugh at Rob so much about

his idea of the Himalayas, I think; because almost any boy who had just been reading Captain Mayne Reid's "Cliff Climbers," would think that there could be nothing in this life half so fine to do as to go to the Himalayas to live. Rob took it very good-naturedly this time, however.

"Not any thing, papa," he replied, "except what is in that book you gave me, the 'Cliff Climbers;' but that says some of the mountains are five miles high, and I thought that would cure the asthma, to go up as high as that. Mamma says that's what we are going to Colorado for, to get up high, to cure your asthma."

"Papa, we're so glad to go if it will make you better," said Nelly, taking hold of her father's hand with both of hers. Mr. March stooped over and kissed Nelly on her forehead.

"I know you are," he said: "you are papa's own little comfort always."

Mr. March loved both of his children very dearly; but Nelly gave him more pleasure than Rob did. He often said to his wife when they were alone: "Nelly never gives me a moment's anxiety. The child has all the traits which will make her a noble and a useful and a happy woman; but I am not so sure about Rob. I am afraid we shall have trouble with him." And Mrs. March always replied: "It is very true all you say about Nelly. She is a thoroughly good child; but you are quite mistaken about Rob. He is very hasty and impulsive; but he will come out all right. He has twice Nelly's cleverness, though he is so backward about his books. You'll see."

"I'm glad too, papa," cried Rob, "just as glad as

any thing.   It will be splendid to live on a farm.   Shall
you wear blue overalls like Uncle Alonzo?   And will
you let me help milk?   And can't I have a bull pup?
I 'm going to call him Cæsar."

"Well, upon my word, young people," said Mr.
March; and he looked at his wife when he spoke,
"you seem to have got this thing pretty well settled
between you.   I don't know that we are going to Colorado at all: after dinner we will all sit down together
and talk it over.   I 've got a letter here." — and he
took a big envelope out of his pocket — "from a gentleman I wrote to in Colorado, and he has sent me
some pictures of different places there, and of some of
the strange rocks.   We can't have our sleigh-ride this
afternoon; it is not going to stop snowing: so we may
as well take a journey to Colorado on paper; perhaps
it will be the only way we shall ever go."

Rob and Nelly could hardly eat their dinner: they
were so eager to see the Colorado pictures and to hear
all about the country.

As Mr. March looked at their eager faces, he sighed,
and thought to himself: —

"Dear little souls!   They have no idea of what is
before them if we go to Colorado.   It is as well they
haven't."

"What makes you look so sad, papa?" said Nelly.

"Did I look sad, Nelly?" replied Mr. March.   "I
didn't mean to.   I was thinking how delighted you and
Rob seemed at the idea of going to Colorado, and thinking that you would probably find it very different from
what you expect.   You would not be so comfortable
there as you are here."

"Isn't there enough to eat out there?" asked Rob, anxiously.

"Oh, yes!" said Mr. March, laughing, "plenty to eat."

"Well, that's all I care for," said Rob. "Oh, papa, do hurry! you never ate your dinner so slow before. I've been done ever so long. Can't I be excused, and go and read till you're ready to show us the pictures?"

"Yes," said Mrs. March, "you may both go up into my room; and, as soon as papa and I have finished our dinner, we will come up there and have our talk."

Mrs. March wished to have a little conversation alone with her husband before their talk with the children. She told him about Nelly's having accidentally overheard what they were saying in the night; "so I thought I would tell them all about it," she said.

"Certainly, certainly," said Mr. March. "There is no reason they should not know. Even if we do not go, no harm can come of it."

Then she told him of the obstinate notion Rob had taken into his head about the Himalayas, and how hard it had been to convince him that they ought not to set off for those mountains at once. Mr. March was laughing very heartily over this as they went up the stairs, and, as they entered the room, Rob said : —

"What are you and mamma laughing so about, papa?"

Mrs. March gave her husband a meaning look, intended to warn him not to tell Rob that they were laughing at him; but Mr. March did not understand her glance.

"Laughing at your fierce desire to start off for the Himalayas, Rob," he said.

"I don't care," said Rob: "I'm going there some day. You just read the 'Cliff Climbers,' and see if you don't think so too. I'll take you and mamma and Nell there when I'm a man and have money enough: see if I don't."

"Well, well, Rob, we'll go when that time comes, if we're not too old when you're rich enough to pay all that the journey costs. I've always thought I should like to go round the world," said Mr. March; "but now we'll look at the Colorado pictures."

Then they sat down, Mr. and Mrs. March on the lounge in front of the fire, Nelly in her father's lap, and Rob perched up on the back of the lounge behind his mother, so that he could look over her shoulder.

The first picture Mr. March took out of the envelope was one which looked like the picture of two gigantic legs and feet wrong side up.

"Oh, what big feet!" exclaimed Rob. "Do giants live in Colorado?"

Mr. March turned the picture the other side up.

"They are rocks, Rob," he said, "not feet; but they do look like feet, that's a fact. These are some of the rocks in a place called Monument Park, because it is so full of these queer rocks. Here are some more of them: they are of very strange shapes. Here are some that look like women walking with big hoop-skirts on, and some like posts with round caps on their heads; and here is a picture of a place where so many of these rocks are scattered among the trees, that they look like people walking about. Here is one group which has been called the 'Quaker Wedding.'"

"Oh, let me see that! let me see that!" exclaimed Nelly. "How queer to call rocks Quakers!"

"I don't see that they look very much like men and women, after all," added she as she studied the picture: "but they don't look like any rocks I ever saw. I think I should be afraid of them. They look alive."

"Pooh!" said Rob, "I shouldn't be. Rocks can't stir. Show us some more, papa."

The next pictures were of beautiful waterfalls: there were three of them, — one of seven falls, one above the other, and one of a beautiful fall very narrow, hemmed in between rocks, with tall pine-trees growing about it. The next was of a high mountain with snow half way down its sides, and a great many lower mountains all around it. This was called Pike's Peak.

"Oh, papa!" said Nelly, "could we live where we could see that mountain all the time?"

"Perhaps so, Nell," answered her father, smiling at her eagerness: "would you like to?"

Nelly was looking at the picture intently, and did not reply for a moment. Then she said: —

"Papa, I think it would keep us good all the time to look at that mountain."

"Why, Nell," said her mother, "I didn't know you cared so much for mountains. You never said so."

"I never saw a real mountain before," said Nelly. "This isn't a bit like Mount Saycross."

The town of Mayfield was in one of the pleasantest counties in Massachusetts. The region was very beautifully wooded, and had several small rivers in it, and one range of low hills called the Saycross Hills; the highest of these was perhaps three thousand feet high, and Nelly had spent many a day on its top: but she had never seen any thing which gave her any idea of the grandeur of a high mountain till she saw this picture of Pike's Peak. It seemed as if she could not take her eyes away from this picture: she looked at it as one looks at the picture of the face of a friend.

"Oh papa!" she exclaimed at last, "let me have this picture for my own: won't you? I'll be very, very careful of it."

"Yes, you may have it if you want it so much," replied Mr. March, "but be very sure not to lose it. I may want to show it to some one, any day."

"I won't lose it, papa," said Nelly, in a tone of so much feeling that her father looked at her in surprise.

"Why Nell," he said, "you must be a born mountaineer I think."

And so she was. From the day she first looked on this picture of Pike's Peak till the day when she stood at the foot of the real mountain itself, it was seldom out of her mind. She kept the little card in the box with Mrs. Napoleon's best bonnet and gown, and she talked so much about it that her father called her his "little Pike's Peak girl."

The rest of the pictures were of some of the towns in Colorado, some ranches, — ranch is the word which the Coloradoans use instead of farm, — and some beautiful canyons. A canyon is either a narrow valley with very high steep sides to it, or a chasm between two rocky walls. The most beautiful and wonderful things in Colorado are the canyons: they all have streams of water running through them; in fact, the canyons may be said to be roads which rivers and creeks have made for themselves among the mountains. Sometimes the river has cut a road for itself right down through solid rock, twelve hundred feet deep. You can think how deep that must be, by looking at the walls of the room you are sitting in, as you read this story. Probably the walls of your room are about ten feet high. Now imagine walls of rock one hundred and twenty times as high as that; and only far enough apart for a small river to go through at the bottom; and then imagine beautiful great pine-trees, and many sorts of shrubs and flowers growing all the way down these sides, and along the upper edges of them, and don't you see what a wonderful place a canyon must be? You mustn't think either that they are just straight up and down walls, such as a mason might build out of bricks, or that they run straight in one direction for their whole length. They are made up often of great rocks as big as houses piled one on top of another, and all rough and full of points, and with big caves in them; and they turn and twist, just as the river has turned and twisted, to the north or south or east or west. Sometimes they take such sharp turns that, when you look ahead, all you can see is the big high wall right before you, and it looks as if you couldn't go any farther; but, when you go a few steps nearer, you will see that both the high walls bend off to the right or the left, and the river is still running between them, and you can go right on. One of the prettiest pictures which Mr. March's friend had sent him was of a canyon called Boulder Canyon. It is named after the town of Boulder, which is very near it. This is one of the most beautiful canyons in all Colorado. It is very narrow, for the creek which made it is a small creek; but the bed of the creek is full of great rocks, and the creek just goes tumbling head over heels, if a creek can be said to have head and heels. Ten miles long this canyon is, and the creek is in a white foam all the way. There is just room for the road by side of the creek; first one side and then the other. I think it crosses the creek as many as twenty-five times in the ten miles; and it is shaded all the way by beautiful trees, and flowers grow in every crevice of the rocks, and along the edge of the water. As Rob and Nelly looked at picture after picture of these beautiful places, they grew more and more excited. Rob could not keep still: he jumped down from his perch behind his mother's shoulder, and ran round to his father's knee. "Papa, papa! say you'll go? say you'll go?" and Nelly said in her quieter way: —

"Oh papa! I didn't know there were such beautiful places in the world. Don't you think we'll go?"

Pretty soon it grew too dark to look at the pictures any longer, and Mrs. March sent the children down-stairs to play in the dining-room by the fire-light.

After they had gone, she said to her husband: "Doesn't it make you more willing to go, Robert, to see how eager the children are for it?"

Mr. March sighed.

"I do not know, Sarah," he said. "Their feelings are very soon changed one way or the other. A little discomfort would soon make them unhappy. I have great fears about the rough life out there, both for them and for you."

"I wish you would not think so much about that," replied Mrs. March. "I am convinced that you exaggerate it. I am not in the least afraid ; and as for the children they are so young they would soon grow accustomed to any thing. Of course there would be no danger of our not being able to have good plain food ; and that is the only real necessity."

"But you seem to forget, Sarah, about schools. How are we to educate the children there?"

"Teach them ourselves, Robert," replied Mrs. March earnestly. "It will be better for them in every way. Such an out-door life as they will lead there is ten times better than all the schools in the world. Oh, Robert! if you can only be well and strong, we shall be perfectly happy. I am as eager to go as the children are."

Mrs. March had been from the beginning in favor of the move. In fact, except for her, Mr. March would never have thought of it. He was a patient and quiet man, and would have gone on bearing the suffering of his asthma till he died, without thinking of the possibility of escaping it by so great a change as the going to a new country to live. It was well for him that he had a wife of a different nature. Mrs. March had no patience with people who, as she said, would "put up with any thing, rather than take trouble." Mrs. March's way was never to "put up" with any thing which was wrong, unless she had tried every possible way of righting it. Then, when she was convinced that it couldn't be righted, she would make the best of it, and not grumble·or be discontented ; which way do you think was the best?— Mr. March's or Mrs. March's? I think Mrs. March's was ; and I think Rob and Nelly were very fortunate children to have a mother who taught them such a good doctrine of life. This is the way she would have put it, if she had been going to write it out in rules.

First. If you don't like a thing, try with all your might to make it as you do like it.

Second. If you can't possibly make it as you like it, stop thinking about it : let it go.

There was a very wise man, who lived hundreds and hundreds of years ago, who said very much the same thing, only in different words. I don't know whether Mrs. March ever heard of him or not. His name was Epictetus, and he was only a poor slave. But he said so many wise things that men kept them and printed them in a book; and one of the things he said was this : —

"There are things which are within our power, and there are things which are beyond our power. Seek at once to be able to say to every unpleasing semblance : 'You are but a semblance, and by no means the real thing.' And then examine it by those rules which you have ; and first and chiefly by this : whether it concerns the things which are within our own power, or those which are not ; and if it concerns any thing beyond our power, be prepared to say that it is nothing to you."

I think this would be a good rule for all of us to copy and pin up on the door of our rooms, to read every morning before we go downstairs. Some of the words sound a little hard to understand at first : but after they are explained to you they wouldn't seem so ; and if we all lived up to this rule, we should always be contented.

Late in the evening, after the children had gone to bed, as Mr. and Mrs. March sat talking over their plans, there came a loud ring at the door-bell.

"I think that is Deacon Plummer," said Mr. March. "He said he would come in to-night and talk over Colorado. He has been thinking for some time of going out there; and, if we go, I think he will go too."

"Will he, really?" exclaimed Mrs. March. "And Mrs. Plummer? What a help that would be!"

"Yes, it would be a great advantage," said Mr. March. "He is the best farmer in all this region, and as honest as the day is long; and, queer as he is, I like him, I believe, better than any deacon I 've ever had."

"And he likes you too," said Mrs. March. "I believe if he goes now, it will be only to go with you; or, at least, partly for that. Mrs. Plummer's health, I suppose, is one reason."

"Yes, that is it," said Mr. March. "The doctors say she must go to Florida next winter: she can't stand another of our winters here; and Mr. Plummer says he 'd rather break up altogether and move to a new place, than be always journeying back and forth."

Just as Mr. March pronounced these words, the door opened, and Deacon and Mrs. Plummer appeared. They were a very droll little couple: they were very short and very thin and very wrinkled. Deacon Plummer had little round black eyes, and Mrs. Plummer had little round blue eyes. Deacon Plummer had thin black hair, which was very stiff, and never would lie down flat; and Mrs. Plummer had very thin white hair, which was as soft as a baby's, and always clung as close to her head as if it had been glued on. It was so thin that the skin of her head showed through, pink, in many places; and, except for the little round knot of hair at the back, you might have taken it for a baby's head.

Deacon Plummer always spoke very fast and very loud; so loud that at first you jumped, and wondered if he thought everybody was deaf. Mrs. Plummer always spoke in a little fine squeaky voice, and had to stop to cough every few minutes, so it took her a great while to say any thing. Deacon Plummer very seldom smiled, and looked quite fierce. Mrs. Plummer had a habit of smiling most of the time, and looked so good-natured she looked almost silly. She was not silly, however: she was sensible, and was one of the best housekeepers and cooks in all Mayfield. She was famous for making good crullers; and, whenever she came to Mr. March's house, she always brought four crullers in her pocket,—two for Rob and two for Nelly. As soon as she came into the room this night, she began fumbling in her pocket, saying:—

"Good evening, Mrs. March. How do you do, Mr. March?" (cough, cough). "I've brought a cruller" (cough, cough) "for the" (cough, cough) "children. Dear me" (cough, cough), "they're crumbled up" (cough, cough). "I got a leetle too much lard in 'em, jest a leetle, and the leastest speck too much lard'll make 'em crumble like any thing" (cough, cough); "but I reckon the crumbs'll taste good" (cough, cough) "if they be crumbled" (cough, cough); and, going to the table, she turned her pocket wrong side out, and emptied upon a newspaper a large pile of small bits of cruller. "Do you think they'll mind their being" (cough, cough) "crumbled up?" (cough, cough) "'t was only my spectacle case" (cough, cough) "did it," she said, looking anxiously at the crumbs.

"Call 'em crumblers! call 'em crumblers," said Deacon Plummer, laughing hard at his own joke, and rubbing his hands together before the fire; "tell the children they 're a new kind, called crumblers."

"Oh! the children won't mind," said Mrs. March, politely, and she brought a glass dish from the closet, and, filling it with the crumbs, covered it with a red napkin, and set it on the sideboard. "There," said she, "as soon as Rob comes downstairs in the morning, he will peep into this dish, and the first thing he will say will be, 'I know who 's been here: Mrs. Plummer 's been here. I know her crullers.' That 's what he always says when he finds your crullers on the sideboard."

Mrs. Plummer's little blue eyes twinkled with pleasure, so that the wrinkles around their corners all folded together like the sticks of an umbrella shutting up.

"Does he now, really?" she said. "The dear little fellow! Children always does like crullers."

"Crumblers; call 'em crumblers," shouted the Deacon. "That 's the best name for 'em anyhow."

"Well, Parson," he said, "how 's Colorado? Heard any thing more? Me an' my wife 's gettin' more 'n more inter the notion of goin', that is, ef you go. We shan't pick up an' go off by ourselves; we 're too old, an' we ain't used enough to travellin': but ef you go, we go; that 's about fixed, ain't it, 'Lizy?" and he looked at his wife and then at Mr. March and then at Mrs. March, with his queer little quick, fierce glance, as if he had said something very warlike, and everybody were going to contradict him at once.

"Yes" (cough, cough), "I expect we 'd better" (cough, cough) "go 'long; 't seems kinder" (cough,

cough) " providential like our all goin' " (cough, cough)
" together so.   Don't you think " (cough, cough) " so,
Mrs. March?   Be ye sure " (cough, cough) " ye 'd like
to have us go?" replied Mrs. Plummer.

" Oh, yes, indeed!" said Mrs. March.   " Mr. March
was just speaking of it when you came in how much he
would like to have Deacon Plummer go.   Mr. March
knows very little about farming, though he was brought
up on a farm, and he will be very glad of Deacon
Plummer's help; and I shall be very glad to see two
Mayfield faces there.   I expect to be lonely sometimes."

" Lonely, ma'am, lonely !" spoke up the Deacon:
" can't be lonely, ma'am.   Don't think of such a thing,
ma'am, with the youngsters, ma'am, and me an' my wife,
ma'am, an' the Parson.   I 'd like to see you have a lonesome minnit, ma'am ;" and the Deacon looked round on
them all again with his quick, fierce look.

Mr. March laughed.   " It seems to be shutting in all
round us, Sarah, to take us to Colorado : doesn't it?"

" It isn't two hours," he continued, turning to Deacon Plummer, " since the children left us to go to bed,
with their heads so full of Colorado and their desire to
set out for the country immediately, that I am afraid
they haven't shut their eyes yet.   And as for Nelly,
she 's gone to bed with a picture of Pike's Peak in her
hand."

" Picture !   Have ye got pictures of the country
round about there?" interrupted the Deacon.   " I 'd
like to see 'em, Parson ; so 'd Elizy.   She was a won-
derin' how 'twould look in them parts.   She hain't travelled none, Elizy hain't, since she was a gal.   I hain't
never been much of a hand to stir away from home, an'

I donno now what 's taken me so sudden to go so far away; but I expect it 's providential."

Mr. March took the Colorado pictures out of the big envelope again, and showed them to Deacon and Mrs. Plummer. They were as interested in them as Rob and Nelly had been, and it made Mrs. March laugh to think how much the old man and his wife, bending over the pictures, looked like Rob and Nelly suddenly changed from ten years old to sixty. Mrs. Plummer did not say much. Her spectacles were not quite strong enough for her eyes. She had been for a whole year thinking of getting a new pair, and she wished to-night she had done so, for she could not see any thing in the stereoscope distinctly. But she saw enough to fill her with wonder and delight, and make her impatient to go to the country where there were such beautiful sights to be seen. As for the Deacon, he could hardly contain himself: in his excitement, he slapped Mr. March's knee, and ex-claimed : —

" By golly, — beg your pardon sir, — but this must be the greatest country goin'. It 'd pay to go jest to see it, ef we didn't any more 'n look round 'n come right home again. Don't you think so, Elizy?"

The enthusiasm of these good old people, and the eager wishes of the children produced a great impression on both Mr. and Mrs. March. It did really seem as if every thing showed that they ought to go; and, before Deacon and Mrs. Plummer went home, it was about decided that the plan should be carried out.

Deacon Plummer was for starting immediately.

" I 'll jest turn the key in my house," he said, " 'n start right along; 'n you 'd better do the same thing;

we don't want to be left without a roof to come back to ef things turns out different from what we expect; ef we settle, we kin come back 'n sell out afterwards; 'n the sooner we git there the better, afore the heavy snows set in."

"But they don't have heavy snows in Colorado, not in the part where we are going," said Mr. March: "the cattle run out in the open fields all winter."

"You don't mean to tell me so!" exclaimed the deacon. "What a country to live in! I should think everybody 'd go into raisin' cattle afore any thing else."

"I think that is one of the best things to do there," replied Mr. March. "I have already made up my mind to that. And there is nothing I should enjoy more. And between your farming and my herds of cattle, we ought to make a good living. Deacon, come round in the morning and we'll talk it over more, and see what time it's best to start."

At breakfast the next morning, Mr. March told Rob and Nelly that it was decided that they would move out to Colorado. The two children received the news very differently. Nelly dropped her knife and fork, and looked steadily in her father's face for a full minute: her cheeks grew red, and she drew in a long breath, and said, "Oh! oh!" That was all she said; but her face was radiant with happiness. Rob bounded out of his chair, flew to his mother and gave her a kiss, then to his father and gave him a great hug, and then he gave a regular Indian war-whoop, as he ran back to his seat.

"Rob! Rob! you must not be so boisterous," exclaimed his mother; but she was laughing as hard as she could laugh, and Rob knew she was not really displeased with him.

"Oh Nell, Nell!" cried Rob, "isn't it splendid? why don't you say any thing?"

"I can't," replied Nelly. But her cheeks were growing redder and redder every minute, and her father saw that tears were coming in her eyes.

"Why, Nell," he said, "you are not sorry, are you? I thought you wanted to go."

"Oh, so I do, papa," exclaimed Nelly; "I want to go so much that I can't believe it."

Mr. March smiled. He understood Nelly better than her mother did.

CHAPTER III.

OFF FOR COLORADO.

IT was finally decided that it would be best not to set out for Colorado until the middle of March. There were many things to be arranged and provided for, and Mr. March did not wish to leave the people of his parish too suddenly. Afterward he wished that he had gone away immediately, as soon as his decision was made; for the ten weeks that he waited were merely ten long weeks of good-bye. Everybody loved him, and was sorry he was going; and there was not a day that somebody did not come in to hear the whole story over again why he was going, when he was going, where he was going, and all about it. At last Mrs. March grew so tired of talking it all over and over, that she said to people: "I really can't talk any more about it. We are not going till the fifteenth of March, but I wish it were to-morrow." After the first two or three weeks, Rob and Nelly lost much of their interest in talking it over; two months ahead seemed to them just as far off as two years; and they did not more than half believe they would ever really go. But when the packing began, all their old interest and enthusiasm returned, and they could not keep quiet a moment.

Nelly's great anxiety was to decide whether she would better carry Mrs. Napoleon in her arms all the way or let her go in a trunk. She said to her mother that she really thought Mrs. Napoleon would go safer in her arms than anywhere else. "You see, mamma, I should never lay her down a single minute, and how could any thing happen to her then? But in the trunk she would be shaken and jolted all the time." The truth was, Nelly was very proud of Mrs. Napoleon, and she secretly had thought to herself, "I expect there 'll be a great many little girls in the cars: in four whole days, there must be; and they would all like to see such a beautiful doll."

Mrs. March understood this feeling in Nelly perfectly well, and it amused her very much to see how Nelly was trying to deceive herself about it.

"But, Nelly," she said, "the cars will be full of cinders and dust, and they will be sure to stick to the wax. Her face would get dirty in a single day, and you can't wash it as you do Pocahontas's. Don't you think you 'd better carry Pocahontas instead?"

Pocahontas was Nelly's next best doll: she was the big one, I told you about; the one that was almost the size of a real live baby; the one which was so big that it made Mrs. March first think of using her father's great stockings to hang up for Christmas stockings for the children.

"Oh, mamma!" said Nelly: "Pocahontas is too heavy; and I don't care half so much for her as for dear beautiful Josephine. I shouldn't care very much if Pocahontas did get broken, but if any thing were to happen to the Empress it would be dreadful. Do let me carry her, mamma. I 'll make her a beautiful water-proof cloak just like mine; and she can wear two veils just as you do on the water."

"Very well, Nelly, you can do as you like," replied her mother; "but I warn you that you will wish the doll out of the way a great many times before we reach our journey's end; and I am afraid her looks will be entirely spoiled."

"Oh, no, mamma!" replied Nelly, confidently. "You 'll see you haven't the least idea what good care I shall take of her."

At last the day came when the last box was shut and nailed and corded, the last leather bag locked, the last bundle rolled up and strapped; and Mr. and Mrs. March, and Rob and Nelly, and little Deacon Plummer and his good little wife, all stood on the doorsteps of the parsonage waiting for the stage, which was to carry them ten miles to the railway station where they were to take the cars. Mrs. Napoleon really looked very pretty in her long water-proof cloak; it was of bright blue lined with scarlet; and she wore a dark blue hat with a little bit of scarlet feather in it, to match her cloak; and she had a dark blue veil, two thicknesses of it, pinned very tight over her face and hat; Nelly held her hugged tight in her arms, and never put her down.

"Oh, my! before I 'd be bothered with a doll to carry," exclaimed Rob, looking at Nelly, — "leave her behind. Give her to Mary Pratt. You won't care for dolls out in Colorado. I know you won't."

Nelly gave Rob a look which would have melted the heart of an older boy; but Rob was not to be melted.

"Oh, you needn't look that way!" he said. "A doll's

a plague: I heard **mamma tell** you so too, so now,
there," he added triumphantly. Nelly walked away in
silence, and only hugged Mrs. Napoleon tighter, and
Mr. March, who had been watching the scene, said to
his wife: "**Look at that** motherly **little thing.** The
doll's the same to her as a baby to you."

"Yes," said Mrs. March, "but Rob's right after all.
It'll be a great bother having that wax **doll** along; but
I thought it was better to let Nelly see for herself. I
dare say she'll forget it, and leave it at the first place
where we change cars."

"**Not she,**" said Mr. **March.** "You **don't know**
Nelly half so well as I do, Sarah, if she is your own
child. Nelly'd carry that doll all round the world and
never lay it down."

"We'll see," said Mrs. March, laughing. Mr. March
was a little vexed at his wife for saying this; and he
privately resolved that he would keep an eye on Mrs.
Napoleon himself all through the journey, and see that
she was not left behind at any station.

Four days and four nights in the cars, going, going,
going every minute, night and day, dark and light,
asleep and awake: nobody has any idea what such a
journey is till he takes it. Poor old Deacon Plummer
and Mrs. Plummer were so tired by the end of the
second day that they looked about ninety years old.

"Deary me!" Mrs. Plummer said a dozen times a
day. "It's a great deal farther than I thought."

"I told you, Elizy, it was four days and four nights,"
the Deacon always replied; "but I suppose you didn't
sense it no more 'n I did. Nobody couldn't believe the
joltin' 'd be so wearin'. I feel's if my bones was all

jelly in my skin," and the poor old man moved as if they were. He reeled when he walked; and, at each lurch the cars gave, he would catch hold of any thing or anybody who happened to be near him. If it were a person, he would apologize most humbly: but if the car gave another lurch, even while he was apologizing, he would clutch hold again, just as hard as before, at which the person would walk away quite offended; and very soon everybody in the car tried to keep out of the old man's way, they were so afraid of being violently laid hold of by him.

Rob and Nelly did not mind the jolting; did not mind the lurches the cars gave; did not mind the cinders, the dust, the noise. They were having the best time they ever had in their lives. For the first two days of their journey, they were in what is called "The drawing-room," in the sleeping-car. I wonder if I could make those of you who have never been in a sleeping-car understand about this little room. I will try.

Most of the sleeping-cars have merely shelves along the sides in the place where the seats are in the ordinary day-cars: curtains are hung in front of these shelves, and they are parted off from each other like the shelves in a long cupboard. In the daytime, these shelves are folded away and fastened up against the walls, and seats left below them. At night when people are ready to go to bed, the shelves are let down, and the curtains put up in front of them, and each person climbs up on his shelf, and undresses behind the curtain, and goes to bed. I forgot to say that a very good little bed is made up on each shelf. A man who has the care of the car, and who is called the porter, makes these beds.

This is the way it is in nearly all the sleeping-cars. But there are some cars which have, besides these, a nice little room walled off at one end. It has seats for two people on each side; and these seats are made into comfortable beds at night. It has two windows which open on the outside of the car, and two which open on the narrow aisle of the car; these four windows are all your own, if you have hired the whole little room for yourself. You can have them either open or shut, just as you like, and nobody else has any right to say any thing about it, which is a great comfort; in the ordinary car, you know there is always somebody just behind you or just before you who is either too hot or too cold, and wants the windows shut when you want them open, or open when you want them shut. This little room has a door at each end of it. One opens into the car where the rest of the people are sitting. The other opens into a nice little closet where there is a wash-bowl and water, and you can take a bath comfortably. At night the porter comes and hangs up curtains across these doors, because they have glass in the tops of them; then he draws the curtains at your windows; then he lights a lamp which hangs in the middle of the ceiling in your room: and there you are shut up in as cunning a little bedroom as you would ever want to see; and almost as snug and private as you could be in your own bedroom. You can undress and go to bed comfortably; and, unless the jolting of the car keeps you awake, you can sleep all night as soundly as you would at home.

Rob and Nelly were delighted with this little room. So was Mrs. March. She hung up their cloaks and hats on the hooks, and took out their books and papers, and made the little room look like home. Nelly propped Mrs. Napoleon up in one corner of one of the red velvet arm-chairs, and took off her blue veils, for there seemed to be no dust at all. "I wish I'd brought Pocahontas too," said Nelly: "there is so much room, and dolls do look so nice travelling like other people."

"People!" laughed Rob. "Dolls ain't people."

"They are too," said Nelly. "People are men and women, and there are boy dolls and girl dolls and women dolls and men dolls."

"Mamma, are dolls people?" asked Rob, vehemently. "Nell says they are, and I say they ain't. They ain't: are they?"

"Not live people," said Mrs. March: "Nell didn't mean that."

"Oh, no!" said Nelly; "but they're play people, and you can't be sure they don't know any thing just because they don't speak. I could go a whole year without speaking if I tried to."

"I believe you could," laughed Mrs. March; "but Rob couldn't."

"Not I," said Rob. "What's the use? I like to talk. Nell's a dumb-cat: that's what she is."

"I can talk if I've a mind to," retorted Nelly; "but I don't want to; that is, not very often: I don't see the use in it."

This is the way it always was with Rob and Nelly. Dearly as they loved each other, they never thought alike about any thing: but for that very reason they did each other good; much more than if they had been just alike.

When it was time for breakfast or for **dinner**, the black porter, **whose name** was Charley, brought in a little square **table and set it up as firm** as he could between **the seats.** Then **Mr. March** lifted up the big luncheon-basket on **one of** the chairs, and **Mrs.** March took out her spirit-lamp, and they had great fun cooking. There was **a** saucepan which **fitted over** the spirit-lamp, and the flame of the spirit-lamp was so large that **water boiled in this** saucepan in a very few minutes. **Mrs. March could make** tea or chocolate or coffee: she **could boil eggs, or** warm up beef soup; then, after they had eaten all they wanted, **they** heated more water **in** the same saucepan and washed their dishes in it. **At** first, this seemed dreadful **to** Nelly, **who was a** very neat little girl.

"Oh, mamma," she said, "how horrid to cook in the same pan you wash dishes in!" But Mrs. March laughed at her, **and told** her that when people were travelling **they could** not afford to be so particular.

It was only for the first two days and nights of their journey that they had this comfortable little **room.** On the morning of the third day they reached Kansas City, and there they had to change cars. They sat in a large and crowded waiting-room, while Mr. March went to see about the tickets. Nelly **and** Rob looked with great astonishment on every thing they saw. They seemed already to have come into a new world. The people looked strange, and a great many of them were speaking German. There were whole families — father, mother, and perhaps half-a-dozen little children — sitting on the railway platforms, on big chests, which were tied up with strong ropes. They had great feather-beds, too, tied in bundles and bulging out all round the ropes. Their faces were very red, and their clothes were old and patched: if Nelly had met them in the lanes of Mayfield, she would have taken them for beggars; but here they were travelling just like herself, going the same way too, for she watched several of them getting into the same train. Then there were groups of men in leather clothes, with their boots reaching up to their knees, and powder-horns slung across their shoulders. They all carried rifles: some of them had two or three; and one of them, as he stepped on the platform, threw down a dead deer; another carried a splendid pair of antlers. Nelly took hold of Rob's hand and walked very cautiously nearer the dead deer.

"Oh, Rob!" she said, "it's a real deer. There is a picture of one in my Geography with just such horns as these."

Nelly was carrying Mrs. Napoleon hugged up very tight in her arms; but she had not observed that, in the jostling of the crowd, Mrs. Napoleon had somehow turned her head round as if she were looking backward over Nelly's shoulder. Neither had she observed that two little girls were following closely behind her, jabbering German as fast as they could, and pointing to the doll. Presently, she felt her gown pulled gently. She turned round, and there were the two little girls, both with outstretched hands, talking as fast as magpies, and much more unintelligibly. Each of them took hold of Nelly's gown again, and made signs to her that she should let them take the doll. They looked so eager that it seemed as if they would snatch the doll out of her hands: the words they spoke sounded so thick and strange that it half frightened Nelly. "Oh, dear me, Rob!" she exclaimed; "do tell them to go away. Go away, good little girls, go away!" she said, pleadingly. "I can't let you take her."

"Clear out!" said Rob, roughly, taking hold of one of them by the shoulder and giving her a shove. No sooner had the words passed his lips than he felt himself lifted by the nape of his neck as if he had been a little puppy: he was in the hands of a great red-faced German, who looked like a scarlet giant to poor Rob, as he gazed up in his face. This was the father of the two little girls; he had seen the shove that Rob gave his little Wilhelmina, and he was in a great rage; he shook Rob back and forth, and cuffed his ears, all the time talking very loud in German. All he said was: —

"You are a good-for-nothing: I will teach you manners, that you do not push little girls who are doing you no harm;" but it sounded in the German language like something very dreadful.

Poor Nelly clung to him with one hand, and tried to stop his beating Rob.

"Oh, please don't whip my brother, sir!" she cried. "He did not mean to hurt the little girl. She was going to snatch my doll away from me."

But the angry German shook Nelly off as if she had been a little fly that lighted on his arm. Rob did not cry out, nor speak a word. He was horribly frightened, but he was too angry to cry. He said afterwards: —

"I thought he was going to kill me; but I just made up my mind I wouldn't speak a single word if he did."

All this that I have been telling you didn't take much more than a minute; but it seemed to poor Nelly a thousand years. She was crying, and the little German girls were crying too: they did not mean to do any harm, and they did not want the little boy whipped. Some rough men and women who were looking on began to laugh, and one man called out: —

"Go it, Dutchy, go it!"

Mr. March, who was just walking up the platform, heard the noise; and, when he looked up to see what it meant, what should he see but his own Rob held away up in the air, in the powerful grip of this tall man, and being soundly cuffed about the ears. Mr. March sprang forward, and, taking hold of Rob with one hand, caught the angry man's uplifted arm in the other.

"Stop, sir," he said; "this is my little boy. What has he done? Leave him to me. What has he done?"

"Nothing, papa," called poor Rob, the tears coming into his eyes at the sight of a protector; "nothing except push that ugly little yellow-haired girl: I guess she is his; she was going to snatch Nell's doll."

The German set Rob down; and, turning towards Mr. March, began to pour out a torrent of words. Luckily, Mr. March understood most of what he said, and could speak to him in his own language. So he explained to him that his little daughters had tried to take Nelly's doll away from her, and that Rob had only intended to protect his sister, as was quite right and proper he should do. As soon as the man understood this, he turned at once to his little girls who stood by crying, and asked them a short question in German.

They sobbed out, "ja, ja" (that means "yes, yes"). In less than a minute he caught up first the elder one, just as he had caught up Rob, and boxed her ears;

then the smaller one, and cuffed her also; and set them both down on the ground, as if he were used to swinging children up in the air and boxing their ears every day. Then he turned to Rob, and, taking him by the hand, said to Mr. March, —

"Explain to your little boy that I ask his pardon. He was doing the right thing: he is a gentleman; and I ask that he accept this horn from me and from my very bad little girls."

So saying, he took out of a great wallet that hung across his back a beautiful little powder horn. It was a horn of the chamois, the beautiful wild deer that lives in the mountains in Switzerland. It was as black as ebony, and had a fine pattern cut on it, like a border round the top; then it had a scarlet cord and silver buckles, to fasten it across the shoulders. Rob's eyes glistened with delight as he stretched out his hand for it.

"Oh, thank you, thank you!" he said. "Oh, papa! please thank him, and tell him I don't mind the whipping a bit now. And," he added, "please tell him, too, that I didn't mean to shove his little girl hard, only just to keep her off Nell."

Mr. March interpreted Rob's speech to the German, who nodded pleasantly and walked off, leading his two little sobbing children by the hand. He was so tall that the little girls looked like little elves by his side, and he looked like the picture of the Giant with his seven-league boots on. When Rob turned to show his beautiful powder horn to Nelly, she was nowhere to be seen.

"Why, where is Nell, papa?" he exclaimed.

Mr. March looked around anxiously, but could see

nothing of her. They hurried back into the waiting-room, and there to their great relief they saw Nelly sitting by her mother's side. Rob rushed up to her, holding up his powder horn, and exclaiming, —

"Why, Nell, what made you come away? That old thrasher was a splendid fellow: see what he gave me, as soon as papa made him understand; and he cuffed those girls well, I tell you, — most as hard as he did me. Why, Nell, what's the matter?" Rob suddenly observed that Nelly was crying.

"Don't talk to Nelly just now," said Mrs. March: "she is in trouble." And she put her arm round Nelly tenderly.

"But what is it, mamma?" exclaimed Rob; "tell me. Is she hurt?"

"What is it, Sarah?" said Mr. March. By this time Nelly was sobbing hard, and her head was buried on her mother's shoulder. Mrs. March pointed to Nelly's lap: there lay a shapeless and dirty little bundle, which Nelly held grasped feebly in one hand. It was the remains of Mrs. Napoleon. The blue waterproof was all torn and grimed with dirt; a broken wax arm hung out at one side; and when Rob cautiously lifted a fold of the waterproof, there came into view a shocking sight: poor Mrs. Napoleon's face, or rather what had been her face, without a single feature to be seen in it, — just a round ball of dirty, crumbling wax, with the pretty yellow curls all matted in it. Mr. March could not help smiling at the sight; luckily, Nelly did not see him.

"Why, how did that happen?" he said.

"What a shame!" exclaimed Rob. "Say, Nell, you shall have my powder horn;" and he thrust it into her hand. Nelly shook her head and pushed it away, but did not speak. Her heart was too full.

Then Mrs. March told them in a low tone how it had happened. When Nelly caught hold of the German's arm, trying to stop his beating Rob, she had forgotten all about Mrs. Napoleon, and let her fall to the ground. Nobody saw her, and, in the general scuffle, the doll had been trampled under foot. Really, if one had not been so sorry for Nelly, one could not help laughing at the spectacle. The scarlet feather and the bright blue cloak, and the golden curls, and the dark blue veils, and the red and white wax, all mixed up together so that you would have hardly known that it was a doll at all, — except that one blue eye was left whole, with a little bit of the red cheek under it. This made the whole wreck look still worse.

"Our first railroad accident," said Mrs. March, laughingly. Nelly sobbed harder than ever.

"Hush," said Mr. March, in a low tone to his wife. "Don't make light of it."

"Nelly, dear," he said, taking hold of the doll gently, "shall not papa throw the poor dolly away? You don't want to look at her any more."

"Oh, no, no!" said Nelly, lifting up the bundle, and hugging it tighter.

"Very well, dear," replied her father, "you shall keep it as long as you like. But let me pin poor dolly up tight, so that nobody can see how she is hurt."

Nelly gave the doll up without a word, and her kind papa rolled the little waterproof cloak tight round the body and arms; then he doubled up the blue veil and pinned it many thicknesses thick all round the head;

and then he took a clean dark-blue and white silk handkerchief of his own and put outside all the veil, and
made it into a snug little parcel, that nobody would
have known was a dolly at all.

"There, Nelly," he said, putting it in her lap, "there
is dolly, all rolled up, so that nobody can look at her."

Nelly took the sad little bundle, and laid it across her
knees.

"Can she ever be mended, papa?" she said.

"No, dear, I think not," said Mr. March; "I think
the sooner you put her out of your sight the better; but
now we must go into the cars."

Poor Nelly! she walked slowly along, carrying the
blue and white package as if it were a coffin, — as indeed it was, a kind of coffin, for a very dead dolly.

As they were going into the car, Mr. March said to
his wife : —

"There is no drawing-room in the sleeping-car which
goes through to-day. I have had to take two sections."

Mrs. March had never travelled in a sleeping-car before, and she did not know how much nicer the little
room was than the "sections." So she replied : "They 'll
do just as well, won't they?"

"I think you will not like them quite so well," replied
Mr. March; "you cannot be by yourself with the children. But it is only for one night; we will make the
best of it. There are our sections, one right opposite
the other; so you will not have strangers opposite
you."

They put their lunch-basket and bags and bundles
down on the floor, and sat down on the two sofas, facing
each other. Nelly put her blue and white parcel in one

corner of the sofa, lay down with her head on it, and was soon fast asleep. There were tears on her cheeks.

"Poor child!" said Mr. March; "this is her first real grief."

"I'm glad I ain't a girl," said Rob, bluntly; "I don't believe in dolls, do you, papa?"

Mr. March answered Rob's question by another.

"Do you believe in babies, Rob?"

"Why, of course, papa! What a funny question! I think babies are real nice. They're alive, you know."

"Yes," said his father; "but dolls are just the same to little girls that babies are to grown-up women. Nelly felt just like a mother to Mrs. Napoleon. She was a very good little mother too."

"Yes," said Mrs. March; "she was. I am very sorry for her."

"I'm real glad Deacon Plummer and Mrs. Plummer weren't here," said Rob.

"Why, why, Rob?" said his mother.

(Deacon and Mrs. Plummer had left the train at Quincy to spend a week with a son of theirs who lived there. They were to join the Marches later, in Denver.)

"Oh, because she'd have said: 'This is — cough — cough — providential.' What does providential mean, anyhow, papa? You never say it. Does it make you cough and sneeze? Mrs. Plummer is always saying it about every thing."

Mr. and Mrs. March laughed so hard at this they could not speak for some minutes. Then Mr. March said : —

"You must not speak so, Rob;" but, before he had

finished his sentence, he had to stop again, and laugh harder than before. "Deacon and Mrs. Plummer are going to be the greatest help to us, and they are as good and kind as they can be."

"Yes, I like her crullers first-rate," said Rob. "What does providential mean, papa?"

Mr. March looked puzzled.

"I hardly know how to tell you, Rob. Mrs. Plummer means by it that God made the thing happen, whatever it is that she is speaking of, on purpose for her accommodation: that is one way of using the word. I do not believe that doctrine: so I never use the word, because it would be understood to mean something I don't believe in."

"I should think God'd be too busy," said Rob, as if he were thinking very hard; "he couldn't remember everybody, could he?"

"Not in that way, I think," said Mr. March; "but in another way I think it is true that he never forgets anybody. It is something like my garden, Rob. You know I've got parsnips, and carrots, and beets, and potatoes, — oh! a dozen of things, all growing together. Now I never forget my garden. I know when it is time to have the corn hoed; and I know, when there hasn't been any rain for a long time, that I must water it. But I don't think about each particular carrot or parsnip in the bed: I could hardly count them if I tried. Yet I mean to take very good care of my garden, and never let them suffer for any thing; and if any one of my vegetables were to be thirsty, if it could speak, it ought to ask me to give it some water."

I am afraid Rob did not listen attentively to this long

explanation. He never thought of any one thing very long, as you know. And he was busy now watching all the people pour into the car. There was a little girl, only about Nelly's age, who had to be carried on a little mattress. She could not walk. Something was the matter with her spine. Her father and mother were with her. And there was a lady with a sweet face, who was too ill to sit up at all. The sofas in her "section" were made up into a bed as soon as she came in; she had a doctor and a nurse with her.

Then there were several couples, who had two or three children with them; and one poor lady who was travelling all alone with five children, and the largest only twelve years old; and there were some Englishmen with guns and fishing-rods and spy-glasses and almost every thing you could think of that could be cased in leather and carried on a journey, — one of them even had a bath-tub, a big, round bath-tub, in addition to every thing else. He had a man-servant with him who carried all these things, or else he never could have got on at all. The man's name was Felix. That is a Latin word which means "happy," but I don't think this poor fellow was happy at all. He was a Frenchman. I don't know how he came to be an Englishman's servant, but I suppose the Englishman had lived a great while in France, and had found him there. Felix's master always talked French with him; so Felix had not learned much English, and it would have made you laugh to see him clap his hand to his head when anybody said any thing he could not understand. He would pound his head as if he could drive the meaning in that way; and then he would pull his thin hair; and then sometimes he would turn round and round as fast as a top two or three times. When he came into the cars loaded down with the guns and the rods and the bundles and the bath-tub, his master would tell him to put them down in the corner; then the porter would come along and say : —

"Look here! you can't have all these things in here;" and then Felix would say : —

"Vat dat you say, sare?"

Then the porter would repeat it; and Felix would say again : —

"Vat dat you say, sare?"

And then the porter would get angry, and pick up some of the things, and lay them on Felix's back, and tell him to carry them off; and there Felix would stand stock-still, with the things on his back, till his master appeared. Then he would pour out all his story of his troubles in French, and the Englishman would be very angry with the porter, and say that he would have his things where he pleased; and the porter would say he should not. He must put them under his berth or in the baggage car; and poor Felix would stand all the while looking first in the porter's face and then in his master's, just like a dog that is waiting for his master to tell him which way to run for a thing. Great drops of perspiration would stand on his forehead, and his face would be as red as if it were August: he was so worried and confused. Poor Felix! he was one of the drollest sights in the whole journey.

The people kept pouring in.

"Mamma, where are they all to sleep?" whispered Rob.

"I'm sure I don't know, Rob," she answered.

At last the train moved off, and the different families arranged themselves in their own sections, and it seemed a little less crowded. But there were not seats enough for all the children, and some of them were obliged to sit on the floor in the middle of the aisle. The lady who had five children had only engaged one berth: that is half of a section.

"How do you expect to manage about sleeping?" said Mrs. March to her.

"Oh, that's easy enough," said she. "We've slept so all the way from New York. I put the three little ones crosswise at the foot, and the two others lie 'longside of me."

Mrs. March did not reply to this; but she thought to herself, "I'd like to see those babies after they are all packed away for the night."

At noon the train stopped for the passengers to take their dinner at a little station. More than half the people in the car went out. Then the porter — the new porter's name was Ben — brought in little tables and put them up between the seats for the people who had their own lunch-baskets and did not want to go out to dinner. In the next section to the Marches were a man and his wife with three children. They had a big coffee-pot full of coffee, and one tin cup to drink it from. They had loaves of brown bread, a big cheese, and a bunch of onions. As soon as they opened their basket, the smell of the onions and the cheese filled the car.

"Ugh!" said Rob; "where does this horrible smell come from?"

Luckily the people who owned the cheese and the onions did not hear him, and before he had time to say any more, his mother whispered to him to be quiet; but Rob's face was one of such disgust, that nobody could have looked at him without seeing that he was very uncomfortable. Mrs. March felt as uncomfortable as Rob did: but she knew that those people had just the same right to have cheese and onions on their table that she had to have chocolate and orange marmalade on hers; so she opened one of the windows wide to let in fresh air, and went on with her dinner. As soon as the spirit-lamp began to burn, the children in the next section exclaimed aloud: " Oh, what is that? what is that?" They had never seen any thing of the kind before. The two eldest, who were boys, jumped down from their seat, each carrying a big piece of bread and of cheese, and came crowding around Mrs. March to look at the lamp. Mrs. March was a very gentle and polite woman, but she could not help being vexed at these ill-mannered children.

" Go away, little boys," she said : " I am very busy now. I am afraid you will upset the lamp, and get burned."

Then she looked at the father and mother, hoping they would call their children back. But they took no notice of them: they went on eating their bread and cheese and onions ; and, at every fresh onion they sliced, a fresh whiff of the strong, disagreeable odor went through the car. Mr. March had been out to the eating-house, to get some milk. Mrs. March had brought a big square glass bottle, which held three pints ; and, whenever they stopped at an eating-house, Mr. March bought fresh milk to fill it, and this was a great addition to their bill of fare. He came into the car at this moment, bringing the milk bottle, and as soon as he opened the car door, he exclaimed, as Rob had done : —

" Ugh !" but in a second more he saw what had made the odor, and he said no more. As he handed the milk to his wife, she said in a low tone : —

" Could we go anywhere else to eat our dinner, Robert ?"

Mr. March looked all around the car and shook his head.

" No," he said; " every seat is taken, and at any moment the people may come back. It is nearly time now for the train to start. We will make a hasty meal; perhaps we can do better at night."

Rob and Nelly were very quiet. They did not like the two strange boys who stood close to their seat staring at them, and at every thing which was on the table. Rob whispered to Nelly : —

" 'Tain't half so nice as it was in the little room : is it, Nell?"

" No," said Nelly.

" Shouldn't you think they'd be ashamed to stare so?" continued Rob, making a gesture over his shoulder towards their uninvited guests.

" Yes," said Nelly. " It's real rude."

Still the boys stood immovable at Mrs. March's knee. At last one of them lifted his head, and, saying " What keeps that thing on there?" pointed to the saucepan standing on the little tripod of the lamp. Just at that moment, his brother accidentally hit his arm and made his hand go farther than he meant : it hit the saucepan and knocked it over ; down went the spirit-lamp, all the alcohol ran out and took fire, and for a few minutes there was a great hubbub I assure you. Mr. March seized their heavy woollen lap-robe, and threw it on the floor above the burning alcohol, and stamped out the flames; and nobody was burned. But the nice chocolate was all lost; it went running down a little muddy stream, way out to the door; and the tumbler which had the butter in it fell to the floor and was broken; and the nice slices of white bread which Mrs. March had just cut were all soaked in alcohol and spoiled; and altogether it was a wretched mess, and all because two little boys had not been taught how to behave properly. They ran off as hard as they could go, you may be sure, back into their own seat, as soon as the mischief was done; and, if you will believe it, their father and mother never even looked round or took any notice of all the confusion that was going on. They sat and munched their onions and brown bread and cheese as if they were in their own house all alone. One sees very queer and disagreeable people in travelling. By the time Mr. and Mrs. March had put out the fire, and picked up all the things and wiped up the chocolate as well as they could with a newspaper, the people who had gone out to get their dinners, all came pouring back, and the cars began to move.

"Oh, dear me!" said Mrs. March: "we shall have to go without our lunch now till tea-time. Here, children, just drink this milk, and eat a piece of bread, and at tea-time, perhaps, we'll have better luck."

"I don't care," said Rob; "I ain't hungry a bit: it's all so horrid in here."

"Neither am I," said Nelly. "Can't we have a little room all to ourselves to-morrow, papa?"

"No, Nell," said her father: "no more little room for us on this journey; this car goes through to Denver. We can't change. But it is only one night and one day: we can stand it."

"I 'm glad part of it is night," said Nelly; "we 'll be by ourselves when we 're in bed."

"Yes," said Mrs. March. "You are to sleep with me, and Rob with papa; and we 'll be all shut in behind the curtains.' I think that will be quite comfortable."

When the train stopped for the passengers to take supper, Mr. and Mrs. March decided that they would go out too, and not try any more experiments with the spirit-lamp while they had such dangerous and disagreeable companions in the next seat.

Nelly and Rob clung to their father's hand as they entered the eating-room. There were four long tables, all filled with people eating as fast as they could eat. Nearly all the men had their hats on their heads, and the noise of the knives and forks sounded like the clatter of machinery. The train was to stop only twenty minutes, and everybody was trying to eat all he could in so short a time. Mr. and Mrs. March, being very gentle and quiet people, did not hurry the waiters as the other people did; and so it happened that their supper was not brought to them for some time. Nelly had eaten only a few mouthfuls of her bread and milk when there was a general rush from all the tables, and the room was emptied in a minute. The conductor of the train was sitting at the table with the Marches, and he said kindly to them: —

"Don't hurry; there is plenty of time; five minutes yet."

"Five minutes!" said Rob, scornfully: "I couldn't take five mouthfuls in five minutes. I'm going to carry mine into the cars." And he began spreading bread and butter.

"A good idea, Rob," said his mother. And she did the same thing; and, as the conductor called "All aboard!" the March family entered the car, each carrying two slices of bread and butter.

"Not much better luck with our supper than with our dinner, Sarah," said Mr. March; "I think you'll have to open your lunch-basket, after all."

"Oh, don't ask me to!" said Mrs. March. "The children have had a good drink of milk. We can get along till morning. I would rather go hungry than take out the things with all those people looking on. We can go to bed early: that will be a comfort."

Mistaken Mrs. March! They sat on the steps of the cars for half an hour to watch the sunset. The brake-man had found out that Mr. March was so careful and Nelly and Rob were such good children that he let them sit there as often as they liked. Nelly loved dearly to sit between her father's knees on the upper step and look down at the ground as it seemed to fly away so swiftly under the wheels. Sometimes they went so fast that the ground did not look like ground at all. It looked like a smooth, striped sheet of brown and green paper being drawn swiftly under the car wheels. It seemed to Rob and Nelly as if they must be going out over the edge of the world. All they could see was sky and ground.

"This is the way it looks when you are out in the middle of the ocean, Nell," said her father; "just the great round sky over your head, and the great flat sea underneath : only the sea is never still, as the ground is ; that is the only difference."

" Still ! " cried Rob. " You don't call this ground under us still, do you? It 's going as fast as lightning all the time."

" No, Rob ! it is we who are going ; the ground is still," said his mother ; " but it does look just as if the ground were flying one way and we the other. It makes me almost dizzy to look down."

Pretty soon the moon came up in the east. It was almost full, and, as it came up slowly in sight, it looked like a great circle of fire. Rob and Nelly both cried out, when they first saw it : —

" Oh, mamma ! oh, papa ! see that fire ! "

In a very few minutes it was up in full sight, and then they saw what it was.

" Dear me ! only the moon, after all," said Rob ; " I hoped it was a big fire."

CHAPTER IV.

A NIGHT IN A SLEEPING-CAR.

THE moonlight was so beautiful that Mrs. March did not like to go back into the car; and Rob and Nelly begged so hard to sit up, that she let them stay long past their bed-time. At last she exclaimed:—

"Come, come! this won't do! We must go to bed," and she opened the car door. As soon as she looked in she started back, so that she nearly knocked Mr. March and Nelly off the platform.

"Why, what has happened?" she said.

Mr. March laughed.

"Oh, nothing," he said: "this is the way a sleeping-car always looks at night."

Curtains were let down on each side the aisle its whole length. It was very dark, and the aisle looked very narrow. Not a human being was in sight.

"Where are our sections?" said Mrs. March.

"These are ours, I think," said Mr. March, pulling open a curtain on the left.

"Let my curtain alone," called somebody from inside. "Go away."

Mr. March had opened the wrong curtain.

"Oh, I beg your pardon, madam," he said, much mortified that he should have broken open a lady's bedroom.

Mrs. March and Rob and Nelly stood close together in the middle of the aisle, at their wits' end. They did not dare to open another curtain, for fear it should be somebody's else bedroom, and not their own.

"I'll call Ben," said Mr. March; "he'll know."

But Ben was nowhere to be found. At last they found him sound asleep in a little state-room at the end of the car.

"Ben, come show us which are our sections," said Mr. March.

Ben was very sleepy. He came stumbling down the aisle, rubbing his eyes.

"Reckon there is your berths; I made 'em up all ready for you," said Ben, and pulled open the very curtain Mr. March had opened before.

"Oh! don't open that one; there's a lady in there," cried Mrs. March; but she was too late. Ben had thrown the curtains wide open.

The same angry voice as before called out: —

"I wish you'd let my curtain alone. What are you about?"

"Done made a mistake this time, sure," said Ben, composedly drawing the curtains together again; but not before Mrs. March and Nelly and Rob had had time to see into the bed, and had seen that it was the mother with five children. There they all lay as snug as you please: the three little ones packed like herrings in a box, across the foot of the bed, and the two others on the inside; and the mother lying on the outer edge almost in the aisle. As Ben pushed back the curtains, she muttered: —

"There ain't any room to spare in this berth, if that's what you're looking for."

Rob and Nelly gave a smothered laugh at this.

"Hush, children!" whispered Mrs. March. "You wouldn't like to be laughed at."

"Oh, mamma, it's so funny!" said Rob. "We can't help it."

Mrs. March did not think it funny at all. She began to be in despair about the night.

The very next section to the one with the five children was one of Mr. March's, and luckily those were the next curtains Ben opened.

"Here you are! you're all right!" he said, cheerfully. "Here's all your things: I done piled 'em up first-rate for you."

Piled up they were indeed. The lunch-basket, the strapped bundle of blankets, the overcoats, the water-proofs, the leather bags, all one above the other on one bed.

"Where are we to sleep, mamma?" exclaimed Nelly.

"On top," said Rob. "Hurrah! hurrah!" and he was about to jump on the top of the pile.

· "Be quiet, Rob," said his father: "we must go to bed as quietly as we can, and not wake people up. We ought to have come earlier. Almost everybody is asleep, I think."

At this point, rose two great snores, so close that Mrs. March started.

"Mercy!" she exclaimed. "How that frightened me!"

Snore! snore! snore! The sounds came as regularly as the striking of a clock: they were most uncommonly loud snores. Mr. March looked at his wife and smiled. Mrs. March did not smile in return: she did not like this state of things at all.

At last they had sorted out the things they needed, and the rest of the things they pushed under their berths, — all but the big lunch-basket: Mr. March had to carry that out to the end of the car, and set it by the stove. Then Mr. March and Rob climbed into their bed, and shut the curtains; and Mrs. March and Nelly climbed into theirs, and shut their curtains, and began to undress. Presently, Mr. March called across in a whisper : —

"Wife, what shall I do with Rob's clothes?"

Mrs. March was at that moment trying to find some place to put Nelly's and hers.

"I 'm sure I don't know," she replied. "There isn't a sign of a hook here to hang any thing on."

"Nor here," replied Mr. March : "I 'll leave them all in a pile on the foot of the bed."

"That 'll do very well for a man's clothes," thought Mrs. March; "but I must hang up our gowns and skirts." At last, she had a bright thought. She stood up on the edge of the bed, and hooked the skirts over the rod the curtains were swung from. It was all she could do to reach it; and, just as she was hooking the last skirt on, the car gave a lurch, and out she fell, out into the aisle, and across it, through the curtains of Mr. March's berth, right on to his bed.

"Goodness alive, Sarah ! is this you?" he exclaimed, jumping up, frightened. He was just falling asleep.

"Well, I believe so," she said : "I 'm not sure."

"Oh, mamma, did it hurt you?" called Nelly, anxiously.

"No, no, dear," replied her mother. "I'm coming right back." But, before she went, she whispered in her husband's ear : —

"Robert March, I think a sleeping-car is the most detestable place I ever got into in my life. Suppose I'd tumbled into some stranger's berth, as I did into yours just now."

Mr. March only laughed, and Mrs. March heard him laughing to himself after she had gone back, and it did not make her feel any pleasanter to hear this. At last she and Nelly were both undressed and in bed. Their clothes and dressing-cases and travelling-bags were piled up on their feet.

"You mustn't kick, Nelly," said Mrs. March. "If you do, you'll upset all the things out on the floor."

"I'm afraid I always kick, mamma," replied honest Nelly. "I won't while I'm awake; but when I'm asleep I don't know."

Nelly was fast asleep in two minutes; but Mrs. March could not sleep. The air in the car was so close and hot it made her head ache. She had pinned her curtains tight together before she lay down, so that nobody could look in on her as she had on the poor lady with five children. Now she sat up in bed and unpinned them, and looked out into the aisle. It was dark : the car was dashing along at a tremendous rate; the air was most disagreeable, and there were at least six people snoring different snores.

"I can't stand this. I must open the window at the foot of the berth," said Mrs. March. So she crept down and tried to open it. She had not observed in the day-time how the windows were fastened : she fumbled about in the dark till she found the fastening; she could not move it; she took the skin off her knuckles; she wrenched her shoulder; all this time sitting cross-legged on the bed. At last she gave a shove with all her strength, and the window flew up: in one second, an icy blast blew in full of smoke and cinders. "This won't do, either," said Mrs. March; and she tried to get the window down. This took longer than to get it up; finally, in despair, she propped it open about two inches with one of her boots; then she sank back exhausted, and came down hard on her watch and broke the crystal: then she had a difficult time picking up all the little bits of glass in the dark, and then, after she had picked them up, she did not know what to do with them. There was some stiff paper in her travelling-bag, if she could only get at it; at last she found it, but, in drawing it out, she knocked the cork out of the hartshorn bottle, and over went the bottle in the bag, all the hartshorn poured out, and such a strong smell of hartshorn filled the berth it waked Nelly up.

"Oh, mamma! what is it? what smells so?" she said, sleepily.

"Only hartshorn, dear," said her mother, in a despairing tone. "I've upset it all over every thing. Go to sleep, dear: it won't smell so very long."

Nelly dozed off again, saying: "I'm going to get up just as soon as it's light. I hate this bed: don't you, mamma?"

"Yes, Nell, I do," said Mrs. March; "I would rather have sat up all night: but I am so tired and sleepy now I shall go to sleep, I think."

When Nelly waked, it was just beginning to be light.

Her mother was sound asleep. Nelly leaned over her, and looked out into the aisle. Nobody was up except Ben, who was blacking boots at the end of the aisle.

"I'll get up as still as I can, and get all dressed before mamma wakes up," thought Nelly. "Poor mamma! What a time she had last night!"

At that moment, as Nelly turned her head, she saw a sight which so frightened her that, in spite of herself, she screamed. "What is it, Nell?" asked her mother, waking instantly. Nelly could not speak, but pointed to the wall at the back of their berth. Mrs. March sat upright in bed, and gazed with astonishment and alarm almost as great as Nelly's. What could it mean? There, in the smooth panel of black walnut, which was almost as shining as a looking-glass, was the reflection of a man's face. It was the face of the man who had been eating the cheese and brown bread and onions. He had a red handkerchief tied about his head for a nightcap; and he was sound asleep, with his mouth wide open. While Mrs. March and Nelly sat gazing breathlessly at this unaccountable sight, the head slowly turned on the pillow, and a hand came up and rubbed one eye. Nelly nearly screamed again. Her mother put her hand quickly over her mouth.

"Hush, Nell!" she said; "do not be frightened. I see how it is."

The partitions which separated the sleeping-berths one from the other did not come up close to the wall of the car. There was room to put your hand through between. The black walnut lining of the car was so polished that it reflected like a looking-glass; so each person could see, in the back of his berth, the face of the person who was lying in the berth next before his.

"Goodness!" exclaimed Mrs. March; "if we can see into that berth, they can see into this one;" and she seized one of the pillows, and set it up against the crack. Then she looked down, and saw a similar opening at the foot of the berth. This one she stopped up with another pillow.

"There, Nell," she said, "now we can dress without being overlooked."

Nelly did not quite understand how these shining black walnut panels could have acted like looking-glasses, and she was a little afraid still that the queer, shaggy face with the red silk nightcap would glare out at her again; but she hurried on her clothes, and in a few minutes was ready to go to the little wash-room which was provided for ladies at the end of the car.

"We are so early," said Mrs. March, "that I think we will be the first ones there."

Ah, how mistaken she was! When they reached the little room, there stood two women waiting for their turn at the wash-stand; a third was washing her face. As Mrs. March and Nelly appeared, one of those who were waiting called out : —

"Come in. Don't go away. If you do, you 'll lose your turn : there 'll be lots more here directly."

"Thank you," said Mrs. March : " my daughter and I will wait there, just outside the door. We will not intrude upon you."

At this, all three of the women laughed, and one said :

"H'm ! there ain't much question of intrudin' in these sleepin'-cars. It's just a kind o' big bedroom, that's all."

Mrs. March smiled, and said : "Yes, I think so;"

and the women went on talking. They were relating
their experiences in the night. One of them said : —

" Well, I got along very well till somebody opened a
window, and then I thought I should ha' froze to death ;
but my husband he called the conductor up, and they
shut all the ventilators up ; but I just shivered all night.
Real good soap this is : ain't it ? "

Mrs. March looked warningly at Nelly, who was just
about to speak. " Keep quiet, Nell," she said. But
Nelly whispered : " Do you suppose that was our window, mamma ? "

" I dare say," answered Mrs. March, in a still lower
whisper : " keep still, Nell."

" Well, I wa'n't too cold," said the woman at the
wash-bowl. She had her false teeth in her hand, and
was washing them under the little slow stream running
from the faucet : so she could not speak very distinctly.
" Well, I wa'n't too cold," she said, " but I 'll tell you
what did happen to me. In the middle o' the night I
felt somethin' against my head, right on the very top
on 't ; and what do you think it was? 'Twas the feet of
the man in the next section to our 'n. ' Well,' says I,
' this is more 'n I can stand ; ' and I gave 'em a real
shove. I reckon he waked up, for I didn't feel 'em no
more."

At this Nelly had to run away. She could not keep the
laugh back any longer. And Mrs. March thought it
better to let her go, for she did not know what might be
coming next in the conversation of these women. At
the other end of the car, Nelly saw Rob, carrying something done up in newspaper in his hand. She ran after
him. He put his finger on his lips as she drew near him,

and made signs to her not to speak. She could not imagine what he was carrying. He went very fast to the outside door of the car, opened it, and threw the parcel out.

"What was it, Rob?" said Nell, eagerly.

"I won't tell you," said Rob: "you'll tell."

"Oh! I won't; I won't; indeed I won't," said Nell.

"Honest Indian?" said Rob.

"Honest Indian," said Nelly.

This was the strongest form of pledge which Rob and Nelly ever gave. It was like a sort of oath among the children in Mayfield. If a child broke his promise after he had said "Honest Indian," there was nothing too bad for him.

"Well," said Rob, coming very close to Nelly, and speaking in a low whisper, "it was those people's string of onions!"

"Why, Rob!" cried Nelly, in a horrified tone, "why, Rob! that's stealing. How could you?"

"'Tain't stealing either, Nell March," said Rob, stoutly; "I haven't got 'em. Stealing is taking things. I haven't got them. I didn't want the old, horrid things. I just threw them away. That ain't taking."

Nelly still looked distressed. "Papa wouldn't like it," she said, "nor mamma either. They were all those people had to eat, except bread and cheese. Oh, Rob! I think it was awful mean in you."

"I don't care: I wish I hadn't told you. I don't think it was mean. It was good enough for them for making such a smell in the cars. I heard some of the gentlemen saying they hadn't any business with onions in the car, — that the conductor ought to make them throw them away. Anyhow, Nell, you promised not to tell."

"Yes," said Nell, "but I never once thought of its being such a thing as this. What do you suppose they'll do? They might have you took up and put in prison, Rob."

Rob looked a little disturbed, but he replied bravely:

"Oh, pshaw! I don't know whose onions they were anyhow. I just found them rolling round on the floor, and I picked them up: they weren't anybody's when they were out loose in the car. I don't care: we won't have such a horrid smell here to-day."

Nelly walked away, looking very unhappy. She disliked the smell of onions as much as Rob did; but she would rather have had the string of onions in her lap all day than have had Rob do such a thing as this; and she felt sure it would all be known, somehow, before the day came to an end, — as you will see that it was.

After everybody had got up, and the beds and pillows and blankets were all packed away in the little cupboards overhead, and the car was put in order for the day, the people who had lunch-baskets began to eat their breakfasts. Nelly sat very still in her seat, and watched to see what would happen when the onions were found to be missing. Rob had walked away, and stood at the farther door of the car. He seemed to be very busy looking out at the scenery.

Mrs. March had a good little breakfast of boiled eggs and bread and butter and tea and milk, all ready on the table.

"Call Rob," she said to Nelly. Nelly walked to the end of the car, and said: —

" Come, Rob. Mamma's got breakfast all ready."

Without looking round, Rob whispered : —

" Have they missed 'em ? "

" I don't know : I haven't heard any thing," answered Nelly, in the same low tone. And they walked back together, Nelly looking much more anxious than Rob did. Mrs. March noticed their grave faces as they took their seats, and she said : —

" You are tired : aren't you, children ? "

" Oh, no, mamma ! " they both exclaimed ; " we aren't a bit tired ! "

But their faces did not brighten. If the whole truth were told, it must be owned that they were both very unhappy. The more Rob thought about those onions, the more he felt afraid that it was stealing to have thrown them away ; and this made him wretched enough.

And the more Nelly thought about it, the surer she felt that Rob was going to get into trouble before the thing was done with. Neither of them ate much breakfast ; they were both listening to what was going on in the next section. They could hear such sentences as : —

" I know I left 'em here last night."

" Perhaps they went out of the window."

" They couldn't : they were on the floor."

" That black rascal's got 'em, you may be sure."

At this last sentence, Nelly gave Rob a push under the table with her foot, and his face turned very red. In a moment more, Ben entered the car ; as he was passing the Marches' table, the angry man from the next section called out, in a very rude way : —

" Here, you nigger, what 'd you do with my onions ? "

Ben stood stock-still, he was so astonished.

"Ungyuns!" he exclaimed; "I never seed no ungyuns."

"Yes, you did! You must have: you 've stowed 'em away somewhere. Now jest you pass 'em out, or I 'll report you."

Ben had never been accused of stealing before. He looked the man full in the face, and said: —

"You can do all the reportin' yer want to, mister. I never seed your ungyuns." And he was about to pass on; but the man was so angry, and so sure that Ben must have taken his onions, that he stood in the middle of the aisle, right in Ben's way, and would not let him pass.

"Hand 'em over now," he said, in the most insulting tone; "hand 'em over."

Mr. March, who had been watching the scene with some amusement, was very much astonished, on looking at Rob at this moment, to see his cheeks flushed, his lips parted as if he were about to speak.

"Why, Rob," he said, "do you know where the onions are?"

"No," said Rob.

Nelly gave an involuntary gasp, under her breath, "Oh!"

Mr. March looked at her in still greater surprise.

"Do you, Nell?" he said.

Nelly did not reply, but looked at Rob, who said: —

"I don't know where they are now." But his expression was a very guilty one.

"Rob!" said his father, sternly, "you know something about those onions: tell me this moment."

Nelly clasped her hands tight, and gave a little cry, "Oh, Rob!"

Now that the final moment had come, Rob spoke up like a man.

"Papa, I threw them out of the car door, — they made such a smell. I found them close to our berth when I first got up, and they smelled so horrid I threw them away. Perhaps they weren't this man's onions," said poor Rob, clutching at a last hope.

Mr. March could hardly believe his ears.

"You! You took what did not belong to you, and then threw it away! Why, Rob! I am ashamed of you! Why, Rob, I wouldn't have believed it!" exclaimed Mr. March. "You will pay for those onions out of your allowance." And he looked at Rob more sternly than he had ever done in his life.

"Come, now, immediately," he continued, "and apologize to the man." And he took Rob by the hand and led him to the next seat.

"I am very sorry to tell you, sir," he said, "that my little boy here took your onions and threw them away. He shall buy some for you at the very first station where we can."

"What 'd yer throw 'em away for?" said the man, looking curiously and not unkindly at Rob, whose face was enough to make anybody sorry for him.

"Because I hate the smell of them so," said Rob, sturdily; "and my mamma hates them too; and I found them rolling round on the floor, by our berth; and I just picked them up and threw them away. I didn't think about their being anybody's, — not until

7

afterwards," he added; "and I 'm very sorry, sir. I 'll buy you some more out of my own money."

Mr. March smiled at this little explanation: he saw that Rob had not really intended to do wrong.

"No, no, my boy, you needn't do that," said the man; "we 're going to get off before dinner time; an' we 've got a bin full o' onions at home. I expect they do smell kind o' strong to folks that ain't used to 'em; but they 're mighty healthy."

Rob walked back to his seat somewhat relieved, but still very much ashamed. He glanced up in his mother's face. She looked mortified; still there was a twinkle in her eyes: in the bottom of her heart, she sympathized with Rob's impulse to be rid of the onions at any cost.

"Oh, Rob!" she said, "how could you do such a thing? You knew they must belong to somebody."

"Well, I did afterwards, — after I told Nell; but, when I picked them up, I didn't think any thing except how they smelt. It was a good riddance anyhow."

The sick lady, who had had to lie down all the way, was in the section next but one to Mr. March's. She had looked much amused during all this conversation, which she could not help hearing. Mrs. March noticed her pleasant smile, and thought she would like to do something for her. So she gave Nelly a nice cup of hot tea to take over to her. The lady was very grateful.

"Oh!" she said, "this is the first good tea I have tasted since I left home."

Then she made Nelly sit down on the bed beside her, and talked to her so sweetly that Nelly felt as if she had known her all her life ; and pretty soon she told her all about Mrs. Napoleon.

"Bring her here. Let me see her," said the lady.

"Oh, I can't bear to have anybody see her!" said Nelly: "she looks awful."

"Never mind : we'll draw the curtains, and nobody else shall see."

So she called her nurse, who was sitting near ; and, as soon as Nelly had climbed up into the berth, the nurse drew the curtains tight and shut them in together. It seemed to Mrs. March a long time before Nelly came out. When she came she had two small parcels in her hands. They were both in nice white tissue paper, tied up with pink ribbon. Nelly looked as if she had been crying, but yet she looked happy ; and the sick lady had a most beautiful smile on her face. Nelly gave one of the parcels to her mother, and said : —

"Mamma, will you please pack this in the bag? It is the Empress's clothes. Perhaps I may have another doll some day that they will fit."

Then she handed the other parcel to her father, and said : —

"Please throw this out of the window, papa?"

"What is it, Nell?" he said, surprised.

Nelly's voice trembled a little ; but she answered bravely.

"Mrs. Napoleon, papa. That nice lady looked at her, and said she never could be mended ; and if she were me, she'd throw her right away. She says I'll feel better as soon as she is out of my sight."

Mr. March looked over at the sick lady and bowed and smiled.

"She is quite right, Nell. You'll forget all about it much quicker. Good-by, Mrs. Napoleon," he said, and threw the white parcel with its pink ribbons as far as he could throw it.

"I don't want to forget about it, papa," replied Nelly, and pressed her face close against the window-pane, so as not to lose the last glimpses of the package.

Never were people gladder to reach any place than Mr. and Mrs. March and Nelly and Rob were to reach Denver. They were so tired that they went right to bed as soon as they entered the hotel. They did not want any supper. The next morning, however, they were up early, all rested and ready to look at every thing. The first thing they saw as they walked out of the hotel door, was a long range of high mountains to the south. They looked down the long street on which the hotel stood, and saw these mountains rising up like a great wall across the end of the street. They were covered with snow two-thirds of the way down. The lower part which was not covered with snow was of a very dark blue color; and the upper part, where the snow lay, shone in the sun so dazzling bright that it made their eyes ache to look at it. The sky was as blue as blue could be, and had not a cloud in it; and some of the sharp peaks of the mountains looked as if they were really cutting through the sky. Mr. and Mrs. March and Nelly and Rob all stood still in the middle of the street looking at the beautiful sight. Several carriages and wagons came very near running over them, but they hardly observed it. No one of them spoke for some minutes: even Rob was overawed by the grandeur of the mountains. But his overawed silence did not last long. In a few minutes, he broke out with : —

"Bully mountains ! ain't they? Come on !" Mr. and Mrs. March laughed.

"Well, Rob," said his father, "you've brought us to our senses : haven't you?   But I do wish you wouldn't talk slang."

"No, Rob," said his mother. "How many times have I asked you not to say 'bully'?"

"I know it, mother," replied Rob; "but you don't tell me any other word to say instead of it. A fellow must say something ; and 'bully''s such a bully word. I don't believe there's any other word that's good for any thing when things are 'bully.'"

"Oh, dear Rob ! dear Rob ! Three times in one sentence ! What shall we do to you? We will really have to hire you to leave off that word, as grandpa hired you to drink cold water, at so much a week."

"Mamma," said Rob, solemnly, "you couldn't hire me to leave off saying 'bully.' Money wouldn't pay me : I try not to say it often, because you hate it so ; but I don't expect to leave it off till I'm a man. I just have to say it sometimes."

"Oh, Rob, you don't 'have' to say it !" exclaimed Nell. "Nobody 'has to say' any thing."

"Girls don't," said Rob, patronizingly : "but girls are different ; I'm always telling you that girls don't need words like boys. It's just like whistling : girls needn't whistle ; but a boy — why, a boy'd die if he couldn't whistle."

"I can whistle," said Nell. "I can whistle most as well as you."

"You can't, Nell," exclaimed Rob, utterly astonished.

For ·reply, Nelly quietly whistled a bar of Yankee Doodle. Rob stared at her.

"Why, so you can!" said he. "I didn't know girls ever whistled : I thought they were made so they couldn't."

"Oh, no!" said Mrs. March; "I used to be a great whistler when I was a girl; but I never let anybody hear me, if I could help it. And Nelly knows that it is not ladylike for a girl to whistle. She likes to whistle as well as you like to say 'bully,' however; so you might leave off that as well as she can leave off whistling."

"But you used to whistle all alone by yourself," persisted Rob; "and it is just as good fun to whistle all alone as with other people; but it wouldn't be any fun to go off all alone, and say 'bully! bully! bully!'"

Mrs. March put her hands over her ears, and exclaimed: "Oh, Rob! Rob! That makes six times! That dreadful word!"

"Oh!" said Rob, pretending to be very innocent, "do you mind my saying it that way? That wasn't saying it really : only talking about it," and Rob gave his mother a mischievous look.

The streets were thronged with people; everybody seemed in a hurry; the shop windows were full of just such things as one sees in shop windows at the East; through street after street they walked, growing more and more surprised every moment.

"Why, Robert," said Mrs. March, "except for the

bustling and excited air of the people, I should not know that I was not in an Eastern city."

"Nor I," said Mr. March: "I am greatly astonished to see such a civilized-looking place."

Just then an open carriage rolled past them. It was a beautiful carriage, lined with red satin.

"Oh, mamma! there is the nice lady who was in the cars," said Nelly: "let me go and speak to her."

The lady saw them and stopped her carriage: she was very glad to see their faces; she felt so lonely in this strange place. She was all alone with her doctor and nurse; and already she was so homesick she was almost ready to turn about and go home.

"Oh! do let your little girl jump in and take a drive with me," she said. "It will be a great favor to me if you will."

"Oh, mamma! let me; let me," cried Nelly; and, almost before her mother had fully pronounced the words giving her permission, she was climbing up the carriage steps. As she took her seat by the lady's side, she looked wistfully back at Rob. Mrs. Williams (that was the lady's name) observed the glance, and said: "Won't you let the little boy come too? Would you like to come, dear?"

"No, thank you," said Rob: "I'd rather walk. I can see better."

"Oh, Rob! how can you?" exclaimed Nelly, but the driver touched his horses with the whip, and they were off.

What a drive that was for Nelly! She never forgot it. It was her first sight of the grand Rocky Mountains. The city of Denver lies on a great plain; about

thirty miles away stands the mountain range ; between
the city and the mountains runs a river, — the Platte
River, — which has green trees along its bank.   Mrs.
Williams took Nelly out on high ground to the east, from
which she could look over the whole city, and the river,
and out to the beautiful mountains.   Some of the peaks
were as solid white as white clouds, and looked almost
like clouds suddenly made to stand still in the skies.
Mrs. Williams loved mountains very much ; and, as she
looked at Nelly's face, she saw that Nelly loved them
too.   Nelly said very little ; but she kept hold of Mrs.
Williams's hand, and, whenever they came to a particu-
larly beautiful view, she would press it so hard that once
or twice Mrs. Williams cried out : " Dear child, you
hurt me : don't squeeze so tight ; " upon which Nelly,
very much ashamed, would let go of her hand for a few
minutes, but presently, in her excitement, would be holding it again as tight as ever.   Mrs. Williams was a widow
lady : she had lost her husband and her only child — a
little girl about Nelly's age — only two years before, and
she had been an invalid ever since.   As soon as she saw
Nelly's face in the cars, she had fancied that she looked
like her little girl who was dead.   Her name was Ellen
too, and she had always been called Elly ; so that Nelly's
name had a familiar sound to her.   Mrs. Williams was
a very rich lady ; and, if Nelly's father and mother had
been poor people, she would have asked them at once to
give Nelly to her.   But, of course, she knew that that
would be out of the question ; so all she could do was
to try to make Nelly have a good time as long as she
was with her.   After they had driven all about the city,
and had seen all there was to see, she said to the driver :

“Now go to the best toy store in the city.” Nelly did not hear this direction : she was absorbed in looking at the mountains. So she was much surprised when they stopped at the shop, and Mrs. Williams said : —

“ Now, Nelly dear, I want you to go in and buy something for me : will you? I can’t get out of the carriage myself.”

“ Yes indeed,” exclaimed Nelly, “ if I can ; but I never went into a shop alone in my life. Mamma always goes with me. Can’t I bring what you want out here for you to look at ? ”

Mrs. Williams laughed.

“ You ’ll be a better judge of it than I, Nell,” she said. “ It is a wax doll I want for a young friend of mine, — just about such an one as you had in the cars.”

Wasn’t Nelly a very simple little girl never to think that Mrs. Williams meant to buy it for her? She never so much as thought of it. “ Oh ! ” said she, “ how glad she ’ll be ! I hope she ’ll have better luck with it than I had. You tell her not to take her on any journeys. Is it your own little girl ? ”

Then Nelly saw the tears come in Mrs. Williams’s eyes : her lips quivered, and she said : —

“ My own little girl is in heaven ; but this doll is for a little girl I love very much, who looks like my little girl. Run in, dear, and see what you can find.”

The shopkeeper looked quite surprised to see such a little girl coming up to the counter, and asking if he had any big wax dolls with eyes which would open.

“ Yes, sis,” he said, “ we have two ; but they cost too much money for you, I reckon.”

Nelly did not like being called “ sis.”

"My name is not sis," she said, "and the doll is for a sick lady out in the carriage. Won't you please bring them out for her to look at?" and Nelly turned, and walked out of the shop.

"Hoity toity!" said the man. "What airs we put on, don't we, for small fry! Eastern folks, I reckon;" but he went to a drawer, and took out his two wax dolls, and carried them to the carriage. Each doll was in a box by itself. One was dressed in pink satin, and one in white muslin.

"Which is the prettiest, Nelly?" said Mrs. Williams.

"Oh, the one in white muslin, — ever so much the prettiest! My mamma says satin is very silly on dolls, and I think so too. Mrs. Napoleon had a blue satin dress, and I gave it to Mabel Martin. She never wore it but once, — the day she came; she had it on when she was in the stocking; but I hated it on her."

"In the stocking!" said Mrs. Williams; "that big doll never went into a stocking. What do you mean?"

"Oh, not into a common stocking!" said Nelly; "into one of my grandpa's stockings. Mamma always hangs his stockings up for us at Christmas."

Mrs. Williams was still more perplexed.

"Why, child," she said, "how big is your grandpa? Is he a giant?"

"Oh, no!" laughed Nelly, "he isn't very big; but these are great stockings he had made to sleep in. They come all the way up his legs, — both parts of his leg, — way up above his knee, as far as his legs go, so as to keep him warm when he's asleep. He doesn't sleep in any night-gown."

Mrs. Williams laughed heartily at this, and was about

to ask Nelly some other questions, when the shopkeeper
interrupted her with : —

"Can't stand here all day, mum. Do ye want the
dolls or not : say quick."

Mrs. Williams was not accustomed to be spoken to
in this manner, and she looked at him in surprise.

"Oh !" he said, in answer to her look, "you ain't in
the East, you 'll find out. We Western men 've got too
much to do to dangle round all day on a single trade.
Do ye want the dolls? If not, I 'll take 'em back."

"I am sorry you are in such a hurry all the time,
sir," said Mrs. Williams, slowly : "it must be very disagreeable. I will take one of these dolls as soon as
this little girl has decided which one is the prettiest."

"Oh, the white-muslin-gown one, ever so much,"
exclaimed Nelly.

"Very well. You may put it up for me," said Mrs.
Williams, taking out her purse. "How much does it
cost?"

"Ten dollars," said the man.

"Oh, oh !" exclaimed Nelly, "mine was only five,
and it was just as big as this one."

The man looked a little embarrassed. The doll did
not really cost ten dollars : it had only cost five ; but
he thought Mrs. Williams looked like a rich lady, and
he might as well ask all he could get.

"Well, this cost me six dollars in New York," he
said ; "but there isn't much sale for them here : you
can have it for seven."

Mrs. Williams paid him the seven dollars, and they
drove away with the box with the doll in it, lying in
Nelly's lap. Presently Nelly said : —

"Oh, Mrs. Williams, won't you let me send all Mrs. Napoleon's clothes to the little girl this dolly's for? I think they'd fit this dolly: don't you?"

"You dear little thing!" exclaimed Mrs. Williams; "would you really send all those pretty clothes to a little girl you don't know?"

"But you know her," said Nelly, "and you said you loved her; so I'd like to have her have them. Besides, I don't believe I'll ever have another dolly like Mrs. Napoleon: at any rate, not for a great many years."

"Very well, dear," replied Mrs. Williams: "I will take them. She will be all the more pleased to get so many extra suits. When we stop at the hotel, you can give them to me."

"The waterproof is torn some," said Nelly: "I guess mamma'll mend it."

"Oh, never mind!" said Mrs. Williams. "This little girl's mamma is a very kind mamma: she can mend it."

When they stopped at the hotel, Nelly raced upstairs and burst into her mother's room.

"Mamma!" she exclaimed almost as breathlessly as Rob was in the habit of speaking, "mamma, give me all Mrs. Napoleon's clothes. The sick lady's bought a beautiful wax doll — just Mrs. Napoleon's size — her name's Mrs. Williams — I asked her — and she's going to send it to a little girl she loves very much — her own little girl's dead — and I want her to have those clothes too, because Mrs. Williams is so kind; oh, she's the sweetest lady! Give me the clothes, quick!"

Mrs. March was looking in a trunk for them while

Nelly ran on. She smiled as she handed them to Nelly.

"Are you sure you will not want them yourself, Nell?" she said; "you might have a doll that they'd just fit."

"I don't believe I ever will, mamma," said Nelly; "and even if I do, I'd rather give these clothes away. Mrs. Williams is such a sweet lady — you don't know, mamma!" And Nelly ran downstairs with the package in her hand. As she left the room, Rob said to his mother: —

"Mamma, I bet she's bought the doll for Nell! Wouldn't that be fun? Nell's such a goose she'd never suspect any thing!"

"Hush, Rob!" said Mrs. March; "don't put such an idea into Nell's head. It isn't at all likely."

"Well, you'll see, mamma. I'll bet you any thing."

"Ladies don't 'bet,' Rob; and you know mamma hates to hear you say the word."

"Oh, dear, mamma!" groaned Rob, "you hate all the nice words! I wish ladies were just like boys!"

Late that evening, after Rob and Nelly were fast asleep, a large parcel was brought to their rooms, addressed to Mrs. March. She opened it, and found inside — sure enough, as Rob had said — the beautiful wax doll which Nelly had told them about; and, in the box with the doll, the little bundle of all Mrs. Napoleon's clothes. A note from Mrs. Williams to Mrs. March was pinned on the outside of the package. She said: —

"My DEAR Mrs. MARCH, — Will you allow me to give this doll to your dear, sweet little daughter, to supply the place of the lost Mrs. Napoleon. If you knew how great a pleasure it is to me to do this, I am sure you would not refuse it. Your little girl reminds me so strongly of my own little Elly, who died two years ago, that I only wish I could have her always with me

"Truly your friend, although a stranger,

"ISABELLA WILLIAMS."

"Well, Rob was right!" exclaimed Mrs. March, as she read this note. "See, Robert, what a beautiful doll has come for Nelly from that invalid lady she went to drive with this afternoon. Rob said she had bought it for Nelly, but I didn't believe it. I don't exactly like to take such a valuable present from a stranger."

Mr. March was reading the note.

"But we could not refuse," he said. "It would be cruel, when she wants to give it to Nelly because she looks so like her little child that is dead."

"No," said Mrs. March; "of course we could not refuse."

"She had one of the sweetest and saddest faces I ever saw," said Mr. March. "I do not think she will live long. I wish we could do something for her."

"I will go and see her to-morrow morning, and thank her for the doll," said Mrs. March; "and then I will find out whether we can do any thing for her or not. I shall not let Nelly know any thing about the doll till we are all settled. I will pack it away in my trunk."

"Yes, that will be much wiser," said Mr. March: "we won't have a second Mrs. Napoleon disaster."

Later in the evening, Deacon and Mrs. Plummer arrived; and the next day was very much taken up in discussing plans with them, and making arrangements for going on their journey; and it was late in the afternoon before Mrs. March found time to go to the hotel where Mrs. Williams was staying. She found, to her great sorrow, that Mrs. Williams had left town at noon. She had gone, the landlord said, to Idaho Springs; where he believed she was to take the hot baths. Mrs. March wrote a note to her immediately, and the landlord said he would forward it; but he was not sure of her address, and Mrs. March was very much afraid it would never reach her.

The Marches stayed in Denver a week, but they did not hear a word from Mrs. Williams, and Mrs. March reproached herself very much for not having gone to see her early the next morning after the doll came.

"It is evident," she said, "that she never got my note; and what must she have thought of us for not acknowledging such a beautiful present. It will worry me always, as often as I see the doll."

CHAPTER V.

FIRST GLIMPSES OF COLORADO AND A NEW HOME.

JUST one week from the day they had reached Denver, they set out again on their journey southward. They were going to a beautiful place in the mountains, called the Ute Pass. It really is a canyon : you remember I tried to explain to you what a canyon is like. This canyon is called the Ute Pass because a tribe of Indians named the Utes used to come and go through it when they were journeying from one hunting ground to another. A little stream comes down through this pass, which is called the Fountain Creek. It leaps and tumbles from rock to rock, and is always in a foam. A great many years ago, some Frenchmen who were here named it "The fountain that boils." Part of the canyon is very narrow, and the rocky walls are very high. There is a good road through it now, close beside the brook ; but when the Indians used to go through it there was no road : they had a little narrow path ; some parts of it are still to be seen, high up on the ledges of the rock, wherever there is room enough for a pony to get foot-hold. It looks like a little, worn track which sheep or goats might have made ; you would never believe, to look at it, that great bands of Indians on ponies used to travel over it. One thing they used to come down for was to drink the waters of some springs which bubble up out of the rocks at the mouth of the canyon. These are very strange. They bubble up so fast that they look as if they were boiling: this is why the Frenchmen called the brook "The fountain that boils." But they are not any hotter than the water in the brook. The Indians found out that this water would cure people who were ill: so they used to wrap their sick people up in blankets, and bring them on ponies over this little narrow path through the pass, and then build their wigwams close to the springs, and stay there for weeks, drinking the water, and bathing in it. The last part of the canyon is not narrow: it widens out; and has little fields and meadows and groves in it. The road through it is lined almost all the way with green trees and bushes of different kinds; and there is a beautiful wild-hop vine which grows in great abundance, and climbs up the trees, and seems to be tying them all up in knots together; the hop blossoms look like green tassels at every knot. Does not this sound like a lovely place to live in? Mr. and Mrs. March thought so; they had seen several pictures of it; and a man who had lived two years there told them about it, and tried to persuade them to buy his house and land. But old Deacon Plummer was too wise to buy till they had tried it.

"No, no," he said; "we'll hire it for six months first, and see how it works. It may be all true as you say about the cattle's grazin' well up and down them rocks; but I'd rather hev medder land any day. We'll hire, to begin with."

So they had rented the man's house and land for six

months, and had bought all his cows: the cows were still on the place. Then they bought a nice wagon, with three seats and a white top to it, very much like the butchers' carts you see going round with meat to sell in country villages. All the farmers in Colorado drive in such wagons. Then they had bought two horses. The horses and the wagon were to go with them on the cars. I must tell you about the horses. They had such queer names! One was-a dark red, and he was called "Fox." He had a narrow head and a sharp nose; and really his face did look like a fox's face. The other horse was of a very queer shade of reddish yellow, with a good deal of white about him; his forefeet were white, and his mane was almost white; and, if you will believe it, his name was "Pumpkinseed"! The man the Marches bought him of did not know why he was called so. He himself had only owned him a year; and, when he asked the man he bought him of how he came to give the horse such a queer name, he said he "didn't know. The old woman named him; mebbe she thought he was kind o' the color of pumpkin-seed, sort o' streaked with yaller 'n' white." Rob was delighted with this name. He kept singing it over and over: "Pumpkinseed! Pumpkinseed! We've got a horse called Pumpkinseed!"—till his mother begged him to stop.

The railroad which runs southward from Denver is the kind of railroad called a narrow-gauge railroad. This means that the track is only about two-thirds the width of ordinary railroad tracks; and the cars and the engines are made small to match the track. You can't think how droll a train of such little cars looks when

you first see it; it looks like a play train. A gentleman
I know said a funny thing the first time he saw a little
narrow-gauge train pulling along behind its little engine;
he turned to his wife: " Look here, wife," said he;
" let's buy that and send it home to the children to
play with."

When Rob and Nelly first stepped into the little car,
they exclaimed, " What a funny car!" On one side
the car there were double seats in which two people
could sit; on the other side were single seats, rather
tight even for one person. Nelly and Rob both ran to
get two of these little seats.

" Hurrah!" said Rob, as he sat down in this; " I'm
going in a high chair! Mamma, ain't this just like a
baby's high chair?"

" Yes, just about, Rob," said Mr. March, who had
taken his seat in one, and found it too tight for comfort.

But they soon ceased to wonder at the little seats, for
they found so much to look at out of the car windows.
The journey from Denver to the town of Colorado
Springs, where they were to leave the cars, takes four
hours and a half: the road lies all the way on the plains,
but runs near the lower hills of the mountain ranges on
the right; about half way, it crosses what is called the
" Divide." That is a high ridge of land, with great
pine groves on it, and a beautiful little lake at the top.
This is over eight thousand feet high.

Down the south side of this, the cars run swiftly by
their own weight, just as you go down hill on a sled:
the engine does not have to draw them at all. In fact,
they have to turn the brakes down some of the time to
keep the cars from going too fast.

Nelly and Rob sat sidewise in their seats, with their faces close to the window, all the way. They had never seen such a country. Every mile new mountain tops came in sight, and new and wonderful rocks. Some of the rocks looked like great castles, with towers to them. More than once Rob called out: —

"There, mamma! that one is a castle: I know it is. It can't possibly be a rock."

And it was hard even for the grown people to believe that they were merely rocks. Old Deacon and Mrs. Plummer were almost as much excited as Rob and Nelly. The Deacon, however, was looking with a farmer's eye at the country. He did not like to find so much snow: as far as he could see in all directions, there was a thin coating of snow over the ground. The yellow grass blades stood up above it like little masts of ships under water. Everywhere he looked he saw cattle walking about. They did not look as if they were contented; and they were so thin, you could see their bones when they came close to the cars.

At last the Deacon said to Mr. March: —

"Here's their stock runnin' out all winter, that we've heard so much on; but it appears to me, it's mighty poor-lookin' stock. I don't see how in natur' the poor things get a livin' off this dried grass, half buried up in snow."

"Ah, sir!" spoke up a man on the seat behind Mr. March; "you do not know how much sweeter the hay is, dried on the stalk, standing. There is no such hay in the world as the winter grasses in Colorado."

"Do you keep stock yourself, sir?" asked the Deacon.

"No, I've never been in the stock business myself,"

the man replied; "but I have lived in this State five years, and I know it pretty well; and it's the greatest country for stock in the world, sir, — yes, the greatest in the world."

Deacon Plummer smiled, but did not ask any more questions. After this enthusiastic man had left the car, the Deacon said quietly, pointing to a poor, lean cow who was sniffing hungrily at some little tufts of yellow grass near the railroad track: "I'd rather have her opinion than his. If the critter could speak, I guess she'd say, 'Give me a manger full of good medder hay, in a Massachusetts barn, in place of all this fine winter grass of Colorado.'"

Rob and Nelly laughed out at this idea of the cow's being called in as witness.

"I guess so too," said Rob; "don't she look hungry, though?"

Just before they reached the town of Colorado Springs, they suddenly saw, a short distance off, on the right-hand side of the railroad track, two enormous red rocks, rising like broken pieces of a high wall; they looked thin, like slabs. One of them was deep brick red, and the other was a sort of pink.

"Oh, mamma! look quick, look quick," exclaimed Nelly: "what can those red rocks be?"

"They are the Gates of the Garden of the Gods," said the conductor. who was passing at that moment; "the Garden lies just behind them, and you drive in between those high rocks."

Even while he was passing, the rocks disappeared from view. Nelly looked at them with awe-stricken eyes.

"The Garden of the Gods, sir!" she said; "what

does that mean? What gods? Do they worship heathen gods in this country?"

A lady who was sitting opposite Nelly laughed aloud at this question.

"I don't wonder you ask such a question," she said: "it is one of the most absurd names ever given to a place, and I cannot find out who gave it. Those high rocks that you saw are like a sort of gateway into a great field which is full of very queer-shaped rocks. Most of them are red, like the gates; some of them have uncouth resemblances to animals or to human heads. There is one that looks like a seal, and another like a fish standing on its tail, and peering up over a rock. There are a good many cedar-trees and pines in this place, and in June a few flowers; but, for the most part, it is quite barren. The soil is of a red color, like the rocks; and the grass is very thin, so that the red color shows through; and you couldn't find a place in all Colorado that looks less like a garden."

"But why did they say 'gods'?" asked Nelly; "did they mean the old gods? My papa has read me about them, — Jupiter, and his wife, Juno. Is this where they lived?"

The lady laughed again. "I can't tell you about that, dear," she said. "I think they thought the place was so grand that it looked as if it ought to belong to some beings greater than human beings: so they said 'gods.' I think myself it would have been a good name for it to call it the 'Fortress of the Gods,' or 'The Tombs of the Giants;' but not the 'Garden of the Gods.' I shouldn't want it even for my own garden; and I'm only a commonplace woman. But it is a very wonderful place to see. You will be sure to go there, for all strangers are taken to see it."

"Do you live in Colorado, madam?" asked Mrs. March.

"Oh, yes!" replied the lady: "Colorado Springs, the little town we are just coming to, is my home."

"Do you like it?" asked Mrs. March, anxiously.

"Like it!" replied the lady; "like is not a strong enough word. I love it. I love these mountains so that, whenever I go away from them, I miss them all the time; and I keep seeing them before me all the while, just as you see the face of a dear friend you are separated from. I should be very ungrateful, if I did not love the place; for it has simply made me over again. I came out here three years ago on a mattress, with my doctor and nurse, and thought it very doubtful if I lived to get here; and I have been perfectly well ever since."

"Did you have asthma?" asked Rob, turning very red as soon as he had asked the question. He was afraid it was improper. "My papa has the asthma."

"Oh, if that is your papa's trouble, he will be sure to be entirely well. Nobody can have asthma in Colorado," replied the lady. "It is the one thing which is always cured here. My own trouble was only a throat trouble."

"I am very glad to hear you speak so confidently about the asthma," said Mrs. March: "my husband has been a great sufferer from it, and it is for that we have come."

"You have done the very wisest thing you could have done," said the lady: "you will never be sorry for it. But here we are; good morning."

The train was already stopping in front of a little brown wooden building, and the brakeman called out: "Colorado Springs."

"What a pleasant lady!" said Nelly to her mother.

"Yes," said Mrs. March; but it was partly because she told us such good news for papa.

As they stepped out on the platform, they were almost deafened by the shouts of two black men, who were calling out the names of two hotels: two omnibuses belonging to the different hotels were standing there, and each black man was trying to get the most passengers for his hotel. Each man called out: —

"Free 'bus — this way to the free 'bus — only first-class hotel in the city."

"Mercy on us!" exclaimed Mrs. March. "Let us go to the one who speaks the lowest, if there is any difference. They must think railroad travellers are all deaf! It makes no difference to which one we go just for a dinner. We shall drive home this afternoon."

So saying, she stepped into the nearest omnibus, and the rest of the party followed her. In a moment more, the driver cracked his whip, and the four horses set off on a full gallop up the hill which lies between the railway station and the town. As they drew near the hotel door, the driver turned such a sharp corner, all at full speed, that the omnibus swung round on the wheels of one side, and pitched so violently that it threw both Nelly and Rob off their seats into· the laps of their father and mother who sat opposite.

"Hullo!" exclaimed Rob, picking himself up, "this is the way the gods drive, I suppose!"

His mother looked reprovingly at him; but he only laughed and said: —

THE UTE PASS. — Page 121.

"They call every thing after the gods, don't they? So I thought that pitch was the same sort."

After dinner, Deacon Plummer harnessed Fox and Pumpkinseed into the new wagon, and they set out for their new home. It was a beautiful afternoon; as warm and bright as a May day in New England. There was no snow to be seen except on the mountains, which rose like a great blue wall with white peaks to the west of the town.

"Now this feels something like," said the Deacon, as they set out; "this is like what they told us. I wonder if it's been this way all winter."

They drove five miles straight towards the mountains. Nelly had taken her picture of Pike's Peak out of the travelling-bag, and held it in her hand. Now she could look up from it to the real mountain itself, and see if the picture were true.

"I don't care for the picture any more, papa," said Nelly, "now I've got the mountain. The picture isn't half so beautiful." And Nelly hardly took her eyes from the shining, snowy summit till they were so close to its base that it was nearly shut out from their sight by the lower hills.

They drove through the little village at the mouth of the Ute Pass. Here they saw two large hotels, and half a dozen small houses and shops. This little village is called Manitou. The Indians named it so. Manitou means "Good Spirit," and they thought the Good Spirit had made the waters bubble up out of the rocks here to cure sick people. A few rods beyond the last house, they entered the real pass. Now their surprises began. On each side of them were high walls

of rock : at the bottom of the right-hand wall was just
room enough for the road ; on the left hand they looked
over a steep precipice down to a brook which was rush-
ing over great stones, and leaping down with much roar
and foam from one basin to another; there was no
fence along this left-hand side of the road, and as Mrs.
March looked over she shuddered, and exclaimed : —

"Oh, Robert, let me get out! I never can drive up
this road ; let us all walk."

Mr. March himself thought it was dangerous ; so he
stopped the horses, and Mrs. March and Mrs. Plummer
and the two children got out to walk. Nelly and Rob
did not look where they were walking ; they were all the
while looking up at the great rocks over their heads,
which jutted out above the road like great shelves :
some rose up high in the air like towers ; they were
all of a fine red color, or else of a yellowish brown ;
and they were full of sharp points, and deep lines cut
in them ; and a beautiful green lichen grew on many of
them. Sometimes they were piled up in piles, so that
they looked as if they might tumble down any minute ;
sometimes they were hollowed out in places that looked
as if they were made for niches for statues to stand in ;
on one high hill was a strange pile, built up so solid
and round it looked like a pulpit. Mrs. March and
Nelly and Rob were standing still, looking at this :
when a man who passed by, seeing they were strangers,
called out : —

"That's Tim Bunker's Pulpit."

"Who's Tim Bunker?" cried Rob ; but the man was
riding so fast he did not hear him.

"Oh, Nell! if it isn't too far we'll climb up there

some day: won't we?" said Rob. "Mamma, don't you suppose we're pretty near our house?"

"I think not, Rob," replied Mrs. March; "there cannot be any place for a house while the pass is so narrow."

"Oh, mamma! mamma! come here!" shouted Nelly. She had taken one step down from the road, and was looking over into the brook. "Here is the most beautiful little fall you ever saw!"

They all climbed carefully down on the broad stone where Nelly was standing, and looked over. It was indeed a beautiful fall: not very high, — but all one white foam from top to bottom; and the water fell into a small pool, where the spray had frozen into a great round rim: it looked like frosted silver.

"That's a pretty silver bowl to catch the water in; ain't it, now?" said Mrs. Plummer. "I'd like a drink of it."

"What a queer country this is!" said Mrs. March; "here we are walking without any outside wraps on, and almost too warm in the sun; and here is ice all round this pool; and I have seen little thin rims of ice here and there on the brook all the way up."

"It's just bully," cried Rob. "Say, mamma, I'm going down to drink out of that bowl;" and, before they could stop him, Rob was half way down the precipice. He found it rougher than he thought; and he had more than one good tumble before he got down to the bed of the brook: but he reached it, dipped his drinking-cup into the pool, broke off a big piece of the frozen spray, and with that in one hand, and his drinking-cup in the other, began to climb up again. This was twice

as hard as to go down, — it made Rob puff and pant,
and he lost his piece of ice before he had gone many
steps, — but he managed to carry the water up, and
very much they all enjoyed it.　"It's the sweetest
water I ever tasted," said Mrs. Plummer.

"Yes," said Mrs. March, "it must be, in good part,
melted snow water out of the mountains : that is always
sweet.　This is the brook, no doubt, which runs past
our house.　You know they said it was close to the
brook."

"Oh, splendid!" cried Rob ; "oh, mamma, isn't this
a gay country? so much nicer than an old village with
streets in it, like Mayfield.　This is some fun."

Mrs. March laughed, but she thought in her heart :

"I hope he'll always find it fun."

"I don't think it's fun, Rob," said Nelly, slowly.

"Why not, Nell?" exclaimed Rob ; "why don't you
like it?"

"I do like it," said Nelly, earnestly ; "I like it better than any thing in all the world ; but I don't think it's
fun.　It's lots better than fun."

"Well, what 'd you call it, if you don't call it fun?"
said Rob, in a vexed tone.

Nelly did not answer.

"Why don't you say?" cried Rob.

"I'm thinking," replied Nelly : "I guess there isn't
any name for it.　I don't know any."

Just at this moment, they heard the tinkle of bells
ahead, and in a second more loud shouts and cries.
They walked faster.　The wagon had been out of their
sight for some time.　As they turned a sharp bend in
the road now, they saw it ; and they saw also another

wagon brought to a dead halt in front of it. The wagon which was coming down was loaded high with packages of shingles. It was drawn by six mules. They had bells on their necks, so as to warn people when they were coming. Mr. March and Deacon Plummer had heard these bells, but they had not known what they meant: if they had, they would have drawn off into one of the wider bends in the road, and waited. Now here the two wagons were, face to face, in one of the very worst places of the road, just where it seemed barely wide enough for one wagon alone. The rock rose up straight on one side, and the precipice fell off sharp on the other. To make matters worse, Pumpkinseed, who hated the very sight of a mule, and who did not like the shining of the bright, yellow shingles, began to rear and to plunge. The driver of the mule team sat still, and looked at Mr. March and the Deacon surlily without speaking. Mr. March and the Deacon looked at him helplessly, and said : —

"What are we going to do now?"

"Didn't yer hear me a-coming?" growled the man.

"No, sir," said Mr. March, pleasantly: "we are strangers here, and did not know what the bells meant."

At this the man jumped down: he was not so angry, when he found out that they were strangers. He walked down the road a little way, and looked, and shook his head; then he walked back in the direction he had come from; then he came back, and said : —

"There's nothin' for it, mister, but you'll have to unharness your team. My mules'll stand; I'll help you."

So they took out Pumpkinseed and Fox, and Mr.

March led them on ahead. Then Deacon Plummer and
the mule-driver pushed the wagon backward down the
road till they came to a place where there was a curve
in the road, and they could push it up so close to the rock
that there was room for another wagon to pass. There
the mule-driver drove his wagon by; and then Mr.
March led Fox and Pumpkinseed down, and harnessed
them to the wagon again: all this time Mrs. March and
Mrs. Plummer and Rob and Nelly stood on the edge of
the precipice, wherever they could find a secure place,
and holding on by each other. As the mule team started
on, the driver called back: "There's three or four more
behind me: you'd better keep a sharp lookout, mister."

"I should think so," exclaimed Deacon Plummer;
"this is the perkiest place for teams to pass in thet ever
I got into. I don't much like the thought o' comin' up
and down here with all our teamin'."

"No," said Mrs. March, "I'll never drive down
here as long as I live."

"Never's a long word, wife," laughed Mr. March.
"If we're going to live in this pass, I don't doubt we
shall get so used to this road, we shan't think any thing
about it."

The road wound like a snake, turning first one way
and then the other, and crossing the brook every few
minutes. Sometimes they would be in dark shadow,
when they were close to the left-hand hill; and then, in
a minute, they would come out again into full sunlight.

"It's just like going right back again from after sundown to the middle of the afternoon: isn't it, mamma?"
said Nelly. "How queer it feels!"

"Yes," said Mrs March, "and I do not like the sundown part. I hope our house is not in such a narrow part of the pass as this."

Presently they saw a white house a little way ahead, on the right-hand side of the road. A high, rocky precipice rose immediately behind it ; and the brook seemed to be running under the house, it was so close to it. The house was surrounded by tall pine and fir trees ; and, on the opposite side of the road, the hill was so steep and high that already, although it was only three o'clock in the afternoon, the sun had gone down out of sight, and the house was dark and cold. The whole party looked anxiously at this house.

" That can't be it, can it? " said Mrs. March.

" Oh, no ! " said Mr. March ; " it isn't in the least such a house as the photograph showed : but I will stop and ask."

A man was chopping wood a few steps from the house. Mr. March called to him.

" This isn't Garland's, is it? "

Instead of replying, the man laid down his axe, and walked slowly out to the road, staring very hard at them all.

" Be you the folks that's comin' to live to Garland's? " he said.

" Yes," said the Deacon ; " and we hope this isn't the place ; if 'tis, we hain't been told the truth, that's all."

" Oh, Lor', no," laughed the man. " This ain't Garland's ; his place's two mile farther on. That ain't no great shakes of a place, either, — Garland's ain't ; but he's got more land 'n we have. There ain't land enough here to raise a ground mole in. I 'm sick on 't."

" You don't get daylight enough here to raise any

thing, for that matter," said Mr. March; "here it is the middle of the afternoon, by the clock, and past sundown for you."

"I know it," said the man; "but there's something in the air here which kind o' makes up for every thing. I don't know how 'tis, but we've had our healths first rate ever since we've lived here. But I'm going to move down to the Springs: it's too lonesome up here, and there ain't nothin' to do. Be you goin' into stock?"

"Not much," said Mr. March. "We are only trying an experiment here: we have bought all Garland's cows."

"Have ye?" said the man. "Well, Garland had some first-rate cattle; but they're pretty well peaked out now. Cattle gets dreadful poor here, along in March and April: ye'd reelly pity 'em. But it's amazin' how they pick up 's soon 's the grass comes in June. It don't seem to hurt 'em none to be kinder starved all winter. Come and see us: we're neighborly folks out 'n this country. My wife she'll be glad to know there's some wimmen folks in the Pass. She's been the only woman here for a year. Garland he bached it: he hadn't no wife."

Rob and Nelly had listened silently with wide-open eyes and ears to this conversation; but at this last statement Rob's curiosity got the better of him.

"What is baching it?" said he, as they drove off.

The man laughed.

"Ask your father: he'll tell you," he said.

"What is it, papa?" said Rob.

"I suppose it is for a man to live all alone, without

any wife. You know they call unmarried men ‘old bachelors,’ after they get to be thirty or thirty-five. But I never heard the word before.”

“Oh!” said Rob; “is that all? I thought ’twas a trade he had, — or something he sold or made.”

“Well,” said the Deacon; “any man that could live up here in this stone gully, without his wife along, I don’t think much of. It’s the lonesomest place, for an out-doors place, that ever I saw.”

“Oh, I think it’s splendid!” said Rob.

“So do I,” said Nelly. “It’s perfectly beautiful!”

“Ain’t it a comfort, Mrs. March,” said Mrs. Plummer, “how children always does take to new places?”

“We don’t either,” cried Rob; “I hate some places I’ve seen. But this is splendid. Just you look at those rocks: you bet I’ll pitch ’em down! I’m going up on to every one of the highest rocks I can find.”

“Oh, Rob! you’ll break your neck,” said Mrs. March. “I shall not allow you to climb, unless your father is with you.”

“Now, mamma” — Rob was beginning when, suddenly catching sight of a house, he exclaimed : —

“There ’tis! That’s like the picture. And there’s the barn! I saw it first! Oh, hurry! hurry!” And in his excitement Rob stood up in the wagon.

Yes, there it was. It had looked better in the photograph which Mr. Garland had showed to Mr. March than it did in reality. It was a small, unpainted pine house; without any piazza or blinds. The windows were small; the front door was very small; there was no fence between it and the road; and all the ground around it had been left wild. It was really a desolate-looking place.

"Why, there isn't any yard!" exclaimed Nelly.

"Yard!" said her mother; "why, it is *all* yard, child. As far as you can see in every direction, it is all our yard."

Mrs. March's heart had really sunk within her at the sight of the place. The house was nothing more than she would have called a shanty at home; but she was resolved, no matter what happened to them, never to let her husband see that she found any thing hard. So she spoke cheerfully about the yard; and, as they were getting out of the wagon, she said: —

"How nice and open it is here! See, Robert, the sun is still an hour high, I should think. This is a lovely place."

Mr. March shook his head. He did not like the appearance of things. Mrs. Plummer had bustled ahead into the house. In a moment she came back, followed by a man. This was the man who had been left by Mr. Garland in charge of the house, and who was to stay and work for Mr. March.

"Bless my eyes!" he exclaimed; "you've took me by surprise. I hain't had no letter from Garland. He said he'd write and let me know when you'd be up. I calculated to have spruced up considerable before you come in. We've bached it here so long 'tain't much of a place for wimmen folks to come to."

"Oh, never mind!" said Mrs. March; "Mr." — she hesitated for a name: "I don't think I've heard your name —"

"Zeb, ma'am; Zeb's my name. Don't go by any

other name since I 've been in these mountains," said
the man, pulling off his old woollen cap, and making
an awkward bow to Mrs. March, whose pleasant smile
and voice had won his liking at once.

" Never mind, then, Zeb," Mrs. March continued :
" we have not come expecting to find things as we had
them at home. We shall call it a picnic all the time."

" Well, that 's about what it is, mum, most generally
in this country 's fur 's I 've seen it," said Zeb, thinking
at that moment, with a dreadful misgiving, that he had
no meat in the house, except salt pork ; and no bread
at all. He had intended to make some soda biscuit for
his own supper. " But she looks like jest one o' them
kind that can't abide soda," thought poor Zeb to himself. " An' where in thunder be they all to sleep?" he
continued ; " Garland might ha' known better than to
let six folks come down on me, this way, without any
warnin'. 'Twas mighty unconsiderate of him ! However, 'tain't none o' my business. I don't keep no
hotel."

While Zeb was pursuing this uncomfortable train of
thought, he was helping Deacon Plummer and Mr.
March unharness the horses ; he seemed silent, and, Mr.
March thought, surly ; but it was in reality only his
distress at not being able to make the family more
comfortable. Finally he spoke.

" Did Garland tell you he 'd written?"

" Oh, yes !" said Mr. March ; " he said he 'd written,
and you would be looking out for us."

" Well, perhaps he wrote, and perhaps he didn't. It 's
as likely as not he didn't. At any rate, if he did, the
letter 's down in that Manitou post-office. I hain't

never seen it: an' I may as well tell you first as last, that I ain't no ways ready for ye. There ain't but two beds in the whole house. I was a calculatin' to bring up one more from the Springs next week; an' I hain't got much in the way of provisions, either, except for the hosses. There's plenty of oats, an' that's about all there is plenty of."

Deacon Plummer and Mr. March were standing in the barn door: the Deacon thrust his hands deep down in his pockets and whistled. Mr. March looked at Zeb's face. The more he studied it, the better he liked it.

"Zeb," said he, "we can stay, somehow, can't we? We men can sleep on the hay for a few nights, if the sleeping 's all. What have you really got in the way of food? That's the main thing."

It pleased Zeb to have Mr. March say "we men." "I guess he 's got some stuff in him, if he is a parson," thought Zeb; and his face brightened as he replied.

"Well, if you can sleep on the hay, it's all right about the sleepin'; but I didn't reckon you could. But that's only part o' the trouble. However, I can jump on to a hoss and ride down to Manitou and pick up suthin', if the wimmen folks think they can get along."

"Get along! of course we can get along!" exclaimed Mrs. March, who had just come out in search of her husband. "There is an iron pot and a tea-kettle and a frying-pan and a barrel of flour and a firkin of Graham meal; what more do we want?" and she laughed merrily.

"Hens, mamma, hens! There are lots of hens here!" shouted Rob, coming up at full speed; "and see this splendid shepherd dog! He knows me already! See! he follows me!" and Rob held his hand high up in the air to a beautiful black and white shepherd dog who was running close behind him.

"Yes; Watch, he's real friendly with everybody," said Zeb. "He's lots o' company, Watch is. He knows more 'n most folks. Here, Watch! give us your paw?"

The dog lifted one paw and held it out.

"No, not that one — the white one!" said Zeb.

Watch dropped the black paw and held up the white one instantly.

"He'll do that just 's often 's you'll ask him," said Zeb; "an' it's a mighty queer thing for a dog to know black from white."

"Oh! let me try him?" said Rob. "Here, Watch! Watch!" Watch ran to Rob at once.

"He does take to you, that's a fact," said Zeb.

"Give your paw, Watch, — your white paw," said Rob.

Watch put his white paw in Rob's hand.

"Now your black paw," said Rob.

Watch put down his white paw and lifted the other.

"White, black! — white, black!" said Rob, as fast as he could pronounce the words; and, just as fast as he said them, the dog changed his paws.

At this moment, Nelly appeared, her cheeks very red, carrying a little yellow and white puppy in her arms.

"Oh! see this dear little puppy!" she said; "doesn't he just match Pumpkinseed?"

"We might call him Pumpkin Blossom," said Mrs. March.

"His name 's Trotter," said Zeb.   "He 's jest got it learned: I guess you can't change it very easy.   Put him down, miss, and I 'll show you what he can do. I hain't taught him much yet; he 's such a pup: but there 's nothin' he can't learn.   Trotter, roll over!"

The puppy lay down instantly and rolled over and over.   "Faster!" said Zeb.

Trotter rolled faster.   "Faster! faster! fast as you can!" cried Zeb; and Trotter rolled so fast that you could hardly see his legs or his tail; he looked like a round ball of yellow hair, with two bright eyes in it.

Nelly and Rob shouted with laughter, and even Mr. March and Deacon Plummer laughed hard.   They had been so busy that they had not observed that it was growing dark.   Suddenly Zeb looked up, and said : —

"Ye 'd better run in : it 's going to be a snow flurry."

"A snow flurry!" exclaimed Mrs. March, looking up at the bright blue sky overhead.   "Where 's the snow to come from?"

"Out o' that cloud, mum," replied Zeb, pointing to a black cloud just coming up over the top of the hill to the west.   "'T 'll be here in less than five minutes; mebbe 't 'll be hail : reckon 't will."

Sure enough, in less than five minutes the cloud had spread over their heads, and the hail began to fall. They all stood at the windows and watched it.   Rattle, rattle, it came on the roof and against the west windows, and the hailstones bounded off from every place they hit, and rolled about on the ground like marbles.   At first they were very small : not bigger than pins' heads; but larger and larger ones came every minute, until they were as big as large plums.   Rob and Nelly had never seen such hailstones; they were half frightened, and yet the sight was so beautiful to watch, that they enjoyed it. The storm did not last more than ten minutes; the hailstones grew smaller again, just as they had grown larger; and then they came slower and slower, till they stopped altogether, and the great black cloud rolled off toward the south, and left the sky clear blue above their heads, just as it was before; and the sun shone out, and every thing glistened like silver from the boughs of the trees down to the blades of grass. The great hailstones were piled up in all the hollow places of the ground, but the hot sun shining on them began to melt them immediately; and, except where they were in the shadow of rocks or trees or piles of boards, they did not last long. Nelly picked up a tin pan and ran out and filled it in a minute: then she passed them round to everybody, saying: "Won't you have some sugared almonds?" and they all ate them and pretended they were candy; and Rob and Nelly rolled them away from the doorstep and made Trotter run after them. In less than ten minutes after the storm had passed, it was so warm that they were all standing in the open doorway, or walking about out of doors.

"Upon my word, what a country this is!" said Mr. March. "Ten minutes ago it was winter; now it is spring."

"Yes," said Zeb. "That's jest the way 'tis all through the winter; but next month ye 'll get some winter in good airnest. April 'n' May 's our winter months. I 've seen the snow a foot 'n' a half deep in this Pass in May."

"What!" exclaimed Mr. March, now really excited. "A foot and a half of snow! What becomes of the cattle then?"

"Oh!" said Zeb, "it never lays long : not over a day or two. This sun 'll melt snow 's quick 's a fire 'll melt grease, 'n quicker."

"Then I suppose it is very muddy," said Mrs. March.

"No, mum, never no mud to speak of; sometimes a little stretch of what they call adobe land 'll be putty muddy for a week or so; but 's a general thing the roads are dry in a day; in fact, you 'll often see the ground white with a little sprinkle of snow at eight o'clock in the morning, and by twelve you 'll see the roads dry, except along the edges : the snow jest kind o' goes off in the air here ; it don't seem 's if it melted into water at all."

"Well, I 'll give it up!" said the Deacon ; "near 's I can make out, this country 's a conundrum."

Mrs. March and Mrs. Plummer now set themselves to work in good earnest to put the little house in order. They had brought with them only what they could carry in valises and hand-bags : all their boxes and trunks were to come in a big wagon the next day ; so there was not much unpacking to be done. The house had only five rooms in it : one large room, which was to be used as the kitchen and dining-room and living-room ; three small rooms which were for bedrooms ; and another room which had been used as a lumber-room. As soon as Mrs. March looked into this room, she resolved to make it into a little sitting-room by and by. It had one window to the east, which looked out on the brook, and one to the south, which had a most beautiful view down the Pass. These rooms had no plaster on the walls, and the boards were very rough; but the Colorado pine is such a lovely shade of yellow that rooms built of bare boards are really prettier than most of the rooms you see which have paper on them.

Poor Mrs. Plummer thought these bare boards were dreadful. She worked on, industriously, helping Mrs. March do all she could; but every few minutes she would give a great sigh, and look up at the walls, or down at the floor, and say: —

"Well, Mrs. March! I never did expect to see you come to this."

Mr. March also wore rather a long face as he stood in the doorway and watched his wife.

"Oh, Sarah!" he said, at last, "I can't bear to have you work like this. I didn't realize it was going to be just such a place. I shall go to the Springs to-morrow and get a servant for you."

"You won't do any such thing, Robert," said Mrs. March. "There's no room for a servant to sleep in; and I don't want one, any way. Mrs. Plummer will give me all the help I need; and Rob and Nelly will help too. Look at Rob now!" At that minute, Rob came puffing and panting in at the door, with his arms full of crooked sticks, stems of vines, and all sorts of odds and ends of drift-wood, which he had picked up on the edge of the brook.

"Here's kindling wood, mamma; lots of it. Zeb told me where to get it. There's lots and lots all along the brook." And he threw down his armful on the hearth, and was going back for more.

"Dear boy! here is enough, and more than enough,"

said Mrs. March. "You can bring me some water next; we dip it out of the brook, I suppose."

"Now, mamma, that 's just all you know about it," replied Rob, with a most exultant air of superiority; "there 's just the nicest spring, right across the brook, only a little bit of ways. Zeb showed me; you come and see, — there 's a bridge."

Mrs. March followed him. Sure enough, there was a nice, fresh spring, bubbling up out of the ground, among the bushes; it was walled around with boards a few feet high, so that the cattle should not trample too close to it; a narrow plank was laid across the brook just opposite it; and it was not twenty steps from the house.

"See, mamma," said Rob, as he dipped in the pail, and drew it out dripping full, "see how nice this is. I can bring you all the water you want."

"Take care! take care, Rob!" shouted his father, as Rob stepped back on the plank. He was too late. Rob in his excitement had stepped a little on one side of the middle of the plank: it tipped; he lost his balance, and in he went, pail of water and all, into the brook. The brook was not deep, and he scrambled out again in less than a minute, — much mortified and very wet. Mrs. March could not help laughing.

"Well, you helped fill the brook instead of my pail; didn't you?" she said.

"But, mamma, I haven't got any dry clothes," said poor Rob: "what 'll I do?"

"That 's a fact, Rob," said his mother. "You 'll have to go to bed while these dry."

"Oh, dear!" said Rob; "that 's too bad!" And he

walked very disconsolately toward the house. Zeb was just riding off, with two empty sacks hanging from his saddle pommel.

"Zeb," called Rob; "I tumbled in the brook; and I've got to go to bed till my clothes are dry."

"Don't ye do no such a thing," cried Zeb; "you jest walk round a leetle lively, and your clothes'll be dry afore ye know it. Water don't wet ye much in this country."

"Come, now, Zeb," said the Deacon, "let's draw a line somewhere! That's a little too big a story. I can believe ye about the snow's not making mud, because I've seen these hail-stones just melt away into nothin' in half an hour; but when it comes to water's not wettin', I can't go that."

"Well, you just feel of me now!" shouted Rob; "I'm half dry already!"

The Deacon and Mrs. March both felt Rob's arms and shoulders.

"'Pon my word, they ain't so very wet," said the Deacon; "was it only just now you tumbled in?"

"Not five minutes ago," said Mrs. March.

"It is certainly the queerest thing I ever saw," she continued, feeling Rob from his shoulders to his ankles: "he is really, as he says, half dry. I'll try Zeb's advice. Rob, you run up and down the road as hard as you can for ten minutes; don't you stand still at all."

Rob raced away, with Watch at his heels, and Mr. and Mrs. March walked into the house, Mr. March carrying the pail filled once more with the nice spring water. In a few minutes, as they were all busily at work, they heard a sound at the door: they looked up; there stood a white cow, looking in on them with a mild expression of surprise.

"Oh!" said Mr. March, "Zeb said the cows 'd be coming home pretty soon. The Deacon and I 'll have to milk."

"Yes, they 're a comin'," called out the Deacon, peering over the back of the white cow, and pushing her gently to one side, so that he could enter the door; " they 're a comin' down the road, and down the hill up there back o' the saw-mill: I jest wish ye 'd come and look at 'em. Don't know as ye 'd better, either, if ye want to have a good appetite for your supper! If ever ye see Pharaoh's lean kine, ye 'll see 'em now."

Mr. and Mrs. March and Mrs. Plummer all ran out and stood in front of the house, looking up the road. There came the cows, one, two, three, all in single file, down the hill, now and then stopping to take a nibble by the way; in the road there were half a dozen more, walking straight on, neither turning to the right nor the left.

" That 's right, ye poor things : make for the barn ; I would if I was you. Perhaps I won't feed you a good feed o' hay 'n' corn-meal to-night, sure 's my name 's Plummer!" The cows were indeed lean : you could count every rib on their bodies, and their hip bones stuck out like great ploughshares.

"What a shame!" exclaimed Mrs. March. " Husband, you were imposed upon. These cows are not worth any thing."

" Oh, yes they be ; they 're first-rate stock," said the Deacon ; " first-rate stock, only they 're so run down.

Ye'll see I'll have 'em so fat in four weeks ye won't know 'em."

The cows gathered together in a little group between the two barns, and looked very hard at these strangers they had never seen before. They knew very well that something had happened, — they missed Zeb, — and began to low uneasily; but when Deacon Plummer came out of the barn with a big pitchfork full of hay, and threw it down before them, all their anxieties were allayed. These were good friends who had come: there was no doubt of that. Nine times the Deacon brought out his pitchfork full of hay, and threw it on the ground, one for each cow: and didn't they fall to and eat!

"H'm!" said the Deacon, as he watched them. "If this is the result of your fine winter grazin', I don't want any thing to do with it. It's just slow starvation to my way o' thinking. Look at them udders! There ain't a quart apiece in 'em. Our milkin' 'll be soon over, Parson."

"The sooner the better for me, Deacon," laughed Mr. March. "I never did like to milk."

"Oh! let me milk! let me milk, papa! please do!" cried Rob, who had returned from his ten minutes' run on the road, as dry as ever.

"And me, too! me too!" said Nelly, who was close behind.

"Not to-night, children. It is late, and we are in a hurry," said Mr. March. Just as he spoke, the sun sank behind the hill. Almost instantly, a chill fell on the air.

"Bless me," said Mr. March, "here we have winter again. Run in, children; it is growing too cold for you to be out. What a climate this is, to be sure! one can't keep up with it."

While Deacon Plummer and Mr. March were milking, they talked over their prospects. They were forced to acknowledge that there was small chance of making a living on this farm.

"We're took in: that's all there is on 't," said the Deacon, cheerily; "but I reckon we can grub along for six months; we can live that long even if we don't make a cent; and now we're here, we can look about for ourselves, and see what we 're gettin' before we make another move."

"Yes," said Mr. March. "That's the only way to do. I confess I am disappointed. Mr. Garland seemed such a fair man."

The Deacon laughed. "Ye don't know human nature, Parson, the way we men do that's knockin' round all the time among folks. Ye see folks always comes to you when they're in trouble, or else when they're joyful, — bein' married, or a baptizin' their babies, — or somethin' o' ruther that's out o' the common line; so you don't never see 'em jest exactly 's they are. Now I kinder mistrusted that Garland from the fust. He was too anxious to sell, to suit me. When a man's got a first-rate berth, he ain't generally so ready to quit."

When the milkers went in with their pails of milk, they found a blazing fire on the hearth, and supper set out on a red pine table without any table-cloth. Mrs. March had made Graham biscuit and white biscuit, and had baked some apples which she had left in her lunch-basket. When she saw the milk, she exclaimed: —

“ Now, if this isn’t a supper fit for a king ! — bread and milk and baked apples ! ”

“ Ain’t there any butter? ” called out Rob.

“ Yes, there is some butter ; but I doubt if you will eat it,” said Mrs. March. “ Zeb is going to buy some better butter at Manitou.”

Rob put some of the butter on his bread, and put a mouthful of the bread in his mouth. In less than a second, he had clapped his hand over his mouth with an expression of horror.

“ Oh ! what ’ll I do, mamma? it ’s worse than medicine ! ” he cried ; and swallowed the whole mouthful at one gulp. “ That can’t be butter, mamma,” he said. “ You ’ve made a mistake. It ’ll poison us : it ’s something else.”

“ Little you know about bad butter, don’t you, Rob? ” said Deacon Plummer, calmly buttering his biscuit, and eating it. “ I ’ve eaten much worse butter than this.”

Rob’s eyes grew big. “ What ’d you eat it for? ” he said, earnestly.

“ Sure enough,” said Mrs. Plummer. “ That ’s what I ’ve always said about butter. If there ’s any thing else set before folks that ’s bad, why they just leave it alone. There isn’t any need ever of eating what you don’t like. But when it comes to butter, folks seem to think they ’ve got to eat it, good, bad, or indifferent.”

“ That ’s so,” said the Deacon ; “ and if I ’ve heard you say so once, Elizy, I ’ve heard you say it a thousand times ; I don’t know how ’tis, but it does seem as if you had to have somethin’ in shape o’ butter, if it ’s ever so bad, to make a meal go down.”

“ I don’t see how bad butter helps make a meal go

down," said Rob. "It like to have made mine come up just now."

"Rob! Rob!" said his mother, reprovingly; "you forget that we are at supper."

"Excuse me, mamma," said Rob, penitently; "but it was true."

CHAPTER VI.

LIFE AT GARLAND'S.

THIS was the first night of the Marches and Plummers in their strange new home in Colorado. When they waked up the next morning, Mr. March and Deacon Plummer rolled up in buffalo robes on the hay in the barn, Mrs. March and Nelly in one bed in one little bedroom, Mrs. Plummer in another opening out of it, and Rob on an old black leather sofa in the kitchen, they could hardly believe their eyes as they looked around them. They all got up very early, and now their new life had begun in good earnest. Immediately after breakfast, Mr. March drove away in the big wagon with Fox and Pumpkinseed. He would not tell his wife where he was going, nor take any one with him. The truth was, that in the night Mr. March had taken two resolutions: one was that he would get a servant for Mrs. March; the other was that he would buy furniture enough to make the house pleasant and comfortable, and china enough to make their table look a little like their old home table. But he knew if he told Mrs. March what he meant to do, she would think they ought not to spend the money. All their own pretty china which they had used at home, she had packed up and left behind them, saying: " We shall not want any thing of that kind in Colorado." Mrs. March did not care about such things half so much as Mr. March and Nelly did; that is, she could do without them more easily. She liked pretty things very much, but she could do without them very well if it were necessary. She watched Mr. March driving off down the road this morning with an uneasy feeling.

"I don't know what Mr. March 's got in his head," she said to Mrs. Plummer; "but I think he is going to do something rash. He looks as children do when they are in some secret mischief."

"Why, what could it be?" said good Mrs. Plummer. "I don't see what there is for him to do."

"Well, we shall see," said Mrs. March. "I wish I 'd made him take me along."

"Made him!" exclaimed Mrs. Plummer. "Can you make him do any thing he 's sot not to? I hain't never been able to do that with Mr. Plummer, not once in all the thirty years I 've lived with him. It 's always seemed to me that men was the obstinatest critters made, even the best on 'em; an' I 'm sure Mr. Plummer 's as good a man 's ever was born; but I don't no more think o' movin' him if his mind 's made up, than I should think o' movin' that rock up there," pointing to a huge rock which was at the top of one of the hills to the south-west of the house.

The day flew by quickly in putting their new home in order. Both Mrs. March and Mrs. Plummer worked very hard, and Rob and Nelly helped them. They swept and washed floors; they washed windows; they washed even the chairs and tables, — which sadly needed it, it must be owned. Rob and Nelly enjoyed it all as a frolic.

"This is like last Christmas, when Sarah was drunk: isn't it, mamma?" said Rob.   "It's real fun."

"Don't you wish Sarah was here to help you, mamma?" said Nelly.

"No, dear," replied Mrs. March, "I do not.   I would rather do all the work ourselves, and save the money."

"Are we very, very, very poor, mamma?" said Nelly, with a distressed face.

"Oh, no, dear! not so bad as that," laughed Mrs. March; "but papa's salary has all stopped now, as I explained to you; and that was the greater part of our income: and, till we have more money coming in regularly from something out here, we must spend just as little as possible."

Just before dinner, Rob came in with a big armful of kindling-wood, and on the top of the wood he carried a long piece of a beautiful green vine.

"Oh, Rob, Rob, let me see that!   Where did you find it?" said his mother.

"Upon the hills, mamma, back of the saw-mill. There's oceans of it up there."

"There *is* oceans, Rob?" said his mother.

"There *are* oceans, then!   You knew what I meant. It's just like a carpet; and you can pull up great, long pieces of it: it comes up just as easy as any thing."

Mrs. March turned the vine over and over in her hands.   It had a small glossy leaf, like the leaf of the box.   Some of the long, slender tendrils of it were bright red.

"The leaf is so thick I think it would keep a long time," said Mrs. March.   "I wish you and Nelly would bring me several armfuls of it. I 'll tack it up all round the room: the walls won't look so bare, then."

"Oh, goody!" said the children; "that's just like Christmas." And they ran off as fast as they could go. In an hour they had heaped the whole floor with piles of the vine. The more they brought, the more beautiful it looked: the leaves shone like satin, and there were great mats of it nearly two yards long. Mrs. March had never seen it before, and did not know its name. Afterward she found out that it was the kinnikinnick vine, and that the Indians used it to smoke in their pipes. Some of the branches had beautiful little red berries like wintergreen berries on it. Nelly sorted these all out by themselves; then Mrs. March stood up on a chair, and some of the time on a table, and nailed a thick border of these vines all round the top of the room; then she took the branches which had red berries on them; and, wherever there was an upright beam in the wall, she nailed on one of these boughs with the red berries, and let it hang down just as it would. Then she trimmed the fireplace and the door and the windows. It took her about two hours to do it. When it was all done, you would hardly have known the room. It looked lovely: the yellow pine boards looked much prettier with the green of the vines than any paper in the world could have looked. Rob and Nelly fairly danced with delight.

"Oh, mamma! mamma! it 's prettier than any Christmas we ever had: isn't it?"

"Yes," said Mrs. March; "if the vines will only last, it is all we need to keep our walls pretty till summer time."

"Well, I never!" said Zeb, who came in at that moment. "If wimmen folks don't beat all! Why, mum, ye look's if you was goin' to have an ice-cream festival."

Zeb's only experience of rooms decorated with green vines had been when he had attended ice-cream festivals, given by churches to raise money.

"Well, we'll have one some day, Zeb," said Mrs. March, laughing; "and we won't charge you any thing. I can make very good ice-cream."

"Oh, to-night! to-night! mamma," exclaimed the children.

"Can't to-night," Mrs. March said; "for the freezer's in the big box with all the other kitchen things."

"I might make some crullers," said Mrs. Plummer.

"Do! do! do!" cried Rob. "Mrs. Plummer's famous for crullers!" And he ran off, singing —

"Plummer!
Cruller!
Plummer!
Cruller!"

at the top of his lungs.

It was nearly dark before Mr. March returned. Rob was the first to spy him.

"Why, there's Pumpkinseed!" he exclaimed. "And what in the world's papa got in the wagon?" And he ran down the road to meet him. All the others ran too. The wagon did indeed present a very singular appearance. Four red wooden legs stuck far out in front; Mr. March was wedged in between them; high above his head bulged out a great roll of bolsters and pillows; and as far as you could see, away back in the wagon, there seemed to be nothing but bed-ticking, and legs of furniture.

"Mercy on us!" exclaimed Mrs. March; "What did I tell you, Mrs. Plummer? That's what he went off for, — to buy furniture. Mr. March always must have things just right. Dear me! I wish he hadn't done it."

But, as I told you long ago, it was Mrs. March's way always to make the best of what couldn't be helped. So she went forward to welcome her husband as pleasantly as if she were delighted to see all this new furniture.

"Ah, Robert," she said, "now I know why you wouldn't take me. You wanted to surprise us all."

"Yes," said Mr. March, his face beaming all over with satisfaction, "I didn't mean you should spend another night in such a desolate hole. There's another wagon load behind."

At this Mrs. March could not help groaning.

"Oh, Robert! Robert!" she said, "what did you buy so much for?"

"Oh, part of the other load is feed for the cattle," said Mr. March. "That I'm responsible to Deacon Plummer for. Those were his orders."

When the two wagons were unloaded, the space in front of the little house looked like an auction. Rob and Nelly ran from one thing to another, exclaiming and shouting. Mr. March had indeed furnished the whole house. He had bought two pretty little single bedsteads for Rob and Nelly, and a fine large bedstead for himself and Mrs. March; he had bought mattresses and pillows and bolsters and blankets; a whole piece of pretty rag-carpet, in gray and red stripes; two large rocking-chairs with arms, two without, and two small low chairs; a work-table with drawers, two bureaus, a wardrobe, and two sets of book-shelves to hang on the walls; two student lamps, and a table with leaves that could open out. Then he had bought a whole piece of pretty chintz in stripes of black and green.

"There, wife," he said, as he showed her this, last of all, "now we can make a decent little home out of it, after a few days."

As he spoke, he stepped into the kitchen: he started back with surprise.

"Why, how perfectly lovely!" he exclaimed; "where did you get it? And what is it? I never saw a place so transformed. Why, it looks even elegant."

"I thought you would like it," said **Mrs. March**, much pleased. "Perhaps if you had seen it so before you went away, you wouldn't have bought so many new things."

"Why, Sarah, I haven't bought a thing that wasn't absolutely necessary," said Mr. March.

"They are all very nice, dear," replied Mrs. March; "and of course we shall be much more comfortable with them. It was very kind of you. But haven't you spent a great deal of money?" she asked anxiously.

"Oh, no!" said Mr. March, "I think not; though things are much higher here than at home. I didn't get the bills; but I don't believe it's over two hundred dollars."

This seemed a great deal to Mrs. March; but she said no more. And the next day, when all the things were arranged, a square of the rag-carpet laid on the floor, and the pretty chintz curtains at the window, she could not help admitting to herself that life looked much easier and pleasanter than it had before.

"And I ought to be thankful that he did not buy more," she thought; "and that he could not find a servant to bring out here."

On inquiring after servants, Mr. March had found that it was almost impossible to get any good ones; and their wages were so high, he had at once given up all idea of hiring one now.

"I'll let you try it, Sarah, for the present," he said; "but, if I see you in the least breaking down, I shall have a servant, if I have to send home for one."

"I won't break down," said Mrs. March; "I never felt so well in my life. I am never tired. I suppose it is the air."

"Yes," said Mr. March; "it must be. I, too, feel like another man. I can draw such full, long breaths; I shouldn't know there was such a thing as asthma in the world."

As day after day went on, they all came to like their new home better and better. The little room which had been a lumber room was made into a sitting-room, and trimmed all round with the kinnikinnick vines; the big table with leaves stood in the centre, and the bookshelves hung on the walls. Zeb and Deacon Plummer built pine shelves across one end of the room, way to the top: these were filled with Mr. March's books. There were two small school-desks by the east window; and at these Rob and Nelly sat for two hours every morning, and studied and recited their lessons to Mr.

March. In the afternoon, they played out of doors; they climbed the hills and the rocks; and, at four o'clock, they went after the cows. This was something they were never tired of, because they never knew just where they should find the cows: they rambled into so many little nooks and corners among the hills; but three of the cows had bells on their necks, and the rest never went far from them. Watch always went with Rob and Nelly, and he seemed to have a wonderful instinct to tell where to look for a cow. Whenever it stormed too much for the children to be out, Zeb went. Sometimes Watch went all alone. He could bring the cows home as well as anybody. But Nelly and Rob never liked to miss it. It was the great pleasure of their day; and the out-door air and the exercise were making them brown and strong. They looked like little Italian peasant children: wherever they went they sang; up hill and down, and on the tops of the highest rocks, their merry voices rang out. Felix — that Frenchman I told you about that they saw in the cars, the one who was servant to the English gentleman — had taught Rob how to make the cry which the Swiss hunters make in the Alps. It is called the "Jodel"— and it sounds very fine among high hill-tops. It is something like this : —

"Yo-ho! yo-ho! yo-ho!" The syllables are pronounced one after the other just as fast as you can, in a high shrill tone, and there is a sort of tune to it which I could not describe; but perhaps you know some traveller who has been in Switzerland, who can describe it to you. Rob used to "jodel" beautifully; and many a time when he was on a high rock, way up above the

road, and saw people riding or driving below him, he
would ring out such a " jodel," that the people would
stop and look up amazed. They could not believe they
were in America. Rob was fast growing as strong and
well as Nelly. He never had sore throats here: and
Mr. and Mrs. March often said that they would be glad
they had come to Colorado, if it were for nothing except that it had made Rob so well. As he grew stronger,
he grew to be a much better boy. He was not selfish
nor cross as he used to be at home ; and he was as full
of fun as a squirrel, all day long. One thing he very
much enjoyed doing, was taking Fox and Pumpkinseed
up to the tops of the high hills to graze. The best
grass grew very high up on the hills ; but neither Fox
nor Pumpkinseed had ever been used to such steep
hills, and they both hated to climb them. Deacon Plummer was very droll about it. " Don't blame 'em," said
he, " don't blame 'em a mite. Who 'd want to be for
ever climbing up garret to get a mouthful of something
to eat?" However, since the food was chiefly " up
garret," as the deacon called it, " up garret" the horses
must go ; and it was somebody's duty every morning to
lead them up. Often, in the course of the day, they
would ramble slowly down : then they would have to be
taken up again ; and Rob was always on the lookout
for a chance to do this. He always took Fox ; he was
easier to lead than Pumpkinseed.   You had to lead only
one : the other would follow ; and it was a funny sight
to see Rob way up on the steep hill, tugging away at
Fox's halter, and Fox half holding back, half going
along, and Pumpkinseed behind, following on slowly
with a most disgusted expression, every now and then

"One thing he very much enjoyed doing, was taking Fox and Pumpkin-seed up to the tops of the high hills to graze." — PAGE 154.

stopping short and looking up at Rob and Fox, as much as to say, " Oh, dear! why will you drag us up this horrible hill?"

The hill opposite the house was so high that when Rob was at the very top of it with the horses, he didn't look bigger than a " Hop-o'-my-thumb," and the horses looked like goats. After he got them fairly up, and saw them grazing contentedly, Rob would run down the hill at full speed. At first he got many a tumble flat on his nose doing this; but after a while he learned how to slant his body backwards, and then he did not tumble.

But while Rob and Nelly were growing well and strong, and having such a good time that they never wanted to go back to Mayfield, I am sorry to say that the grown people were not so contented. In the first place, good old Mrs. Plummer could not sleep. Her cough was all gone; and if she could only have slept, she would have been as well as anybody; but her heart beat too fast all the time, and kept her awake at night. She did not know that she had any trouble with her heart when she was at home; and nobody had told them that people with heart-trouble could not live in Colorado: but that is the case; the air which is so pure and dry is also so light, that it makes your pulse beat a good many times more a minute, and it takes a good strong heart to bear this. You know your heart is nothing but a pump that pumps blood to go through your veins, just as water goes through pipes all over a house; and the pump has to be very strong to pump so many strokes a minute as it does in Colorado. So poor Mrs. Plummer, instead of growing better, was growing worse; and this made them all unhappy.

Then Deacon Plummer and Mr. March had to acknowledge that they were paying out more money than they took in, and this worried them both.

"We've got to get out on't somehow, that's clear and sartin," said the deacon. "It won't take very long at this rate to clear us both out. I hate to give up. I'm sure there must be better places in the country somewhere for stock raisin' than this is; but we won't stir till warm weather sets in. Then we'll look round."

The last week in April and the first in May were hard weeks. Snow-storm after snow-storm fell. At one time, all travel through the pass was cut off for two days. The snow lay in great drifts in the narrowest places. In such weather as this, all the cattle had to be kept in the barns and yards, and fed; hay was very dear; and as Deacon Plummer said, "It don't take a critter very long to eat its own head off, and after it's eaten it off six times over, its head's on all the same for you to keep a feedin'."

When June came in, matters brightened. The cows had plenty of grass, gave good milk, and Mrs. March and Mrs. Plummer made a good many pounds of butter each week, which they sold at Manitou without difficulty. Here at last was a regular source of income; but it was small: "a mere drop in the bucket," Mrs. March said when she was talking over matters with Mrs. Plummer. I must tell you how this butter was made, because it was such a pleasure to Rob and Nelly to watch it. It was made in a little shed which joined on to the old saw-mill, and the old saw-mill wheel did the churning. Wasn't that a funny way? We must give Zeb the credit of this. He was turning the grindstone

one day for Deacon Plummer to sharpen up the axes.
It is very hard work to turn a grindstone, and Zeb was
very tired before the axes were half ground. Suddenly
the thought popped into his head, "Why shouldn't I
make that old water-wheel turn this grindstone for us?"
After dinner he went up to the saw-mill and looked at
it. There was the old wooden wheel as good as ever;
the gate which had shut the water off and let it on was
gone; "but that's easy fixed," said Zeb, and to work
he went; and before sundown, he had the water-wheel
bobbing round again as fast as need be. The next day
he took the grindstone and sunk it in between two old
timbers in a broken place in the floor, just back of the
wheel; then he put a strap round the grindstone and
fastened it to the water-wheel; then he pulled up the
little gate, and let the water on the water-wheel. Hurrah! round went the water-wheel, and round went the
grindstone keeping exact pace with it! Zeb clapped
his knee, which was the same thing as if he had patted
himself on the shoulder. "Good for you, Abe Mack!"
he said. Then he looked around frightened, to see if
anybody had heard him. No one was near. He drew
a long breath. "Lord!" he said; "to think o' my
saying that name out loud after all this time!" and he
wiped his forehead with the back of his hand. "I'd
better be more keerful than that," he said. "I'll get
tracked yet, if I don't look out." Two years before,
in a fight in a mining town a great many miles north
of his present home, Zeb had had the misfortune to kill
a man. He never intended to do such a thing. He
really drew his pistol in self-defence; but he could not
prove this, and he had fled for his life, and had been

ever since living hidden away on this lonely farm in the mountains. He had intended to go still farther away where there would be no possibility of his ever being seen by any of the men who had known him before, but he had fallen so in love with these hills he could not tear himself away from them. But he had never told his true name to any one, and when he pronounced it now the sound of it frightened him almost as if it had been a sheriff who was calling him by it.

After dinner, Zeb invited the whole family out to see his new water-works. They all looked on with interest and pleasure. Mr. March had often looked at the old mill and wished he had money enough to put it in order.

"Well done, Zeb!" he said. "You've turned the old thing to some account, haven't you? That's a capital idea; we'll grind knives and axes now for anybody who comes along."

"Zeb," said Mrs. March, "can't you make it churn the butter for you?"

Zeb was struck by the idea.

"Lor, ma'am," he said; "I never heard o' such a thing! but I don't know why not. I'll try it, sure's my name's—" he stopped short, and gasped out "Zebulon Craig."

No one observed his agitation. They were all too busy watching the grindstone and the water-wheel. The next day and the next, Zeb was seen steadily at work in the saw-mill. He would not let the children stay with him.

"Run away! run away!" he said. "I've got a job o' thinkin' to do: can't think with you youngsters a lookin' on."

Rob and Nelly were almost beside themselves with curiosity.

"Zeb's making a churn to go by water like the grindstone: I know he is," said Rob. "It's real mean for him not to let us see."

"But, Rob," said the wise Nelly, "he says he can't think if we're round. He'll show it to us 's soon 's it's done."

"I don't care," said Rob; "I want to see how he does it;" and Rob hovered round the mill perpetually, much to Zeb's vexation.

Late in the second afternoon, Zeb called out: —

"Rob, go fetch me the churn, will you?"

Rob was only too happy to be admitted into the partnership on any terms. The churn was quite heavy, but he rolled it and tugged it to the shed-door. Zeb lifted it over the threshold: and then Rob saw that there was a long slender beam fastened to the water-wheel, and reaching half way across the wall of the shed; an upright beam was fastened to this, a hole was cut in the shed wall, and another beam run through this hole, and fastened to the upright beam on the other side. When the water-wheel turned round and round, it made this upright beam go up and down. Zeb took the dasher of the churn and fastened it to this beam: up and down, up and down it went, faster than anybody could churn.

"'Tain't quite long enough," said Zeb. "We'll have to stand the churn on something." Then he ran back to the house and asked Mrs. Plummer for some cream. She gave him about three gallons; he put it into the churn, raised the churn a little higher, and set the machinery in motion. In about ten minutes he looked in.

"It's comin'! it's comin'!" he cried. "Run, call all the folks, Rob."

Rob ran, and in a few minutes the whole family were looking on at this new mode of churning. It worked beautifully; in fifteen minutes more the butter was made.

"There!" said Zeb, as he drew up the dasher with great solid lumps of butter sticking to it. "If that ain't the easiest churned three gallons o' cream ever I see!"

"Yes, indeed, Zeb," said Mrs. March, "it is. We shan't dread churning-day any more."

Mr. March examined the machinery curiously. "Zeb," he said, "if we had two good iron wheels we could make shingles here, couldn't we? I believe it would pay to rig the old place up again."

"Yes, sir," said Zeb. "There's nothin' ye can't make with such a stream o' water's that if ye've got the machinery to put it to. It's only the machinery that's wantin'. We've got water power enough here to run a factory."

You would not have thought so to look at it; the water did not come right up out of the brook; it came through a wooden pipe, high up on wooden posts. It was taken out of the brook a mile or two farther up the Pass, where the ground was a great deal higher than it was here at the mill. So it came running all the way down through this pipe, high up above the brook, and when it was let out it fell with great force. The pipe was quite old now, and it leaked in many places; in one place there was such a big leak it made a little waterfall; this water dripping and falling into the brook beneath made it sound like a shower, and all the bushes and green things along the edges of the brook were dripping wet all the time. There was a big pile of the old sawdust on the edge of the brook; this was of a bright yellow color: the old saw-mill had fallen so into decay that three sides of it were open, and it looked hardly safe to go into it. You had to step carefully from one beam to another: there was not much of the floor left. But it was a lovely, cool, shady place, and almost every day some of the teamsters who were driving heavy teams through the Pass would stop here to take their lunch at noon: often Rob and Nelly would go out and talk with them, and carry them milk to drink. Zeb kept out of sight at such times. He was always in fear of being seen by somebody who had known him in the northern country.

As the summer came on, all sorts of beautiful flowers appeared along the edges of the brook, in the open clearings, and even in the crevices of the rocks. Nelly gathered great bunches of them every morning. She loved flowers almost as well as she loved mountains. She used to go out late in the afternoon and gather a huge basketful of all the kinds she could find, — red and white, and yellow and blue, — then she would set the basket in the brook and let the water run through it all night, keeping the stems of the flowers very wet. In the morning they would look as fresh as if she had just picked them. Remember this, all of you little children who love flowers and like to pick them. If you pick them in the morning, they will wither and never

revive perfectly, no matter how much water you put
them in. Pick them at sundown, and leave them in a
great tub full of water out of doors all night, and in the
morning you can arrange them in bouquets, and they
will keep twice as long as they would if you had not
left them out of doors all night. Nelly used to sit on
the ground in the open space west of the saw-mill and
arrange her bouquets; sometimes she would tie up as
many as eight or ten in one morning, and sometimes
travellers driving past would call to her and ask her to
sell them: but Nelly would not sell them; she always
gave them away to anybody who loved flowers. Rob
thought she was very foolish. "Nell, why didn't you
take the money?" he would say. "It's just the same
to sell flowers as milk: isn't it?"

"No," said Nelly, "I don't think it is. The flowers
are not ours."

"Whose are they?" exclaimed Rob.

"God's," said Nelly, soberly. Rob could not appre-
ciate Nelly's feeling.

"Well, what makes you steal 'em, then?" he asked,
in a satirical tone.

"God likes to have us pick them: I know he does,"
said Nelly, earnestly. "He gives them all to us for
every summer as long as we live."

"Oh, pshaw, Nell!" said Rob. "He don't do any
such thing. They just grow: that's all."

"Well, papa says that God makes them grow on
purpose for us to see how pretty they are. They aren't
of any other use: they aren't the same as potatoes.
And don't you know the little verse, —

> " ' God might have made the earth bring forth
> Enough for great and small ;
> The oak tree and the cedar tree,
> Without a flower at all.'

I 'm always thinking of that. 'Twould be horrid here if we didn't have any thing but things to eat."

CHAPTER VII.

A HUNT FOR A SILVER MINE.

ONE morning, early in June, Nelly was sitting out by the old mill, with her lap full of blue anemones and white daisies: the anemones were hardly out of their gray cloaks. The anemones in Colorado come up out of the ground like crocuses; the buds are rolled up tight in the loveliest little furry coverings almost like chinchilla fur. I think this is to keep them warm, because they come very early in the spring, and often there are cold storms after they arrive, and the poor little anemones are all covered up in snow.

Nelly heard steps and voices and the trampling of hoofs. She sprang up, and saw that a large blue wagon, drawn by eight mules, had just turned in from the road, towards the brook, and the driver was making ready to camp. He came towards Nelly, and said, very pleasantly : —

"Little girl, do your folks live in yonder?" pointing to the house.

"Yes, sir," said Nelly.

"Do they ever keep folks?"

"What, sir?" said Nelly.

"Do they ever keep folks, — keep 'em to board?"

"Oh, no! never," replied Nelly.

The man looked disappointed. "Well," he said,

“ I 've got to lie by here a day or two, anyhow. I was in hopes I could get took in. I 'm clean beat out ; but I can sleep in the wagon.”

“ My mamma will be glad to do all she can for you if you 're sick, sir, I 'm sure,” said Nelly ; “ but we haven't any spare room in our house.”

The driver looked at Nelly again. He had once been a coachman in a gentleman's family at the East, and he knew by Nelly's voice and polite manner that she was not the child of any of the common farmers of the country.

“ Have you lived here long ? ” he said.

“ Oh, no ! ” replied Nelly : “ only since last spring. We came because my papa was sick. He has the asthma.”

“ Oh ! ” said the man : “ I thought so.”

Nelly wondered why the man should have thought her papa had the asthma ; but she did not ask him what he meant. In a few minutes, the man lay down in his wagon and fell fast asleep, and Nelly went into the house. After dinner, she told Rob about the man, and they went out together to see him. They peeped into the wagon. It was loaded full of small bits of gray rock : the man was rolled up in a buffalo robe, lying on top of the stones, still fast asleep. His face was very red, and he breathed loud.

“ Oh, dear ! ” said Nelly, “ how uncomfortable he must be ! He looks real sick.”

“ I bet he 's drunk ! ” said Rob, who had unluckily seen a good deal of that sort of sickness since he had lived on a thoroughfare for mule-wagons.

“ Is he ? ” said Nelly, horror-stricken. “ No, Rob,

he can't be, because he talked with me real nice this morning.   Let's go and tell mamma."

Mr. March went out, looked at the man, and woke him up.   He found that he was indeed ill, and not drunk.   The poor fellow had been five days on the road, with a very heavy cold; and had taken more cold every night, sleeping in the open air.   Walking all day long in the hot sun had also made him worse, and he was suffering severely.

"Come right into the house with me, my man," said Mr. March; "my wife'll make you a cup of hot tea."

"Oh, thank you!" said the man.   "I've been thinkin' I'd give all the ore in this 'ere wagon for a first-rate cup of tea.   I don't never carry tea: only coffee; but I've turned against coffee these last two days;" and he followed Mr. March into the house.

"What'd you say you had in your wagon?" asked Rob, who had been standing by.

"Ore," said the man.

The only word Rob knew which had that sound was "oar."

"Oar!" he said.   "Why, I didn't see any thing but rocks."

Mr. March and the man both laughed.

"Not 'oar,' to row with, Rob," said Mr. March; "but 'ore,' to make money out of."

"Silver ore, I suppose," he added, turning to the man.

"Yes," he said; "from the Moose mine, up on Mount Lincoln."

Rob's eyes grew big.   "Oh! tell me about it," he said.   And Nelly, coming up closer, exclaimed, in a tone unusually eager for her, "And me too. Is the mountain made of silver, like the mountains in fairy stories?"

The man was drinking his tea, and did not answer. He drank it in great mouthfuls, though it was scalding hot.

"Oh, ma'am," he said, "I haven't tasted any thing that went right to the spot's that does, for months; if it wouldn't trouble ye too much, I'd like one more cup." He drank the second cup as quickly as he had the first; then he leaned his head back in the chair, and said: "I feel like a new man now. I guess that was the medicine I needed. I reckon I can go on this afternoon."

"No," said Mr. March: "you ought to stay here till to-morrow. There is an old leather-covered settee in the barn you're welcome to sleep on. It will be better than the ground; and we'll doctor you with hot tea, night and morning."

"You're very kind," said the man: "I don't know but I'd better stay."

"Oh, do! do!" said Rob; and "do! do!" said Nelly. "Stay and tell us all about the mountain of silver and the Moose; does the Moose draw out the silver?"

You see Rob and Nelly couldn't get it out of their heads that it was all like a fairy tale. And so it is when you think of it, more wonderful than almost any fairy tale, to think how great mountains are full of silver and of gold, and men can burrow deep down into them, and get out all the silver and gold they need.

"Oh, there isn't any real Moose," said the man.

"That's only the name of the mine. I don't know why they called the mine the Moose mine. They give mines the queerest kind o' names."

"What is a mine, anyhow?" asked Rob.

"Oh," said the man, "I forgot you didn't know that. A mine's a hole in the ground, or in the side of a mountain, where they dig out gold or silver. There's mines that's miles and miles big, underground, with passages running every way like streets."

"How do they see down there?" said Rob.

"They carry lanterns, and there are lanterns fastened up in the walls."

"Is your wagon all full of silver?" asked Nelly, in a low tone.

"Not exactly all silver yet," the man said, laughing; "there's a good deal of silver in it: it's very good ore."

"It looked just like gray rock," said Rob.

"Well, that's what it is," replied the man; "it's gray rock. It's got to be all pounded up fine in a mill, and then it's got to be roasted with salt in a great oven, and then it's got to be mixed with chemicals and things. I don't rightly know just what it is they do do to it; it's a heap of work I know, before it ever gets to be the pure silver."

"Some day I will take you, Rob," said his father, "where you can see all this done: I want to see it myself. Run out, now, you and Nelly, and play, and let the driver rest. He is too tired to talk any more."

Rob and Nelly went back to the wagon. All Nelly's anemones and daisies were lying on the ground, withered. Even this one short hour of hot sun had been enough to kill them.

“Oh, my poor, dear flowers!” said Nelly, picking them up. “How could I forget you!” and she looked at them as sorrowfully as if they were little babies she had neglected.

“Pooh, Nell,” cried Rob. “They’re no good now. Throw them in the brook, and come look at the silver.”

They both climbed up on the tongue of the wagon and looked in at the front.

“I can’t see any silver about it,” said Nelly; “it don’t look like any thing but little gray stones, all broken up into bits.”

“No,” said Rob: “it don’t shine much;” and he picked up a bit and held it out in the sun.

“Oh, take care! take care, Rob!” cried Nelly. “Don’t lose it; it might be as much as a quarter of a dollar, that bit.”

“Nell,” said Rob, earnestly, “don’t you wish papa had a mine, and we could dig up all the money we wanted? oh, my!” and Rob drew in his breath in a long whistle.

“Yes,” said Nelly: “I mean to look for one. Do you find the holes already dug, do you suppose? Perhaps that place where old Molly tumbled in was a mine.”

Old Molly was one of their cows, who had tumbled one day into a hole made by a slide of earth; and Zeb had had to go down and tie ropes around her to pull her up.

“Yes,” said Rob: “I bet you any thing it is. Let’s go right up there now, and see if we can find some rock like this. I’ll carry this piece in my pocket to tell by. I’ll only borrow it: I’ll put it back.”

"Let me carry it then," said Nelly. "I 'm so afraid you 'll lose it."

So Nelly tied the little bit of gray rock in a corner of her pocket-handkerchief, and then crammed her handkerchief down tight in her pocket, and they set off at a swift pace, towards the ravine where Molly had had her unlucky fall.

When dinner-time came, the children were nowhere to be found. Zeb went up and down the brook for a mile, looking and calling aloud. Watch and Trotter had both disappeared also.

"Ye needn't worry so long 's the dogs is along, ma'am," said Zeb, when he returned from his bootless search. "If they get into any trouble, Watch 'll come home and let us know. He 's got more sense 'n most men, that dog has."

But Mrs. March could not help worrying. Never since they had lived in the Pass had Nelly and Rob gone away for any long walk without coming and bidding her good-by, and telling her where they were going. The truth was, that this time they had entirely forgotten it: they were so excited by the hopes of finding a mine. They had walked nearly a mile when Nelly suddenly exclaimed: "Oh, Rob! we didn't say good-by to mamma! She won't know where we are."

"So we didn't!" said Rob. "What a shame! But we can't go back now, Nell: it 's too late; we 've come miles and miles; we 'd better keep on; she 'll know we 're all right; we always are. We 're most there now."

It was the middle of the afternoon before Rob and Nelly got home. Mrs. March had been walking up and down the road anxiously for an hour, when she saw the two little figures coming down the very steepest of the hills. They walked very slowly; so slowly that she felt sure one of them must be hurt. The dogs were bounding along before them. As soon as the children saw their mother, Rob took off his hat, and Nelly her sun-bonnet, and waved them in the air. This relieved Mrs. March's fears, and the tears came into her eyes, she was so glad. "Oh, Robert, there they are!" she exclaimed to Mr. March, who had just joined her. "See! there they are, way up on that steep hill. Thank God, they are safe!"

Mr. and Mrs. March both stood in the road, shading their eyes with their hands, and looking up at the children.

As they drew nearer, Mrs. March exclaimed: "Why, what are they carrying?" Mr. March burst out laughing, and said: "They look like little pack mules." In a few minutes, the hot, tired, dusty little wanderers reached the road, and ran breathlessly up to their father and mother: "Oh, mamma!" cried Rob; and "Oh, papa!" cried Nelly. "We've found a mine; we've got lots of ore; now we can get all the money we want. You see if this isn't almost exactly like the stuff in the man's wagon!" and Nelly emptied her apron on the ground, and Rob emptied his jacket; he had taken it off and carried it by the sleeves so as to make a big sack of it. Mr. and Mrs. March could hardly keep from laughing at the sight: there were the two piles of little bits of stone, and the children with red and dirty faces and the perspiration rolling down their cheeks, getting down on their knees to pick out their choicest specimens. Nelly was fumbling deep down in her pocket; presently she drew out her handkerchief all knotted in a wisp, and out of the last knot she took the little bit of ore which they had borrowed from the wagon for a sample. This she laid in her father's hand: "There, papa," she said, "that's the man's: we borrowed it to carry along to tell by."

"They don't look so much like it as they did," she added, turning sorrowfully back to the poor little pile of stones. Rob was gazing at them too, with a crest-fallen face.

"Why, they don't shine a bit now," he said; "up there they shone like every thing."

Mr. March picked up a bit of the stone and looked closely at it.

"Ah, Rob," he said, "the reason it doesn't shine now, is because the sun has gone under a cloud. There are little points of mica in these stones, and mica shines in the sun; but there isn't any silver here, dear. Did you really think you had made all our fortunes?"

Rob did not speak. He had hard work to keep from crying. He stood still, slowly kicking the pile of stones with one foot. His father pitied him very much.

"Never mind, Rob," he said; "you're not the first fellow that has thought he had found a mine, and been mistaken."

Rob stooped down and picked up two big handfuls of the stones and threw them as far as he could throw them.

"Old cheats!" he said.

"Yes, real old cheats!" said Nelly; and she began to scatter the stones with her foot. "And they were awful heavy. Oh, mamma, I'm so hungry!"

"So 'm I," said Rob. "Isn't it dinner-time?"

"Dinner-time!" exclaimed their mother. "Did you really not have any more idea of the time than that! Why, it is three o'clock! Where have you been?"

"Not very far, mamma," answered Nelly; "only up where old Molly tumbled in. Rob thought perhaps that hole was a mine. It's all full of these shining stones. Isn't it too bad, mamma?"

"Isn't what too bad, Nell?" said Mrs. March.

"Why, too bad that they ain't silver," replied Nelly. "We thought we could all have every thing we wanted."

Mrs. March laughed.

"What do you want most of all this minute?" she said.

"Something to eat, mamma," said Nelly.

"Well, that you can have; and that I hope we can always have without any silver mine: and to-day we have something very good to eat."

"Oh! what, mamma, what? say, quick!" said Rob.

"Chicken pie," said Mrs. March, in a very comical, earnest tone.

"Chicken pie!" shouted Rob. "Hurrah! hurrah!" and both he and Nelly ran toward the house as hard as they could go.

"There is a wish-bone drying for you on the mantel-piece," called out Mr. March.

"They 'll both wish for a silver mine, I expect," laughed Mrs. March, as she and her husband walked slowly along. "What a queer notion that was to come into such children's heads!"

"I don't know," said Mr. March, reflectively; "I

think it 's a very natural notion to come into anybody's head. I 'd like a silver mine myself, very much."

"We mightn't be any happier if we had one, nor half so happy," replied Mrs. March. "I 'd rather have you well, and the children well, than have all the silver mines in Colorado."

"If you had to choose between the two things, I dare say," answered Mr. March; "but I suppose a person might have good health and a silver mine besides. How would that do?"

"Well, I 'll make sure of the health first," said Mrs. March, laughing. "I 'm not in so much hurry for the silver mine."

After Rob and Nelly had eaten up all the chicken pie which had been saved for them, they took down the wish-bone from the mantel-piece, and prepared to "wish."

"It 's so dry, it 'll break splendidly," said Rob. "I know what I 'm going to wish for."

"So do I," said Nelly, resolutely; "I 'm going to wish hard."

They both pulled with all their might. Crack went the wish-bone, — no difference in the length of the two pieces.

"Pshaw!" cried Rob; "how mean! one or the other of us might have had it."

Nelly drew a long sigh. "Rob," said she, "what did you wish for?"

"A silver mine," said he, "both times."

"So did I," said Nell. "I thought you did, too. I guess we shan't either of us ever have one."

"I don't care," said Rob; "there 's plenty of money

besides in mines. I'm going to have a bank when I'm
a man."

"Are you, Rob?" said Nell. "What's that?"

"Oh, just a house where you can go and get money,"
replied Rob, confidently. "I used to go with papa
often at home. They gave him all he wanted."

Nelly looked somewhat perplexed. She did not
know any thing about banks: still she thought there
was a loose screw somewhere in Rob's calculations; but
she did not ask him any more questions.

After tea. Mr. March walked away with the driver
of the mule team. They did not come back until it
was dark. Mr. March opened the door of the sitting-
room, and said, "Sarah, I wish you'd come out here
a few minutes." When she had stepped out and closed
the door, he said, "I want you to come up where the
wagon is: there's a nice bonfire up there, and it isn't
cold; I want this man to tell you all he's been telling
me about a place down South, — a hundred miles below
this. If it's all's he says, that's the place we ought
to go to. But I wanted you to hear all about it before
I said any thing to the Deacon."

The driver's name, by the way, was Billy; he was
called "Long Billy" on the roads where he drove, because his legs were so long, and his body so short. He
had made a splendid bonfire on the edge of the brook,
and Mr. March and he had been sitting there for an
hour, on a buffalo robe spread on the ground. Mrs.
March sat down with them, and Long Billy began his
story over again. It seemed that he had formerly been
a driver of a mule team on another route, much farther
south than this one. He had "hauled ore," as he

called it, from a little town called Rosita, to another town called Canyon City. There the ore was packed on cars and sent over the little narrow-gauge railroad up to Central City, where the silver was extracted from the rock, and moulded into little solid bricks of silver ready to be sent to the mint at Philadelphia to be made into half dollars and quarters.

This town of Rosita lay among mountains: was built on the sides of two or three narrow gulches, in the Wet Mountain range; at the foot of these mountains was the beautiful Wet Mountain Valley, — a valley thirty miles long, and only from five to eight miles wide; on the side farthest from Rosita this valley was walled by another high mountain range, the Sangre di Christo range. This means "The blood of Christ." The Spaniards gave this name to the mountains when they first came to the country. All the mountains in the Sangre di Christo range are over eight thousand feet high, and many of them are over twelve thousand; their points are sharp like the teeth of a saw, and they are white with snow the greater part of the year. The beautiful valley lying between these two long lines of mountains was the place about which Long Billy had been telling Mr. March, and now began to tell Mrs. March.

"Why, ma'am," he said, "I tell ye, after coming over these plains, it is jest like lookin' into Heaven, to get a look down into that valley; it's as green as any medder land ye ever laid your eyes on; I 've seen the grass there higher 'n my knee, in July."

"Oh!" said Mrs. March, with a sigh of satisfaction at the very thought of it, "I would like to see tall grass once more."

"Yes, indeed, wife," said Mr. March; "but think what a place that would be for cattle, and for hay. Farming would be something worth talking about; and Billy says that the farmers in the valley can have a good market in Rosita for all they can raise. There are nearly a thousand miners there; and it is also only a day's journey from Pueblo, which is quite a city. It really looks to me like the most promising place I've heard any thing about here."

"It's the nicest bit of country there is anywhere in Colorado," said Billy, "'s fur's I've seen it. Them mountains 's jest a picture to look at all the time; 'n' there's a creek, — Grape Creek, they call it, because it's just lined with wild grape-vines, for miles, — runs through the valley; 'n' lots o' little creeks coming down out o' the mountains, 'n' empties into 't. I wouldn't ask nothin' more o' the Lord than that He'd give me a little farm down in Wet Mountain Valley for the rest o' my life. I know that."

"Do you think there are any farms there that could be bought," asked Mr. March, anxiously. "I should think such desirable lands would be all taken up."

"Well, they're changin' round there a good deal," said Billy. "Ye wouldn't think it; but men they git discontented a hearing so much talk about silver. They're always a hoping to get hold on a mine 'n' make a big fortin' all in a minnit; but I hain't seen so many of these big fortin's made off minin' 'n this country. For one man thet's made his fortin', I've known twenty that's lost it. Now I think on 't I did hear, last spring, that Wilson he wanted to sell out; 'n' if you could get his farm, you'd jest be fixed first rate. There's the

best spring o' water on his place there is in all the
valley ; and it ain't more 'n four miles 'n' a half from his
place up into Rosita : ye 'd walk it easy."

Mr. March looked at his wife. Her face was full of
excitement and pleasure.

"It sounds perfectly delightful, Robert," she said ;
"but you know we thought just so about this Pass.
The pictures were so beautiful, and all they told us
sounded attractive."

Billy made a scornful sound almost like a snort.

"H'm !" he said, "anybody that recommended ye
to settle this low down in the Ute Pass for stock-raisin'
or farmin' must ha' been either a knave or a fool : that 's
certain."

"A knave, I think," said Mrs. March. "He tried
very hard to sell us the whole place."

"I 'll be bound he did," sneered Billy ; "cheap
enough he 'll sell it, too, afore ever he gets anybody to
buy."

"Say, mister," he continued, "you jest come along
with me to-morrow : I 'd like to take a run down to
Rosita, first rate ; 'n' I 've got to lay by a few days
anyhow. I 'll get this load o' ore board the cars at the
Springs, 'n' then I 'll jest quit work for a week ; 'n' I 'll
go down with yer to Rosita. There 's somebody there
I 'm wantin' to see putty bad." And Billy's burnt face
grew a shade or two deeper red.

"Ah, Billy, is that it?" said Mr. March.

"Well, yes, sir. We 're a calculatin' to be married
one o' these days 's soon 's I get a little ahead. It 's
slow work, though, layin' up money teamin', 'n' I won't
take her out of a good home till I can give her one o'

her own's good. Her father he's foreman 'n one o' the mines there; 'n' he's always been a real forehanded man. She's well off: she's got no occasion to marry anybody to be took care of." And Billy smiled complacently in the thought that it must have been for pure love that the Rosita young lady had promised to marry him.

"Sarah, what do you think of my going?" said Mr. March.

"Go, by all means!" said Mrs. March. "The little journey will do you good, even if nothing comes of it. We need not say any thing about the reason for your going, till you get back. If you decide to move down there, that will be time enough to explain."

"And Mrs. Plummer will say that it was all 'providential,'" laughed Mr. March.

"And so shall I, Robert," said Mrs. March, very earnestly.

The next morning Mr. March and Long Billy set off together at seven o'clock. It was the first time Mrs. March had been separated from her husband in this new country, and she dreaded it.

"Good-by! good-by!" called the children, in their night-gowns, at the bed-room window; "good-by, papa."

"Good-by!" said the Deacon; "reckon your bones 'll ache some, before ye get to the Springs, a ridin' that wheeler." Mr. March was riding the near wheeler, and Long Billy was walking by his side.

"Not if he don't walk any faster than this," said Mr. March. "And I shall walk half of the time."

"Ye needn't walk a step if ye'd rather ride," said

Billy. " I 'm all right this mornin'. "Tain't only about ten miles down to Colorado Springs. I don't think nothin' o' walkin' that fur, especially when I 've got company to talk to. Mules is dreadful tiresome critters. Now a hoss 's real good company ; but a mule ain't no company 't all."

CHAPTER VIII.

THE MARCHES LEAVE GARLAND'S.

IT was on a Wednesday morning that Mr. March and Long Billy set out for Rosita. The next week, on Thursday evening, just at sunset, Mrs. March heard the sound of wheels, and, looking up, saw a white-topped wagon, drawn by two mules, coming up the road. In the next instant, she saw Rob and Nelly running, jumping, and clapping their hands, and trying to climb up into the wagon.

"Why, that must be Mr. March," she exclaimed, and ran out of the door.

"Why, that's queer," said the Deacon, following slowly; "he said he'd write the day before he was a-comin'; and we were to go down 'n' meet him at the Springs."

"And if he hasn't brought that long-geared fellow back with him, I declare!" continued the Deacon, as he walked on: "I'd like to know what's up now."

Mrs. March had already reached the wagon, and was welcoming her husband. Long Billy interrupted her greetings.

"Well, mum," he said, "I s'pose you're surprised to see me back again. But me 'n' him" — nodding to Mr. March — "'s struck up a kind o' 'liance, an' I'm to your service now: me 'n' my mules."

"I know what that means," thought Mrs. March: "we're going to move down to that valley, post haste." But all she said was: —

"Very well, Billy; I'm glad to see you. Mr. March's friends are always mine."

"What are you going to do with that Long Legs, Parson?" said Deacon Plummer, as soon as he found a chance to speak to Mr. March alone; "seems to me we haven't got work for another hand: have we?"

"Not on this farm: that's a clear case, Deacon," replied Mr. March; "but it's too long a story to enter on now. After supper I'll tell you my plans."

The Deacon took out his red silk handkerchief, and rubbed his forehead.

"Oh, Lord!" said he to himself; "what's that blessed man been and done now? He ain't noways fit to go off by himself. I'll bet he's been took in worse 'n ever."

After supper Mr. March told his story. He had bought a farm in the Wet Mountain Valley, and he proposed that they should all move down there immediately. The place had more than equalled all Long Billy's descriptions of it; and Mr. March's enthusiasm was unbounded. Deacon Plummer listened to all his statements with a perplexed and incredulous face.

"Did you see that medder grass's high's a man's knee?" he asked.

"Waded in it, Deacon," replied Mr. March; "but that isn't all: I've got a wisp of it in my pocket."

Long Billy chuckled, as Mr. March drew the crumpled green wisp out of his pocket, and handed it to the Deacon.

" 'Twas I put him up to bringin' that," said Billy.
" Sez I, ' there ain't nothin' so good for folks 's seein'
with their own eyes.' I kind o' misgave that the old
man wouldn't be for believin' it all."

The Deacon unfolded the grass ; back and forth, back
and forth, he bent it, and straightened it out across his
knees. He looked at it in silence for a minute ; then
he said : —

" Well, that beats me ! Acres like this, you say ? "

" Miles, Deacon," said Mr. March.

" Miles 'n' miles," said Billy ; " 's fur 's you can see
it wavin' in the wind ; 't looks like wheat, only puttier.
P'raps you 'd better show him the wheat now ? "

Mr. March pulled out of his other pocket a similar
wisp of wheat, and handed it to the Deacon. This he
straightened out, as he had the grass, across his knees,
and looked at it in silence for a moment ; then he tasted
the kernel ; then he rolled up both wheat and grass
together, and handed them back to Mr. March, saying :

" I 've got nothin' more to say. Seein' 's believin'."

Long Billy nodded his head triumphantly, and winked
at Mr. March.

" But," continued the Deacon, " for all that I don't
feel it clear in my mind about our goin'. 'Twouldn't
make any difference to ye, Parson, anyway, if Elizy 'n'
I didn't go ; would it ? "

Mr. March was much surprised.

" Why, Deacon ! " he said, " we should be very sorry
to have you separate from us. You surely can't stay
on in this place ! "

" Oh, no ! " replied the Deacon ; " we hain't the
least idea o' that. The fact is, I expect we ought to go

home : Elizy 's so poorly. We 've been thinkin' on 't for some time. But we was so kind o' settled here, and all so home-like, we hated to stir. But if you 're goin' to break up, and go to a new place, I expect we 'd better take that time to go home."

This was not wholly a surprise to Mr. and Mrs. March, for they had themselves felt that old Mrs. Plummer would after all be better off in her comfortable home in Mayfield. They saw that she was growing slowly more feeble : the climate did not suit her.

" I reckon we 're kind o' old for this country," said the Deacon. " It don't seem to me 's I feel quite so fust-rate 's I did at home. Trees gets too old to transplant after a while."

" That 's so ! that 's so ! " exclaimed Billy. " I 've never yet seen the fust time, old folks adoin' well here. The air 's too bracin' for 'em. They can't get used to it, — no offence to you, sir," — looking at Deacon Plummer.

" Oh, no offence, — no offence at all," replied the Deacon. " I don't make any bones about ownin' that I 'm old. Me 'n' my wife 's both seen our best days ; 'n' I reckon we 're best off at home. I think we 'd better go, Parson. We 're mighty sorry to leave you ; but when you move South, we 'll start the other way towards home. Ain't that so, Elizy ? " Mrs. Plummer had been rocking violently for the last few minutes, with her face buried in her handkerchief.

" Yes," she sobbed, " I expect so. It 's just providential, the hull on 't."

" Dear Mrs. Plummer, do not cry so ! " exclaimed Mrs. March. " We have had a very pleasant time.

It is only a few months; and when you get home, it will only seem as if you had taken a six months' journey. I really think you will be better in Mayfield than here."

"Oh, I 've no doubt on 't," said Mrs. Plummer, still crying in her handkerchief; "but I thought we was a goin' to live with you all the rest o' our lives. It 's a awful disappointment to me. But it 's all providential. It 's a comfort to know that."

When Zeb heard the news that the family would break up in a few days, — the Marches to move down to Wet Mountain Valley, and the Plummers to go back to Massachusetts, — he was very sorry. He turned on his heel without saying a word, and went into the barn.

"Just your luck, Abe Mack!" he said, under his breath; "you don't no sooner get used to a place 'n' to folks, 'n' feel real contented, than somethin' happens to tip ye out. Ye 're born onlucky; I reckon there 's no use fightin'. They 're so took up with this long-legged spindle of a mule-driver I expect they won't want me; 'n' I don't want to go down into no minin' country, nuther, — 'tain't safe. I 'll see if the old man won't take me back to the States. I 've got enough to pay my way, if he 'll give me work after I get there; and I reckon I 'd be safe from any o' them Georgetown fellers in Massachusetts."

The Deacon was very glad to take Zeb back with him. He had learned to like the man, and he needed such a hand on his farm.

And so it was all settled, and everybody went to work as hard as possible to get ready for the move. Nelly and Rob hardly knew whether to be glad or sorry.

They loved the hills so much, they were afraid they would not love the valley so well. Yet their heads were nearly turned by Long Billy's stories of the wonderful mines in Rosita; of the machinery in the stamp-mill where they crushed the ore and got the silver out; of the delicious wild grapes on Grape Creek; and the trout, and the flowers on the hills.

"Yer hain't ever seen any flowers yet," said Billy, when Nelly tried to tell him how many flowers grew in the pass; "ye jest wait till I take ye up on Pine's ranch, some Sunday. I'll show ye flowers then: sixty odd kinds in one field, — yes, sure! I counted 'em; and old Pine he counted 'em too. And he sent 'em off by express once, some of each kind, to the folks at Washington. You'll see!"

Just three weeks from the day Long Billy first drove into the shadow of the old saw-mill to camp, the March and Plummer family set out on their journeys: Fox and Pumpkinseed drawing one big white-topped wagon, in which were Mrs. March, Deacon and Mrs. Plummer, Nelly and Rob. Billy's two mules drew the other big wagon, which was loaded down very heavily with the furniture Mr. March had bought. Mr. March drove this; and Billy, mounted on a new horse which he had bought, was driving all the cattle before him. Zeb sat by Mr. March's side in the mule wagon. He and Deacon and Mrs. Plummer were to take the cars at Colorado Springs, and go to Denver. Mr. and Mrs. March had begged them to come down with them into Wet Mountain Valley, and make a visit. But the Deacon said "No."

"The fact is," he said, "I may's well own it: now

that we 're really started for home, we 're dreadful homesick. I didn't know 's I had felt it so much. Can't
transplant old trees, Parson, no use ! It 's a good country for young folks, — a good country ; I shall tell the
boys about it. But give me old Massachusetts. I just
hanker after a sight o' the old buryin'-ground, 'n' that
black elder-bush in the corner on 't."

When they parted at the little railroad station in Colorado Springs, Mrs. Plummer broke down and cried.
Nelly cried a little too, from sympathy ; and even Watch
whined, seeing that something unusual and uncomfortable was going on. Luckily, however, good-byes at
railway stations always are cut short. The engine-
bell rings, and the cars move off, and that puts an end
to the last words. Mr. and Mrs. March were sorry
to part from these good old people ; and yet, if the
whole truth were told, it must be owned that they felt
a sense of relief when they were gone. They had felt,
all the while, a responsibility for their comfort, and a
fear lest they should be taken ill, which had been bur-
densome.

"We shall miss them : shan't we ? " said Mrs. March,
as the train moved off.

"Yes," said Nelly ; "I 'm real sorry they 're gone.
I like Zeb too."

"We 'll miss the crullers," said Rob. "Say, mamma,
didn't she show you how to make 'em ? "

"Rob," said his father, "you ought to be a Chinese."

"Why ? " asked Rob.

"Because they think the seat of all life is in the
stomach ; and they give great honor to people with very
big stomachs," answered his father.

Rob did not know whether his father were laughing at him or not.   He suspected he might be.

" I don't know what you mean, papa," he said : " you like crullers, anyhow."

" Fair hit, Rob ! " said Mrs. March.   " Fair hit, papa ! "

The journey to Rosita took six days : they had to go very slowly on account of the cattle.   The weather was perfect ; and every night they slept on the ground, in a tent which Mr. March had bought in Colorado Springs. Rob rode on Pumpkinseed's back a good part of the way, like a little postilion.   Before the end of the journey, they were all so burnt by the sun that they looked, Mrs. March said, " a great deal more like Indians than like white people."   They drove into Rosita just at sunset.   I wish I could tell you how beautiful the whole place looked to them.   You go down a steep hill, just as you come into the town of Rosita.   On the top of this hill, Mr. March called out to his wife to stop.   She was driving Fox and Pumpkinseed ; and he was following behind with the mules.   He jumped out, and came up to the side of her wagon.

" There, Sarah ! " he said, " did you ever see any thing in your life so beautiful as this ? "

Mrs. March did not speak ; both she and Nelly and even Rob were struck dumb by the beauty of the picture.   They looked right down into the little village. It was cuddled in the ravine as if it had gone to sleep there.   The sides of the hills were dotted with pine-trees ; and most of the little houses were built of bright yellow pine boards : they shone in the sun.   Just beyond the village they could see a bit of a most beautiful green valley; and, beyond that, **great** high mountains, half covered with **snow.**

"That is the valley," said Mr. March: "that **bit** of bright green, way down there **to** the west."

Nelly was the first to speak.

"Papa," said she, "it looks just like a beautiful green bottom to a deep well: doesn't it?"

"Yes, this little bit that you see of it from here, does," said Mr. March; "but, after you get into it, it doesn't **look so.** It is thirty miles long; and so level, you would think you were **on the plains.** And oh, Nell! you can **see your** dear Pike's Peak grandly there! It looks twice as high here **as** it does from any place **I** have seen it."

"Oh, I'm so glad!" said Nelly.

Still, Mrs. March did not speak. Her husband turned to her at **last, anxiously,** and said: —

"Don't you like it, Sarah?"

"Oh, Robert!" she said, "it is so beautiful it doesn't look to me like a real place. It looks like a painted picture!"

"That'll do! that'll do!" laughed **Mr.** March; "I'm satisfied. Now we'll go down the hill."

Rob nudged Nelly. They were on the back seat of the wagon.

"Nell," he whispered, "did you ever see any thing like it? I see lots of silver mines all round on the hills. Billy told me how they looked. Those piles of stones are all on top of mines; that's where they throw out the stones. I'll bet we'll find a mine."

"Oh," said Nelly, "wouldn't that be splendid! Let's go out the first thing to-morrow morning."

Mr. March had planned to stay in Rosita a couple of
days, before going down to his farm in the valley. He
wished to become acquainted with some of the Rosita
tradesmen, and to find out all about the best ways of
doing things in this new life. Long Billy proved a
good helper now. Everybody in Rosita knew Long
Billy and liked him ; and, when he said to his friends,
confidentially : —

" This is a first-rate feller I 've hired with : he does
the square thing by everybody, I tell you. There 's
nothin' narrer about him ; he 's the least like a parson
of any parson ye ever see," — they accepted Billy's
word for it all, and met Mr. March with a friendliness
which would not usually have been shown to a new-
comer.

The next morning after they reached Rosita, Long
Billy proposed to take Mr. March out and introduce
him to some of the people he knew. When Mr. March
came downstairs, he was dressed in a good suit of
black, and wore a white collar : on the journey, he had
worn his rough working-clothes, and a flannel shirt.
Long Billy looked him up and down, from head to foot,
with an expression of great dissatisfaction ; but did not
say any thing. Then he walked out on the piazza of
the hotel, and stood still for some minutes, in deep
thought. Then he said to himself : —

" Hang it all ! I 'll have to speak to him. What 'd
he want to go 'n' spruce hisself all up like that for ?
'T 'll jest ruin him in this town, oncet for all ! I 'll have
to speak to him. I 'd rather be scotch-wollopped."

What scotch-wollopped means I do not know : but it
was a favorite expression of Long Billy's. So he walked

back into the hotel, and beckoned Mr. March out on the piazza.

"Look here, Parson," he said, speaking very fast, and looking very much embarrassed, — which was an odd thing for Billy, — "look here, Parson, you ain't goin' to preach to-day, be yer?"

"Why, no, Billy," said Mr. March; "why did you ask?"

"Ain't these yer preachin' clo'es?" replied Billy, pointing to the black coat.

Mr. March laughed.

"Why, yes, I have preached in them, Billy; but I do not expect ever to again. I must wear them out, though."

"Not in these parts, Parson," said Billy, solemnly, shaking his head. "Yer don't know minin' towns so well's I do. Ef I was to take you down town in that rig, there wouldn't one o' the fellers open his head to yer. They'd shet up jest like·snappin' turtles. Ye jest go upstairs 'n' put on the clo'es ye allers wears: won't ye?" said Billy, almost pleadingly.

"Why, certainly, Billy, if you really think it would make any difference about my making friends with the people. I don't want to offend anybody. These are pretty old clothes, though, Billy, if they only knew it. It was to save my others that I put them on. But I'll change them, if you say so." And Mr. March ran upstairs much amused. When he came down in his rough suit and his blue flannel shirt, Billy smiled with pleasure.

"There," he said, "you look like a man in them clo'es, Parson. Excuse my bein' so free; but I allers did think that the parsons' clo'es had a good deal to do with fellers despisin' 'em 's they do. They allers call 'em ' Tender-feet.' "

" Tender-feet !" exclaimed Mr. March ; " what does that mean, Billy ? "

Billy did not answer immediately. He was puzzled to think of any definition of " Tender-feet."

" Well," he said at last, " don'no' as I can say exactly what it does mean ; but 'tain't because I don't know. Any feller that 's over-particular about his clo'es, 'n' his way o' livin', 'n' can't rough it like the generality o' folks in Colorado, gets called a ' Tender-foot ' ! Lord, I 'd rather be called a thief, any day ! "

Mr. March laughed heartily.

" I see ! I see ! " he said. " Well now, Billy, you don't think there 'd be any danger of my ever being called a ' Tender-foot :' do you ? "

" Not a bit of it, Parson," said Billy, emphatically, " when a feller came to live with yer ; but to see yer jest a walkin' round in them black clo'es o' yourn, you 'd get took for one. Yer would : that 's a fact. I should take yer for one myself. Yer may 's well give that suit up, oncet for all, Parson, for this country, I tell ye," added Billy, thinking he would make sure that the danger did not occur again. " Thet is," he continued, " except Sundays. I don't suppose 'twould do ye any harm to be seen in it Sundays, or to a dance."

" I don't go to dances, Billy," said Mr. March ; " perhaps I 'll give the suit away : that 'll save all trouble."

As they left the hotel, they saw Rob and Nelly walking hand in hand up the steep road down which they had come the night before, entering the village.

"Where can the children be going?" said Mr. March.
"Rob! Nelly!" he called. They both turned and said:
"What, papa?" but did not come towards him.

"Where are you going?" he said.

"Oh, only a little way up this road," replied Rob.

"Don't you want to come with me?" said Mr. March.
The children hesitated.

"Do you want us, papa?" said Nelly.

"Why, no, certainly not," replied Mr. March, "unless you want to come. I thought you would like to see the town: that's all."

"We'd rather go up on the hill, papa," said Rob.
"Mamma said we might, if we wouldn't go out of sight of the hotel. Good-by!"

"Good-by, papa!" called Nelly. And they both trudged off with a most business-like air.

Long Billy laughed.

"Them youngsters got silver on the brain," he said.
"Thet's what's the matter with them. I've seen plenty o' grown folks jest the same way in this country: a walkin', walkin' by the month to a time, a pokin' into every hole, 'n' a hammerin' every stone,—jest wild after gold 'n' silver. There's plenty on 'em's jest wasted time enough on 't to ha' made a considerable money, if they'd stuck to some kind o' regular work. That little chap o' yourn, he's a driver: he hain't never let go the idee of findin' a silver mine, sence the day they hauled all them mica stuns down, back there 'n the pass. They're a rare couple, he 'n' Nelly: they are."

"Yes, they are good children," said Mr. March:
"good children; but I don't want them to get possessed with this desire for money." And he looked anxiously

up the hill, where he could see Rob and Nelly striking off from the road, and picking their way across the rough ground towards a great pile of gray ore, which had been thrown out of one of the mines.

Long Billy also looked up at them.

"The little sarpents!" he said. "They're a makin' for the Pocahontas mine, straight. Rob, he was a askin' me all about the piles o' ore 'n' the engines in the mines, yesterday."

"Is there any danger of their being hurt?" said Mr. March.

"Oh, no! I reckon not. That Nelly, she's jest the same's a grown woman. I allers notice her a holdin' the little feller back. She won't go into any resky places no more 'n her ma would. She's got a heap o' sense, that little gal has."

While Mr. March and the children were away, Mrs. March sat at the west window of her room, looking off into the beautiful valley. I wish I could make you see just how it looked from her window; however, no picture can show it, and I suppose no words can tell it; but if you really want to try to imagine how it looked just ask somebody who is with you while you are reading this page, to explain to you how high a thousand feet would seem to you. If you can see the spire of the church, and can know just how high that is, that will help you get an idea of a thousand feet. Then you can imagine that you are looking off between two high hills, right down into a bit of green valley one thousand feet lower down than you are. Then try to imagine that this bit of green valley looked very small; and that, beyond it, there were grand high mountains, half còvered with snow. The lower half of the mountains looked blue: on a sunny day, mountains always look blue in the distance; and the upper half was dazzling white. This is the best I can do towards making you see the picture which Mrs. March saw as she sat at her western window. After all, I think Nelly's sentence was worth more than all mine, when she said, "Oh, papa, it looks like a beautiful green bottom to a deep well." The picture was so beautiful that Mrs. March did not want to do any thing but sit and look at it, and when her husband returned from his walk in the village, she was really astonished to find that she had sat at the window two whole hours without moving. The children did not come home until noon. Their faces were red and their eyes shone with excitement: they had had a fine time; they had rambled on from one mine to another on the hill; whenever they saw a pile of the gray ore, and a yellow pine building near it, they had gone into the building and looked into the shaft down which the miners went into the ground. They had found kind men everywhere who had answered all their questions; and Rob had both his pockets full of pieces of stone with beautiful colors, like a peacock's neck. Rob had forgotten the name of the stone: so had Nelly.

"It sounded something like prophets," said Nelly, "but it couldn't have been that;" she handed a bit of the stone to Long Billy.

"Oh," said he, glancing at it carelessly, "that's nothing but pyrites; that's no account; they'll give you all you want of that."

"I don't care:" said Rob, "it's splendid. I'm

going to make a museum, and I shall have the shelves full of it. But, mamma," he said sadly, "there isn't any use in our looking for a mine. When I told one of the men that we were going to see if we couldn't find a mine, he just laughed, and he said that every inch of the ground all round here belonged to people that thought they 'd got mines. All those little bits of piles of stones, with just a stick stuck up by them, every one of those means that a man 's been digging there to find silver; and they 're just as thick! why, you can't go ten steps without coming on one! They call them ' claims.' "

" That 's so," said Long Billy; " and I 'll tell ye what I call 'em. I call 'em gravestones, them little sticks stuck up on stone heaps: that 's what most on 'em are, graves where some poor feller 's buried a lot o' hope and some money."

Nelly turned her great dark eyes full on Long Billy when he said this. Her face grew very sad: she understood exactly what he meant. Rob did not understand. He looked only puzzled.

" Graves!" exclaimed he. " Why, what do you call them graves for, Billy? There isn't any thing buried in them."

Billy looked a little ashamed of his speech: he did not often indulge in any thing so much like a flight of fancy as this.

" Oh, nothin'!" he said. " That 's only a silly way o' puttin' it."

" I don't think so, Billy," said Nelly. " I think it 's real true. Don't you know, Rob, how awfully you and I felt when we thought we 'd found that mine up in the pass, and it turned out nothing but mica? We felt just as if we 'd lost something."

"I didn't," said Rob; "I just felt mad; and it makes me feel mad now to think of it: how we lugged those heavy old stones all that way. I wish I 'd saved some for my museum though. All the boys here have museums, a man told me, and perhaps I won't find any of that kind of stone here."

After dinner, they all drove down into the valley to look at their new home. The road wound down in a zigzag way among a great many low hills. Sometimes for quite a distance among these hills, you cannot see the valley at all; and then all of a sudden you look right out into it. As they went lower, they saw more and more of it, until at last they reached it and came out on the level ground, where they could look up and down the whole length of the valley. Long Billy was driving them: when they reached the spot where the whole valley lay in full view, he stopped the horses, and, turning round to Mrs. March, said : —

"Well, mum, did I tell the truth or not?"

"No, Billy, you did not," replied Mrs. March, very gravely.

Billy looked surprised, and was just about to speak, when Mrs. March continued : —

"You did not tell half how beautiful it is."

"Ah!" said Billy. "Well, that kind o' lie I don't mind bein' charged with."

"Oh, papa! let me get out!" cried Nelly. "I want to walk in this grass. Is this our grass?"

The road was winding along between two fields of high grass, which waved in the wind. As it waved,

Nelly saw bright red and blue flowers among it; some tall, and some low down close to the ground as if they were hiding.

"Yes, this is where our land begins," said her father; "this is our own grass: but I don't want you to run in it; we must mow it next week."

"Oh, let us, papa; just a little bit—close to the fence. You can spare a little bit of hay," pleaded Nelly; "we'll step light."

"Do let them, Robert," said Mrs. March. "I should like to do it myself."

"Very well: keep close to the fence, then," said Mr. March, and reined up the horses. Rob and Nelly jumped out, and had clambered over the fence in a second, and waded into the grass. It was nearly up to their shoulders, and they looked very pretty moving about in it, picking the flowers. As Mrs. March was watching them, she suddenly saw a brown bird with yellow breast fly out of the grass, and perch on one of the fence-posts.

"Oh, don't stir, children! don't stir!" she cried: "see that bird!"

Rob and Nelly stood perfectly still. And what do you think that bird did?—opened his mouth and sung the most exquisite song you ever heard. The canary bird's song is not half so sweet. The bird was not ten steps away from the carriage or from the children: there he sat, looking first at one and then at the other like a tame bird. In a few seconds he sang again: then he spread his wings and flew a little way into the field, and alighted on a tall, slender, grass stalk, and there he sat, swinging to and fro on the grass, and sang again; then he flew away. Nobody drew a long breath till he had gone.

"That's a lark," said Billy; "this country's full on 'em; they're the tamest birds for a wild bird I ever see. They'll sing to ye right under your feet."

"Well, he's a glorious chorister," said Mr. March.

"If he's a chorister, I'd like to go where he keeps his choir," said Rob. "I mean to catch one, and have him to sing in my museum."

"Oh, no, Rob," said Nelly; "don't!"

"They won't never sing in cages," said Billy. "I've seen it tried many a time. They jest walk, walk, walk up and down, up and down in the cage the hull time, and beat their wings. They can't stand bein' shut up, for all they're so tame actin' while they're free."

The children climbed back into the wagon now, with their hands full of flowers; and Billy whipped up the horses.

"Git up, Pumpkinseed! git up, Fox!" he said: "there's a crib o' corn ahead for you."

Very soon the new home came in sight. It looked, when they first saw it, as if it were half buried in green grass; but, as they came nearer, they saw that the enclosure in which the house and barns stood was entirely bare of grass. This gave it a naked and barren look which was not pleasing, and disappointed Mrs. March very much. However, she said nothing; only thought to herself, "I'll have green grass up to that very door-step, before another year's out."

The house was very much like the one they had lived in, in the Ute Pass, except that it was larger; there were three log-cabin barns, two of which were very large;

and a queer-shaped log-house, bigger at the top than at the bottom, standing up quite a distance from the ground, on posts. This was for wheat. Then there were two dog-houses, and a great place built round with palings, to keep hens in; and one or two large open sheds where wagons and carts stood. Billy looked round on all these buildings with great pride.

"I declare," said he, "there ain't such a ranch 's this in all the valley. What a dumb fool that Wilson was to go 'n' leave it. He 's put all he 's worth, except this farm, into a mine up in Central; 'n' now he 'll go 'n' put the money for this in too, and 's like 's not he 'll never see a dollar on 't again 's long 's he lives. This minin' jest crazes folks."

"Did ye ever see a puttier farm 'n this, mum?" he asked, turning to Mrs. March.

Mrs. March could not say that she had not. To her eye, accustomed to Massachusetts green yards, shaded by elms and maples, this little group of rough houses and sheds, standing in an enclosure with hardly a green thing, only a few tufts of coarse grass, and weeds growing around it, was very unsightly. But she did not want to say this; so she said: —

"It is much the nicest place I have seen in Colorado, Billy; and this valley is perfectly beautiful. But where is the creek?"

"Right there, mum, just a few rods beyond that fence to the west, — where you see that line of bushes."

"I don't see any water," said Nelly.

"No, you can't till yer come right on it," said Billy; "'tain't very wide here, 'n' it jest slips along in the bushes 's if it was tryin' to hide itself."

"Papa," whispered Nelly, "doesn't Billy say queer things about things, just as if every thing was alive, and had feelings as we do? I like it."

Mr. March smiled, and took Nelly's hand in his.

"Girlie," he said, "Billy's a little of a poet, in his rough way."

"He doesn't make verses: does he?" asked Nelly, reverentially. To make verses had always been the height of Nelly's ambition, as many a little roll of scribbled paper in her desk would show. But there was one great trouble with Nelly's verses thus far: she never could find any words that rhymed; and now to hear Billy called a poet seemed very strange to her.

"I never should have thought he could make verses," she continued.

"Oh! making verses is the smallest part of being a poet, Nelly," said Mr. March. "You can't understand that yet; but you will some day."

Then they all went into the house, and looked at room after room, thinking what they would do with each. The rooms were sunny and bright, but were so dirty that Mrs. March groaned.

"Oh, how shall we ever get this place clean!"

"I'll tell you," said Billy. "If ye don't mind the expense o' stayin' at the hotel a week, an' if ye'll buy me a little paint, I'll have this hull place so ye won't know it, in a week's time. There's nothin' I can't turn my hand to; an' I'd like to fix things up here for you, first rate. I saw up 't the other place about how you like things."

Billy had a quick eye for every thing that was pretty. He had never seen any house in Colorado which was so cosey and pretty as the Marches' house in the Ute Pass ; and he **was thinking now in his heart how** he would like to make this new one as pretty as that.

"Mebbe you couldn't trust **me,**" he said, seeing that Mrs. March hesitated.

"Oh, yes, I could, Billy," she replied; "I have no doubt you could put it all in beautiful order. I was thinking whether we ought **to stay**" — she was going to say, "**stay a whole week at** the hotel" — but, just at that minute, there came piercing shrieks in Rob's voice :

"**Papa! papa! Billy! come! come!**"　　.

The shrieks came from the direction of the creek.

"**Oh, my God!** he's fallen into the creek!" cried **Mrs. March, as she** tried **to run** towards the spot. Long **Billy** dashed **past her, with his** great strides, and said, as he passed : —

"Don't be skeered, mum ; **in** the mud, most likely."

The cries came feebler and feebler, and stopped altogether, — then a loud **burst** of laughter from Billy, which brought **the life** back to Mrs. March. She was clinging to the fence, nearly senseless with terror ; Nelly stood close by, her face white, and tears rolling down her cheeks : when they heard Billy's laugh, **they** looked at each other in amazement and relief.

"He can't be in the creek, mamma," said Nelly : "Billy wouldn't laugh."

Then they heard Mr. March laugh, and say : —

"Hold on, Rob: don't be frightened ; we'll get a rail."

Then Billy came striding back out of the bushes, still laughing. **When he saw Mrs.** March's and Nelly's agonized **faces, his** own sobered instantly.

"'Twas too bad, mum," he exclaimed, "to give ye such a skeer. He's in the slough, thet's all; he's putty well in, too; he'll be a sight to see when we get him fished out. He's in putty well nigh up to his arms."

Mrs. March could not help laughing; but Nelly only cried the more.

"Poor dear Rob!" she said: "how he will feel!" And she began to climb the fence.

"Oh, Lor'! don't any more on ye come over here," cried Billy: "it's all we can do to get round. The creek's overflowed: 'n' it's all quakin' tussocks here; that's the way he went in, a jumpin' from one to another."

While Billy was speaking he was tearing off two of the top rails from the fence. He seemed to be as strong as a giant. In a very few minutes, he had two rails over his shoulder, and had plunged back among the bushes. In a few minutes more, out they all came; Rob being led between Mr. March and Billy. He was indeed, as Billy had said he would be, "a sight to behold." Up to his very arms he was plastered with black, slimy mud.

"Oh, mamma, it smells horrid," was his first remark. "I wouldn't mind if it didn't smell so."

Nelly ran up as close to him as she dared.

"Oh, Rob," she said, "how could you go in such a place! Why didn't you stay with us?"

"I wanted to see if there were any grapes yet," said Rob; "and you couldn't have told yourself, Nell, that it wouldn't bear. Ugh! What'll I do, mamma?"

"I'm sure I don't know, Rob," said Mrs. March:

she was at her wit's end. She looked helplessly at
Billy: Billy was rubbing his left cheek with his right
forefinger, — his invariable gesture when he was perplexed. Mr. March also stood looking at Rob with a
despairing face.

"I wish you wouldn't all look so at me," cried Rob,
half crying: "it's horrid to be stared at. What'll I
do, mamma?"

It was indeed a dilemma. Rob's trousers and jacket
were dripping wet, and coated thick with the muddy
slime; his shoes were full of it; as he walked about it
made a gurgling noise, and spurted up; his face was
spattered with it; his hands were black; even his hair
had not escaped.

"There's lots o' hay in the barn," said Billy; "we
might rub a good deal off on him with that. Me 'n'
you'd better take him," said Billy, nodding to Mr.
March. "No, mum, ye stay where ye be; we'll manage better without ye, this time," continued Billy,
waving Mrs. March back, as she set out to follow them.

Poor Rob looked back, as Billy led him off towards
the barn; the tears ran down in the mud on his cheeks,
and made little white tracks all the way.

"I think you're real mean to laugh, mamma," he
said.

Mrs. March was sorry to hurt his feelings, but she
could not help laughing. Nelly did not laugh, however:
she looked almost as wretched as Rob did. It seemed
an age before any one came back from the barn. Then
Mr. March and Billy came out alone: Mr. March carried Rob's trousers on a stick, and Billy carried the
jacket and the stockings and shoes.

"Why, what have you done with the child!" exclaimed Mrs. March: "he will take cold, without any clothes on."

Mr. March's eyes twinkled.

"Well, he has some clothes on, such as they are," he said. "Billy raised a contribution for him: my under-drawers and vest, and Billy's coat; he 's all rolled up in the hay, and you 'd better go and sit by him now."

Mrs. March and Nelly hurried in. There lay Rob, all buried up in hay: only his face to be seen. He looked very jolly now, and said he felt perfectly comfortable.

"Now tell me a story, mamma! tell me a story. You 've got to tell me stories as long as I stay here."

So Mrs. March sat down on one side, and Nelly on the other, and Mrs. March told them the story of the Master Thief, out of the Brothers Grimm's "Fairy Stories of All Lands;" and, just as she got to where the Master Thief was planning to steal the bottom sheet from off the king's bed, she looked up and saw that Rob was fast asleep.

"Oh, that 's good," she said; "that 's the best thing that could have happened to him. Now we 'll go out and look at the house again."

"But, mamma," said Nelly, "I think I 'll stay here. If he should wake up, he would feel so lonely here; and he can't get out of the hay."

"Thank you, dear: that is very kind of you," replied Mrs. March. And, as she went out of the barn, she said to herself, "What a kind, thoughtful child Nelly is. She really is like a little woman."

Mrs. March could not find her husband and Billy anywhere; so she sat down on the door-step of the house to wait for them. She looked up and down the beautiful valley: it seemed a great deal more than thirty miles long. The mountains at the south end of it looked blue and hazy; the great Sangre di Cristo Mountains, which made the western wall, looked very near; the snow on them shone so brightly it dazzled Mrs. March's eyes to look at it. After a time, she got up from the door-step and walked round to the north side of the house.

"Oh, there is Nelly's mountain!" she said. There stood Pike's Peak, in full sight, to the north-east. It looked so grand and so high at first, Mrs. March did not know it. This, too, had a great deal of snow on it, and there were white clouds floating round the top; it was the grandest sight in the whole view. There were no other houses near; she could see only a few in the valley; and she could not see Rosita at all. The road down which they had come seemed to end very soon among the hills.

"We shall not have much more to do with neighbors here than in the pass," thought Mrs. March. "But I do not care for that. One could never be lonely with these mountains to look at."

"Well, mum, here's the little feller's clo'es," said Billy, coming up at this moment, with Rob's clothes hanging in a limp wet bundle over his arm. "Now I'll jest make a rousin' fire back here, 'n' you'll be astonished to see how quick they'll dry. I've washed 'em in about five hundred waters, — that medder mud's the meanest stuff to stick ye ever see, — but they'll be dry in no time now."

"Mamma!" called Nelly, from the barn; "Rob's awake. He wants to get up: he says he won't lie here another minute."

"I'll show him his clo'es," said Billy. "I guess that'll convince him," and Billy carried the wet bundle into the barn. Shouts of laughter followed, and in a minute more Billy came out again, shaking all over with laughter. "I jest offered 'em to him," said he, "'n' told him he could get up 'n' put 'em on ef he wanted to; but I rayther thought he'd better let 'em dry some fust."

"What did he say?" asked Mrs. March.

"He wanted to know how long it would take 'em to dry, 'n' I told him the best part of an hour; 'twill be some longer 'n that, but I couldn't pretend to be exact to a minnit, 'n' he laid back on the hay 'n' sez he: 'You tell my mamma to come right here 'n' finish that story she was a tellin'.'"

When Mrs. March went back into the barn, she shouted aloud as soon as she saw Rob. He had crawled out of his hay bed. It was too warm: there he sat bolt upright, with his legs straight out in front of him. Nelly had drawn the white drawer legs out to their full length, and set Rob's shoes, toes up, in the hay at the end of them, so it looked as if his legs were all that length; then Mr. March's gray waistcoat came down nearly to his knees, and Billy's old brown coat hung on his shoulders as loosely as a blanket. He looked up at his mother with a perfectly grave face, and did not speak. Nelly was laughing hard. "Isn't he too funny, mamma?" said she.

"You can laugh now if you want to, mamma," said

Rob, politely. "I don't mind your laughing at papa's drawers and waistcoat and Billy's old coat. That's quite different from laughing at me."

"Thank you, dear," said Mrs. March: "you're very kind; but I can get along very comfortably without laughing at you now. You're not half so funny as you were when you were covered with the mud."

It took so long to dry Rob's clothes, that it was nearly dark when they got back to Rosita.

"Well, I reckoned you liked your house so well you weren't coming back to us at all," said the landlord, as they drove up.

"Oh, no, sir," cried Rob, "that wasn't it. I fell into the mud by the creek: I always fall into the water each new place we go to. I did it the first thing up in the Pass."

The landlord looked closely at him. "What! you been into the creek in them clothes?"

"Billy washed them," said Nelly; "they were all black as mud."

"Oh!" said the landlord. "Well, there ain't any thing under Heaven that Long Billy can't do: that's certain."

Mr. and Mrs. March thought so too, when one week later they drove down to take possession of their home. Billy had pleaded so earnestly to be allowed to do all the work himself that Mr. March had consented; and had even promised him that they would not come near the house until he invited them. Then Billy set to work in good earnest, and Miss Lucinda Harkiss set to work with him. This was the young woman to whom Billy was engaged. She was coming to be Mrs. March's servant. A very good time Lucinda and Billy had all that week. It was almost like going to housekeeping together for themselves. The first day, Lucinda swept and scrubbed the floors, and washed the windows till they shone; then Billy stained all the floors dark brown, and painted the window-sashes and the door-frames brown; and this brown color was so pretty with the yellow of the pine, that it made the rough boarded rooms look almost handsome. While the paint was drying, Lucinda and Billy drove over to Pine's ranch at the foot of one of the Sangre di Christo mountains. They knew old **Mr. Pine** very well; and he was very glad to have them make him a visit. All one day Billy worked hard digging up young pine-trees, and Lucinda gathered a great quantity of the kinnikinnick vines. Billy had told her how Mrs. March had had them nailed up on the walls in the other house. The next day they drove home early in the morning, and in the afternoon Billy set out a row of the little pine-trees all round the house. "Even if they don't grow, they'll look green for a spell," he said to Lucinda; "an' ye never see a woman hanker arter green stuff 's Miss March does. There wan't a livin' thing growin' in that Ute Pass, but what she had it in a pitcher or a tumbler or a tin can, a settin' round in her house. And as for that Nelly, she'd bring in her arms full o' flowers every day o' her life. You'll like 'em all, Lucinda, see if you don't. They ain't like most o' the folks out here."

Lucinda had a good many fears about coming to live with Mrs. March. She had never been a servant; but she wanted to be married to Billy as much as he wanted to be married to her, and she thought if she could earn good wages and lay all the money up, they could be married sooner.

"I shall like them well enough, I dare say," said Lucinda; "but I don't know how I'll stand being ordered round."

"Ordered round!" said Billy, in a scornful tone. "I tell you they ain't the orderin' round kind; they 're the reel genuwine fust-class folks; an' genuwine fust-class folks don't never order nobody to do nothing: I tell you I shouldn't stand no orderin' any more 'n you would. Mr. March he always sez to me, 'We 'd better do so and so,' if there 's any thing he wants done; 'n' he works 's hard as I do, any day, 'n' Miss March she 's jest like him. You 'll see how 'twill be. I ain't a mite afeared."

After the paint was dry, they nailed up the vines; and Billy added to them some pine boughs with great clusters of green cones on them which were beautiful. Then they unpacked the boxes of furniture; and Billy showed Lucinda how to put up the chintz curtains in the sitting-room, and the white ones in the bedrooms, and, when it was all done, it looked so pretty that Billy could not help saying : —

"Don't you wish it was our house, Luce?" He always called her Luce for short. "Can't take time for no three-storied names 'n this country," said Billy; "two 's too many."

Lucinda blushed a little, and said : —

"We can make ours just as pretty some day, Billy."

"That 's so, Luce," said Billy: "you 'll get lots o' idees out o' Miss March. She 's what I call a reel home-y woman. I hain't never seen nobody I 've took to so since I left hum."

When every thing was ready, the house and the barns and sheds all in order, and the whole enclosure raked over and made as tidy as possible, Billy said : —

" Now, we 'll jest keep 'em waitin' one more day. You make up a lot o' your best bread, and churn some butter ; 'n' I 'll go over to Pine's and pick two or three gallons o' raspberries. They 're just ripe to pick now, 'n' this is the last chance I 'll get. Then you 'n' Miss March can preserve 'em. I know she wants some. I heared her say so when we was a comin' up Hardscrabble Canyon."

Something besides raspberries Billy brought back from Pine's ranch that night, — something that he never dreamed of getting, something which pleased him so greatly he fairly snapped his fingers with delight, — it was a little pet fawn. " Old-man Pine " had had it for several months ; it had strayed down out of the woods, when it was too young to find its way back ; he had found it early one morning lapping milk out of the milk-pan he kept outside his cabin-door for his dog Spotty. He had caught it without difficulty, and tamed it, so that it followed him about like a puppy. Sometimes it would disappear for a few days, but always came back again. It was a lovely little creature, almost white under its belly, and on the under side of its legs ; but all the rest of a beautiful bright red. When Billy told old Mr. Pine about the March family, and about the twin brother and sister, who were such nice children, the old man said : —

" Don't you think they 'd like to have the fawn? It 's a pesky little thing, for all it 's so pretty, an' I 'm tired on 't. There was a man offered me seven dollars for it, a while ago, but I thought I didn't want to let it go; but ye may have it for them children if ye want it. Ye can tell 'em I sent it to 'em; an' I 'm the oldest settler in this valley, tell 'em. Yer must bring 'em over to see me some time."

Billy promised to do so.

"They 'll go clean out o' their heads when they see the critter," he added. "They 've been a talkin' about deer ever since they come: deer an' silver are the two things they 're full of. They 've pretty near walked their little feet off by this time, I expect, lookin' fur a mine. They took the idee 's soon 's they see the wagon-load o' ore I was a haulin' through the Ute Pass: that 's when I fust knew 'em; an' I declare to you, the young-sters hain't never let go on 't, 'n' I donno 's they ever will."

"Mebbe, then, they 'll find a mine yet," said old Pine. "There 's one o' the best mines in all Californy was found by a little feller not more 'n ten years old. He jest hauled up a bush with solid gold a stickin' in the roots."

"You don't say so!" said Billy. "Well, there ain't no such free gold 's that in this country; but I wouldn't like any thing much better, next to findin' a mine myself, than to have Mr. March's folks find one. They 're the sort o' folks ought to have money."

Billy worked very late that night fencing a little bit of the green meadow nearest the house, to keep the fawn in. The little creature seemed shy and fright-ened; and, when Billy drove away in the morning to bring the family down, he charged Lucinda to go out often and speak to it and feed it with sugar.

"I'd like to have it get over its scare before Nelly sees it," he said; "for, if it don't seem to be happy, she's just the gal to go on the sly and let the critter out, so it could go where it wants to."

Billy was much disappointed, when he reached the hotel, to learn that Mr. and Mrs. March and the children were out. They had gone to one of the mines, and would not be back till dinner-time; for they were going down into the mine.

"I never see any thing in all my life like that little chap," said the landlord. "He don't rest a minute. I believe he 'n' his sister have walked over every foot o' ground within five miles o' this house; 'n' there ain't a workin' mine in all these gulches that he don't know by name; 'n' he'll tell you who's the foreman 'n' how many workmen are on; 'n' he's got about a wheelbarrow full o' specimens o' one sort 'n' another, for his museum, 's he calls it. The little girl she seems a kind o' nurse to him, she's so steady; but they say they're twins: you wouldn't ever think it."

"No, that you wouldn't," replied Billy; "but they are. I like the gal best myself. She don't say much; but there ain't nothin' escapes her, 'n' she's just the sweetest-tempered little thing that was ever born. She's too good: that's the worst on 't. I don't like to see youngsters always doin' right; 't don't look healthy."

Poor Lucinda's nice dinner was almost spoiled, — it had to wait so long before the family came. Billy had not once thought of the possibility of his not finding them at home, and had called out to Lucinda, as he drove off: —

"Now, mind, Luce, you have all ready at one, sharp. We'll be here before that time."

So, when Billy drove into the yard, at half-past two o'clock, he felt quite crest-fallen, and half afraid to see Lucinda's face in the doorway. But she smiled pleasantly, and only said : —

"How punctual you are, to be sure! Dinner won't be very good."

"Never mind, Lucinda," said Mrs. March. "We were not at home. It wasn't Billy's fault. He has been worrying about you for an hour. It will taste very good to us all, for we are hungry."

Mrs. March praised every thing in the house, till Billy's face and Lucinda's grew red with pleasure ; and Mr. March also praised every thing out of doors.

"Didn't I tell you, Luce," said Billy, at the first chance he found to whisper in her ear, " didn't I tell you they was nice folks to work for? They don't let you slave yourself to death for 'em like some folks, 'n' never say so much 's a thank you."

The delight of Rob and Nelly in the fawn was greater than could be told in words. They ran round and round the enclosure, to see it upon all sides ; they fed it, till it would not eat another mouthful; they stood still, gazing at it with almost unbelief in their faces.

"Oh, is it really our own? Will it always stay?" they cried. "It is too good to be true."

I don't believe there was in all Colorado a happier family than went to sleep under Mr. March's roof that night. Everybody was entirely satisfied with the home and with everybody in it. Even Watch and Trotter sat in the low-arched doors of their new houses, and held their heads up, and looked around them with an air of contentment and pride. They had never had houses of their own before. They had slept on the great pile of saw-dust by the old mill; but they walked straight into these little houses and took possession of them as naturally as possible. They almost made you think of people who, when they come into possession of things much finer than they have been accustomed to, try very hard to act as if they had had them all their lives.

CHAPTER IX.

WET MOUNTAIN VALLEY.

AND now my story must skip over three whole years. There is so much to tell you about Nelly, and her life in the Wet Mountain Valley, that, if I do not skip a good deal, the story will be much too long. The first year was a very happy and prosperous one. There were big crops of wheat and of hay, and they were sold for good prices, so that Mr. March had more money than he needed to live on, and he was so pleased that he spent it all for new things, — some new books, some new furniture, and a nice new carriage much more comfortable for Mrs. March to drive in than the white-topped wagon. Mrs. March felt very sorry to have this money spent; she wanted it put away to keep; but, as I told you before, Mr. March always wanted to buy every thing he liked, and he thought that there would always be money enough.

"Why, Sarah!" he said; "here's the land! It can't run away! and we can always sell the hay and the wheat; and the cattle go on increasing every year. We shall have more and more money every year. By and by, when we get things comfortable around us, we can lay up money; but I really think we ought to make ourselves comfortable."

So Mr. March bought every thing that Billy said he

would like to have to work on the farm with, and he
sent to Denver for books and for clothes for Rob and
Nelly, and almost every month he added some new and
pretty thing to the house. Thus it went on until at the
end of the year, all the money which had been made
off the farm was gone, and all their own little income
had been spent too. Not a penny had been laid up in
the house except by Billy and Lucinda. They had laid
up two hundred and fifty dollars apiece. They had
each had three hundred and had spent only fifty.

"Luce," said Billy, "one more such year 's this, an'
we can take that little house down to Cobbs's, and farm
it for ourselves."

"Yes," said Lucinda, hesitatingly, "but I 'd a most
rather stay 's we are. I don't ever want to leave Mrs.
March 'n' the children; and you 'n' I couldn't be together any more 'n we are now."

"Why, Luce!" said Billy; and he walked out of
the kitchen without another word. He was grieved.
Lucinda ran after him.

"Billy!" she said.

"What?" said Billy, chopping away furiously at a
big pine log.

"I didn't mean that I wouldn't go if you thought
best; only that I hated to leave the folks. Of course,
I expect we 'll go when the time comes. You needn't
get mad."

"Oh, I ain't mad," said poor Billy; "but it sounded
kind o' disappintin', I tell yer. I like the folks 's well
's you do; but a man wants to have his own place, and
his children a growin' up round him; but I shan't ask
you to go till you 're ready: you may rest 'sured o'

that." And with this half way making up), Lucinda had to be satisfied.

Before the second summer was over, Mr. March was quite ready to acknowledge that it would have been wiser to follow his wife's advice, and lay up all the money which they did not absolutely need to spend. Just as the crops were well up, and bidding fair to be as large as before, there came all of a sudden, in a night, a great army of grasshoppers and ate every thing up. You little children at the East who have seen grasshoppers only a few at a time, as you walk through the fields in the summer, cannot have the least idea of how terrible a thing an army of grasshoppers can be. It comes through the air like a great cloud : in less than a minute, the ground, the fences, the trees, the bushes, the grass, the doorsteps, the outsides of the windows, are all covered thick with them ; millions and millions of millions, all eating, eating as fast as they can eat. If you drive over a road where they are, they rise up in great masses, their wings making a whistling noise, and horses are afraid to go along. Think of that : a great creature like a horse afraid of such little creatures as grasshoppers ! Nobody would believe without seeing it, how a garden or a field looks after one of these grasshopper armies has passed over it. It looks as bare and brown as if it had been burned with fire. There is not left the smallest bit of green leaf in it. This is the way all Mr. March's fields looked in one week after the grasshoppers came into the valley. All the other farmers' fields were in the same condition. It was enough to make your heart ache to look at them. After there was nothing more left to eat, then the great army spread its wings and moved on to the South.

Mr. March looked around him in despair. It had all happened so suddenly he was confused and perplexed. It was almost like having your house burn down over your head. In one week he had lost a whole year's income. It was too late for the things to grow again before the autumn frosts which come very early in the valley.

This was real trouble. However, Mr. and Mrs. March kept up good courage, and hoped it would never happen again. They sold their pretty new carriage and all the other things that they could spare, to get money to buy food for themselves and for the cattle; and they told Billy and Lucinda that they could not afford to keep them any longer.

" We must do all our own work this winter, Billy," said Mr. March; " if you don't get any thing better to do, I 'll be glad of you next summer; but this winter we have got to be as saving as possible. Rob will help me, and Nelly 'll help her mother: we must put our shoulders to the wheel like the rest."

Billy was not surprised to hear this. On the morning the grasshoppers appeared, he had said to Lucinda : —

" Luce, do you see those pesky varmints? They 'll jest clean out this valley in about ten days, 'n' you 'n' me may 's well pack our trunks. There won't be victuals for any extra mouths here this year, I tell you ; I should-n't wonder if it jest about broke Mr. March up. He hain't got any ready money to fall back on. He paid down about all he had for this place, 'n' he 's spent a sight this last year. Blamed if I don't wish I hadn't asked him for a thing. He 's the generousest man ever was. It 's a shame he should have such luck. I don't count on next summer nuther, for the ground 'll be chuck full of the nasty beasts' eggs: ten to one they 'll be worse next year than they are this: there 's no knowin'. We might 's well get married, Luce, an' if there 's any thing doin' in the valley at all, I can allers get it to do."

So, early in the autumn Billy and Lucinda were married, and went to live in " Cobbs's Cabin," a little log cabin about two miles from Mr. March's place, on the road to Rosita. The winter was a long and a hard one: hay was scarce and dear; and all sorts of provisions were sold at higher prices than ever before. The March family, however, were well and in good spirits. Nelly and Rob enjoyed working with their father and mother, — Rob in the barn and out in the fields, and Nelly in the house. They still studied an hour every day, and recited to their father in the evening. Rob studied Latin, and Nelly studied arithmetic; and their mother read to them every night a few pages of history, or some good book of travels. Rob did not love to study, and did only what he must; but Nelly grew more and more fond of books every day. She did not care for her dolls any longer. Even the great wax doll which Mrs. Williams had given her was now very seldom taken out of the box. All Nelly wanted to make her happy was a book: it seemed sometimes as if it did not make much difference to her what sort of a book. She read every thing she could find in the house; even volumes of sermons she did not despise; and it was an odd thing to see a little girl twelve years old reading a big, old leather bound volume of sermons. Rob used to laugh at her and say: —

"Oh, pshaw, Nell! what makes you read that? Read Mayne Reid's stories: they 're worth while. What do you want to read sermons for, I 'd like to know?" And Nelly would laugh too, and say : —

"Well, Rob, they aren't so nice as stories ; but I do like to read them. It 's like hearing papa preach."

To which Rob would reply, in a cautious whisper : —

"Well, I 'm glad we don't have to hear papa preach any more. I hate sermons. I 'm never going to church again 's long 's I live ; and, when I 'm a man, I shan't make my boys go to church if they don't want to."

The third summer began just as the one before it had begun, with a great promise of fine crops ; but they were no sooner fairly under way, than the grasshoppers came again, and ate them all up. This was very discouraging. Mr. March did not know what to do. He sold a good many of his cows ; and, before the summer was over, he sold some of his books ; but that money did not last long, and they were really very poor. Now came the time when Nelly's little head began to be full of plans for earning money. She asked her mother, one day, to let her go up into Rosita and sell some eggs.

Mrs. March looked at her in surprise.

"Why, Nell," she said, "you couldn't walk so far."

"Oh, yes, I could," said Nelly. "Rob and I often walk up to the top of the hill: it 's only a little way from Billy's house, and we often go there ; and I know I could sell all our eggs, — and some butter too, if we could make enough to spare. I 'd like to, too. I think it would be good fun."

"I 'll ask your father," replied Mrs. March. "I don't think he 'd be willing : but if we could get a little money that way, it would be very nice. We don't need half the eggs."

When Mrs. March told her husband of Nelly's proposition, his cheeks flushed.

"What a child Nelly is!" he exclaimed. "I can't bear to have her go round among those rough miners. I've often thought myself of carrying things up there to sell; but I thought my time was worth more on the farm than any thing I could make selling eggs. Oh, Sarah!" he exclaimed, "I never thought we should come to such a pass as this."

"Now, Robert, don't be foolish," said Mrs. March, gayly. "There isn't the least disgrace in selling butter and eggs. I'd as soon earn a living in that way as in any other. But I wouldn't like to have Nelly run any risk of being rudely treated."

"I don't believe she would be," said Mr. March: "her face is enough to make the roughest sort of a man good to her. You know how Billy worshipped her; and he's a pretty rough fellow on the surface. I think we might let her try it once, and see what happens."

And so it came to pass, that, early in the third summer of their stay in Wet Mountain Valley, Nelly set off one morning at six o'clock with a basket on her arm, holding three dozen of eggs and two pounds of butter, which she was to carry up into Rosita to sell. Rob pleaded hard to go too, but his father would not consent.

"Nelly will do better by herself," he said. "You will be sure to get into some scrape if you go."

"I don't care," said Rob, as he bade Nelly good-by: "you just wait till trout time: see if I don't make him let me go then. I can make more money selling trout than you can off eggs, any day. A gentleman told me one day when he drove by where I was fishing, one day last summer, that he 'd give me forty cents a pound for all I had in my basket; and I told him I wasn't fishing to sell: I was real mad. I didn't know then we were going to sell things; but, if we are, I may as well sell trout; the creek's full of them."

"Well, we are going to sell things, I tell you," said Nelly: "I don't know what else there is for us to do. We haven't got any money; I think papa's real worried, and mamma too; and you and I 've just got to help. It 's too bad! I don't see what God made grasshoppers for."

"To catch trout with," said Rob, solemnly: "there isn't any thing else half so good."

Nelly laughed, and set off at a brisk pace on the road to Rosita. Her father stood in the barn door watching her. As her little figure disappeared, he said aloud: —

"God bless her! she 's the sweetest child a man ever had!"

It was almost five miles from Mr. March's house to Rosita. For the first half of the way, the road lay in the open valley, and had no shade; but, as soon as it began to wind in among the low hills, it had pine-trees on each side of it; the little house where Billy and Lucinda lived stood in a nook among these pines. Nelly reached this house about seven o'clock, just as Billy and Lucinda were finishing their breakfast. She walked in without knocking, as she always did.

"Bless my soul alive!" exclaimed Billy. "Why,

what on airth brings you here, to this time o' day, Nelly?"

Nelly had placed her basket on the floor, and sat down in a rocking chair, and was fanning herself with her sun-bonnet. Her face was very red from the hot sun, but her eyes were full of fun.

"Going up to Rosita, Billy," she said. "Guess what I've got in the basket."

"A kitten," said Lucinda: "your mother promised me one."

"Oh, dear, no!" said Nelly; "a weasel ate them up last Saturday night: all but one; and that one the old cat must keep. Guess again."

Billy did not speak. He guessed the truth.

"Your luncheon," said Lucinda.

"Yes," said Nelly, "my luncheon's in there, on the top; but underneath I've got eggs and I've got butter. I'm going to sell them in Rosita, and mamma said I was to stop and ask you what price I ought to tell the people. She didn't know."

Billy walked hastily out of the room and slammed the door behind him. This was what Long Billy always did when he felt badly about any thing. His first idea was to get out in the open air. Lucinda looked after him in astonishment. She did not think of any reason why he should feel sorry about Nelly's selling the butter and eggs, but she saw something was wrong with him.

"Why, you don't say so, Nelly!" she replied. "Well, I dare say you'll make a nice little penny. Eggs is thirty cents, and butter thirty-five to forty: your mother's ought to be forty. What're you goin' to do with the money?"

"Why, it isn't for myself!" said Nelly, in a tone of great astonishment: "it's for papa and mamma. I don't want any for myself. But you know we don't have hardly any money now; and I asked mamma to let me see if I couldn't get some in Rosita. Rob's going to sell trout too, by and by: as soon as they're plenty."

Billy came back into the room now; and, looking away from Nelly, he said: —

"See here, child: you let me carry them things up to town for ye. Ye stay here with Luce. I've got to go up anyway to-day or to-morrow. It's too fur for ye to walk."

"Oh, no, Billy, thank you!" said Nelly. "It isn't too far. I've often and often walked up to the hill where you look right into the streets. And I want to go; I wouldn't miss it for any thing."

"Well, I'm goin' along with yer, anyhow," said Billy. "Luce, you get me that flour-sack." And, as Lucinda went into the closet to get it, he followed her in and shut the door.

"Ain't that a shame, Luce," he said, "to have that little thing go round sellin' eggs? I expect they're awful hard up, or they wouldn't ever have done it. I tell you it jest cuts me. Mr. March don't know them miners's well's I do. I shall tell him it ain't no place for gals."

"You're jest off all wrong now, Billy," replied Lucinda. "It's you that don't know miners. There wouldn't a man in Rosita say a rough word before Nelly no sooner 'n you would. They'll jest all take to her: you see if they don't. And it's a real sensible thing for the children to do. I 've been thinking o' doing the same thing myself. There 's lots o' money to be made off eggs."

Billy was unconvinced ; but he was too wise to say so.

"Well, well," he said, "we shall see. I 'll go up with her to-day, and tell her which houses are the best houses to go to. If she 's going to do it regular, she 'd better have regular houses, and not be a gaddin' all about town, knockin' at doors. Oh, I tell you, Luce, it just cuts me ! I can't stand it."

"Well, I don't see nothin' so very dreadful in it," replied Lucinda. "The gal 's got the sense of a woman : she 'll look out for herself as well as if she was twenty ; and there 's lots o' money to be made off eggs ; I tell you that."

Nelly trudged along by Billy's side as cheery as a lark. She showed him a little brown-silk bag she had to bring home the money in ; it was in a pocket in her petticoat, and she had to lift up her gown to get at it.

"Mamma put that in yesterday," she said : "I asked her to. I saw a lady in the cars once, Mrs. Williams : such a beautiful lady, — she gave me that big wax doll. She carried all her money in a pocket in her petticoat, under her gown ; because, she said, nobody could get at that to steal it."

Billy laughed immoderately. The idea of a little girl's pocket being picked on the road from Rosita down into Wet Mountain Valley was very droll.

"Well, Nelly," he said, "you 've got a long head o' your own ; but I reckon you took a little more pains than you needed to, that time. Nobody's goin' to think o' such a thing as pickin' your pocket here."

“Mamma thought it was a very good plan,” said Nelly, with an air of dignity; “and I think so too. Men can’t tell about women’s pockets: pockets in trousers are much harder to get at.” At which Billy only laughed the harder; and at night, when he went home and told Lucinda, he had another fit of laughter over it.

“To think o’ that little mite standin’ out to me that I couldn’t jedge about women’s pockets, pockets in trousers was so different! Oh, Lord!” said Billy, stretching his long legs out on the wooden settee: “I thought I should ha’ died. You was right though, Luce, about the men. I’ll own up. That child can go from eend to eend o’ thet town’s safe’s if she was one o’ the Lord’s angels in white, — if that’s what they wear, — an’ wings on her shoulders: only I never did believe much in the wings. But you oughter’ve seen how the men looked at her. You know she’s got a different look about her somehow from most gals: she ain’t pretty, but you can’t take your eyes off her; an’ she’s so pretty spoken: that does it, more ’n her looks. When we come by the stamp-mill, at noon, the men was all pourin’ out; and afore I knew it we was right in the midst on ’em: a runnin’ an’ cuffin’ and tumblin’ each other, and not choosin’ their words much. Nelly she took right hold o’ my hand, but she never said nothin’.

“ ‘Hullo, sis,’ sez Jake Billings; and he pushed her little sun-bonnet back off her head. I declare I’d a notion to knock him over; but Nelly she looked up at him an’ jest laughed a little, and sez she: —

“ ‘Oh, please, sir, don’t: you’ll make me drop my

eggs.'   And he looked as ashamed as I ever see a man. And he put her bonnet right back on her head agin, and sez he : —

"'Let me carry 'em : won't ye, sis?'

"Ye see she wouldn't let me so much's touch the basket all the way, though I kept askin'. She said she was goin' to carry it always, an' she might as well begin : an' it wan't heavy ; but I know 'twas, for all her sayin' 'twan't, heavy, that is, for her little pipes o' arms.

"'No, thank you,' said she to Jake : 'Billy wanted to carry them for me ; but I wouldn't let him. I like to carry them all the way myself, to see if I can. I'm going to come every week, perhaps twice a week.'

"'Be ye?' said Jake. 'Whose little gal are ye, and where do ye live?'

"Then I told him all about her folks ; and all the rest o' the men they walked along with us 's quiet and steady you wouldn't ha' known 'em ; and Jake he took her right into that Swede's house, you know : Jan, the one that boards some o' the hands."

"Oh, yes!" said Lucinda ; "and Ulrica, his wife 's the nicest woman among the whole set."

"Well," continued Billy, "Jake he took her right in there. 'Jan 'll buy all your eggs,' sez he : 'he 's allers wantin' eggs.' I followed on : Nelly she was goin' with Jake, jest as if she 'd ha' known him all her life ; but she looked back, an' sez, in that little voice o' hern, jest like the sweetest fiddle I ever heard : —

"'Come along, Billy,' sez she, 'and see if I can't sell eggs.'

"An' as soon as she got inter the house, she walked right up to Ulrica, and held out her basket, and sez : —

" ' Would you like to buy some eggs to-day, ma'am? I 'm selling 'em for my papa and mamma : and they 're thirty cents a dozen.'

" Ulrica don't understand English much, and Nelly's words didn't sound like the English she was used to ; an' she couldn't make her out : but Jan he stepped up, and explained to her ; and then Ulrica took hold o' Nelly's long braids o' hair, and lifted 'em up, and said something to Jan in their own language ; an' he nodded his head, an' looked at Nelly real loving : and sez he to me, in a whisper like : —

" ' The wife thinks she looks like our little Ulrica : and she ain't unlike her, that 's true ; though she 's big-ger 'n our little girl was when she died.'

" All this time Nelly was a lookin' from one to the other on 'em with her steady eyes, an' makin' em out. They took all her eggs ; but the butter they said she 'd better take up to Mr. Clapp's, the owner o' the Black Bull Mine. Mis Clapp was very particular about her butter, an' 'd give a good price for it. So we went up to his house ; and just as soon as Mis Clapp sot her eyes on Nelly, I could see how she took to her, by the way she spoke : an' she took the butter and paid her the eighty cents ; and you 'd oughter to seen Nelly a liftin' up her caliker gown to get to her petticoat, and drawin' out her little silk bag, an' putting in the money, — countin' it all as keerful as any old woman. Mis Clapp she laughed, and sez she : —

" ' You 're a real little business woman : ain't you ? '

" ' Yes 'm,' sez Nelly, as grave as a jedge, ' I 'm goin' to be. Would you like some more butter next week ? I can bring some on Saturday.'

"Then Mis Clapp she jest engaged three pounds a week regular: an' Nelly thought that 'd be all they could spare now."

"Pshaw!" interrupted Lucinda; "Mis March ain't no hand to skimp: but they might spare four 's well 's not."

"Well," said Billy, "I guess they will when they see the money a comin' in so easy. That 'll be one dollar and sixty cents a week; and the eggs 'll be say one dollar an' eighty more: that 'll putty nigh keep 'em in meat 'n' flour. I 'm real glad they thought on 't. But I expect it goes agin Mr. March dreadful. That gal 's the apple o' his eye: that 's what she is."

"Well, he might go hisself, then," said Lucinda, scornfully, "if he thinks it 's too lowerin' for his gal: I don't see nothin' to be ashamed on in 't myself. If sellin' is honorable business for men, I don't see why it ain't for women 'n' gals."

"Now, Luce," exclaimed Billy, "don't be contrary. You know 's well 's I do what I mean. There 's plenty o' things you don't want gals to do that 's honorable enough, so fur 's thet goes. But I must tell ye what Ulrica did 's we were comin' out o' town. There she stood waitin' in her door. She 'd been watchin' for us all the arternoon; an' 's soon 's she see us, she began a beckonin' and a callin'; an' we crossed over, 'n' there she hed a little picture o' their gal that was dead; an' sez she, holdin' it up to me an' pointin' to Nelly: —

"'Is it not the same face? Do you not see she haf the same face as mine child?' And then she gave Nelly such a hug and kiss, and Nelly she kissed her back just as kind 's could be, and sez she: —

"'I am glad I look like your little girl; but you mustn't cry, or I shall not come again.'

" 'Oh, yes, yes, come again : all days come again !' sez Ulrica : and she was cryin' too all the time. Then she gave Nelly a paper bag full of queer little square cakes with a picture stamped on 'em. They have 'em at Christmas, she said, in her country. Nelly wan't fur takin' 'em ; but I nudged her, 'n' told her to take 'em, — Ulrica 'd be hurt if she didn't. After we got away from the house, Nelly sez to me, kind o' solemn, sez she : —

" 'Billy, I don't like to look like so many dead little girls. Isn't it queer? That was what Mrs. Williams said, — that nice lady : she used to cry, and say I looked like her little girl that was dead ; and now it 's a little girl way off in Sweden. Isn't it queer?'

" But I tried to put it out of her head ; but she kept talking about it all the way. I think people needn't say such things to children ; it jest makes 'em gloomy for nothing."

The account Nelly gave to her father and mother of her day in Rosita was almost as graphic as Billy's. She had thoroughly enjoyed the day. She was pretty tired ; but not too much so to have a fine scamper with Rob and the pet deer in the paddock after tea. And the air castles that she and Rob built that night after they had gone to bed were many stories high. Nelly was sure that if her mother would only make butter enough, and her father would buy some more hens, she could earn all the money they needed to have.

"Why, Rob," she said, "you see I had more than two dollars to-day ; and the basket wasn't a bit heavy :

I could have carried twice as much. If I could make
four dollars each day, don't you see how soon it would
be hundreds of dollars? hundreds, Rob!"

"Yes," said Rob; "and I could make as much more
by the trout: and there would be hundreds and hundreds. And strawberries, Nell! Strawberries! why
couldn't we sell strawberries? Old Mr. Pine said we
could have all we could pick."

"I thought of that," replied Nelly: "but we haven't
any horses now to carry us over there. You know we
always went in the wagon."

"Pooh!" said Rob, "we could go just as well in the
ox-cart."

"But wouldn't it take all day to get there?" said the
wise Nelly: "to get there and back?"

"Oh," said Rob, "I never thought of that. Perhaps
Mr. Scholfield would lend us his horses some day."

"I don't believe papa would — like — to — borrow,"
said Nelly, drowsily; and in a second more she was
sound asleep.

Mr. and Mrs. March, also, were building some air
castles, resting on the same foundations as Rob's and
Nelly's. Nelly's happy and animated face when she
returned, and her enthusiastic account of her day's
work, had surprised both her father and mother.

"I thought she would be so tired out she would never
want to go again," said Mrs. March: "but she is full
of the idea of going twice a week, all the time."

"The exercise is not bad for her," replied Mr. March,
hesitatingly: "I have no fears about that. And I suppose it is a false pride which makes me shrink so from
letting her carry about things to sell. We are very

poor, and we do need the money; and the child's impulse to help us is a true and noble one; but I can't be wholly reconciled to the idea yet. If we do permit it, I shall keep an exact account of every penny the dear child brings into this house; and, if we are ever in comfortable circumstances again, I shall pay it all back to her with interest. I have made up my mind to that."

"It will be a nice fund to pay for her having a year or two at some good school, when she is older," said Mrs. March, cheerfully; "and I do not feel as you do about her selling things. I think it will never do her the least harm in any way. Some of the best and noblest people in the world have gone through just such struggles in their youth. I see no disgrace in it: not the least; and I have perfect faith in Nelly's good behavior under all circumstances."

"Yes," said Mr. March, "she can be trusted anywhere. I only wish Rob had half her steadiness of head."

"Rob will come out all right," said Mrs. March: "you don't do justice to him. His heart is in the right place."

Mr. March laughed.

"You never will hear a word against Rob," said he.

"Nor you against Nelly," replied Mrs. March. "Now I think Nelly's obstinacy is quite as serious a fault as Rob's hasty impulsiveness."

"Nelly's obstinacy!" exclaimed Mr. March: "what do you mean? I never saw a trace of it."

"No: you never would," said Mrs. March, "because you never have occasion to deal with her in little matters. To me she is always obedient; but with Rob she is as unyielding as a rock in the most trifling matters. When they were little it was quite different, — while he was ill so much, you know; then she used to give up to him so much I thought it would spoil him. But now she literally rules the boy; and I can't help it. Why, the other day they had a really serious quarrel as to where their hair-brushes should be kept. I don't know what made Rob stand out so: usually he gives up. I did not interfere, because I wish them to settle all such matters themselves; but I heard Nelly say : —

" ' Rob March ! you can move those hair-brushes just as often as you please : it won't make the least difference. I shall move them right back again into this drawer, if it 's every day of your life till you 're fifty years old !'

" ' I shan't live with you when I 'm fifty,' said Rob : ' so you 'll have to leave off before then. And I won't have the hair-brush box in the drawer. It doesn't look bad on the top of the bureau; and I want it where I can get at it easy.'

" ' I 'll take it out for you,' said Nelly, ' as often as you want it, if you 're too lazy; but it 's going to be in the drawer.' "

Mr. March laughed heartily.

" Well, wasn't Nelly right?" he said. " If I recollect right, the box is a shabby old box, much better out of sight."

" Oh ! of course you 'd take Nelly's part," said Mrs. March, half playfully, half in earnest.

" Well, which won?" said Mr. March.

" Oh, Nelly, of course. She always does," replied Mrs. March.

"I'm glad of it," laughed Mr. March. And there the conversation dropped.

The next day Nelly followed her father out to the barn after breakfast.

"Papa," said she, "I want to ask you something."

"What is it, little daughter?" he replied.

"If I could get four dollars each time I went to Rosita, and should go twice every week, how much would that be in a year?" said Nelly.

"Four hundred dollars, my child," replied Mr. March.

"Is not that a good deal of money?" said Nelly: "wouldn't it buy almost all we want?"

"It would buy enough food for us to eat, dear," said Mr. March: "not much more than that."

"Well, Rob could get a good deal for trout too," said Nelly, resolutely: "he's going to fish, next week: and they're forty cents for one pound; and I'm going to take Rob up with me, the next time, and show him how to sell things. It is very easy."

"Do you like it, Nell, — really like it?" said her father.

"Oh, yes!" replied Nelly; "it's splendid! It's the nicest thing I ever did. I like to see the people, and to count the money; and then it is so nice to help too, papa! Oh! you will let us help: won't you?"

"Yes, my child, we will let you help us this summer, because we are really very poor just now; but I hope next year we will not be in such straits. You and Rob are dear, good children to want to work. Papa will never forget it."

Nelly put her hand in her father's, and walked along

in silence by his side for a few minutes. Then suddenly
catching sight of Rob in the field, she exclaimed: —

"Oh! there's Rob going down to the creek now to
fish. I will go and tell him it is all settled. I can help
him fish. I shall put the grasshoppers on the hook: I
hate it, and I said I'd never do it again; but now that
it's for the money, I shall." And she ran off as fast
as she could, to join Rob.

All that morning, Rob fished and Nelly stuck grasshoppers on the hooks for him. At noon, they were
miles away from the house: they had followed up the
creek without noticing how far they were going.

"Oh, dear!" said Rob, looking up at the sun, "look
at that old sun: he's just galloped all this morning.
I think his horses are running away. Did papa show
you that picture of him in the 'Mythology'? It was a
splendid man, in a chariot, standing up, and driving
four horses. They thought the sun was really a man.
Say, Nell, let's don't go home yet."

"I'm so hungry!" said Nelly, whose share of the
amusement was not so exciting as Rob's.

"Pshaw!" said Rob: "I wonder what's the reason
girls get hungry so much sooner than boys."

"They don't," said Nelly, doggedly: "they've got
stomachs just alike. You're as hungry now as you can
be; only you won't say so. I know you are."

Rob did not deny it; in fact, as soon as Nelly had
said the word "hungry," he had begun to feel a dreadful gnawing in the region of his stomach.

"I'll tell you, Nell," he exclaimed: "we'll cook a
trout on a hot stone. I know how. Billy did it one
day last summer. You just get a lot of dried sticks

and things, and pile them up; and I 'll find a flat stone."

In a few minutes, they had a big fire, and a large flat stone standing up in the hottest part of the blaze.

"There!" said Rob, rubbing his hands: "now you 'll see a dinner fit for a king. We 'll have a trout apiece."

"Good big ones!" said Nelly. "How do you tell when the stone is hot enough?"

"Oh! if it burns a stick to hold it on it, it 's too hot, and you let it cool a while," replied Rob, with a patronizing tone; as much as to say, "Girls did not know much about cooking on hot stones."

Girls knew more about getting hot stones out of fires, however, than boys did, in this instance. Poor Rob burnt his fingers badly, trying to pull the stone out by taking hold of it with a handful of thick green leaves.

"Oh, Rob! Rob!" screamed Nelly: "you 'll burn you!"

But it was too late. Rob had grasped the stone with all his usual impetuosity, and the leaves had shrivelled up instantly, like cobwebs, the stone was so hot. He let it fall back into the fire, and danced about, shaking his burnt fingers, and screwing up his face very hard, to keep from crying.

"Oh, that was too bad, Rob!" cried Nelly. "Why didn't you let me get it out?"

"You get it out!" cried Rob, quite angry; "you get it out! I 'd like to see you! That 's the way Billy took his out. There isn't any other way."

Nelly had run off a few steps for a big stick. Presently she came back; and, without saying a word to Rob, put the end of the stick under the stone, and lifted it up and rolled it over and over, till she had it entirely out of the ashes and hot brands, and on a smooth, clean place in the grass. Then she took a little twig, and held it close to the stone, to see if it were still too hot. The twig smoked.

" Oh ! it 's lots too hot," said Rob, meekly. " What made you think of that way of getting it out, Nell?"

" I don't know," said Nelly : " your burning your fingers, I guess."

Then they cut open two nice trout, and Rob scraped them clean with his knife ; and, as soon as the stone was cool enough, they laid them on the hot stone. Oh, how good they smelled as soon as they began to cook, and the fat began to ooze out ! When the under side was nice and brown, Rob turned them over with two sticks carefully ; and, in a few minutes more, they were done. Then he stuck a pointed stick through the biggest one, and handed it very politely to Nelly, saying : —

" Won't you be helped to some fish, Miss Nelly March?"

Nelly held out two pointed sticks to take it ; and then she ran round and round with it, for a minute, to cool it ; and then she took it by the tail and ate it up in less time than it has taken to write this page. Rob ate his more slowly.

" Oh ! I wish we had cooked four," said Nelly.

Rob looked at his basket. It was not much more than half full.

" I can't fish any more," he said : " my fingers hurt so. Don't let 's eat up any more. We can have a good supper when we get home. Let 's keep all these to sell."

"Of course we will, Rob," said Nelly, quite ashamed: "I was a pig."

"Pigs don't eat trout, I guess," said Rob, laughing.

"No," said Nelly; "but they always want more. I was a real pig. Now let's hurry home. I'm afraid we're a long way off."

"Well, they know we're fishing," said Rob: "they won't worry. It's good mamma's got over worrying about my falling into the creek."

CHAPTER X.

ROB AND NELLY GO INTO BUSINESS.

THEY were indeed a long way from home; much farther than they dreamed. It was past four o'clock when they reached the house, and Mrs. March had begun to be a little anxious about them. She was much pleased when she saw the basket of trout.

"Oh, what a nice supper we will have!" she exclaimed.

Rob and Nelly looked at each other and at her.

"Oh, mamma!" Nelly began, but checked herself at once, and looked again at Rob.

"Why, what is the matter, children?" said Mrs. March.

"Nothing. You can have them if you want them," said Rob, rather forlornly.

"Why, child, what else did you get them for?" exclaimed their mother, who had forgotten all about Rob's plan of selling trout.

"To sell," said Rob. "There's as many as four pounds there, I guess: that's most two dollars; but you can have them. I don't care. I'll go get some more to-morrow, if my hand's well."

"Oh!" said Mrs. March, "I had forgotten about it. So you mean to be a little fish-merchant, do you?"

"Yes. Nelly's an egg-merchant, an egg and butter

merchant; and I'm going to be a fish and fruit merchant: and we're going to take care of you and papa that way," said Rob, in an excited tone. "And I was going to begin to-morrow; but I can begin next day, just as well: let's have these for supper; they're splendid; we've cooked two already."

The tears came into Mrs. March's eyes.

"We'll ask papa, and see what he **says**," she said. "If we're really going to be merchants, we mustn't **eat up all our goods: that's certain.** But what fruits **do you propose** to deal in, Mr. March? Fruits seem to me rather scarce in this valley."

"Oh! strawberries, next month," said Rob; "and then raspberries, and then wild currants, and then wild grapes. There are lots and lots of them on the creek, you know. And we can get carried up **to Mr. Pine's,** and pick berries up above his ranch. He said we might have all **we could** pick."

When they **asked Mr. March** about the trout, he laughed, and said : —

"I think **we must take a** vote of all the partners. This family is a partnership **now**; the 'March firm' we **must call** ourselves; four partners, all working to make money for the firm : **now let's vote.** All that are in favor **of eating the** trout for supper, **hold up their** right hand."

Nobody's hand went up but Rob's.

"Three against **you,** Rob," said his father : "you'll have to go without your trout this time. **It is voted by** a majority of the firm that the **trout** be sold."

"I didn't want"—Rob began, but checked himself, and looked at **his mother.** She nodded and smiled, but

said nothing. A little while afterward, when she found
Rob alone, she put her arms round him, and kissed
him, and said : —

"I understood about the trout, Rob. You thought
I wanted some for my supper : didn't you?"

"Yes, mamma," said Rob : "that was it. I didn't
care so much about them ; but it seemed awful mean
to keep you from having them. Nelly and I had each
had one ; they were splendid. Next time I'll just catch
one basketful to sell, and one to eat."

The next day, Rob and Nelly set off together at six
o'clock for Rosita : Rob with his trout, and Nelly with
eggs and butter. They stopped a minute to speak to
Lucinda and Billy, as they passed their house. Billy
was not there. He had gone to work for Mr. Pine,
Lucinda said, and would not be at home for a week.

"You like it : don't you, Nelly?" she said.

"Yes, indeed!" said Nelly : "I think it's fun. And
the people are all so kind : that Swede woman kissed
me because I look so much like her little girl. I am
going there again to-day. They keep boarders, you
know ; and she wants eggs every time I come, she said.
I thought perhaps they'd take Rob's trout too."

"Oh, no! they won't," said Lucinda. "Trout is too
dear eatin' for such boarders 's they keep. You take
the trout right up to Miss Clapp's. She'll take 'em all,
an' as many more 's you can ketch."

By the middle of the afternoon, the children were at
Lucinda's door again. They both ran in shouting : —

"Lucinda! Lucinda! we've sold every thing ; and
we've got five dollars and seventy-five cents! Now
what do you say? Won't mamma be glad? Couldn't

anybody get very rich this way, if they only kept on?
Isn't it splendid?"

"You dear little innocent lambs," said Lucinda:
"it's much you know about gettin' rich, or bein' poor."

"Why, we are poor now; very, very poor: papa
said so," interrupted Nelly. "That's the reason he
lets us sell things."

"Oh, well! your pa don't know nothin' about bein'
real poor," said Lucinda: "and I don't suppose he ever
will; but it's a good thing you're a bringin' in somethin' this year. It's a dreadful year on everybody."

"Yes; papa said we were a real help," said Nelly:
"he said so last night."

"Luce," exclaimed Rob, "what do you think Jan
is going to make for us? He's taken the measure of
us to-day; he showed us a picture of a man and a
woman with them on. They're real nice to carry
things with: you don't feel the weight a bit, he says.
In his country, everybody wears them on their shoulders, — everybody that has any thing heavy to carry.
They're something like our ox-yoke, — only with a
straight piece, that comes out; and we can hang a
basket on each end, and run along just as if we weren't
carrying any thing. They're real nice folks, Jan and
his wife. They're the nicest folks in Rosita."

"Oh! not so nice as Mrs. Clapp, Rob," said Nelly.

"Yes, they are too; lots nicer. They don't speak
so fine and mincing: but I like them lots better; they're
some fun. And Luce," he continued, "they've got a
picture-book full of pictures of the way people dress in
their country; and they let us look at it. It was splendid. And Ulrica she keeps taking hold of Nelly's hair,

and lifting up the braids and looking at them, and talking to Jan in her own language.”

“It makes her cry, though,” said Nelly. “I wish she wouldn’t.”

“But what is this Jan is going to make you? ” asked Lucinda: “a real yoke, such as I’ve seen the men wear to bring up two water-buckets to oncet? I don’t believe your pa and ma ’ll let you wear it.”

“Why not?” said Nelly: “does it look awful on your shoulders? ”

“Well, you know how the ox-yoke looks on old Starbuckle and Jim,” said Rob. “It’s a good deal like that: I saw one in the picture-book.”

“But we ’re not going to be yoked together,” said Nelly. “It can’t look like that.”

“No, no,” said Lucinda, “ not a bit. They ’re real handy things. Lots o’ the men have them, to carry water-buckets up the hill with in Rosita. They just make ’em out of a bent sapling, with two hooks at each end. You ’ll find them a heap o’ help.”

“Then I shall wear it, no matter how it looks,” said Nelly, resolutely.

“We needn’t wear them in the streets,” said Rob: “we can take them off just outside the town, and hide them among the trees.”

“Now, Rob,” exclaimed Nelly, “I’d be ashamed to do that! That would look as if we were too proud to be seen in them. I shall wear mine into all the houses.”

“Wait till you see how it feels, Nelly,” said Lucinda. “Perhaps you won’t like it so well ’s you think.”

When Nelly and Rob told their father and mother

about the shoulder-yokes that the Swede Jan was going to make for them, both Mr. and Mrs. March laughed heartily.

"Upon my word," said Mr. March, "you are going to look like little merchants in good earnest: aren't you?"

"Don't you suppose they will hurt your shoulders?" asked Mrs. March.

"Ulrica said they didn't," replied Nelly. "She said she had worn one a great deal. She puts a little cushion under the place where they come on your neck. She says we can carry twice as much on those as we can in our hands."

It was arranged now that Rob and Nelly should, for the present, go up to Rosita twice a week, on Tuesdays and Fridays. Mr. March reckoned that they would be able to spare butter and eggs enough to bring them five or six dollars each week. The money from the trout they did not allow themselves to count on, because it would be uncertain; but Rob made most magnificent calculations from it. "Four dollars a week, at least," he said; "and that will be one way to pay off those old grasshoppers. I'll make a good many of them work for us: see if I don't!"

The next time Rob and Nelly went to Rosita, when they bade their mother good-by, they said: —

"Be on the lookout for us, mamma, this afternoon. You'll see us coming down the road with our yokes on."

So Mrs. March began to watch, about three o'clock; and, sure enough, about four, there she saw them coming down the lane which led from the main road to their house. They were coming very fast, at a sort of hop-skip-and-jump pace, but keeping step with each other exactly. A sort of slender pole seemed to be growing out of each shoulder; from this hung slender rods, and on the end of each rod was fastened a basket or a pail. Rob's yoke had two pails; Nelly's had two baskets. As the children ran, they took hold of the rods with their hands, just above the baskets and pails. This steadied them, and also seemed to be a sort of support in walking. As soon as the children saw their mother, they quickened their steps, and came into the yard breathless.

"Oh, they are splendid!"

"Why, they're just as light as any thing!"

"They don't hurt your neck a bit!"

"See the nice baskets Ulrica gave us! Jan made them himself out of willows," shouted they, both talking at once, and each out of breath. Then Nelly slipped off her yoke, and, before her mother knew what she was about, had tried to put it on her shoulders; but her mother was too tall: Nelly could not reach up.

"Oh! do try it on, mamma," she said: "just to see how nice it is."

Mrs. March tried; but the yoke had been carefully adjusted to Nelly's slender little figure, and Mrs. March could not put it on.

"Well, if you only could, mamma, you'd see how easy it is," said Nelly, slipping it on her shoulders again, and racing down to the gate to meet her father, who was just coming in.

Mr. March stopped short, and stared at Nelly for a minute.

" Why, Nell," he said, " I did not know what you were. I thought you were some new kind of animal, with horns growing out lengthwise from your shoulders."

" So we are ! so we are !" shouted Rob, running up so fast that the pails on the rods of his yoke swung back and forth high up in the air. " We are the four-armed boy and girl of Rosita. They 'll want us for a show. Four arms on a boy are as wonderful as two heads on a calf."

How Mr. March did laugh ! The children's fun was contagious. He seized Rob's yoke, and tried to put it on his own shoulders ; but it was as much too small for him as Nelly's had been for her mother. Then he sat down on the fence, and examined the yokes carefully. They were beautifully made out of very slender young aspen-trees, which could be easily bent into place. The wood was almost white, and shone like satin : Jan had rubbed it so long.

" He says when the white gets dirty he will paint them for us," said Nelly : " all bright colors, as they have them in Sweden. But while they keep clean they are prettier white."

Ulrica had put a soft cushion of red cloth at the place where the yoke rested on the neck behind ; also, on each rod just where the hands grasped them. Mrs. March examined them carefully.

" This is beautiful cloth," she said : " I wonder where the woman got it."

" Oh ! she has a big roll of it in a chest," said Nelly. " I saw it ; and a big piece of beautiful blue, too. It was made in Sweden, she says ; and she has a queer gown, which was her little girl's that is dead, all made of this red and blue cloth, with—oh!—millions of little silver buttons sewed on it, all down the front. She wanted me to try it on; but I did not like to. It was too small, too: not too short; I think it would have come down to my feet. Do little girls in Sweden wear long gowns, like grown-up ladies, mamma?"

"I don't know, dear," said Mrs. March.

"She has some of the little girl's hair in the same chest; and she took it out, and held it close to mine."

"Yes," said Rob: "I didn't want her to. How did we know she was clean?"

"Oh, for shame, Rob!" cried Nelly: "they're all as clean as pins; you know they are. But I didn't like her to do it, because it made her cry."

After supper they had a great time deciding where to keep the yokes. Rob wanted them hung up on the wall.

"They look just as pretty as the antlers old Mr. Pine has upon the wall in his house," said Rob; "and we can't ever have any antlers, unless we shoot a deer ourselves. Mr. Pine said a man offered him fifty dollars for them; but he wouldn't take it. I think our yokes look just about as pretty."

"Oh, Rob!" exclaimed Nelly, "how can you talk so? They are not pretty a bit; and you know it!"

"I don't either!" said Rob: "I do think they're pretty; honest, I do."

While they spoke, Mrs. March was hanging one of the yokes up on the wall, by a bit of bright red tape, tied in the middle. She hung it quite low, between the door and the south window. Then she hung Nelly's sun-bonnet on the nail above it, and Nelly's little red shawl over one end of the yoke.

"There," she said, "you are right, Rob. It makes quite a pretty hat-rack."

"So it does," said Mr. March. "Now we'll put the other one up the other side the door; and that shall be Rob's, to hang his coat and jacket on."

"My jacket isn't pretty, though, like Nell's shawl," said Rob, wistfully. "Why don't men wear red jackets in this country? In that book of Jan's ever so many of the men have red jackets on, with silver buttons; and they're splendid. Jan has one too in the chest; but he doesn't wear it here, because it would make the folks laugh, he says: it is so different from our clothes here. He put it on for us while Ulrica was showing Nelly the little girl's gown. It did.look queer; it came down most to his knees, and had great flaps on the side, and big silver buttons on the front, as big as dollars. But it was splendid: a great deal handsomer than the uniform the Mayfield guards wore."

When Billy came home from Mr. Pine's, Lucinda told him about the yokes which Jan had made for the children to wear, to carry their baskets and pails on. Billy listened with a disturbed face.

"Miss March 'll never let 'em wear 'em: will she?"

"I donno," said Lucinda: "Miss March's got heaps o' sense; an' the children was jest tickled to death with them. They come racin' down the hill with 'em on, 's proud as militia-men on trainin'-day. But how 'twill be about wearin' 'em round town I donno."

"It'll never do in the world," said Billy. "The boys 'll all follow 'em, and hoot and halloo; and Rob 'll be fightin' right an' left, the fust thing you know.

It's a bad business, bad business. I donno what put it into that pesky Swede's head, anyhow."

"Oh! jest to help the children," said Lucinda. "From what the children say, Jan an' his wife both seem to have kind o' adopted 'em. You know how she takes on over Nelly, 'cause she looks so like her own little gal."

"I know it," said Billy. "Blamed if I don't wish I hadn't taken 'em there. You'll see they can't wear the things in Rosita."

This time Billy was right. He had been mistaken in thinking that the miners would treat Nelly roughly; but he was right now about the boys. The next time Nelly and Rob went up to Rosita, they entered the town a little before nine o'clock: it was just the time when all the children were on their way to school. As soon as Rob and Nelly appeared with their little yokes on their shoulders, and a basket and pail swinging from each rod, the boys on the street set up a loud shout, and all rushed towards them.

"Hullo, bub! what kind o' harness 've you got on?"

"Did your pa cut down his ox-yoke to fit ye?"

"Oh, my! look at the gal wearin' one too," they cried; and some of the rudest of the boys pressed up close, and tried to take off the covers of the baskets and pails. In less than a second, Rob had slipped his yoke off his shoulders, and thrown it on the ground, baskets and all; and sprung in front of Nelly, doubling up his fists, and pushing the boys back, crying : —

"You let us alone, now: you'd better!"

"Hush! hush! Rob," said Nelly, who was quite white with terror. "Come right into this store: the

" In less than a second, Rob had slipped his yoke off his shoulders, and sprung in front of Nelly." — PAGE 250.

gentleman that keeps the store won't let them touch us."

And Nelly slipped into the store, and as quick as lightning took off her yoke and put it on the floor ; and, saying to the astonished storekeeper, "Please let my things stay there a minute ; the boys are tormenting my brother," she ran back into the centre of the crowd, snatched up both Rob's baskets of trout, and, pushing Rob before her, came back into the store. The crowd of boys followed on, and were coming up the store steps ; but the storekeeper ordered them back.

"Go away!" he said: "you ought to be ashamed of yourselves, tormenting these children so. I'd like to thrash every one of you! Go away!"

The boys shrank away, ashamed ; and the storekeeper went up to Nelly, who was sitting down on a nail-keg, trembling with excitement.

"What is this thing, anyhow?" said he, taking up the yoke. "Oh! I see, — to carry your pails on."

"Yes, sir," said Nelly ; "and it's a great help. We have to walk so far the baskets feel real heavy before we get here. Jan, the Swede man, made them for us. It is too bad the boys won't let us wear them."

"Are you Mr. March's little girl?" said the shopkeeper.

"Yes," said Nelly ; "and that's my brother," pointing to Rob, who was still standing on the steps, shaking his fists at the retreating boys and calling after them.

"He'd better let 'em alone," said the shopkeeper. "The more notice ye take of 'em, the more they'll pester ye. But I reckon ye can't wear the yokes any more ; I wouldn't if I was you. You tell your father that

Mr. Martin told ye to leave 'em off. Ye can leave 'em here, if ye 're a mind to. Some time when your father 's a drivin' in he can stop and get 'em."

"Yes," said Nelly : " I hadn't any thought of wearing them again. All I wanted was to get in here and be safe, so they shouldn't break my eggs : I 've got four dozen eggs in one pail. I think it is real cruel in the boys to plague us so." And Nelly began to cry.

"There, there, don't ye cry about it ; 'taint any use. Here 's a stick of candy for ye," said the kind-hearted Mr. Martin. " The Rosita boys are a terrible rough set."

"We might take care not to get into town till after they 're in school," said Nelly, taking the candy and breaking it in two, and handing half of it to Rob. "Thank you for the candy, sir. I 'm sorry I cried : I guess it was because I was so frightened. Oh ! there 's Ulrica now !" And she ran to the door, and called, "Ulrica ! Ulrica !"

Ulrica came running as fast as possible, soon as she heard Nelly's voice. She looked surprised enough when she saw the two yokes lying on the floor, and Nelly's face all wet with tears, and Rob's deep-red with anger. When Nelly told her what the matter was, she said some very loud words in Swedish, which I am much afraid were oaths. Then she turned to Mr. Martin, and said : —

" Now, is not that shame — that two children like this will not be to be let alone in these the streets? I carry the yokes myself. Come to mine house."

So saying, Ulrica lifted both the yokes up on her strong shoulders, and, taking Nelly's biggest pail in one hand, strode away with long steps.

"Come on mit me," she said; "come straight. I like to see the boy that shall dare you touch." And as she passed the boys, who had gathered sullenly in a little knot on the sidewalk, she shook her head at them, and began to say something to them in her broken English; but, finding the English come too slow, she broke into Swedish, and talked louder and faster. But the boys only laughed at her, and cried: —

"Go it, old Swedy!"

"Oh, Ulrica! don't let's speak to them," whispered Nelly. "Be quiet, Rob!" And she dragged Rob along with a firm hand.

"Now I goes mit you to the houses mineself," said Ulrica. "It shall be no more that the good-for-nothings have room that to you they one word speak."

So Ulrica put on her best gown, and a clean white handkerchief over her head, and her Sunday shoes, which had soles almost two inches thick; then she took one of the baskets and one of the pails, and, giving the others to Nelly and Rob, she set off with them to walk up to Mrs. Clapp's, where the butter and trout were to be left. Mrs. Clapp was astonished to see Ulrica with the children. Ulrica tried to tell her the story of the yokes; but Mrs. Clapp could not understand Ulrica's English, and Nelly had to finish the story.

"It was too bad," said Mrs. Clapp: "but my advice to you is, to give up the yokes. It would never be quite safe for you to wear them here: the boys in this town are a pretty lawless set."

"Oh, no, ma'am!" replied Nelly, "I haven't the least idea of wearing them again. It would be very silly. But it is a dreadful pity: they did help so much, and Jan took so much trouble to make them for us."

Rob hardly spoke. He was boiling over with rage and mortification.

"I say, Nell," he began, as soon as they got outside Mrs. Clapp's gate: "you might have let me thrash that boy that spoke last, the one that called out at you. I'll die if I don't do something to him. And I'm going to wear my yoke: so there! They may's well get used to it. I'll never give up this way!"

"You'll have to, Rob," answered Nelly. "I hate it as much as you do; but there's no use going against boys, — that is, such boys as these. The Mayfield boys'd never do so. They'd run and stare, perhaps: I expected any boys would stare at our yokes; but they'd never hoot and halloo, and scare you so. We'll have to give the yokes up, Rob."

"I won't," said Rob. "I'm going to wear mine home, and ask papa. I know he'll say not to give up."

"No, he won't, Rob." persisted Nelly. "I shall tell him what the kind shopkeeper said, and Mrs. Clapp too. You might know better yourself than to go against them all. They know better than we do."

"I don't care," said Rob. "It's none of their business. I shall wear my yoke if I've a mind to. At any rate, I'll wear it once more, just to show them."

"Papa won't let you," said Nelly, quietly, with a tone so earnest and full of certainty that it made Rob afraid she must be right.

When Mrs. March saw the children coming home without their yokes, she wondered what could have happened. But almost before she had opened her lips to ask, Rob and Nelly both began to tell the story of their adventures.

"Gently! gently! one at a time," cried Mrs. March; but it was impossible for the children to obey her, they were both so excited. At last Mrs. March said: —

"Rob, let Nelly speak first: ladies before gentlemen, always." And the impatient Rob reluctantly kept silent while Nelly told the tale.

Mrs. March's face grew sad as the story went on. It was a terrible thing to her to think of her little daughter attacked in the street in that way by rude boys.

"Now, oughtn't I to have thrashed them, mamma?" cried Rob, encouraged by the indignation in his mother's face: "oughtn't I to? But Nell she just pulled me into the store by main force; and I felt so mean. I felt as if I looked just like Trotter when he puts his tail between his legs and runs away from a big dog. I don't care: I'll thrash that ugly black-eyed boy yet, — the one that spoke to Nelly; sha'n't I, mamma? Wouldn't you? I know you would! And mayn't I wear the yoke again, just to show them I ain't afraid?"

"Keep cool, Rob," said Mrs. March; "keep cool!"

"I can't keep cool, mamma," said Rob, almost crying; "and you couldn't, either, — you know you couldn't!"

"Perhaps not, dear; but I'd try," replied his mother. "Nothing else does any good ever."

"Well, mayn't I wear the yoke, anyhow?" said Rob. "I won't go into Rosita ever again unless I can!"

"Rob," said his mother, earnestly, "if you were going across a field where there was a bull, you wouldn't wear a red cloak: would you? It would be very silly: wouldn't it?"

"Yes," said Rob, slowly and very reluctantly. He saw what his mother meant.

"That's just what I said," interrupted Nelly: "I said it would be very silly to wear them any more. The boys would never let us alone if we did."

"Nelly is right," said Mrs. March: "it would be just as silly as to carry a piece of red cloth and flourish it in the eyes of the bull, when you know that the sight of red cloth always makes bulls angry."

"I don't care if it does make them all set on me," said Rob: "after I've thrashed them once, they'll let me alone. Anyhow, I won't go unless I can wear it; I know that much: I'd feel such a sneak."

"Of course you'll do as you like about that, my dear boy," replied Mrs. March: "you never need go up to Rosita, if you would rather not. You know it was all your own plan, yours and Nelly's, going up there to sell things. Your papa and I would never have thought of it."

"Well," said Rob, half crying, "but there's all the money I make: we'd lose all that, if I don't go. Nell couldn't carry the trout besides all the butter and eggs."

"I know it," replied his mother; "but that isn't any reason for your doing what you feel would make you seem like a sneak. We wouldn't have you feel like that for any thing."

Poor Rob was very unhappy. He didn't see any way out of his dilemma. He wished he hadn't said he would not go up into Rosita without his yoke.

"Anyhow, I'll ask papa," he said.

"Yes," replied his mother, "of course you will talk it all over with him; and perhaps you'll feel differently about it after that. Let it all go now, and try to forget it."

"I 'm not going to think any more about it," said Nelly. "I don't care for those boys: they 're too rude for any thing. I sha'n't ever look at one of them; but you wouldn't catch me wearing that yoke again, I tell you!"

"That 's because you 're a girl," said Rob. "If you were a boy, you 'd feel just exactly as I do. Oh, goodness! don't I wish you had been a boy, Nell? If you had, we two together could thrash that whole crowd quicker 'n wink!"

"I shouldn't fight, if I were a boy," said Nelly: "I think it is beneath a boy to fight. It 's just like dogs and cats: they fight with their teeth and claws; and boys fight with their fists."

"Teeth, too," said Rob, grimly.

"Do they?" cried Nelly, in a tone of horror. "Do they really? Oh, Rob! did you ever bite a boy?"

"Not many times," said Rob; "but sometimes you have to."

"Well, I 'm glad I 'm not a boy," said Nelly: "that 's all I 've got to say. The idea of biting!"

To Mrs. March's great surprise, she found, when she talked the affair over with her husband, that he was inclined to sympathize with Rob's feeling.

"I don't like to have the boy give it up," said Mr. March. "You don't know boys as well as I do, Sarah. They 'll taunt him every time he goes through the street. I half wish Nelly hadn't hindered him from giving one of them a good, sound thrashing. He could do it."

"Why, Robert!" exclaimed Mrs. March: "you

don't mean to tell me that you would be willing to have your son engage in a street fight?"

"Well, no," laughed Mr. March: "not exactly that: but there might be circumstances under which I should knock a man down: if he insulted you, for instance; and there might come times in a boy's life when I should think it praiseworthy in him to give another boy a thrashing, and I think this was one of them."

"Well, for mercy's sake, don't tell Rob so," said Mrs. March: "he's hot-headed enough now; and, if he had a free permission beforehand from you to knock boys down, I don't know where he'd stop."

While Mr. and Mrs. March were talking, Billy came in. He had heard the story of the morning's adventures from a teamster who had been on the street when it happened; and Billy had walked all the way in from Pine's ranch, to — as he said in his clumsy, affectionate way — "see ef I couldn't talk the youngsters out o' their notion about them yokes."

"'Tain't no use," he said: "an' ye won't find a man on the street but 'll tell ye the same thing. 'Tain't no use flyin' in the face o' natur' with boys; and the Rosita boys, I will say for 'em, is the worst I ever did see. Their fathers is away from hum all the time, and wimmen hain't much hold on boys after they get to be long from twelve an' up'ards; an' the schools in Rosita ain't no great things, either. 'S soon 's I heard about them yokes, I told Luce the children couldn't never wear 'em: the boys 'n the street 'd plague their lives out on 'em. I don't know as I blame 'em so much, either, — though they might be decent enough to let a little gal alone; but them yokes is awful cur'us-lookin' things.

I never see a man a haulin' water with 'em, without laughin': they make a man look like a doubled-up kind o' critter, with more arms 'n he 's any right to. You can't deny yourself, sir, thet they 're queer-lookin'. Why, I 've seen horses scare at 'em lots o' times."

Billy's conversation produced a strong impression on Mr. March's mind. Almost as reluctantly as Rob himself, he admitted that it was the part of wisdom to give up the yokes.

"It 's no giving up for Nelly," said Mrs. March: "she said herself that nothing would induce her to wear it in again."

"And I think Rob would better not go in for a little while, till the boys have forgotten about it," said Mrs. March.

"And not at all, unless he himself proposes it," added Mr. March. "I have never wholly liked the plan, much as we have been helped by the money."

"I 've got an idee in my head," said Billy, "thet I think 'll help 'em more 'n the yokes, — a sight more. I mean to make 'em a little light wagon. Don't tell 'em any thing about it, because it 'll take me some little time yet. I 've got to stay up to Pine's a week longer; an' I can't work on't there. But I 'll have it ready in two weeks, or three to the farthest."

"Thank you, Billy," said Mr. March: "that is very kind of you. And a wagon will be much better than the yokes were: it will save them fatigue almost as much, and not attract any attention at all. You were very good to think of it."

"Nothin' good about me," said Billy, gruffly: "never was. But I do think a heap o' your youngsters, specially

Nelly, Mr. March. It seems to me the Lord don't often send just sech a gal's Nelly is."

"I think so too, Billy," replied Mr. March. "I have never seen a child like Nelly. I'm afraid sometimes we shall spoil her."

"No danger! no danger!" said Billy: "she ain't the kind that spoils."

"Now, you be sure an' not let on about the wagon: won't you, sir," he added, looking back over his shoulder, as he walked away fast on his great long legs; which looked almost like stilts, they were so long.

"Oh, yes! you may trust me, Billy," called Mr. March. "I won't tell. Good-by!"

CHAPTER XI.

HOW TO FIND A SILVER MINE.

WHEN Nelly set off on her next trip to Rosita, she felt a little sad and a little afraid. It had been decided that it would not be best for Rob to go at present, even if he had wished to; that it would be better to wait until the boys had forgotten the fight about the yokes before he was seen in town again. Rob walked with Nelly as far as Billy's cabin. Here they waited awhile for Nelly to rest, and to make sure that she did not get into town till after nine o'clock, after the boys were all safe inside the school-house. In the bottom of her heart, Nelly was really afraid of seeing them again. She would not own, even to herself, that she felt fear; but she could not help wondering all the time what the boys would do, — if they would say any thing when they saw her walking along all alone, and without her yoke on her shoulders. Rob was to spend the day with Lucinda, and be ready to walk home with her in the afternoon. He too felt very uncomfortable about being left behind; and there were two sad little faces which looked wistfully into each other, as the good-byes were being said.

"I 'll come part way and meet you," said Rob. "It 's too mean!"

" No, don't ! " said Nelly : " the sun will be so hot ; and perhaps I sha'n't come till late.   Good-by ! "

Nelly wore on her head a man's hat, with a brim so broad you could hardly see her face at all.   She had had to wear this ever since the summer weather began : the sun is so hot in Colorado that no one can bear it on his head or face in the summer.   On Nelly's arm swung her neat white sun-bonnet, tied by its strings, and pinned up in paper.   When she reached the last hill before entering the town, she always took off her hat, and hid it in a hollow place she had found in the root of a great pine-tree ; then she wore her sun-bonnet into town, and people sometimes said to her : —

" Why, Nelly, how do you keep your sun-bonnet so clean, after this long, dusty walk ? "

But Nelly never told her secret.   She was afraid some boy might hear it, and go and find the hiding-place of her hat.

There wasn't a boy to be seen when Nelly entered the town this morning.   How relieved her heart was you can imagine.   She just drew a long breath, and said to herself, " Oh ! but I 'm thankful.   Poor Rob ! he might as well have come as not."

Then she ran on to Ulrica's house.   Ulrica was very busy ironing some fine white clothes for a young lady who was visiting in Rosita : Ulrica was the only nice washerwoman in the town.   Nelly stood by the ironing-board, watching Ulrica flute the pretty lace ruffles. Presently she sighed, and said : —

" Mamma has ever so many pretty things like these put away in a trunk.   I used to wear such ruffles on my aprons and in my neck every day at home.   But mamma does all our washing now, and it is too much trouble to iron them. So we don't wear them any more."

"Ah, the dear child!" exclaimed Ulrica. "Bring to Ulrica: she will them do; it are not trouble; look how quick can fly the scissors." And in five minutes she had fluted the whole of one neck-ruffle.

"Oh! would you really, Ulrica?" said Nelly. "We could pay you in the eggs."

"Pay! pay!" said Ulrica, angrily: "who did say to be paid? No pay! no pay! Ulrica will do for you: not'ing pay. You are mine child."

"I'm afraid mamma would not like to have you do them without pay," said Nelly. "She would not think it was right to take your time."

"It is not'ing; it is not time: bring them to Ulrica," was all Ulrica would say. And Nelly ran on, resolving to ask her mother, that very night, for some of the old ruffles she used to wear in the necks of her gowns. After she had left the butter and eggs for Mrs. Clapp, and had sold the rest of her eggs at another house near by, she walked slowly down the hill past the hotel. Just below the hotel was a little one-story wooden building, which had a sign up over the door —

"WILHELM KLEESMAN,

"ASSAYER."

While the Marches were staying at the hotel, Nelly had often seen old Mr. Kleesman sitting on the steps of his little house, and smoking a big brown pipe. The bowl of the pipe had carved on it a man's head, with a long, flowing beard. Mr. Kleesman himself had a long, flowing beard, as white as snow, and his face did not look unlike the face on the pipe ; and the first time Rob saw him smoking, he had run to call Nelly, saying : —

"Come here, Nell! come quick! There's a man out there smoking, with his own portrait on his pipe."

Mr. March had explained to Nelly and Rob that "Assayer" meant a man who could take a stone and find out whether there were really any silver and gold in it or not. This seemed very wonderful to the children ; and, as they looked at the old gentleman sitting on his door-step every evening, smoking, they thought he looked like a magician, or like Aladdin who had the wonderful lamp. Rob said he meant to go and show him some of his stones, and see if there were not silver in some of them ; but his father told him that it took a great deal of time and trouble to find out whether a stone had silver in it or not, and that everybody who had it done had to pay Mr. Kleesman three dollars for doing it.

"Whew!" said Rob : " supposing there shouldn't be any silver at all in their stone, what then?"

"They have to pay three dollars all the same," said his father ; "and it is much cheaper to find out that way, than it is to go on digging and digging, and spending time and money getting stones out of the earth which are not good for any thing."

After that, Rob and Nelly used to watch the faces of all the men they saw coming out of Mr. Kleesman's office, and try to guess whether their stones had turned out good or not. If the man looked sad and disappointed, Nelly would say : —

"Oh! see that poor man : his hasn't turned out good, I know."

And, whenever some one came out with a quick step and a smiling face, Rob would say : —

"Look! look! Nell. That man's got silver. He's got it : I know he has."

As Nelly walked by Mr. Kleesman's house this morning, she saw lying on the ground a queer little round cup. It was about half as big as a small, old-fashioned teacup ; it was made of a rough sort of clay, like that which flower-pots are made of ; the outside was white, and the inside was all smooth and shining, and of a most beautiful green color.

"Oh, what a pretty little cup!" thought Nelly, picking it up, and looking at it closely. "I wonder how it came here! Somebody must have lost it ; some little girl, I guess. How sorry she will be!"

At that minute, old Mr. Kleesman came to his door. When he saw Nelly looking at the cup, he called out to her : —

"Vould you like more as dat? I haf plenty ; dey iss goot for little girls."

Mr. Kleesman was a German, and spoke very broken English.

Nelly looked up at him, and said : —

"Thank you, sir. I should like some more very much. They are cunning little cups. I thought somebody had lost this one."

Mr. Kleesman laughed, and stroked his long, white beard with his hand.

"Ach! I throw dem away each day. Little girls come often to mine room for dem : I have vary goot customers in little girls. Come in ! come in ! you shall have so many that you want." And he led Nelly into a small back room, where, in a corner on the floor, was a great pile of these little cups : some broken ones ; some, like the one Nelly had, green on the inside ; some brown, some yellow, some dark-red. Nelly was delighted. She knelt down on the floor, and began to look over the pile.

"May I really have all I want ?" she said. "Are they not of any use ?"

"Only to little girls," said Mr. Kleesman : " sometimes to a boy ; but not often a boy ; mostly it is for little girls ; they are my goot customers."

Nelly picked out six. She did not like to take more, though she would have liked the whole pile. Mr. Kleesman stood watching her.

"Vy not you take more as dem ?" he said.

"I am afraid there will not be enough for the other little girls," replied Nelly.

Mr. Kleesman laughed and shook till his white beard went up and down.

"Look you here," he said, and pointed behind the door. There was another pile, twice as big as the one which Nelly was examining.

"Oh, my !" said Nelly : " what a lot ! I 'll take a few more, I guess."

"I gif you myself. You haf too modest," said the old gentleman. And he picked up two big handfuls of the cups, and threw them into Nelly's basket. Then he sprang to a big brick stove which there was in the room, and opened its iron door and looked in. A fiery heat filled the room, as he opened the door.

" Oh ! " said Nelly, " I wondered what made it so hot in here. Why do you have a fire in such hot weather? " she said.

" To make mine assays," replied Mr. Kleesman. " I haf made three to-day already. I shall make three more. I haf big fire all day. You can look in if you like. Do you like? "

" Very much," said Nelly. Mr. Kleesman lifted her up on a block of wood, so that her face came directly opposite the door into the furnace. Then he gave her a piece of wood shaped like a shovel, with two round holes in it. He told her to hold this up in front of her face, so to keep off the heat, and then to look through the two holes into the furnace. Nelly did so ; and, as soon as she looked into the fiery furnace, she gave a little scream. The fire was one mass of glowing red coals. In the centre, on a stand, stood three little cups, the same size as those she had. In these cups was something which was red hot, and bubbling in little bubbles.

" Oh ! what is it in the cups? " she cried.

" Silver ore," replied Mr. Kleesman. " It have to be burnt and burnt wiz fire before I can tell if it are good. It are done now. I take out." Then with a long pair of tongs he took out one cup after another, and set them all on an iron block on the table.

Nelly stood on tiptoe, and looked into the little cups. The fiery red color died away very quickly ; and there, in the bottom of each cup, was a tiny, little round speck of silver. One was as big as the head of a common-sized pin, and one was a little smaller, and the third one was so small you could but just see it. In fact, if it had been loose on the floor or on a table, you would not have noticed it at all.

"That is not goot for any t'ing," said Mr. Kleesman, pointing to this small one. "I tell the man ven he bring his ore, I think it are no good."

Nelly did not speak; but her face was so full of eager curiosity that Mr. Kleesman said : —

"Now I show you how I tell how much silver there will be in each ton of the ore."

Then he went into the front room, and Nelly followed him. On a table in the window stood a long box; its sides and top were made of glass, set in narrow wooden frames. In this box was a beautiful little pair of brass scales; and in one of these scales was a tiny silver button. One side of this glass box drew up like a sliding door. Mr. Kleesman set his little cups down very carefully on the table; then he sat down in a chair opposite the glass box, and told Nelly to come and stand close to him.

"Now I weigh," he said, and pulled up the sliding side of the glass box; then with a very fine pair of pincers he took up one of the little buttons which had come out of the furnace, and laid it in the empty scale.

"See which are the heaviest," he said to Nelly.

Nelly strained her eyes; but she could hardly see that one scale was heavier than the other.

"They are alike," said Nelly.

Mr. Kleesman laughed.

"Ah, no! but they are not," he said. "Look! here it is written." And he pointed to a little needle which was fastened on the upright bar from which the scales swung. This needle was balanced so that the very smallest possible weight would make it move one way or the other, and point to figures printed on a scale behind it, — just as you have seen figures on the scales the cooks weigh sugar and butter on in the kitchen. Mr. Kleesman took off the glasses he was wearing, and put on another pair. "These are my best eyes," he said, "to read the small figures with." Then he peered a few minutes at the needle; then he shut down the glass slide, and watched it through the glass.

"Even my breath would make that it did not swing true," he said.

Presently he pushed up the slide, and took out the little button with his pincers, and put it up on a bar above the scales, where there were as many as a dozen more of the little buttons, all arranged in a row, — some larger, some smaller. Then he wrote a few words in a little book.

"There," he said, "I haf good news for two men, and bad news for one man, — the man who haf the little button; his mine are not goot. The other two can make twelve dollars of silver from one ton of ore."

By this time Nelly looked so hopelessly puzzled, that the old gentleman laughed, and said : —

"You haf not understand : is that so?"

"Oh, no, sir!" said Nelly : "I have not understood at all. Could I understand?"

"Ach, yes! it is so simple, so simple; the smallest child shall understand, if I show him. Stay you here till afternoon, and I show you from beginning," said Mr. Kleesman. "I make two more assays this afternoon."

"Thank you, sir," replied Nelly : "I should like to

stay very much; but my brother is waiting for me. I must hurry home. Some other day, if you will let me, I will come. May I bring my brother?"

"Is he goot like you; not to touch, and not ask the questions that are foolish?" said Mr. Kleesman.

Nelly colored. She was afraid Rob would not be able to keep as quiet as she had, or to refrain from touching things. Yet she wanted to have him see the curious sight.

"I think he will not touch any thing if you ask him not to; and I will try to keep him very still," said Nelly.

"Vary goot: he may come. Little one, it will be to me pleasure to show you all. You are like German child, not like American child," replied Mr. Kleesman, whose heart warmed towards Nelly more and more the longer he watched her quiet ways and her thoughtful face.

Nelly was so full of thoughts about the fiery furnace, the wonderful little silver buttons in the glowing red cups, and the kind old man with the white beard, that, for the first time all summer, she forgot Ulrica, and set out for the valley on a shorter road, which did not pass Ulrica's house. Poor Ulrica stood in her door, watching for a long time, till she grew anxious; at last, she pinned her white handkerchief over her head, and walked up into the town to see what had become of the child.

"If it is that she haf again to be frighted by the bad boys," said Ulrica, doubling up her fist, as she strode along, "I will make Jan that he go to the town-master, and haf punish them all."

No Nelly was to be found. Each person that Ulrica asked had seen Nelly early in the forenoon ; but no one had seen her since. At last, a man who was driving a long string of pack-mules overheard Ulrica's questions, and stopped his mules to say : —

" Is it that little brown-eyed gal o' March's, down in the valley, you 're asking after ? "

" Yes, yes, it are she ! " exclaimed Ulrica : " haf you saw ? "

" Yes," said the man : " I met her two hours ago well down the valley road, most to Cobb's cabin, — she an' her brother."

" Ach ! " said Ulrica, and turned away without another word. Nor did she speak to a soul all the way home. She was hurt and offended. " It are first time," she said ; " but it will not be last time. She haf found more as Ulrica," and poor Ulrica brooded over the thing till she made herself very unhappy. She would have been quite comforted if she had known that Nelly was feeling almost as badly about it as she did. Nelly did not remember, till she was half way to Lucinda's cabin, that she had not stopped to say good-by to Ulrica. As soon as she thought of it, she stood still, in the middle of the road, and said, " Oh, dear ! " out loud. At first, she had half a mind to go back ; but she knew that would be silly. So she trudged along, trying to hope that Ulrica would not have been watching for her. As soon as she saw Rob, she exclaimed : —

" Oh, Rob ! I forgot to come by way of Ulrica's, as we always do. I 'm afraid she is watching for me. If it hadn't been so far, I 'd have gone back."

Rob looked astonished.

"Why, what in the world made you forget it?" he asked. "You don't like goat's milk as well as I do, or you wouldn't ever forget to go to Ulrica's!"

"Well, you 'd have forgotten it yourself, this time," said Nelly, "I know, if you 'd seen what I have."

Then she showed him the cups, and told him all about the good time she had had in Mr. Kleesman's rooms.

"What! that jolly old fellow with the pipe that looked like Santa Claus?" cried Rob. "Oh, Nell! don't you believe papa 'll let me go in with you, next time?"

"I guess so," said Nelly. "I didn't see a boy to-day, not one, when I first went in; and at noon they didn't take any notice of me. Mrs. Clapp says they forget every thing very soon."

"Well, they don't!" said Rob, firing up at this statement about boys; "and Mrs. Clapp needn't think so. I guess I know. You 'll see they 'll pitch into us again yet, — at least, into me. I dare say they won't bother you. But I 'm going in, anyhow. It 's too mean."

"I 'll ask papa to let you," said Nelly. "We might go just in time to get in about nine, and we could stay at Mr. Kleesman's at twelve o'clock; and then we needn't see them at all. Say, Rob, do you suppose Ulrica 'll care much because I didn't stop?"

"Why, no!" said Rob: "why should she? You saw her in the morning?"

"Yes," said Nelly: "but we always did stop, you know; and she was always standing in the door watching for us, don't you know? I 'm awful sorry!"

"Oh, pshaw!" said Rob: "you 're always thinking of things, Nell."

It seemed very long to Rob and Nelly before the day came round to go up to Rosita again. It was only two days; but it seemed as much as a week to them both. That is one of the queerest things in this life, I think, that time can seem both so much longer and so much shorter than it really is. Haven't you known Saturday afternoons that didn't seem one bit more than a minute long? I have; and I remember just as well all about them, as if it were only this very last Saturday.

At last, the day came. It was Friday, and a lovely, bright day. Mr. March had said that Rob might go too; and both the children were awake long before light, in their impatience to be off.

"It would do just as well if we got up there early enough to be all through with selling things, and get in to Mr. Kleesman's before nine o'clock: wouldn't it, Nell?" said Rob.

"Why, yes," said Nelly, "of course it would. That's splendid. Let's get right up now. It's beginning to be light."

When Mrs. March heard their feet pattering about, she called from her room: —

"What in the world are you about, children?"

"Getting up, mamma," answered Nelly. "We're going up to town real early, so as to get out of the way of the boys, and have a good long time at Mr. Kleesman's. It takes about three hours to do what he does to the ore. Can't we go?"

"I have no objection," replied Mrs. March; "but you must have some breakfast. I will get right up."

"Oh, no! no! please, dear mamma, don't!" cried Nelly. "It's only four o'clock, by the clock downstairs : I 've just been down. We can get plenty to eat without you. There is beautiful cream in the pantry ; and a whole lot of cold potatoes."

Mrs. March laughed, and said : —

" I don't think cold potatoes are a very good breakfast."

" Why, mamma ! mamma ! " cried Rob, " cold potatoes are splendid. I like them best cold, with lots of salt. Please don't you get up."

Mrs. March was very sleepy ; so she turned over in bed, and went sound to sleep. When Nelly was dressed, she peeped cautiously in at the door of her mother's room, which stood open.

" They 're both sound asleep, Rob," she whispered : " let 's take off our shoes."

" What fun ! " whispered Rob ; and the two children stole downstairs in their stocking-feet, like two little thieves ; then they drank a good tumbler of cream, and ate the cold potatoes with salt, and some nice brown bread, and butter.

" I don't think a king need have a better breakfast than this," said Rob.

" I do ! " said Nelly. " If I were a queen, I 'd have a better one."

" What would you have, Nelly ? " said Rob, earnestly.

" Cold roast turkey," said Nelly, " and bread and honey."

" Pooh ! " said Rob, " I hate honey. It has such a twang to it. I 'd have melted maple sugar always on my bread, if I were a king. I 'd have maple sugar packed up in little houses, as they pack the ice in ice-houses, and just cut out great square junks, to melt up."

As the children went out of the house, the sky in the east was just beginning to be bright red. The sun was not up; but it was very light, and Pike's Peak shone against the red sky like a great mountain of alabaster. The peaks of the mountains in the west were rosy red; all their tops were covered with snow, and in the red light they looked like jewels.

"Oh, Rob, look! look!" cried Nelly: "isn't it perfectly lovely! Let's always come early like this."

Rob looked at the mountains and the sky.

"Yes, 'twould be pretty if 'twould stay so," he said; "but 'twon't last a minute."

Even while he spoke, the red color faded; the mountains began to look blue; and, in a minute more, up came the sun over the Rosita hills, and flooded the whole valley with a yellow light. All along the sides of the road were beautiful flowers, — blue, pink, white, yellow, and red. It had rained in the night; and every flower was shining with rain-drops, and as bright as if it had just been painted.

"Oh, Rob," said Nelly, "I'll tell you what we'll do: we'll pick a perfectly splendid bouquet for Ulrica. I know she'd like it. That'll show her I'm sorry I didn't stop. You pick white and blue, and I'll pick red and yellow; and then we'll put them all together. Have you got any string?"

Rob had a big piece. So they picked a big bunch of flowers; and then they sat down on a log, and Nelly arranged them in a beautiful pyramid: the white ones in the middle, then the blue, then the yellow, and then the red. Last, she put a border of the fine, green young shoots of the fir around it, and it was really superb. Then with some stout twine she swung it on her neck, so that it hung down on her shoulders behind.

"There!" she said; "I don't feel the weight of it a bit, and that 'll keep it out of the sun too."

When they reached Ulrica's house, not a window was open. Jan and Ulrica were still asleep. There had been a dance in Rosita the night before; and they had danced nearly all night, and were not likely to wake up very early after such a night as that.

"Nell, hang it on the door," said Rob, "so they 'll find it when they first open the door."

"Somebody might steal it," replied Nelly.

"Pshaw!" said Rob: "who 'd want it?"

"I 'm sure anybody would," retorted Nelly: "it 's perfectly splendid."

"You just tie it on," said Rob: "nobody 'll touch it."

Nelly had run around to the back side of the house. A small window, which opened from a sort of closet where Ulrica kept milk, was open a little way. Nelly squeezed the bouquet in, and ran back to Rob.

"I 've thrown it in at the closet window," she said. "What do you suppose she 'll think when she sees it? She 'll think fairies brought it. Ulrica believes in fairies: she told me so."

"She don't, though: does she?" exclaimed Rob. "What a goose!"

"I think it would be nice to believe in them," replied Nelly. "I do, just a little, wee wee bit. I don't mean really believe, you know; but just a little bit. I guess there used to be fairies, ever so many, many years ago;

oh! longer ago than our great, great, great grand-mother: don't you?"

"No!" said Rob, very contemptuously: "there never could have been any such thing, not since the world began. It's just made-up stories for girls."

"Oh, Rob!" cried Nelly: "you used to like to hear the story about the singing tree, the talking bird, and the laughing water; don't you know?"

"That ain't a fairy story," said Rob: "it's a — a — I forget what mamma called it. Don't you recollect how she explained it all to us? — how it was all true?"

"Oh! you mean a parable," said Nelly. "That's what mamma said, — that it meant that we should all find singing trees and talking birds and laughing water, if we loved them enough. But it's a fairy story too, besides all that."

The children had a droll time going to people's houses so early. Nobody was up. At Mrs. Clapp's, they had to pound and pound, before they could wake anybody. Then Mr. Clapp put his head out of a window to see what had happened.

"Goodness!" he said: "here are the children with the butter. How did they ever get up here so early." And he ran down to open the door.

"Ask them to stay to breakfast," said Mrs. Clapp. "The poor little things must be faint."

Nelly and Rob thanked Mr. Clapp, but said they could not stop.

"We had a splendid breakfast at home," said Rob, triumphantly.

When Mr. Clapp went back to his room, he said to his wife: —

"Poor little things, indeed! You wouldn't have called them so, if you 'd seen them. Their eyes shone like diamonds, and their cheeks were just like roses; and they looked as full of frolic as kittens. I declare I do envy March those children. That Nelly 's going to make a most beautiful woman."

Rob and Nelly reached Mr. Kleesman's door at eight o'clock. His curtains were down: no sign of life about the place.

"I say, Nell, aren't the Rosita people lazy!" exclaimed Rob. "What 'll we do now?"

"Sit down here on the step and wait," said Nelly. "He always comes out here, the first thing, and looks off down into the valley, and at the mountains. I used to see him when we were at the hotel."

How long it seemed before they heard steps inside the house; and then how much longer still before the door opened! When Mr. Kleesman saw the little figures sitting on his door-step, he started.

"Ach, my soul!" he exclaimed: "it is the little one. Good morning! good morning!" And he stooped over and kissed Nelly's forehead.

"This is my brother, sir," said Nelly. "We are all done our work, and have come to see you make the assay. You said you would show us."

"Ach! ach!" cried the old gentleman; and he looked very sorry. "It is one tousand of pities: it cannot be that I show you to-day. My chimney he did do smoke; and a man will come now this hour to take out my furnace the flue. It must be made new. Not for some day I make the assay more."

Nelly and Rob looked straight in his face without

speaking : they were too disappointed to say one word. Kind old Mr. Kleesman was very sorry for them.

"You shall again come : I will show the very first day," he said.

"Thank you, sir," said Nelly. "We always come into town Tuesdays and Fridays. We can come to your house any time." And she took hold of Rob's hand, and began to go down the steps.

"Vait! vait!" exclaimed Mr. Kleesman : "come in, and I show you some picture. You will not have seen picture of Malacca. I did live many years in Malacca."

Rob bounded at these words. His whole face lighted up.

"Oh, thank you! thank you!" he said : "that is what I like best in all the world."

"Vat is dat you like best in all the vorld : Malacca?" said the old gentleman. "And vy like you Malacca?"

Rob looked confused. Nelly came to his rescue.

"He doesn't mean that he likes Malacca, sir," she said : "only that he likes to hear about strange countries, — any countries."

"Ach!" said Mr. Kleesman : "I see. He vill be one explorer."

"Indeed I will that!" said Rob. "Just as soon as I'm a man I'm going all round this world."

Mr. Kleesman had lived ten years in Malacca. He had been in charge of tin mines there. He was an artist too, this queer old gentleman ; and he had painted a great many small pictures of things and places he saw there. These he kept in an old leather portfolio, on a shelf above his bed. This portfolio he now took down, and spread the pictures out on the bed, for Rob and Nelly to look at. There was a picture of the house he lived in while he was in Malacca. It was built of bamboo sticks and rattan, and looked like a little toy house. There was a picture of one of the queer boats a great many of the Malay people live in. Think of that: live in a boat all the time, and never have a house on land at all. These boats are about twenty feet long, and quite narrow ; at one end they have a fireplace, and at the other end their bedroom. The bedroom is nothing but a mat spread over four poles ; and under this mat the whole family sits by day and sleeps by night. They move about from river to river, and live on fish, and on wild roots which they dig on the banks of the rivers.

"My servant lif in that boat," said Mr. Kleesman. "He take wife, and go lif in a boat. His name Jinghi. I write it for you in Malay."

Then Mr. Kleesman wrote on a piece of paper some very queer characters, which Nelly said looked just like the letters on tea-chests.

"Could you write my name in Malay?" asked Nelly, timidly.

"Yes, yes," said Mr. Kleesman: "I write." And he handed Nelly a card with the following marks on it:—

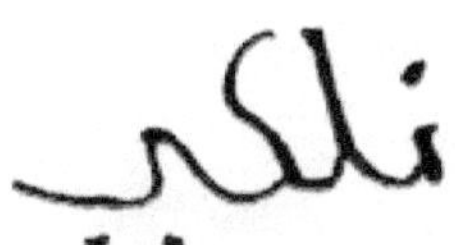

"Dear me!" said Nelly: "is that all it takes to write 'Nelly'? It is a quicker language than ours: isn't it? May I have the paper?"

"I write you better," said Mr. Kleesman; and wrote it over again on a card, which Nelly wrapped up carefully and put in her pocket.

Rob wanted to ask for his name too, but he did not dare to; and Mr. Kleesman did not think of it. He meant to be kind to Rob; but he was thinking most of the time about Nelly. Nelly seemed to him, as he said, like a little girl of Germany, and not of America; and he loved to look at her, and to hear her talk.

There were dozens of pictures in the portfolio; more than I could tell you about: pictures of streets in Malacca; pictures of the people in their gay-colored clothes, — they looked like negroes, only not quite so black; pictures of palm-trees, with cocoa-nuts growing on them; pictures of pine-apples growing; and pictures of snakes, especially one of a deadly snake, — the cobra.

"Him I kill in my own house, close by my veranda," said Mr. Kleesman: "and I draw him with all his colors, while he lie there dead, before he are cold."

While they were talking, there came in a man in rough clothes, a miner, carrying a small bag of stout canvas. He opened it, and took out a handful of stones, of a very dark color, almost black.

"Would you dig where you found that?" he said, holding out the stones to Mr. Kleesman.

Mr. Kleesman took them in his hand, looked at them attentively, and said: —

"Yes, that is goot mineral. There might be mine vere dat mineral is on top. We haf proverb in our country, 'No mine is not wort not'ing unless he haf black hat on his head.'"

The man put his stones back in his bag, nodded his head, and went out, saying : —

" I reckon we 'll buy that claim.   I 'll let you know."

A small piece of the stone had fallen on the floor. Nelly eyed it like a hawk. She was trying to remember where she had seen stones just like it. She knew she had seen them somewhere : she recollected thinking at the time how very black the stones were. She picked up the little piece of stone, and asked Mr. Kleesman if it were good for any thing.

" Oh, no, for not'ing," he said, and turned back to the pictures. Nelly's interest in the pictures had grown suddenly very small. The little black stone had set her to thinking. She put it in her pocket, and told Rob it was time to go home.

" Ven vill you again come," said Mr. Kleesman.

" Next Tuesday," replied Nelly. " That is our day."

" Perhaps it vill be done den ; perhaps not : cannot tell.   But ven is done, I show you all how I make mine assay," said Mr. Kleesman, and kissed Nelly again as he bade them good-by.

" Now we 'll go down to Ulrica's," said Nelly, " and eat our lunch on her porch. I wonder what she thought when she saw the flowers."

When the children reached Ulrica's house, they found the door open, and Ulrica sitting on the door-step, picking the feathers off a white hen. As soon as she saw Nelly, she jumped up and dropped the hen. The feathers flew in all directions ; but Ulrica did not mind : she darted up to Nelly, and threw her arms round her neck, and spoke so fast, — half in Swedish, half in broken English, — that Nelly could not understand what she said. However, she knew she was thanking her for the flowers; and so she replied : —

"I am glad you like them, Ulrica. But are you not ashamed to be asleep.at six o'clock? And Rob and I had walked all the way from the valley, and you were asleep! and Jan too!"

Then Ulrica told them about the dance; and how they had been up so late it had made them sleepy. And then she whisked up the white hen again, and began tearing off its feathers in the greatest hurry.

"Vat is it you came so soon?" she said. "You must to dinner stay. I kill dis for you, — for your dinner, I not tink you come till sun high."

"Oh, stay! stay, Nell! let's stay!" cried Rob, who had tasted Ulrica's stewed chicken once before, and had never forgotten how good it was. Ulrica always boiled her chickens with a few cranberries, as they cook it in Sweden. You would not think it would be good : but it is delicious.

Nelly thought a minute.

"It will not make us any later than if we had stayed at Mr. Kleesman's," she said. "Yes, I think we will stay."

Ulrica clapped her hands when Nelly said this.

"Goot! goot!" she said, "mine child." And she looked at Nelly with tears in her eyes, as she so often did. Then she gave Rob the book of Swedish pictures to look at, and he threw himself at full length on the floor with it. You could 'have eaten off the boards of Ulrica's house, she kept them so clean. Nelly sat in the wooden rocking-chair, and watched Ulrica getting the dinner. Pretty soon Nelly began to nod; and in a few minutes she was fast asleep. Ulrica took her up in her great, strong arms, as easily as if she were a baby, and carried her across the room and laid her on the bed.

" Hullo ! " said Rob, when he looked up from his book and saw Ulrica carrying Nelly : " what 's the matter with Nell ? "

" Sh ! sh ! make not noise," whispered Ulrica. " She haf sleep. She haf tire in the sun."

" We got up before four o'clock," whispered Rob : " but I ain't sleepy a mite."

" Dat iss, that you are man and not girl," said Ulrica ; which pleased Rob immensely.

After Ulrica had laid Nelly on the bed, she went to the big chest in the corner, and took out a fine red woollen blanket, with bright blue figures in the corners. This she spread over Nelly ; and then she stood looking at her for some minutes. Nelly's face, when she was asleep, looked much older than it really was. Her eyes were large, and her mouth was large, and her cheek-bones were high.

" Mine child ! mine child ! " muttered Ulrica, under her breath, and brushed the tears out of her eyes with the back of her hard hand, as she went back to her work.

When Nelly waked up, dinner was all ready ; and Jan and Ulrica were discussing whether they should wake Nelly or not.

" Oh ! " exclaimed Nelly, sitting up and rubbing her eyes, " how came I here ? Where 's Rob ? "

Ulrica sprang to her, and took her little hand in hers.

"Mine child, you haf sleep in chair. I bring you in mine arms here. Haf you rest? Come eat." And she picked her up again, and ran laughing back and forth two or three times across the room with her in her arms.

"She is like baby in arms: she is so light," said Ulrica to Jan in Swedish. "She has too much work."

"No, no," said Jan: "she is all right. She is at the age to be thin." But Ulrica shook her head.

How good that dinner was, and how nice it looked! There was no cloth on the table; but the wood was white as pine wood could be. On one end stood Nelly's pyramid of bright flowers; and, on the other, the great platter of stewed chicken, with the red cranberries floating in the white gravy. Then there was a big plate of rye cakes, baked in the ashes; and two pitchers of milk, one of cow's milk and one of goat's. Jan always bowed his head down and said a short blessing in Swedish, before they began to eat; and Nelly and Rob liked this, because, as Nelly said:—

"It makes you feel as if Jan were just as good as papa: doesn't it, Rob?"

And Rob said "Yes;" but in a minute afterward he added: "Don't you suppose any bad men say grace, Nell?"

"No," said Nelly; "not real grace, real earnest, like papa and Jan. Perhaps they make believe say grace."

After dinner, Nelly showed Ulrica and Jan her little card, on which Mr. Kleesman had written her name in Malay. As she took it out of her pocket, the black stone fell out and rolled away on the floor. She sprang to catch it.

"What's that?" said Rob.

"A piece of black stone," replied Nelly.

"What's it for?" said Rob.

"Oh, I just wanted it," said Nelly.

"But what did you want it for, Nell?" persisted Rob.

CHAPTER XII.

NELLY'S SILVER MINE.

NELLY would not give any reason, but put the stone carefully back in her pocket. She was determined not to tell Rob any thing about it, unless she found the stones; and the more she racked her brains the more confused she became as to where it was she had seen them. All the way home she was in a brown study, trying to think where it could have been. She was in such a brown study that she was walking straight past Lucinda's door without seeing her, when Lucinda called her name aloud.

"Why, Nelly," she said, "ain't you going to stop long enough to speak?"

"She hasn't spoken a word all the way," said Rob, discontentedly. "I can't get any thing out of her. She's real cross."

"Oh, Rob! Rob! how can you!" cried Nelly: "I wasn't cross a bit."

"Then you 're sulky," retorted Rob; "and mamma says that 's worse."

"Tut, tut," said Lucinda: "Nelly doesn't look either sulky or cross. I guess you 're mistaken, Rob."

Nelly felt a little conscience-stricken. She knew she had been thinking hard, all the last hour, about the black stones.

"Never mind, Rob!" she said: "I'll talk now." And she began to tell Lucinda all about the pictures they had seen at Mr. Kleesman's.

"Oh, yes!" said Lucinda: "I know all about those. My little sister's got one of them: Mr. Kleesman gave it to her. He's real fond of little girls. It's a picture he made of the black nurse he had for his little boy. She's got the baby in her arms."

"Why, has Mr. Kleesman got any children?" exclaimed Nelly, very much surprised.

"Oh, yes!" said Lucinda: "he's got a wife and two children over in Germany. That's what makes him so blue sometimes. His wife hates America, and won't come here."

"Then I should think he'd stay there," said Nelly.

"So should I," said Lucinda; "but they say it's awful hard to make a living over there; and he's a layin' up money here. He'll go back one of these days."

"Oh! I wish he'd take me with him," said Rob.

"Rob March! would you go away and leave papa and mamma and me?" said Nelly.

Rob hung his head. The longing of a born traveller was in his eyes.

"I should come back, Nell," he said. "I shouldn't stay: only just to see the places."

"Well," said Nelly, slowly, "I wouldn't go away from all of you, not to see the most beautiful things in all the world; not even to see the city of Constantinople."

Rob did not answer. He was afraid that there must be something wrong about him, to be so willing to do

what seemed to Nelly such a dreadful thing. To see
Constantinople, and hear the muezzins call out the
hours for prayers from the mosques, Rob would have
set off that very minute and walked all the way.

After Nelly went to bed that night, she lay awake a
long time, still thinking about the black stones. She
had put the little piece of stone on the bureau, and
while she was undressing she hardly took her eyes off
it. She recollected just how the place looked where
she saw them. It was in a ravine: there were piles of
stones in the bottom of the ravine, and a good many
scattered all along the sides. There were pine-trees
and bushes too: it was quite a shady place.

"I should know it in a minute, if I saw it again,"
said Nelly to herself; "but where, oh! where was it!"

At last, all in one second, it flashed into her mind.
It was one day when she had started for Rosita later
than usual, and had thought she would take a short cut
across the hills; but she had found it any thing but a
short cut. As soon as she had climbed one hill she
found another rising directly before her, and, between
the two, a great ravine, down to the very bottom of
which she must go before she could climb the other hill.
She had crossed several of these ravines, — she did not
remember how many, — and had come out at last on
the top of the highest of all the hills above the town:
a hill so steep that she had always wondered how the
cows could keep on their feet when they were grazing
high up on it. It was in one of these ravines that she
had seen the black stones; but in which one she could
not be sure. Neither could she recollect exactly where
she had left the road and struck out to cross the hills.

"I might walk and walk all day," thought Nelly, "and never find it. How shall I ever manage?"

Fortune favored Nelly. The very next day, Billy came to the house to ask if Mrs. March could spare Nelly to go and stay two days with Lucinda, while he was away. He had an excellent chance to make some money by taking a party of gentlemen across the valley and up into one of the passes in the range, where they were going to fish. He would be at home the second night: Nelly need stay only over one night. Lucinda was not well, and Billy did not like to leave her alone.

Mrs. March said, "Certainly: Nelly could go."

As soon as she told Nelly of the plan, Nelly's heart seemed to leap in her bosom with the thought: —

"Now that's just the chance for me to look for the stones."

She set off very early, and reached Lucinda's house before eight o'clock. After she had unpacked her bag, and arranged all her things in the little room where she was to sleep, she asked Lucinda if there were any thing she could do to help her.

Lucinda was quilting a big bedquilt, which was stretched out on chairs and long wooden bars, and took up so much of the room in the kitchen it was hard to get about.

"Mercy, no, child!" said Lucinda. "I hain't got nothin' to do but this quilt, an' I expect you ain't much of a hand at quiltin'. 'Twan't my notion to have ye come, — not but what I'm always glad to see ye; ye know that, — but I wan't afraid to be alone. But Billy he's took it into his head 'tain't safe for me to be alone here nights. Now if there's any thing ye want to do, ye jest go 'n' do it."

"Would it make any difference to you if I were gone all day, so I am here to sleep?" said Nelly.

"Why, no," replied Lucinda; "not a bit. Did ye want to go into the town?"

"No," said Nelly; "but I wanted to find a place I saw once, on the way there. It was a real deep place, almost sunk down in the ground, full of pines and bushes: a real pretty place. But it wasn't on the road. I don't know 's I can find it; but I 'd like to."

"All right," said Lucinda: "you go off. I 'll give ye some lunch in case ye get hungry. Ye won't be lonesome, will ye, without Rob?"

"Oh, no!" said Nelly: "I like to be all alone out doors."

Then she bade Lucinda good-by, and set off. For a half mile or so, she walked in the road toward Rosita. She recollected that she had passed Lucinda's before she turned off from the road. But the more she tried to remember the precise spot where she had turned off the more confused she became. At last she sprang out of the road, on the left hand side, and began running as fast as she could.

"I may as well strike off in one place as another," she thought, "since I can't remember. It cannot be very far from here."

She climbed one steep hill, and ran down into the ravine beyond it; then another hill, and another ravine, — no black stones. The sun was by this time high, and very hot. Nelly had done some severe climbing.

"On the top of the next hill I 'll eat my lunch," she thought.

The next hill was the steepest one yet. How Nelly

did puff and pant before she reached the top; and when she reached it, there was not a single tree big enough to shade her!

"Oh, dear!" said Nelly; and looked up and down the ravine, to see if she could spy any shade anywhere. A long way off to the north, she saw a little clump of pines and oaks. She walked slowly in that direction, keeping her foothold with difficulty in the rolling gravel on the steep side of the hill. Just as she reached the first oak-bush, her foot slipped, and she clutched hard at the bush to save herself: the bush gave way, and she rolled down, bush and all, to the very bottom of the ravine. Luckily, it was soft, sandy gravel all the way, and she was not in the least hurt: only very dirty and a good deal frightened.

"I'll walk along now at the bottom, where it is level," said Nelly, "and not climb up till I come to where the trees are."

There had been at some time or other a little stream in this ravine, and it was in the stony bed of it that Nelly was walking. She looked very carefully at the stones. They were all light gray or reddish colored: not a black one among them. She had in her pocket the little piece Mr. Kleesman had given her: she took it out, and looked at it again. It was totally unlike all the stones she saw about her.

"Oh, dear!" sighed Nelly: "I expect I won't find it to-day. I'll come again to-morrow. At any rate, I'll go to that nice, shady place to eat my lunch."

It was further than she thought. In Colorado, every thing looks a great deal nearer to you than it really is: the air is so thin and light that mountains twenty miles

away look as if they were not more than three or four;
and there are a great many funny stories of the mis-
takes into which travellers are led by this peculiarity of
the air. They set off before breakfast, perhaps, to walk
to a hill which looks only a little way off; and, after
they have walked an hour or two, there stands the hill,
still seeming just as far off as ever. One of the fun-
niest stories is of a man who had been cheated in this
way so often that at last he didn't believe his eyes any
longer as to whether a distance were long or short; and
one day he was found taking off his shoes and stockings to wade through a little ditch that anybody could
easily step over.

"Why, man alive!" said the people who stood by,
"what are you about? You don't need to wade a little
ditch like that! Step across it."

"Ha!" said he, "you needn't try to fool me any
more. I expect that ditch is ten feet wide."

Nelly walked on and on in the narrow stony bed of
the dried-up stream. The stones hurt her feet, but it
was easier walking than on the rolling gravel of the
steep sides above. She stopped thinking about the
black stones. She was so hot and tired and hungry, all
she thought of was getting to the trees to sit down.
At last she reached the place just below them. They
were much higher up on the hillside than she had supposed. She stood looking up at them.

"I expect I'll tumble before I get up there," she
thought. It looked about as steep as the side of the
roof to a house. But the shade was so cool and in-
viting that Nelly thought it worth trying for. Half-
way up her feet slipped, and down she came on her

knees. She scrambled up ; and, as she looked down, what should she see, in the place where her knees had pressed into the gravel, but a bit of the black stone ! At first she thought it was the very piece she had had in her pocket ; but she felt in her pocket, and there was her own piece all safe. She took it out, held the two together, looked at them, turned them over and over : yes ! the stones were really, exactly the same color ! Now she was so excited that she forgot all about the heat, and all about her hunger.

"This must be the very ravine !" she said, and began to look eagerly about her for more of the stones. Not another bit could she find ! In her eager search, she did not observe that she was slowly working down the hill, till suddenly she found herself again at the bottom of the ravine, in the dried bed of the brook. Then she stood still, and looked around her, considering what to do. At last she decided to walk on up the ravine.

"The big pile of them was right in such a deep place as this," thought Nelly : "I guess it's farther up."

It was very hard walking, and Nelly was beginning to grow tired and discouraged again, when lo ! right at her feet, in among the gray stones and the red ones, lay a small black one. She picked it up : it was of the same kind. A few steps farther on, another, and another : she began to stoop-fast, picking them up, one by one. She had one hand full : then she looked ahead, and, only a little farther on, there she saw the very place she recollected so well, — the ravine full of bushes, and low pine-trees, and piles of stones among them. She had found it ! Can you imagine how Nelly felt? You see she believed that it was just the same thing as if she had found a great sum of money. How would you feel if you should suddenly find at your feet thousands and thousands of dollars, if your father and mother were very poor, and needed money very much? I think you would feel just as Nelly did. She sat straight down on the ground, and looked at the stones, and felt as if she should cry, — she was so glad! Then the thought came into her mind : —

" Perhaps this land belongs to somebody who won't sell it. Perhaps he knows there is a mine here!" She looked all about, but she could not see any stakes set up to show that it was owned by any one : so she hoped it was not.

Now that the excitement of the search was over, she began to feel very hungry again, and ate her lunch with a great relish. The thoughtful Lucinda had put in the basket a small bottle of milk. Nelly thought she had never tasted any thing so good in her life as that milk. When you are very thirsty, milk tastes much better than water. After Nelly had eaten her lunch, she filled her basket with the black stones, and set off for home. Presently she began to wonder if she could find her way back again to the spot.

" That would be too dreadful," thought she : " to lose it, now I 've just found it." Then she recollected how, in the story of Hop o' My Thumb, it said that when he was carried off into the forest he slyly dropped beans all along the way, to mark the path, and thus found his way back, very easily by means of them. So she resolved to walk along in the bed of the stream, till it was time to climb up and strike off toward Lucinda's, and then to drop red stones all along the way

she went, till she reached the beaten road. She took
up the skirt of her gown in front, and filled it full with
little red stones. Then she trudged along with as light
a heart as ever any little girl had, scattering the stones
along the way, like a farmer planting corn.

When she reached the road, she was surprised to see
that she had come out the other side of Lucinda's house,
full quarter of a mile nearer home.

"Now this isn't anywhere near where I left the road
before," she said. "How 'll I ever tell the place?"

At first she thought she would put a bush up in the
crotch of a little pine-tree that stood just there.

"No, that won't do," she said: "the wind might
blow it out."

Then she thought she would stick the bush in the
sand; but she feared some horse or cow might munch
it and pull it up. At last she decided to break down a
small bough of the pine-tree, and leave it hanging.

"We can't make a mistake, then, possibly," she
thought.

When she reached the house, Lucinda had cleared
the bedquilt all away, and had the table set for supper,
though it was only half-past four o'clock. Nelly was
not hungry. It seemed to her only a few minutes since
she ate her lunch.

"Did you find the place, Nelly?" said Lucinda.

"Yes," said Nelly.

"Was it as pretty as it was before?" Lucinda asked.

"Oh, yes!" said Nelly; "but it was awful steep getting down to it. I kept tumbling down."

"Well, you 're the curiousest child ever was!" exclaimed Lucinda. "Anybody 'd think you got walkin'
enough in a week without trampin' off this way."

Nelly did not reply. She felt a little guilty at letting Lucinda think it was only to find a pretty place she had gone; but she was sure it would not be best to tell anybody about the black stones till she had told her father. She had hid them all in a pile near the pine-tree whose branch she had broken down; and she meant to pick them up on her way home the next night. In the morning it looked to Nelly as if it never would be night, she was in such a hurry to see her father.

"Oh, Lucinda," she said, "do give me something to do! I don't want to go off to-day. I want to stay with you." So Lucinda gave her some brown towels to hem, and also let her snap the chalked cord with which she marked out the pattern on her quilt; and, by help of these two occupations, Nelly contrived to get through the day, till four o'clock, when she set out for home. As good luck would have it, when she was within quarter of a mile from home she saw her father at work in a field. She jumped over the fence and ran to him.

"Papa! papa!" she said, breathless: "look here!" And she held up her basket of black stones. "This is the kind of stone that comes where the silver is. There is a mine underneath it always: Mr. Kleesman said so. And I've found a mine: I'll show you where it is."

Mr. March laughed very heartily.

"Why, my dear little girl!" he said, "what ever put such an idea into your head? I don't believe those stones are good for any thing."

Nelly set down her basket, and pulled her pocket-handkerchief out of her pocket: the little piece of black stone she had got from Mr. Kleesman was tied firm in one corner.

"Look at that, papa," she said, "and see if the stones in the basket are not just like it." Then she told her father all about the man's coming into the assayer's office with a bag of stones like that one, and what Mr. Kleesman said to him.

"Don't you see, papa," she said, vehemently, "that it must be a mine? Why, there are piles of it: it has all slipped down into the bottom of this steep place; there used to be a brook down there. I know it 's a mine, papa! And if I found it, it 's ours: isn't it?"

Nelly's cheeks were red, and her words came so fast they almost choked her.

"Nelly, dear," said her father, "don't you recollect that once before you thought you had found silver ore, you and Rob, up in the Ute Pass?"

Nelly looked ashamed.

"Oh, papa," she said, "that was quite different. That was when we were little things. Papa, I know this is a mine. If you 'd heard what Mr. Kleesman said, you 'd think so too. He said in his country they had a proverb, that no mine was good for any thing unless it had a black hat on its head; and that meant that there were always black stones on top like this."

Mr. March turned the little bit of black stone over and over, and examined it carefully.

"I do not know much about minerals," he said. "I think I never saw a stone like this."

"Nor I either, papa," exclaimed Nelly: "except in this one place. I know it 's a mine, and I 'll give it to you all for your own. It 's mine, isn't it, if I found it?"

"Yes, dear, it 's yours, unless somebody else had found it before you."

"I don't believe anybody had," said Nelly; "for there weren't any stakes stuck down anywhere near; and all the claims have stakes stuck down round them. Oh, papa! isn't it splendid! now we can have all the money we want."

Mr. March smiled half sadly.

"My dear little daughter," he said, "there are a great many more people who have lost all the money they had in the world trying to get money out of a mine, than there are who have made fortunes in that way. You must not get so excited. Even if there is a mine in the place where you found these stones, I don't think I have money enough to open it and take out the ore. But I will show these stones to Mr. Scholfield. He knows a great deal about mines."

"Oh, do! do! papa," exclaimed Nelly. "I know it's a mine."

"I am going down there to-night," said Mr. March. "I will carry your stones, and see what he says. In the mean time, we will not say any thing about it to anybody. You and papa will just have a little secret."

When Nelly kissed her father for good-night, she nodded at him with a meaning glance, and he returned the nod with an equally meaning one.

"What are you two plotting?" cried Mrs. March. "I see mischief in both your eyes."

"Oh, it's a little secret we have, Nelly and I," said Mr. March. "It won't last long: we'll tell you to-morrow."

It turned out that Mrs. March did not have to wait till the next day before learning the secret. Mr. March got home about midnight from Mr. Scholfield's. Mrs.

March had been sound asleep for two hours: the sound of Mr. March's steps wakened her.

"Is that you, Robert?" she called.

"Yes," he said. There was something in the tone of his voice which was so strange that it roused her instantly. She sat up straight in bed and exclaimed: —

"What is the matter?"

"Nothing," said Mr. March.

"Nonsense!" said Mrs. March: "you can't deceive me. Something has happened. Come in here this minute and tell me what it is."

Then Mr. March told her the whole story. He had taken Nelly's stones to Mr. Scholfield, who had said immediately that there was without doubt a mine in the place where that mineral was found; and, when Mr. March had told him as nearly as he could from Nelly's description where the spot was, he had said that no mines had yet been discovered very near that place, and no claims were staked out.

"Scholfield says we must go immediately and stake out our claim. He 'll go shares with me in digging; and at any rate will see what 's there," said Mr. March.

"Do you believe in it yourself, Robert?" asked Mrs. March. She was much afraid of new schemes for making money.

"Why, I can't say I'm very enthusiastic about it," replied Mr. March; "but then I don't know any thing about mines, you see. Scholfield was near wild over it. He says we 've got silver there sure."

"Will you have to find money to begin with?" asked Mrs. March, anxiously.

"Well, Sarah, considering that we haven't got any

money, I don't see how I can : do you?" laughed Mr.
March. "But Scholfield says that if I will give him
a third of the mine, he 'll take another man in, and they
two 'll pay for the working it at first. That seems very
fair : doesn't it?"

"I don't know," said Mrs. March. "If the mine
really does turn out to be very valuable, it is giving him
a good deal."

"That is true," replied Mr. March. "But, on the
other hand, perhaps it is not worth any thing; and, in
that case, Scholfield has the worst of the bargain. He
says, though, he can tell very soon. He has been in
mining a good deal; and he can make his own assays
with the blow-pipe. We 're to start very early in the
morning, and take Nelly along to show us the way.
The dear child was nearly beside herself last night."

"So that was your secret : was it?" said Mrs. March.

"Yes, and a very hard one it was for the child to
keep too," said Mr. March. "She was half crazy to
tell Rob."

"You 'll take him along too : won't you?" asked
Mrs. March.

"Oh, yes," said Mr. March : "no more secrets now ;
that is, not in this house. We won't have it talked
round, if we can help it. Scholfield says that the minute it is known we 've found silver there, those ravines
will just swarm with men prospecting for more claims."

The next day, Mr. March and Mr. Scholfield and Rob
and Nelly set out immediately after breakfast for the
ravine. They stopped at Billy's house and took him
with them. Mr. Scholfield had said to Mr. March, as
they walked along : —

"If Long Billy 'll go in with us, I 'd rather have him than any man I know about here. He 's as honest's daylight; I don't think he 's doing much this summer; I think he 'll go to work digging right away."

Wasn't Nelly a proud little girl as she walked ahead of the party? She kept hold of Rob's hand, and every now and then they would run so fast that the older people had to run, too, to keep up with them.

"How do you know the way so well, Nelly?" said Mr. Scholfield.

Nelly laughed.

"If you watch closely, you can see what I tell by," she said. "It 's in plain sight."

"Yes, plain sight! plain sight!" shouted Rob, to whom Nelly had pointed out the little red stones. "It 's out of a story."

Mr. Scholfield and Mr. March and Billy all looked around, perplexed; but they could see nothing.

"Oh, tell us the secret, Guide," said Mr. March. "We are stupid: we can't find it out."

Then Nelly told them; and as soon as she pointed to the red stones they wondered very much that they had not noticed them before.

It seemed a very short way to the ravine, this time. Nelly had reached it before she thought of its being near.

"Why, here it is," she said; "I didn't think we were half way there."

Then she and Rob sat on the ground and watched the others. Rob was very quiet. He was a good deal overawed at the idea of a real silver mine all for their own.

"Do you suppose it's right here, right under our feet, Nell?" said he, stamping his foot on the ground.

"I dare say," said Nelly. "Perhaps it is all over round here: some of them are as big as a mile."

"I wonder if they'll let us go down as often as we want to," said Rob. "They'll have to, won't they, if it's our own mine?"

"That'll be for papa to say," answered Nelly, decidedly. "I've given it to him. It's his mine."

While the children were thus building their innocent air-castles in a small way, the brains of the older people were building no less actively, and on a larger scale. Both Billy and Mr. Scholfield were much excited. Billy ran from spot to spot, now hammering a stone in two with his hammer, now digging fiercely into the ground with his pick-axe. Mr. Scholfield went about picking up the black stones, and piling them together, till he had quite a monument of them.

"I declare," he said at last, "it beats me that this place hasn't ever been found before, much's this country's been prospected over and over. I don't know what to make of it. But there isn't a sign of a claim here for miles: I know that."

"Well, I'll tell yer what I'm a thinkin'," said Billy. "I'm a thinkin' that's fur back's them fust prospectin' days there was a creek in here; 'n' thet's the reason there didn't nobody look here. I've heern it said hundreds o' times in town thet there wan't no use lookin' along these ridges; they'd all been looked over thorough, 'n' there wan't nothin' in 'em. But we've struck a silver mine, sure: I hain't any doubt of it. Let's name her 'The Little Nelly.'"

Mr. March's face grew red. He did not like the idea of having a mine called after Nelly; but he did not want to hurt Billy's feelings. Before he could speak, Mr. Scholfield cried out : —

"Good for you, Billy! That's what we'll call it! That's a name to bring good luck. 'The Little Nelly!' and may she turn out not so 'little,' after all; and the first bucketful of ore we draw up, Nelly, we'll drink your health, and christen the mine."

Nelly did not quite understand what all this meant.

"Did you mean that I am to name the mine, sir?" she said.

"No," said Mr. Scholfield : "we meant that we were going to name it for you, by your name. But you can name it, if you like. That would be luckier still. Don't you like to have it called by your name?"

Nelly hesitated.

"I think I would rather not have it named after me," she said : "some of the mines have such dreadful names. But I know a name I think would be a real pretty name."

"What's that," said her father.

"The Good Luck," said Nelly.

Billy clapped his knee hard with his hand.

"By jingo!" said he, "that's the best name ever was given to a mine yet. 'The Good Luck' it shall be; and good luck it was to you, Nelly, the day you struck it. Old Pine he said, one day last spring, mebbe you'd find a mine, when I was a tellin' him how you 'n' Rob was allers lookin' for one."

"But I wasn't looking for this, Billy," said Nelly. "I gave up looking for one a long time ago, when we began to sell the eggs. It was just an accident that I happened to remember the black stones in here."

"That's the way some of the best mines have been found," said Mr. Scholfield: "just by sheer accident. There was a man I knew, in California, had his mule run away from him one day: it was somewhere in that Tuolomne region; and if that mule didn't run straight down into a gulch that was just washed full of free gold, — and the fellow had been walking in it some time before he noticed it! There's a heap o' luck in this world."

"Yes," said Mr. March, "there's a great deal of luck; but there is a great deal which is set down to luck which isn't luck. Now, if my little girl here hadn't had the good-will and the energy to try to earn some money for her mother and me, she wouldn't have been searching for a short cut to Rosita over these hills, and would never have found this mine."

"That's so," said Mr. Scholfield, looking admiringly at Nelly. "She's a most uncommon girl, that Nelly of yours. I think we ought to call the mine after her: it's hers."

"No," said Mr. March: "I like her name for it best. Let us call it 'The Good Luck.'"

Mrs. March was watching for her husband and children when they came down the lane. She had been much more excited about the silver mine than she had confessed to Mr. March. All day long she had been unable to keep it out of her mind. The prospect was too tempting. "Why should it not have happened to us, as well as to so many people," she thought. "Oh! if we only could have just money enough to give Rob and

Nelly a good education, I would not ask for any thing
more. And, even if this is not very much of a mine,
it might give us money enough for that." With such
hopes and imaginations as these Mrs. March's mind
had been full all day long; and, when she saw Mr.
March and Rob and Nelly coming toward the house,
she felt almost afraid to see them, lest she should see
disappointment written on their faces.

Not at all. Rob and Nelly came bounding on ahead,
and, as they drew near the door, they shouted out:—

"The Good Luck! The Good Luck! It is named
'The Good Luck.'"

"They wanted to call it 'The Little Nelly,' but Nelly
wouldn't," said Rob. "I don't see why. If I'd found
it, I'd have called it 'The Rob,' I know. They didn't
ask me to let them call it for me. If they had, they
might and welcome."

"It is really a mine, then?" said Mrs. March, looking at her husband.

"Yes, Sarah, I think it is," he replied. "If Scholfield and Billy know,—and they seem to be very sure,
—there is good promise of silver there; and Nelly
herself has named it 'The Good Luck.'"

"Oh, Nelly! did you, really?" exclaimed Mrs.
March. "You dear child!" And she threw both
arms around Nelly, and gave her a great hug. "That's
a lovely name. I do believe it will bring luck."

"I didn't want it named after me," said Nelly. "It
isn't as if it was a live thing —"

"Subjunctive mood, dear! 'as if it were,'" interrupted Mrs. March.

"As if it were," repeated Nelly, looking confused.

"I wish they'd left the subjunctive mood out of the grammar. I shan't ever learn it! It isn't as if it were a live thing, like a baby or a kitten. I wouldn't mind having such things called after me, but some of the mines have the awfullest names, mamma: real wicked names, that I shouldn't dare to say."

"Well, they'll call it after you, anyhow, Nell," cried Rob. "Billy said so, coming home."

"They won't either," said Nelly, "when it was my own mine, only I gave it to papa, and I asked them not to; I think it would be real mean."

"Oh, I don't mean Mr. Scholfield and Billy," said Rob: "they called it 'The Good Luck' as soon as you said so; but the men round town. They'll hear it was you found it; and they'll call it 'The Nelly,' always: you see if they don't."

"Rob, don't tease your sister so," said Mrs. March.

"Why, does that tease you, Nell?" asked Rob, pretending to be very innocent. "I was only telling you what Billy said."

"I don't believe it, anyway," said Nelly: "do you, papa?"

"No," replied Mr. March. "I do not see why they should give it any other name than the one the owners give it."

"Well, you'll see," said Rob. "There are ever so many mines that go by two or three different names. There's one way off in the north somewhere, where Billy used to haul ore, is called 'Bobtail,' some of the time, and 'Miss Lucy,' some of the time. They tried to change 'Bobtail' into 'Miss Lucy,' and they couldn't."

" Couldn't!" exclaimed Nelly: " what do you mean by that?"

" Why, the people wouldn't," said Rob, saucily: " that's all."

" 'That's all' about a great many things in this world, Rob," laughed his mother.   " 'Couldn't' is very apt to be only another word for 'wouldn't' with a little boy I know."

Rob laughed, and left off teasing Nelly about the name of her mine.

CHAPTER XIII.

"THE GOOD LUCK."

BILLY went to work the very next day at "The Good Luck." First, he put up a little hut, which looked more like an Indian wigwam than any thing else. This was for him and Mr. Scholfield to sleep in.

"We can't take time to go home nights till we get this thing started," said Billy. "If we 've got ore here, the sooner we get some on 't out the better; an' if we hain't got ore here, the sooner we find that out the better."

All day long, day after day, Billy and Mr. Scholfield dug, till they had a big hole, as deep as a well, dug in the ground. Then they put a windlass at the top, with a long rope fastened to it, and a bucket on the end of the rope. This bucket they lowered down into the hole, just as you lower a water-bucket down into a well; then they filled it full of the stones which they thought had silver in them, and then turned the windlass and drew it up.

Mr. Scholfield pounded some of these stones very fine, and melted it with his blow-pipe, and got quite big buttons of silver out of it. He gave some of these to Mr. March. When he showed these to Nelly, she exclaimed: —

"Oh! these are a great deal bigger than any I saw

in Mr. Kleesman's office.　Our mine must be a good one."

Mr. Scholfield was in great glee.　He made the most extravagant statements, and talked very foolishly about the mine : said he would not take half a million of dollars for his third of it ; and so on, till old, experienced miners shook their heads and said he was crazy.　But, when they saw the round buttons of shining silver which he had extracted from the stones, they stopped shaking their heads, and thought perhaps he was right.　The fame of " The Good Luck " spread all over town ; and, as Billy had said there would be, there were many who persisted in calling the mine " The Nelly."　Almost everybody in Rosita knew Nelly by sight by this time ; and it gave the mine much greater interest in their eyes that it had been found by this good, industrious little girl, whom everybody liked.　Whenever Nelly went to town now, people asked her about her mine.　She always answered : —

" It isn't my mine : it is my papa's."

" But you found it," they would say.

" I found the black hat it wore on its head," was Nelly's usual reply : " that is all.　Mr. Scholfield and Billy found the silver."

It happened that it was nearly three weeks before Rob and Nelly went to Mr. Kleesman's house again. They had now a new interest, which made them hurry through with all they had to do in Rosita, so as to have time on their way home to stop at " The Good Luck," and watch Billy and Mr. Scholfield at work.　It was an endless delight to them to see the windlass wind, wind, wind, and watch the heavy bucket of stone slowly coming up to the mouth of the hole. Then Billy would let Rob take the bucket and empty it on the pile of shining gray ore which grew higher and higher every day. Sometimes the children stayed here so late that it was after dark when they reached home ; and at last Mrs. March told them that they must not go to the mine every time they went to Rosita : it made their walk too long. She said they might go only every other time.

"Let's go Tuesdays," said Rob.

"Why?" said Nelly.

"It never seems half so long from Tuesday till Friday as it does from Friday to Tuesday," said Rob.

"Why, why not?" asked Nelly.

"Oh, I don't know," said Rob. "Sunday's twice as long as any other day : I guess that's it."

"But you 've got the Sunday each week," exclaimed Nelly : "it isn't any shorter from Tuesday to Tuesday than from Friday to Friday : what a silly boy ! The Sunday comes in all the same. Don't you see?"

Rob looked puzzled.

"I don't care," he said : "it seems ever so much shorter."

The first day that they were not to go to the mine, Rob said : —

"See here, Nell : if we can't go to the mine, let's go and see old Mr. Kleesman. His furnace must be done by this time. Perhaps he 'll be making an assay to-day."

"Oh, good !" said Nelly. "I declare I 'd almost forgotten all about him : hadn't you?"

"No, indeed !" said Rob : "I liked the mine better ; but let's go there to-day."

"And we'll go and eat our lunch at Ulrica's too," said Nelly. "We haven't taken it there for ever so long: she said so Tuesday. We'll go to-day."

"So we will," said Rob. "Perhaps she'll have stewed chicken."

"Oh, for shame, Rob!" said Nelly.

"What for?" said Rob: "I don't see any shame. Where's the shame?"

"Shame to think about something to eat when you go to see people," replied Nelly.

"Now, Nell March, didn't you think of it, honest Indian?" said Rob.

"Well, it's worse to say it," stammered Nelly. "Perhaps I did think of it, just a little, little bit; but I always try not to."

"Ha! ha! Miss Nell! I've caught you this time; and I don't think it's a bit worse to say it: so, there! Stewed chicken! stewed chicken!" And Rob danced along in front of Nelly, shouting the words in her very face. Nelly could not help laughing, though she was angry.

"Rob," she said, "you can be the worst torment I ever saw."

"That's only because you haven't had any other torment but me," cried Rob, still dancing along backwards in front of Nelly.

"Hullo! hullo!" said a loud, gruff voice just behind him: "don't run me down, young man! Which side of the way will you have, or will you have both?"

Very much confused, Rob turned and found himself nearly in the arms of an old man with rough clothes on, but with such a nice, benevolent face that Rob knew he was not going to be angry with him.

"I beg your pardon, sir," he said. "I didn't see you."

"Naturally you didn't, since you have no eyes in the back of your head," said the old man. "Do you always walk backwards, or is it only when you are teasing your sister?"

Nelly hastened to defend Rob.

"Oh, sir," she said, "he was not really teasing me: he was only in fun."

The old man smiled and nodded.

"That's right! that's right!" he said.

They had just now reached Mr. Kleesman's steps. Rob sprang up, two steps at a time.

"What!" said the old man, "are you going in here? So am I." And they all went in together.

Mr. Kleesman was very glad to see Nelly.

"I haf miss you for many days," he said. "Vy is it you not come more to see assay?"

"We have been very busy," said Nelly: "and have not stayed in town any longer than we needed to sell our things."

"I know! I know!" said Mr. Kleesman: "you haf been at the Goot Luck mine!"

"Why, who told you about it?" exclaimed Rob.

"Ach!" said Mr. Kleesman, "you tink dat mines be to be hid in dis town? Not von but knows of 'Goot Luck,' dat the little maid-child haf found;" and he looked at Nelly and smiled affectionately. "And not von but iss glad," he added, patting her on the head.

Then he turned to the old man who had come in with the children, and said, politely: —

"Vat can I do for you, sir?"

The man took off his hat and sat down, and pulled out of his pocket a little bag of stones, and threw it on the table.

"Tell me if that's worth any thing," he said.

Mr. Kleesman took a small stone out of the bag, and called : —

"Franz! Franz!"

Franz was Mr. Kleesman's servant. He tended the fires, and pounded up the stones fine in an iron mortar, and did all Mr. Kleesman's errands.

Franz came running; and Mr. Kleesman gave him the stone, and said something to him in German. Franz took the stone, and disappeared in the back room.

"After he haf make it fine," said Mr. Kleesman, "I shall assay it for you." Then, turning to Nelly and Rob, he said : —

"Can you stay? I make three assay now in three cups."

"Yes, indeed, we can!" said Nelly: "thank you! That is what we came for. We thought the furnace must be mended by this time."

While Franz was pounding the stone, the old man told Mr. Kleesman about his mine. Nelly listened with attentive ears to all he said: but Rob was busy studying the pretty little brass scales in the glass box. The man said that he and two other men had been at work for some months at this mine. The other two men were sure the ore was good; one of them had tried it with the blow-pipe, he said, and got plenty of silver.

"But I just made up my mind," said the man, "that, before I put any more money in there, I'd come to somebody that knew. I ain't such a sodhead as to think I can tell so well about things as a man that's studied 'em all his life ; and I asked all about, and they all said, 'Kleesman's the man: he'd give you an honest assay of his own mind if he could get at it and weigh it.'"

Mr. Kleesman laughed heartily. He was much pleased at this compliment to his honesty.

"Yes, I tell you all true," he said. "If it be bad, or if it be good, I tell true."

"That's what I want," said the man.

Then Franz came in with the fine-powdered stone in a paper. Mr. Kleesman took some of it and weighed it in the little brass scales. Then he took some fine-powdered lead and weighed that. Then he mixed the fine lead and the powdered stone together with a knife.

"I take twelve times as much lead as there iss of the stone," he said.

"What is the lead for?" asked Nelly.

"The lead he will draw out of the stone all that are bad : you will see."

Then he put the powdered stone and the lead he had mixed together into a little clay cup, and covered it over with more of the fine-powdered lead. Then he put in a little borax.

"He helps it to melt," he said.

Then he went through into the back room, carrying this cup and two others which were standing on the table already filled with powder ready to be baked.

Rob and Nelly and the old man followed him. He opened the door of the little oven and looked in : it was glowing red hot. Then he took up each cup in tongs, and set it in the oven. When all three were in,

he took some burning coals from the fire above, and put
them in the mouth of the oven, in front of the cups.

"Dat iss dat cold air from door do not touch dem,"
he said. Then he shut the door tight, and said: —

"Now ve go back. Ve vait fifteen minute."

He held his watch in his hand, so as not to make a
mistake. When the fifteen minutes were over, he
opened the oven-door to let a current of cool air blow
above the little cups. Nelly stood on a box, as she
had before, and looked in through the queer board with
holes in it for the eyes. The metal in the little cups
was bubbling and as red as fire. Rob tried to look, but
the heat hurt his eyes so he could not bear it.

"Ven de cold air strike the cups," said Mr. Kleesman, "then the slag are formed."

"Oh, what is slag?" cried Rob.

"All that are bad go into the slag," said Mr. Kleesman.

Then he put on a pair of thick gloves, and a hat on
his head, and went close up to the fiery oven door, and
took out the cups, and emptied them into little hollow
places in a sheet of zinc. The instant the hot metal
touched the cool zinc, it spread out into a fiery red
rose.

"Oh, how lovely!" cried Nelly.

"By jingo!" said Rob.

Even while they were speaking, the bright red rose
turned dark, — hardened, — and there lay three shining
buttons, flat and round. Their rims looked like dark
glass; and in their centres was a bright, silvery spot.

Mr. Kleesman took a hammer and pounded off all
this dark, shining rim. Then he pounded the little

silvery buttons which were left into the right shape to
fit into some tiny little clay cups he had there. They
were shaped like a flower-pot, but only about an inch
high.

"Now these must bake one-half hour again," he said ;
and put them into the oven. Pretty soon he opened
the oven-door to let the cold air in again, as he had
done before. That would make all the lead go off, he
said : it would melt into the little cups, and leave nothing but the pure silver behind.

"Now vatch! vatch!" he said to Nelly. "In von
minute you shall see a flash in de cups, like lightning,
just one second : it are de last of de lead driven avay ;
den all is done."

Nelly watched with all her might. Sure enough,
flash! flash! flash! in all three of the cups it went ;
the cups were fiery red ; as Mr. Kleesman took them
out, they turned yellow ; they looked like the yolk of a
hard-boiled egg hollowed out, — and there, in the bottom of each, lay a tiny, tiny silver button! Mr. Kleesman carried them into the front room and weighed
them. Two of them were heavy enough to more than
weigh down the little button which was always kept in
the left-hand scale. That showed that the ore had
silver enough in it to make it worth while to work it.
The third one was so small you could hardly see it.
That was the one which belonged to the old man.

"Your ore are not wort not'ing," said Mr. Kleesman to him. Nelly looked sorrowfully at the old man's
face ; but he only smiled, and said : —

"Well, that's just what I've suspicioned all along.
I didn't believe much in all that blow-pipe work. I'm

out about a hundred dollars, — that's all, — not countin'
my time any thing. It's the time I grudge more'n the
money. Much obliged to ye, sir." And the philo-
sophical old fellow handed out his five dollars to pay
for the assay, and walked off as composedly as if he
had had good news instead of bad.

Nelly looked very grave. She was thinking of what
her father had said about Mr. Scholfield's blow-pipe.

"Perhaps Mr. Scholfield was all wrong too, just like
this other man. Perhaps our mine isn't good for any
thing."

Nelly's face was so long that kind-hearted Mr. Kleesman noticed it, and said : —

"You haf tired : it are too long that you look at too
many t'ings. You shall sit here and be quiet."

"Oh, no, thank you," said Nelly : "I am not tired.
I was only thinking."

Mr. Kleesman really loved Nelly, and it distressed
him to see her look troubled. He wanted to know what
troubled her ; but he did not like to ask. He looked
at her very sympathizingly, and did not say any thing.

"Is not a blow-pipe good for any thing to tell about
silver?" said Nelly, presently.

"Oh, ho !" thought Mr. Kleesman to himself : "now
I know what the little wise maiden is thinking : it is
her father's mine. It did not escape her one word
which this man said."

But he replied to her question as if he had not thought
any thing farther.

"Not very much : the blow-pipe cannot tell true. It
tell part true : not all true."

Nelly sighed, and said : —

"Come, Rob: it is time for us to go. We are very much obliged to you for letting us see the assay. It is the most wonderful thing I ever saw. It is just like a fairy story. Come, Rob."

Rob also thanked Mr. Kleesman; and they went slowly down the steps.

"Stay! stay!" said Mr. Kleesman. "Little one, vill you not ask your father that he send me some of the ore from the Goot Luck mine? I shall assay it for you, and I vill tell you true how much silver there should come from each ton, that you are not cheated at the mill vere dey take your ore to make in de silver brick."

Nelly ran back to Mr. Kleesman, and took his hand in hers.

"Oh, thank you! thank you!" she said: "that was what I was thinking about. I was thinking what if our mine should turn out like that man's that was here this morning."

"Oh, no: I t'ink not. Every von say it iss goot, very goot," said Mr. Kleesman. "But I like to make assay. You tell your father I make it for not'ing: I make it for you."

"I will tell him," said Nelly; "and I am sure he will be very glad to have you do it. I will bring some of the ore next time. Good-by!" And she and Rob ran off very fast, for it was past Ulrica's dinner-time.

When they reached the house, it was shut up: the curtains down, and the door locked. Ulrica had gone away for the day, to do washing at somebody's house; and Jan had taken his dinner to the mill. The children sat on the doorstep and ate their lunch, much disappointed. Then they tried to think of some way to let Ulrica know they had been there.

"If we only had a card such as ladies used to leave for mamma when she was away," said Rob, "that would be nice."

"I'll tell you," said Nelly: "we'll prick our names on two of the cottonwood leaves in the top of your hat: they'll do for cards."

Rob always put a few green leaves in the top of his hat, to make his head cool. It keeps out the heat of the sun wonderfully. One variety of the cottonwood leaf is a smooth, shining leaf, about as large as a lilac leaf, and much like it in shape. This was the kind Rob had in his hat. Nelly picked out the two biggest ones, and then with a pin she slowly pricked " Nelly " on one and " Rob " on the other.

"There!" she said, when they were done: "aren't those nice cards? Now I'll pin them on the door, close above the handle, so that Ulrica can't open the door without seeing them."

"What fun!" said Rob. "I say, Nell, you're a capital hand to think of things."

Nelly laughed.

"Why, Rob," she said, "sometimes you find fault with me just because I do ' think of things,' as you call it."

"Oh, those are different things," said Rob. "You know what I mean: bothers. Such things as these cards are fun."

When Ulrica came home at night from her washing, she was very tired ; and she put her hand on the handle of her door and turned it almost without looking, and

did not at first see the green leaves. But, as the door
swung in, she saw them.

"Ah, den! vat is dat?" she exclaimed. "Dem boys
at deir mischiefs again!" And she was about to tear
the leaves down angrily, when she caught sight of the
fine-pricked letters. She looked closer, and made out
the word "Nelly;" then on the other one "Rob."

"Ach! mine child! mine child!" she exclaimed.
"She haf been here: she make that the green leaf say
her name to me. Mine blessed child!" And Ulrica
took the leaves and laid them away in a little yellow
carved box, in the shape of a tub, which she had
brought from Sweden. When Jan sat down at his
supper, she took them out, and laid them by his plate,
and told him where she found them. Jan was much
pleased, and looked a long time curiously at the pricked
letters. Then he laid the leaves back in the box, and
said to Ulrica : —

"Why do you not make for the child a gown, such
as the Swede child wears, of the blue and the red?
Think you not it would please her?"

"Not to wear," said Ulrica. "She would not like
that every one should gaze."

"Oh, no, not to wear for people to see," said Jan;
"but to keep because it is strange and different from
the dress of this country. The rich people that did
come travelling to Sweden did all buy clothes like the
Swede clothes, to take home to keep and to show."

"Yes! yes! I will!" exclaimed Ulrica, much delighted at the thought; "but it shall have no buttons:
we cannot find buttons."

"Wilhelm Sachs will make them for me out of tin:

that will do very well, just for a show," said Jan. "It is not for money; but only that they shine and be round."

So after supper Ulrica took the roll of blue cloth out of the chest, and began to measure off the breadths.

"How tell you that it is right?" said Jan.

"By my heart," said the loving Ulrica: "I know mine child her size by my heart. It vill be right."

But for all that it turned out that she cut the breadths too long, and had to hem a deep hem at the bottom; which wasted some of the cloth, and vexed Ulrica's economical soul. But we have not come to that yet. We must go home with Nelly and Rob.

Nelly had made up her mind not to tell her father any thing about Mr. Kleesman's proposal to make the assay until she could see him all alone; but she forgot to tell Rob not to speak of it; and they had hardly taken their seats at the tea-table when Rob exclaimed: —

"Papa! don't you think Mr. Kleesman says a blow-pipe isn't good for any thing to tell about silver with. And there was a man there to-day, with ore out of his mine, and it hadn't any silver at all in it, — not any to speak of, — and he thought it was splendid: he and two other men; they had tried it with a blow-pipe."

Mr. Scholfield was taking tea with the Marches this night. He listened with a smile to all Rob said. Then he said: —

"That 's just like Kleesman. He thinks nobody but he can tell any thing. It 's the money he 's after. I see through him. Now I know I can make as good an assay with my blow-pipe as he can with all his little cups and saucers and gimcracks, any day."

Nelly grew very red. She did not like to hear Mr. Kleesman so spoken of. She opened her mouth to speak: then bit her lips, and remained quiet.

"What is it, Nelly?" said her father.

"Nothing, sir," replied Nelly: "only I don't think Mr. Kleesman is like that. He is very kind."

"Oh, yes, he's kind enough," said Mr. Scholfield: "he's a good-natured fellow. But it's all moonshine about his being the only one who can make assays. There's a plenty of mines working here to-day that haven't ever had any assay made except by the blow-pipe. There's no use in paying a fellow three or four or five dollars for doing what you can do yourself."

"But that man said —" began Rob.

"Be quiet now, Rob," said Mr. March. "We won't talk any more about it now."

After Mr. Scholfield had gone away, Mr. March called Nelly out of the room.

"Come walk up and down in the lane with me, Nell," he said, "and tell me all about what happened at Mr. Kleesman's."

Then Nelly told her father all about it, from beginning to end.

"Upon my word, Nell," he said, "you seem to have studied the thing carefully. I should think you could almost make an assay yourself."

"I guess I could if I had the cups and things," said Nelly: "I recollect every thing he did. But, papa, won't you let him take some ore from our mine, and let him see if it is good by his way? He won't ask us any thing: he said he was doing it every day, and he could put in one more cup as well as not. Oh, do, papa!"

"I 'll think about it," said Mr. March.

That night he talked it over with Mrs. March, and she was as anxious as Nelly that he should let Mr. Kleesman make the assay. This decided Mr. March; and the next morning he said to Nelly: —

"Well, Nelly, you shall have your way, — you and mamma. I will take some of the ore to your old friend. I shall go up with you to-morrow myself, and carry it. I do not like to send it by you."

"Oh, good! good!" cried Nelly, and jumped up and down, and ran away to find Rob and tell him that their father would walk into town with them the next day.

When Nelly walked into Mr. Kleesman's room, holding her father by the hand, she felt very proud. She had always thought her father handsomer and nicer to look at than any other man in the world; and, when she said to Mr. Kleesman, "Here is my father, sir," this pride was so evident in her face that it made Mr. Kleesman laugh. It did not make him love Nelly any less, however. It only made him think sadly of the little girl way off in Germany, who would have just as much pride in his face as Nelly did in her father's. Mr. Kleesman's love for Nelly made him treat Mr. March like an old friend.

"I am glad to see you here," he said. "I haf for your little girl von great friendship: she iss so goot. I say often to myself, she haf goot father, goot mother. She iss not like American childs I haf seen."

Mr. March was glad to have Nelly liked; but he did not wish to have her praised in this open way. So he said, very quickly: —

"Yes, Nelly is a good girl. I have come to talk to

you, Mr. Kleesman, about our mine : perhaps you have heard of it, — 'The Good Luck.'"

"Yes: I hear it is goot mine, very goot," replied Mr. Kleesman. "I ask the child to bring me ore. I assay it for you. It vill be pleasure to me."

"That is what I was going to ask you to do," said Mr. March. "I would like to know the exact truth about it before I go any farther. Scholfield is pressing me to put in machinery; but I do not like to spend money on it till I am sure."

"Dat iss right," said Mr. Kleesman. "Vait! vait! It is always safe to vait. Haf you brought with you the ore?"

"Yes, I have it here," replied Mr. March, and took a small bag of it from his pocket. Mr. Kleesman examined it very carefully. His face did not look cheerful. He took piece after piece out of the bag, and, after examining them, tossed them on the table with a dissatisfied air.

"Is it all as dis?" he said.

"Yes, about like that," replied Mr. March.

Nelly watched Mr. Kleesman's face breathlessly.

"I know he don't think it is good," she whispered to Rob.

"I cannot tell till I make assay," said Mr. Kleesman. "But I t'ink it not so very good. To-morrow I vill know. To-day I cannot do. I send you vord."

"Oh, no, you need not take that trouble," said Mr. March. "The children will be in day after to-morrow. They can call."

"No, I send you vord," repeated Mr. Kleesman. "I send you vord. Dere are plenty vays. I send you vord to-morrow night. Alvays men go past my door down to valley. I send you vord."

"What do you suppose is the reason he did not want us to call for it?" said Rob, as they walked down street.

"I know," said Nelly.

"What?" said Rob, sulkily. His pride was a little touched at Mr. Kleesman's having so evidently preferred to send the message by some one else rather than by them.

"Because," said Nelly, "he is so kind he doesn't want to tell us to our face the mine isn't good."

"Oh, Nell!" exclaimed Rob, in a tone of distress, "do you think it's that?"

"I know it's that," said Nelly, calmly. "It couldn't be any thing else: you'll see. He doesn't believe that ore's good for any thing. I know by his face he doesn't. I've seen him look so at ore before now."

"Oh, Nell!" cried Rob, "what'll we do if it turns out not to be good for any thing?"

"Do!" said Nelly; "why, we shall do just what we did before. But I'm awful sorry I ever told papa about the old thing. It's too mean!"

"We haven't spent any money on it: that's one good thing," said Rob.

"Yes," said Nelly; "and it's lucky we happened in at Mr. Kleesman's just when we did: there was some good luck in that, if there isn't any in the mine."

"But I don't see why you're so sure, Nell," cried Rob: "Mr. Kleesman said he couldn't tell till he tried it."

"Well, I *am* sure," said Nelly: "just as sure's any thing. I know Mr. Kleesman thinks it isn't good for any thing; and if he thinks so just by looking at the stone, won't he think so a great deal more when he has burnt all the bad stuff away?"

"Well, anyhow, I shan't give up till he sends 'vord,' as he calls it," said Rob. "I guess it 'll be good for a little if it isn't for much. Everybody says Mr. Scholfield knows all about mines."

"You 'll see!" was all Nelly replied; and she trudged along with a very grave and set look on her face. Mr. March was to stay in town later, to see some farmers who were coming in from the country: so the children had a lonely walk home. They stopped only a moment at Ulrica's and at Lucinda's; and both Ulrica and Lucinda saw that something was wrong. But Nelly had cautioned Rob to say nothing about the ore, and she herself said nothing about it; and so the two faithful hearts that loved them could only wonder what had happened to cloud the usually bright little faces.

When it drew near to sunset, the time at which the farmers who had been up into Rosita usually returned into the valley, Rob and Nelly went down the lane to the gate, to watch for the messenger from Mr. Kleesman. The sun set, and the twilight deepened into dusk, and no messenger came. Several farm wagons passed; and, as each one approached, the children's hearts began to beat quicker, thinking that the wagon would stop, and the man would hand out a letter; but wagon after wagon passed, — and no letter. At last Nelly said : —

"It is so dark we really must go in, Rob. I don't believe it 's coming to-night."

"Perhaps his furnace is broken again, and he couldn't do it to-day," said Rob.

"Perhaps so," said Nelly, drearily. "Oh, dear! I wish the old mine was in Guinea. Weren't we happier without it, Rob?"

"Yes, lots!" said Rob; "and we're making a good lot of money off the butter and eggs and trout. I don't care about the old mine."

"I do!" said Nelly: "if it was a good mine — if it were a good mine, I mean, because then we could all have every thing we want, and papa wouldn't have to work. But I know this mine isn't a good one, and I ain't ever going to look for another 's long as I live. Nor I won't tell of one, if I find it, either!"

"Pshaw, Nell! don't be a goose," said Rob. "If this one isn't good for any thing, it don't prove that the next one won't be. I'll find all I can, and try 'em one after the other."

"Well, you may: I won't!" said Nelly.

Bedtime came: still no letter. All through the evening, the children were listening so closely for the sound of wheels, that they could not attend to any thing else. Even Mr. March found it rather hard to keep his thoughts from wandering down the lane in expectation of the message from Rosita. But it did not come; and the whole family finally went to bed with their suspense unrelieved.

The next morning, while they were sitting at breakfast, and not thinking about the message at all, a man knocked at the door and handed in a letter. He had brought it from Rosita the night before, but had forgotten all about it, he said, till he was a mile past the house; and he thought as he would be going in again early in the morning, it would do as well to bring it then.

"Oh, certainly, certainly!" said Mr. March: "it was not on any pressing business. Much obliged to you, sir. Sit down and have some breakfast with us: won't you?"

The man was an old bachelor, — a Mr. Bangs, — who lived alone on a farm some six miles north of Mr. March's. He looked longingly at the nice breakfast, and said to Mrs. March: —

"Well, I had what I called a breakfast before I left home; but your coffee does smell so tempting, I think I'll take a cup, — since you're so kind."

Then he drew up a chair and sat down, and began to eat and drink as if he had just come starved from a shipwreck.

Mr. March laid the letter down by his plate, and went on talking with Mr. Bangs as politely as if he had nothing else to do.

Rob and Nelly looked at the letter; then at each other; then at their father and mother: Rob fidgeted on his chair. Finally, Nelly put down her knife and fork, and said she did not want any more breakfast. Mrs. March could hardly keep from laughing to see the children's impatience, though she felt nearly as impatient herself. At last she said to the children: —

"You may be excused, children. Run out into the barn and see if you can find any eggs!" Rob and Nelly darted off, only too glad to be free.

"Did you ever see such a pig!" exclaimed Rob. "He'd had his breakfast at home? I don't see what made papa ask him!"

"He ate as if he were half starved," said Nelly. "I guess old bachelors don't cook much that's good. Oh! I do wish he'd hurry."

Mr. Bangs had no idea of hurrying. It was a long time since he had tasted good home-made bread and butter and coffee, and he knew it would be a still longer time before he tasted them again. He almost wished he had two stomachs, like a camel, and could fill them both. At last, when he really could eat no more, and Mrs. March had poured out for him the last drop out of the coffee-pot, he went away. The children were watching in the barn to see him go. As soon as he had passed the barn-door, they scampered back to the house.

Their father had the open letter under his hand, on the table. He was looking at their mother, and there were tears in her eyes. He turned to the children, and said, in a voice which he tried hard to make cheerful : —

"Well, Nelly, are you ready for bad news?"

"Oh, yes!" interrupted Nelly, "indeed I am, all ready. I knew it would be bad news! I knew it when we were at Mr. Kleesman's."

"Pshaw!" said Rob, and sat down in a chair, and twirled his hat over and over between his knees: "I don't care! I'm going fishing." And he jumped up suddenly, and ran out of the room.

Mrs. March laughed in spite of herself.

"That is to hide how badly he feels," she said. "Let's all go fishing."

Nelly did not laugh. She stood still by the table, leaning on it.

"It's all my fault," she said. "If I hadn't found the mine, we shouldn't have had all this trouble."

"Why, child, this isn't trouble," exclaimed her father :

"don't feel so.   Of course we're all a little disappointed."

"A good deal!" interrupted Mrs. March, smiling.

"Yes, a good deal," he continued; "but we won't be unhappy long about it.   We're no worse off than we were before.   And there's one thing: we are very lucky to have got out of it so soon, — before we had put any money into it."

"What does Mr. Kleesman say?" asked Nelly.

"He says that there is a little silver in the ore, but not enough to make it pay to work the mine," replied her father; "and he says that he is more sorry to say this than he has ever been before in his life to say that ore was not good.   I will read you the letter."

Then Mr. March read the whole letter aloud to Nelly. The last sentence was a droll one.   Mr. Kleesman said : —

"I have for your little girl so great love that I do wish she may never have more sorrow as this."

"What does he mean, papa?" asked Nelly.

"Why, he means that he hopes this disappointment about the mine will be the most serious sorrow you will ever know: that nothing worse will ever happen to you," replied Mr. March.

"Oh," said Nelly, "is that it?   I couldn't make it mean any thing.   Well, I hope so too."

"So do I," said Mrs. March.

"And I," said Mr. March.   "And if nothing worse ever does happen to us than to think for a few weeks we have found a fortune, and then to find that we haven't, we shall be very lucky people."

So they all tried to comfort each other, and to con-

ceal how much disappointed they really were; but all
the time, each one of them was very unhappy, and
knew perfectly well that all the rest were too. Mr.
March was the unhappiest of the four. He had made
such fine plans for the future: how he would send Rob
and Nelly to school at the East; build a pretty new
house; have a nice, comfortable carriage; have Billy
and Lucinda come back to live with them; buy all the
books he wanted. Poor Mr. March! it was a very
hard thing to have so many air-castles tumble down all
in one minute!

Mrs. March did not mind it so much, because she
had never from the beginning had very firm faith in
the mine. And for Rob and Nelly it was not nearly so
hard, for they had not made any definite plans of what
they would like to do; and they were so young that
each day brought them new pleasures in their simple
life. Still it was a great disappointment even to them,
and I presume would have made them seem less cheerful and contented for a long time, if something had not
happened the very next day to divert their minds and
give them plenty to think about.

CHAPTER XIV.

AN OLD ACQUAINTANCE.

EVER since they had lived in the valley, it had been Nelly's habit, when she got up in the morning, to go at once to the eastern window in her room and look out at Pike's Peak. She loved the mountain now just as much as she had when she first saw it; and her first thought in the morning always was : —

"I wonder if Pike is clear."

The next morning after Mr. Kleesman's letter came, Nelly slept late. She had been out all the day before with Rob, who had fished far down the creek, and led her a long, hard chase through the grape thickets and wet meadows. They had caught two basketsful of trout, which were pretty heavy to lug home; and both Rob and Nelly were so tired that they went to bed the minute they had eaten supper, and hardly spoke while they were undressing. When Nelly waked, she knew by the light in her room that it must be late. She sprang up and ran to the window. As soon as she looked out, she exclaimed "Why!" and rubbed her eyes and looked again. She could not believe what she saw.

"Rob! Rob!" she called. But Rob was fast asleep, and did not hear her. She slipped her feet into her slippers, and ran into his room (he slept in a tiny room opening out of hers: it was not much bigger than a closet, and only held a little narrow bed and one chair).

"Rob! Rob!" she said, shaking him, "get up! Come look out of the window."

"You let me be," said Rob, sleepily: "what is it?"

"Tents! Rob, tents! Four splendid great tents, right close to the wheat-barn. Do get up! Who do you suppose it is?"

"Tents!" cried Rob, as wide awake in one second as if the house were on fire, "tents! hurrah! I hope it's those men with instruments that came last summer. I'm going right down to see." And Rob bounced out of bed, and began to toss his clothes on at a furious rate. Nelly also made great haste; and, in less time than you would have thought possible, the two children were dressed and out in the lane, walking toward the tents. When they got there, they had had their walk for their pains: the tents were all closed up tight, — not a sign of life about one of them. Rob and Nelly walked round and round, like two little spies, trying to find out some sign by which they could tell what sort of people had come into their territory; but they could not.

"I know one thing," said Rob: "they've got splendid wagons and horses." There were six fine horses grazing in the field; and there was a nice covered carriage, besides the heavy white-topped wagon.

"What do you suppose the other two horses are for?" said Nelly. "They don't have four to draw the wagon: do they?"

"I guess they 're horses to ride," said Rob: "one of them isn't much bigger than a pony. Oh, dear! I think they 're real lazy people not to get up." And Rob and Nelly walked back to the house quite discontented. When they told their mother about the tents, she said: —

"Oh, yes, I know it. The party came late last night, after you had gone to bed. They sent up to the house for milk; they were very tired; they had come all the way from Canyon City. There 's a little lame boy in the party; and the motion of the carriage hurts him. He was quite sick last night, the nurse said."

"Oh!" said Nelly: "poor little fellow! That 's the reason they weren't up, then. I 'm real sorry for him. Can't we go down there, by and by, and see him?"

"Yes, I think so," said her mother: "this afternoon, perhaps."

Rob and Nelly sat down on the barn-doorsteps, and watched the tents. It seemed a long time before anybody stirred. At last, a man came out of the tent which was nearest the barn. He stood still for a minute, looking up and down the valley. Then he gave a great stretch and yawned very loud, and walked off towards the field where the horses were.

"That 's their man," said Rob: "he 's going to water the horses. I mean to go and talk to him."

"Oh, no, don't!" said Nelly: "let 's see who comes out next."

In a few minutes more, there came out of the next tent a stout woman, with a white cap on her head. The cap had thick fluted ruffles all round the front.

"Oh! what a funny cap!" said Rob. "That must be the little boy's mother."

"No," said Nelly, "I don't think so.　I think that's
. the nurse.　Mamma said there was a nurse."

"Oh, yes!" said Rob; "she must be the nurse."

The nurse stood looking, just as the man had, up and
down the valley.　Nobody could see that beautiful view
without wanting to stand still and look at it.

"She's looking at Pike now," said Nelly.　"I wonder if she ever saw such a mountain before."

The woman stood a long time without moving: then
she turned and walked slowly back to the tent.　As she
walked she kept looking back over her shoulder at the
mountains.

"Ah! ah!" said Nelly; "see how she looks at the
mountains!"

"I should think she would," said Rob.　"But I wish
the boy'd come out."

The nurse went into the tent; and presently came
out, bringing a chair all folded up into a flat shape:
this she set down on the ground in the shadow of the
tent, and unfolded it, and kept on unfolding it, till it
was about as long as a lounge.

"Hullo!" said Rob, "what sort of a chair is that?"

"For the sick boy, I guess," said Nelly.　"It's a
kind of bed."

Then the nurse brought out pillows and blankets, and
put them in it, and then she brought out two pretty
bright rugs, and spread them down, one in front of the
chair and one at its side.　Next she brought out a little
table, and set it close to the chair.　On this she spread
a white cloth.

"I guess he's going to have his breakfast on that,"
said Nelly.

Then the woman went into the tent, and did not come back again. In a few minutes another man came out of the tent out of which the first man had come. This man did not look about him at all. He ran to the place where the stove stood, and began making a fire in a great hurry.

"Oh, ho!" cried Rob: "two men! I say, Nell, they must be awfully rich folks. They 've got a cook, and a driver, besides the nurse. I wish that boy 'd come out."

"I guess if he 's sick he won't get up early," said Nelly. "Don't you remember how you used to have to lie in bed when we were at home, Rob?"

"Oh, my! I guess I do!" said Rob. "Wasn't it horrid! I 'd as lieve die as be like that again. I haven't been sick once since we came to Colorado: have I, Nell?"

"No," said Nelly. "Don't you remember you used to say I ought to be sick half the time: it wasn't fair for me not to be sick any and for you to be sick all the time?"

"Did I?" said Rob: "that was real mean of me. I wouldn't say so now."

While they were talking, they suddenly saw the nurse come out again, and call the cook. He went into the tent with her, and, in a moment more, they came out again, bringing in their arms a little boy about Rob's size.

"Oh, goodness!" cried Rob: "can't he walk? Pshaw! I hoped he 'd go fishing with me! He won't be any fun."

"Why, Rob March!" exclaimed Nelly: "you 're a

selfish thing. How 'd you like to be lame like that and not have anybody sorry for you?"

"Why, Nell, I am real sorry for him: I mean I expect I should be if I knew him; but I did hope he 'd go round some with me. I haven't had a boy since we came to Colorado."

Nelly looked hurt.

"I 'm sure I go everywhere that you do," she said. "You don't ever have to be alone."

"I know it, Nell," replied Rob, meekly: "you 're as good as any girl can be, — lots better than most girls; but a boy 's different. You 'd like a girl sometimes yourself: you know you would."

"I wouldn't either," retorted Nelly: "I 'd rather have you than any girl in the whole world."

The little sick boy had sharper eyes than the nurse had. She had not seen the two children sitting on the barn-doorsteps: but the boy spied them in a minute, and said to his nurse: —

"There are a boy and a girl sitting in that barn-door. Give me my opera-glass: I want to see what they 're like."

Then Nelly and Rob saw the boy lift up a round thing to his eyes, and point it at them.

"He 's looking at us, Rob," said Nelly, "through that thing: I saw a gentleman have one in the cars. I shall go away: I don't want him to look at us."

"Stop!" said Rob: "he 's put it down. He 's talking to his nurse."

This is what the boy was saying: —

"Flora, please go across there and ask that boy to come here: I want to see him. Tell him I 'm sick. I want to ask him if there are any birds here, — if he can't get me a lark."

"Now, Master Arthur," the nurse replied, "you just wait till your mamma gets up, and ask her. Perhaps she wouldn't want you to have that boy play with you."

"You go along this minute," said Arthur, beginning to cry: "if you don't I'll cry. You know the doctor said I was not to be crossed in any thing. You go along quick! Stay! you tell them both to come here."

The nurse walked away, muttering under her breath:

"And a fine life ye'll lead them, if ye get them under your thumb, to be sure! It's a thousand pities you ever heard that speech of the doctor's, you poor thing."

"She's coming over here, Rob," said Nelly, as she saw the woman walking in their direction: "what do you suppose she wants?"

"Milk or eggs, I guess," said Rob. "I can get her some splendid fresh eggs right behind this door. Old Spotty's got her nest in there now. The weasels got into her old nest and she won't lay there any more."

When the nurse reached the door, she said very politely to the children: —

"Good morning, children. Do you live here?"

"No, ma'am," said Rob, gravely.

Nelly looked at him indignantly.

"Why, Rob!" she began. But Rob went on: —

"Our oxen and cows and hens live here: we live in the house over yonder."

Nelly laughed out, and so did the nurse.

"You have a droll tongue in your head, my boy," she said. "I came to ask you if you wouldn't come over to the tent there and see Master Arthur. He's in the chair there: see him? He's lame: he can't walk."

“ What 's the matter with him ? ” asked Nelly. “ Was he always lame ? ”

“ Oh, no ! ” said the nurse : “ he got a fall when he was about six years old, and he 's been lame ever since : he 's twelve now. But I must go right back : he don't like to be alone a minute. Will you come across ? ”

Rob looked at Nelly.

“ Mamma said we might go this afternoon,” he said : “ do you think she 'd care if we went now ? ”

“ We 'd better go and ask her,” answered Nelly. “ You tell the little boy we 've gone to ask our mother if we may come,” she said to the nurse, and ran off with Rob to the house as fast as feet could go.

The nurse looked after them, and sighed.

“ Well, those are well-brought-up children, whoso-ever they are, to be found out in this wilderness. Oh, but I 'd like to see Master Arthur run like that.”

Flora had been little Arthur's nurse ever since he was a baby ; and, though she was often out of patience with him, she loved him dearly. When she went back and told him what the children said, he muttered fretfully : —

“ Oh, dear ! they needn't have gone to ask. Can't they go two steps without getting leave ? I should think they were babies. They looked as old as I am.”

“ They 're older, Master Arthur,” replied Flora. “ I think they are as much as thirteen : the girl is, at any rate.”

“ Is the boy nice ? ” asked Arthur.

Flora laughed.

“ He 's funny,” she replied. And then she told Ar-thur what Rob had said when she asked him if he and his sister lived there.

Arthur smiled faintly: he hardly ever laughed. His back ached all the time, so that he could very seldom forget it; and this constant pain made him very nervous and irritable.

"You go up to the house and ask their mother to let them come," he said.

"Well, dear," Flora replied, "I will, if they don't come in a few minutes. But I'm sure they'll come, for they said their mother had told them they might come this afternoon; and I'm sure she'll let them come now instead."

"They can come in the afternoon too," said Arthur. "I want them all the time."

"Well, well: I dare say they'll like to stay with you, and read your books, and see your things, very much," said Flora.

"I'll show them my microscope," said Arthur: "that's the only thing I've got that's good for any thing. The books are no good."

Just now the cook came up, bringing Arthur's breakfast on a tray. It looked very nice: milk-toast, and baked apples, and poached eggs, and a cup of nice cocoa. It was wonderful what good things Ralph used to cook, in that little bit of a camp stove, out of doors. Ralph had lived in the family as long as Flora, and loved poor Arthur just as well as she did. It was into the area in front of the basement that Arthur had fallen when he got his terrible hurt; and Ralph had picked him up and carried him in his arms upstairs, thinking all the way that he was dead. Ralph often said that he'd never forget that time, — not if he should live to be a thousand years old! He often told the story to

people they met on their journeys. Everybody took an
interest in poor Arthur, and wanted to know how he
came to be so lame; but nobody liked to ask his father
or mother: so they would ask Flora or Ralph. Ralph
was an Englishman, and he had a very queer pronuncia-
tion of all words beginning with *h.* He dropped the
h's off such words, and he put it on to other words;
which made his sentences sound very queer indeed.

" It was just about height o'clock," he would say, " an'
I 'd just in my 'and the 'ot water for the master's shaving;
an' Thomas 'ee was a takin' hof it out o' my 'and, when
we 'ears such a screech, such a screech, and the missus
she come a flyin' hover the stairs, — I 'm blessed hif 'er
feet so much as lighted hon 'em, — an' she screechin',
screechin', an' 'ollerin'; an' the same minute I 'ears a
noise to the front o' the 'ouse, an' a perliceman a knockin' at the airy door, an' the missus she got to 't fust;
an' if it wan't a meracle wat was it, for 'er to 'ave come
down two flights o' 'igh stairs in less time than I could
'urry across the 'all? An' I takes Master Harthur out
o' the perliceman's 'ands; an' 'is little 'ead a 'anging
down 's if 't 'a' been snapped off. Oh! if it seemed
one minute afore I got 'im hup to the nursery it seemed
a 'underd years; an' the missus she was never 'erself
again, — not till she died. She allers said as 'ow she 'd
killed 'im 'erself. You see 'ee was all alone with 'er in
'er bedroom, an' she never noticed that 'ee 'ad gone to
the window. She was never 'erself again, — never:
she 'd sit an' look at 'im, an' look at 'im, an' the tears 'd
run down 'er face faster 'n rain. But she couldn't 'old a
candle to this missus, in no respects: not to my way o'
thinkin'. It's a 'ard thing to say of 'er, bein' she 's

dead; but it's my 'onest opinion that she's better in 'eaven than hearth, an' all parties better suited."

This was Ralph's story of the accident, and he told it wherever they went. Every one was much surprised to hear that Mrs. Cook was not Arthur's own mother; for no own mother could have shown more patience and love than she did. She had never left Arthur for a whole day or a whole night since she became his mother; and it seemed as if she really thought of little else except how to invent some new thing to amuse him, and keep him from remembering his pain.

Just as Arthur had begun to eat his breakfast, he looked up and saw Rob and Nelly coming out of the door of the house. He pushed away his plate, and cried : —

"Take it away! take it away! I won't eat another mouthful. That boy and girl are coming. Take it away!"

"Oh, Master Arthur," said Flora : "indeed you must eat some more. You'll never get well if you don't eat."

"I won't! I won't! I tell you take it away," screamed Arthur. "I am not hungry. I hate it!"

Poor Arthur never was really hungry.

"Your mamma will be very unhappy when she comes out if you have not eaten any thing," said Flora.

Arthur's face fell.

"Well, give me the cocoa, then, quick!" he said: "I'll drink that, just to please mamma: that's all. She don't make me eat when I don't want to."

At that moment Mrs. Cook came out of her tent, and hurried to Arthur's chair.

"My darling," she said, "mamma was a lazy mamma, wasn't she, this morning? Have you had a nice breakfast? Papa will be out in a minute."

"Mamma! mamma!" cried Arthur, "see that boy and girl, the other side of the fence: they're coming over to see me. I sent Flora after them. I wish they'd hurry. Don't they walk slow?"

Mrs. Cook looked inquiringly at Flora, who explained that Master Arthur had spied the children sitting in the barn-door, and that nothing would do but she must go over and ask them to come and see him.

"They seem to be most uncommon nice-spoken children for these parts, ma'am," said Flora; "and the little girl she wouldn't come, nor let her brother come, till she'd gone into the house and asked leave of their mother."

Mrs. Cook was gazing very earnestly at the children, as they walked slowly towards the tent. In a moment more she sprang to her feet, and took two or three steps forward, and exclaimed, "Why, it is! it is my little Nelly!" and, to Arthur's great astonishment, he saw his mother run very fast to meet the children, and throw her arms round the little girl's neck, and kiss her over and over again.

Nelly was so astonished and bewildered she did not know what to do. She could not see the face of the lady who was kissing her, for she held her so tight she could not look up; and, when she did look up, she did not at first know who the lady was.

"Why, Nelly, Nelly!" she cried; "have you forgotten me? Don't you remember I came on in the same car with you? Why! I've been looking for you and asking for you all over Colorado."

Then Nelly remembered; but still she looked bewildered.

"Oh, yes! Mrs. Williams. I remember you very, very well," she said; "but you don't look a bit as you used to."

"Come here! come here!" shouted Arthur; "come right here, all of you! Mamma, who is this girl, and what makes you kiss her?"

Arthur had been so long used to being the only child, and having all his mother's affection showered upon him, that he really felt uncomfortable to see her kiss another child.

"Why, Arthur! Arthur!" exclaimed his mother, leading Nelly and Rob towards him; "don't speak so. These are old friends of Mamma's, that she knew before she ever saw you. Don't you recollect my telling you about the little boy in the cars, that threw away the onions, and the little girl that had the nice wax doll all broken in the crowd? These are those very same children; and isn't it wonderful that we should have found them here? I am very glad to see them: Nelly, Rob, this is my little boy, Arthur, and he will be more glad to know you than you can possibly imagine; for he can't run about as you do. He has to lie in this chair all day."

While she was speaking, Arthur had been looking very steadily at Rob. He did not take much notice of Nelly. As soon as his mother stopped speaking, Arthur said to Rob: —

"How do you do? Mamma told me all about your throwing away the man's onions ever so long ago, and I used to make her tell me over and over and over again, till she said it was almost as bad as having onions in the house. Didn't you have fun when you did it?" and Arthur laughed harder than he had been seen to laugh for a long time.

"Why, no!" said Rob; "I don't think it was much fun. I don't remember much about it now; but I know I felt awfully mean: you see I felt like a thief when the man began to look for his onions."

Nelly was standing still, close to her new-found friend. She was thoroughly bewildered; she looked from Mrs. Williams to Arthur, and from Arthur to Mrs. Williams, and did not know what to make of it all: and no wonder. When Mrs. Williams bade Nelly good-by in Denver three years before, she was a thin, pale lady, dressed in the deepest black, and with a face so sad it made you feel like crying to look at her. She wore a widow's cap close around her face, and a long, black veil; and she was all alone with her nurse; and she had no little boy. Now she was a stout, rosy-faced lady; and she wore a bright, dark-blue cloth gown, looped up over a scarlet petticoat; and on her head she wore a broad-brimmed straw hat with scarlet poppies and blue bachelor's buttons round the crown. At last Nelly could not contain her perplexity any longer.

"Oh! Mrs. Williams," she exclaimed; "what does make you so pretty now?"

"That isn't my mamma's name," cried Arthur; "her name is Mrs. Cook. Wasn't she pretty when you saw her in the cars? She's always pretty now."

Mrs. Williams laughed very hard, and told Nelly she did not wonder that she was surprised to see her look so differently.

"I often think, when I look in the glass now," she said, "that I shouldn't know my own self, if I hadn't seen myself since three years ago."

Then she led Nelly to one side, and explained to her that she had met Arthur and his papa up at Idaho Springs, where she had gone immediately after leaving Nelly in Denver. Mr. Cook had taken Arthur there, to see if the water in the Idaho Springs would not cure his lameness. They had all lived in the same hotel at Idaho all winter, and in the spring Mrs. Williams had been married to Mr. Cook, and had thus become Arthur's mother. Mr. Cook's home was in New York; but they had come to Colorado every summer for Arthur's sake. He always was much better in Colorado. While they were talking, Mr. Cook came out of his tent; and surprised enough he looked to see his wife sitting on the ground with a little stranger girl in her lap, and Arthur in eager conversation with a boy he had never seen before. He stood still on the threshold of the tent for a moment, looking in astonishment at the scene.

"Oh, Edward! Edward!" exclaimed Mrs. Cook, "this is my little friend! Think of our having found her at last, way down in this valley!"

"Is it possible!" said Mr. Cook. "Why, I am as glad to see you, my little girl, as if I were your own uncle. I didn't know but I should have to go journeying all about the world, like my famous ancestor, Captain Cook, to find you; for my wife has never given up talking about you since I have known her."

Mr. Cook was so tall and so big Nelly felt half afraid of him. He was as tall as Long Billy, and twice as big: he had a long, thick beard, of a beautiful brown

color, and his eyes were as blue as the sky. Nelly
thought he looked like one of the pictures, in a picture-
book Rob had, of "Three Giant Kings from the North
who came Over the Sea." But when he smiled you
did not feel afraid of him; and his voice was so good
and true and kind that everybody trusted him and liked
him as soon as he spoke.

"Was Captain Cook really an ancestor of yours?"
asked Nelly, eagerly.

"Oh!" cried Rob, bounding away from Arthur, and
looking up with reverence into this tall man's face, "are
you a relation of Captain Cook? Have you got any of
his things? Did you know him? Did he ever tell you
about his voyages? We've got the book about them:
I know everywhere he went."

Mr. Cook lifted Rob up in his arms, and tossed him
over his shoulders, and whirled round with him, and set
him down on the ground again, before he answered.
This was a thing Mr. Cook loved to do to boys of Rob's
size. Boys of that age are not used to being picked
up and tossed like babies; but Mr. Cook was so strong
he could toss a big boy as easily as you or I could a little
baby.

"No, sir, I am not a relative of Captain Cook's, so
far as I know, nor of any other Cook, except of all
good cooks: I am a first cousin and great friend and
lover of all good cooks," shouted this jolly, tall man,
whose very presence seemed like sunshine. "Ralph,
you cook of cooks and for all the Cooks, is our breakfast ready?"

Ralph chuckled with inward laughter as he tried to
answer with a quiet propriety. Long as he had lived

with Mr. Cook, he had never grown accustomed to his droll ways.

Rob and Nelly looked on with amazement. This was a sort of man they had never seen.

"Oh, I wish papa was like this," thought Rob: in the next second he was ashamed and sorry for the thought. But from that moment he had a loving admiration for Mr. Cook, which was about as strong as his love for his own father.

As soon as Mr. and Mrs. Cook had eaten their breakfast, they walked up to the house with Nelly. Rob stayed behind with Arthur, entirely absorbed in the microscope. Nelly's feet seemed hardly to touch the ground: she was so excited in the thought of taking Mrs. Cook to see her mother. She utterly forgot all the changes which the three years had brought to them : she forgot how poor they were, and that her mother was at that moment hard at work churning butter. She forgot every thing except that she had found her old friend, and was about to give her mother a great surprise. She opened the door into the sitting-room, and, crying, "Mamma! mamma! who do you think is here?" she ran on into the kitchen, turning back to Mr. and Mrs. Cook and crying, "Come out here! Here she is!"

Mrs. March looked up from her churning, much astonished at the interruption, and still more astonished to see two strangers standing in her kitchen doorway, and evidently on such intimate terms with Nelly. Mrs. March had on a stout tow-cloth apron which reached from her neck to her ankles ; this was splashed all over with cream. On her head she had a white handkerchief, bound tight like a turban. Altogether she looked

as unlike the Mrs. March whom Mrs. Cook had seen in
the cars as Mrs. Cook looked unlike the Mrs. Williams.
But Mrs. Cook's smile was one nobody ever forgot. As
soon as she smiled, Mrs. March exclaimed : —

" Why, Mrs. Williams ! how glad I am to see you
again. Pray excuse me a minute, till I can take myself
out of this buttery apron : walk back into the sitting-
room."

" No, no ! " laughed Mr. Cook, " I know a great deal
better than that ! I was brought up on a farm. You
can't leave that butter ! Here ! give me the apron,
and let me churn it : it 's twenty-five years since I 've
churned ; but I believe I can do it." And, without
giving Mrs. March time to object, he fairly took the
apron away from her, and tied it around his own neck,
and began to churn furiously.

" Now you two go in and sit down," he said, " and
leave this little girl and me to attend to this butter.
You 'll see how soon I 'll ' bring ' it ! " And indeed he
did. His powerful arms worked as if they were driven
by steam ; and in less than a quarter of an hour the
butter was firm and hard, and Nelly and Mr. Cook had
become good friends. He liked the quiet, grave little
girl very much ; but, after all, his heart warmed most
to Rob, and the greater part of his talk with Nelly was
about her brother.

In the mean time, Mrs. Cook and Mrs. March were
having a full talk about all that had happened. There
was something about Mrs. Cook which made people tell
her all their affairs. She never asked questions or
pried in any way, but she was brimful of sympathy
and kindly intent ; and to such persons everybody goes

for comfort and advice. **Mrs.** March had always remembered her with affectionate gratitude **for** her goodness to Nelly, and she was glad **of the opportunity, even three** years late, to thank **her for that beautiful wax doll.**

"It is as good as new now," she said. "Nelly keeps it rolled in tissue paper, in the box. She does not play with dolls any more, **but it is** still her **chief treasure.**"

"Not play with dolls!" exclaimed Mrs. Cook: "why, she is not fifteen."

"I know it," replied Mrs. March, "but our hard-working life here has made both the children old for their **years**: especially Nelly. She was naturally a thoughtful, care-taking child. Rob is of a more mirthful, adventurous temperament. He has taken the jolly side **of the** life here; but Nelly has grown almost **too** sober and wise. She is a blessed child."

"Yes, indeed, she is," replied Mrs. Cook; "and she was so when I first knew her. I never could forget her earnest face. I want you to let her and Rob too be with us just as much as possible while we are here. We shall stay a month: perhaps six weeks, if it does not grow too cold. We find it is much better for Arthur to stay quietly in one place than it is to move about. He gains much more. Travelling tires him dreadfully."

"I shall be more than glad to have the children with you as much as possible," replied Mrs. March; "but that will not be so much as I could wish: for we are all working very hard now; and two days each week the children go to Rosita, to sell eggs and butter. That is the greater part of our income this summer."

Mrs. March said this in a cheerful tone, and as if it were nothing worth dwelling upon, and Mrs. Cook did not express any surprise; but in her heart she was much grieved and shocked to find that the Marches were so poor, and as soon as she was alone with her husband she told him of it with tears in her eyes.

"Only think, Edward," she said, "of those sweet children going about selling eggs and butter in the town."

Mr. Cook was a very rich man; but his father and his grandfather had been farmers; and in Mr. Cook's early years he had driven the market-wagon into town many a time and sold potatoes and corn in the market. It did not, therefore, seem so dreadful to him as it did to his wife that Rob and Nelly should carry about eggs and butter to sell in Rosita.   Still, he was sorry to hear it, and exclaimed: —

"Do they really? The plucky little toads! That's too bad — for the girl: it won't hurt the boy any!"

"Oh, Edward!" said Mrs. Cook, "you wouldn't like to have Arthur do it."

"No, I wouldn't like to have him do it," replied Mr. Cook: "most certainly I wouldn't like to have him; but that wouldn't prove that it mightn't be better for him in the end if he had to. But fate has taken all such questions as that out of our hands, so far as poor Arthur is concerned." And Mr. Cook sighed heavily. Arthur's condition was a terrible grief to his father. All the more because he was so well and strong himself, Mr. Cook had a dread of physical pain or weakness. Many times a day he looked at his helpless son, and said in his inmost heart: —

"Rather than be like that, I would die any death that could be invented."

It was a mercy that Arthur did not inherit his father's temperament. He was much more like his mother: so long as he could be amused, and did not suffer severe pain, he did not so much mind having to lie still. When Rob said to him, one day: —

"Oh, Arthur, doesn't it tire you horribly to stay in that chair?" Arthur answered: —

"Why, no: it's the easiest chair you ever sat in. You just try it some day. I had one before this that did tire me, though: it was a horrid chair. It wasn't made right; but this is a jolly chair. It's better than the bed."

Rob, who had felt guilty the moment he had asked the question, thinking it was not kind, was much relieved at this answer, and thought to himself: —

"Well, that's lucky. He didn't mind my asking him one bit. I guess it's because he's been sick so long he doesn't remember how it felt to run about."

CHAPTER XV.

CHANGES IN PROSPECT.

I COULD not tell you one half of the pleasant things that happened in the course of the next month to Rob and Nelly. They had such good times that they hardly ever thought of their disappointment about the mine. And even Mr. and Mrs. March thought less and less about it every day, they were so much interested in talking with Mr. and Mrs. Cook. Mr. March and Mr. Cook became good friends very soon. Mr. Cook would often work all day long in the fields with Mr. March. He said it made him feel as if he were a boy again, on his father's farm. The days that Rob and Nelly went to Rosita were very long days to Arthur. He was so lonely that Mrs. Cook proposed to her husband one day that they should let Thomas, the driver, take the children up to town in the carriage, and bring them right back again.

"They need not be gone more than two hours in all," she said. "It is that tiresome walk that takes so long."

But Mr. Cook was too wise to do this.

"That would not be any true kindness to the children," he said. "It is much better that they should keep on with the regular routine of their life, just as they did before. If they were to have the carriage to take them up to town for a month, it would only make the walk seem very long and hard to them after we are gone. We will give them all the pleasure we can, without altering their way of living."

"The mere fact of our being here alters their whole life," said Mrs. Cook. "They have now constant companionship, and a variety of amusements and interests, in Arthur's toys and books, which are all new to them. Before we came, they had solitude, absolutely no amusements, and no occupation except hard work. Nelly told me the other day that she had read every book in their house, twice over."

"There are not very many books," said Mr. Cook: "I don't know how March comes to have so few."

"Oh, they had to sell ever so many last summer: Mrs. March told me so," replied Mrs. Cook.

"By Jove! did they?" exclaimed Mr. Cook. "That was too bad. I wonder if March would take it amiss if I sent him out a box of books this autumn."

"I don't know," Mrs. Cook said thoughtfully. "They haven't a particle of false pride, about their work, or selling things, or any thing of that kind; but I doubt their liking presents. They are very independent."

The weeks slipped by as if they weren't more than three days long. Rob and Nelly got up before daylight every morning, so as to hurry through their work and go down to the tents, — down to "Arthur's," they always called it, as if it were a house. Sometimes they stayed all day, till it was time for Rob to go for the cows. They read, or they played dominoes or chequers or backgammon; or they put dissected maps together; or they looked at all sorts of things under the microscope ; or they painted flowers : this was the nicest thing of all. Mrs. Cook drew and painted beautifully. She had taught Arthur, so that he could paint a little simple flower really very well ; and he had a beautiful paint-box, full of real good paints, such as artists use, — not such as are put in toy-boxes for children. This was the thing Nelly enjoyed best. Then Ralph, the cook, used to go off gunning every day ; and he brought home beautiful birds, and Arthur and Rob used to nail the wings on boards to dry. Arthur had a little table that fitted across his chair, and on this table he could pound pretty hard ; and he made a good many pretty things out of wood. It seemed to Rob that there wasn't any thing in the whole world which Flora could not bring out of the two big black boxes which stood in her tent, and held Arthur's things. As for books, he had fifty : every one of Mayne Reid's. When Rob saw those he was delighted.

"Oh, Arthur ! Arthur ! ain't they splendid ! I 've had ' The Cliff Climbers.' "

" I don't think so," said Arthur. " They 're all about hunting and fighting, and such things."

" Oh, my ! " said Rob, " don't you like that ? That 's just what I like. I 'll read some of 'em to you. I bet you 'd like them." And when Rob read them to him, Arthur really did like them. He could not help sharing Rob's enthusiasm ; but when Rob exclaimed : —

" Oh, Arthur, don't you wish you could go to the Himalayas ? "

Poor Arthur only shuddered, and said : —

" No, indeed ! it shakes you so awfully to go in the cars."

Rob did not ask him again; but he told Nelly at night what Arthur had said, and he added: —

"Say, Nell, if I should **ever get to be like Arthur,** I 'd take poison."

"Why, Rob!" cried Nelly, "that 's awfully wicked! You wouldn't ever dare to!" And Nelly turned pale with fright.

"I expect it is," said Rob; "but I reckon I 'd do it! Why, Nell, I 'd just have to!"

Mrs. Cook sat with the children hours at a time, and listened to their talk and play. She and her husband took a drive or a ride every afternoon; but the rest of the time she did not leave Arthur. The more she saw the influence of Rob and Nelly upon him, the more grateful she felt for the strange chance which had brought them together. Arthur was really growing better. He had more color, more appetite, and very seldom complained of pain. He had something to think of beside himself; and he was happy, — the two best medicines in all the world: they will cure more diseases than people dream.

One day, Flora said to Mrs. Cook: —

"I suppose, ma'am, ye 'll be going soon. There was quite a frost in the north o' the valley last night, Thomas was telling me. They say there 'll be snow here before long."

"Yes, Flora, I suppose we will have to go very soon: week after next, Mr. Cook thinks," replied Mrs. Cook.

Arthur was lying back in his chair, with his eyes shut. They thought he was asleep; but at the sound of these words he opened his eyes, and cried out: —

"I won't go away, mamma! I won't go! You can't

make me. I 'm not going away ever. I 'm going to stay here."

" Why, Arthur dear ! " said his mother, " you wouldn't like to stay here without papa and without me ; and you know papa must go home."

" Yes, I would ! " cried Arthur : " I 've been thinking about it for ever so long. Flora can stay : she can dress and undress me ; and I can live in Mrs. March's house, and sleep in Rob's bed. I asked Nelly, and she said I could. Rob can sleep on the lounge. I shan't go home. I hate New York ; and if you take me back there I 'll get sicker and sicker, and die ; and I don't care if I do, if I can't stay here ! "

Mrs. Cook was grieved and shocked. She had often thought to herself that there was danger that Rob and Nelly would be discontented and lonely when Arthur went away ; but strangely enough she had never thought of any such danger for Arthur. She had often wished she could take Nelly home with her to live ; but she had dismissed it from her mind as an impossible thing. Now she began to think of it again. She sat a long time in silence, turning it over and over.

" Why don't you speak, mamma ? " asked Arthur : " are you angry with me ? "

" No, dear," replied Mrs. Cook : " I am not angry : only very, very sorry ; and I am trying to think what we can do to make you happy when we go away. I shall be very sorry if all our pleasant time here only makes you unhappier after you go home. You were very contented before we came here."

" I don't think I was very, mamma," said Arthur, sadly. " I always wanted a boy or a girl ; and none of the boys and girls in New York cared any thing about me, — only my things; but Nelly is just like my own sister, — at least I guess that's the way sisters are, — and Rob is just like my brother. Mamma, I can't go away! I don't see why you can't leave me. You and papa would come back in the spring. Oh, mamma, let me! let me!" And poor Arthur began to cry.

Mrs. Cook put her arms around him, and laid her face down close to his.

"My darling child!" she said, "haven't papa and I done every thing we possibly could to make you happy always?"

"Yes," sobbed Arthur; "and that's why I think you might leave me here."

"Dear boy, you don't seem to think," said his mother, "how lonely papa and I would be without you."

"Oh, mamma, would you, really? How could you be? I'm only a bother: I can't go round with you or any thing. I think you'd have a great deal better time without me. Perhaps I'd get so I could walk if I stayed here all winter. You know one doctor said I ought to stay a whole year."

"Arthur, dear," said Mrs. Cook, earnestly, "do not talk any more about this now. Promise mamma that you will try not to think about it either; and I promise you I will talk to papa and see what he thinks can be done. All we want in this world is to make you happy, and do what is best for you."

"Will you ask him to let me stay?" cried Arthur.

"I will tell him how you feel about being separated from Nelly and Rob," replied his mother; "and I think we can arrange in some way."

Mrs. Cook had already made up her mind what she would do. She would ask Mrs. March to let Nelly go back with them to New York for the winter. She knew that Mr. Cook would be willing; and she believed that Mrs. March might be persuaded to consent, on account of the advantage it would be to Nelly. But she would not mention this plan to Arthur now, because he would only be all the more disappointed if it failed. Arthur leaned his head back in his chair, and shut his eyes again.

"Oh, dear!" he said, "crying does always make my head ache so!"

"Yes, dear," said his mother, "that is reason enough, if there were no other, why you should try hard to behave like a man always, and never let any little thing upset you enough to make you cry."

"I know it," said Arthur, forlornly; "but you cry before you think you 're going to; and then you can't stop."

As soon as Mrs. Cook was alone with her husband, she told him what Arthur had said.

"I am not at all surprised," he replied: "I have been expecting it."

"Of course it would never do to leave the child here," said Mrs. Cook.

"Of course not," said Mr. Cook. "But I 'll tell you what we might do: take Rob and Nelly home with us for the winter. I think their father and mother would let them go."

"Rob too?" said Mrs. Cook.

"Rob too!" echoed Mr. Cook. "Why, if I could have but one Rob would be the one; but if we take one we 've got to take both : you might as well propose to separate the Siamese twins."

" I was thinking of proposing to take Nelly," said Mrs. Cook. " I don't see how Mrs. March could spare them both."

" She could easier let them both go than have one left behind to pine. I don't know but it would kill them to be apart from each other. I don't see, though, how you can prefer Nelly to Rob?"

" And I don't see how you can prefer Rob to Nelly," answered Mrs. Cook : " as a companion for Arthur, Nelly is twice as good as Rob."

" Does Arthur like her better?" asked Mr. Cook.

" Yes, I think he does," replied Mrs. Cook : " he seems to lean on her. He is very fond of Rob, too. He said to-day that they were just like his sister and brother."

" Let us go down to-night and ask Mr. and Mrs. March about it," said Mr. Cook. " The sooner it is settled the better. If Arthur has got this crotchet in his head about staying, he won't be easy a minute."

After tea, Mr. and Mrs. Cook walked down to the house, and proposed the plan. At first, Mr. March said no, most decidedly. But Mrs. March begged him to consider the thing, and not decide too hastily.

" Think what a splendid thing it would be for the children," she said.

" But think what a desolate winter you would have here without them," said Mr. March.

" Oh, no, not desolate!" said Mrs. March : " not desolate with you here. Nelly would write every week. The winter would soon pass away. And, Robert, they may never have another such opportunity in their lives. I think it would be wrong for us to refuse it for them."

"Why not consult them?" said Mr. Cook.

"I know beforehand what they would say," answered Mr. March. "Nelly would say stay here, and Rob would say go. No: we must decide the question ourselves; and Mrs. March is right: we ought not to decide too hastily. We will let you know in the morning."

"You understand, I hope," said Mrs. Cook, "that it is a very great favor, for sake of our helpless boy, that we ask it. It is really asking you to give up your two children for a time, just to make our one happy."

"I understand that," replied Mr. March; "but you must know that it is also a very great obligation under which we lay ourselves to you. I feel it to be such, and I confess I shrink from it: I can never repay it."

"Nonsense!" said Mr. Cook. "The obligation is all on our side; and if you had ever had a poor helpless child like Arthur, you could realize it. Why, March, I'd give all my fortune this moment, and begin at the bottom and make it all over again, if I could see Arthur well and strong as your Rob." And the tears filled Mr. Cook's eyes, as he shook hands with Mrs. March, and bade her good-night.

Mr. and Mrs. March talked nearly all night before they could come to a decision about this matter. It was a terrible thing to them to look forward to a whole winter without the children. But Mrs. March continually said: —

"Robert, suppose we never have another chance to give either of them such an opportunity of pleasure and improvement as this. How shall we feel when we look back? We should never forgive ourselves."

So it was decided that the children should go.

In the morning Mrs. March said to Nelly : —

" You 'll miss Arthur when he goes : won't you ? "

Nelly hesitated, and finally said : —

" Arthur says he won't go ! "

" Won't go ! " exclaimed Mrs. March : " what does he mean ? "

" He is going to ask his father to ask you to let him stay here with us," replied Nelly. " I thought he might sleep in Rob's bed. Rob says he 'd just as soon sleep on the lounge ; and I thought you 'd be willing. He 's such a poor dear ! I could take all the care of him."

" Would you really like to have him ? " said Mrs. March.

" Oh, yes, indeed, mamma, ever so much ! I love him as well as I do Rob, — almost : not quite, I guess, because he isn't my own brother ; but it is so hard for him to be sick, that makes me love him more."

" Mr. and Mrs. Cook came down here last night to ask us to let you and Rob go back to New York with them for the winter," said Mrs. March, very quietly, watching Nelly's face as she spoke.

It turned scarlet in one second, and the voice was almost a shriek in which Nelly cried out : —

" Oh, mamma ! how perfectly splendid ! Can we go ? "

Then in the very next second she said : —

" But you couldn't spare us : could you ? You couldn't stay here all alone." And her face fell.

" Yes, I think we could spare you ; and we have said you might go," said Mrs. March, smiling.

Nelly's arms were round her mother's neck in one moment, and she was kissing her and half laughing and half crying.

"Oh, mamma! mamma!" she said, "I can't tell whether I am glad or sorry. I don't want to go away from you; but oh! if you only could hear Arthur tell of all the beautiful things in New York! Oh! I don't know whether I am sorry or glad!"

But Mrs. March knew very well that she was glad, and this made it much easier for her to bear the thought of the separation.

If Nelly, the quiet Nelly, were as glad and excited as this, how do you suppose the adventurous Rob felt, when he heard the news? The house wouldn't hold him. He had to run out and turn summersaults on the grass. Then he raced off down to the tents, and told Flora and Ralph and Thomas. It was early in the morning, and Arthur was not up. All the servants were glad. They all liked Rob and Nelly, and they all saw how much better Arthur had grown since he had had children to play with.

"Ah, Master Rob," said Thomas, "just wait till I drive ye all out in the Park: that's a place worth looking at, — all beautiful green grass, and lakes, and roads as smooth and hard as a beach, and groves of trees, — not like this bare wilderness, I can tell ye."

"Are there mountains there, Thomas?" asked Rob.

"Mountains! no! The Lord be praised: never a mountain!" exclaimed Ralph; "and if ever I 'm thankful for any thing, it is to get out of sight of the ugly sides of 'em!"

"Oh, Ralph!" was all Rob could say at hearing such an opinion of mountains.

When Flora and Thomas brought **Arthur** out of the tent, Rob ran towards them.

" Oh, Arthur — " he began.

" I know all about it," said Arthur : " Nelly and you are going home with us. I 'd rather stay here, but they won't let me ; **and** having you go **home with us** is next best."

Rob thought **this was** rather an ungracious way for Arthur to speak, and so it was.

" You wouldn't like it here in the winter **half so** well as you **do now, Arthur,"** he said. " **It** 's awfully cold sometimes ; and real deep snow. You 'd be shut up in the house **lots."**

" So I am at **home,"** said Arthur : " weeks and weeks."

" But your house is nicer to be shut up in than **ours,"** continued **Rob.**

" I don't care," said Arthur : " I wanted to stay. But I 'm real glad you and Nelly are going. Can Nelly skate ? We 'll **go and see** her skate in the Park."

" No, she can't ; but I **can,"** said **Rob.** " Is there good skating there ? "

" Oh, goodness, Rob ! " exclaimed Arthur, " didn't you know about the skating in Central **Park? Well,** you 'll see ! We drive up there every pleasant day. I 'm sick of it. But the skating 's some fun : I wish I could skate."

" Perhaps you 'll get strong enough **to,** pretty **soon,"** said **Rob,** sympathizingly.

" If they 'd let me stay here I might," said Arthur, fretfully ; " but they won't."

The nights grew cool so fast that Mr. and Mrs. **Cook**

began to be impatient to set out for home. At first, Mr. and Mrs. March pleaded with them to stay longer; but one morning Mrs. March said suddenly to her husband : —

" Robert, I 've changed my mind about the children's going : I think the sooner they go the better. It is just like having a day set for having a tooth pulled : you suffer all the pain ten times over in anticipating it. I can't think about any thing else from morning till night. Oh, I do hope we haven't done wrong !"

" It isn't too late yet to keep them at home," said Mr. March. " Don't let us do it if your mind is not clear. I don't think Nelly more than half wants to go now."

" Oh, yes, she does !" replied Mrs. March. " She is so excited in the prospect that she talks in her sleep about it. I heard her, last night."

" The dear child !" said Mr. March. " It was Nelly that they really wanted most."

" Not at all," said Mrs. March, quickly : " Mr. Cook told me that he would have only asked for Rob, but he knew the children could not be separated."

" Well, that 's odd," said Mr. March. " Mrs. Cook told me that she had been long thinking that she wished she could have Nelly, but she knew it would be out of the question to separate the children."

Mrs. March laughed.

" I see," she said : " they disagree about the children, just as you and I do. Mrs. Cook likes Nelly best, and Mr. Cook likes Rob."

" Why, Sarah !" exclaimed Mr. March, " what do you mean? We love the children just alike."

" Yes, perhaps we love them equally," replied Mrs.

March ; " but we don't like them equally. I like Rob's ways best, and you like Nelly's. It's always been so, ever since they were born. You'll see Nelly will make a good, loving, lovable woman ; but Rob will make a splendid man. Rob will do something in the world : you see if he does not!"

Mr. March smiled.

" I hope he will," he said. " But as for my little Nelly, I wouldn't ask any thing more for her than to be, as you say, ' a good, loving, lovable woman.' "

CHAPTER XVI.

"GOOT-BY AND GOOT LUCK."

WHEN Nelly heard that they were to set out in three days, she exclaimed : —

"Why, I didn't bid Ulrica good-by, or Mr. Kleesman, or Billy and Lucinda. I thought we weren't going for two weeks. Mayn't I go up to-morrow, mamma? I can sell some eggs, too, even if it isn't the regular day. Ever so many people ask me for them always. Hardly anybody keeps hens in Rosita."

Mrs. March said she might go. So, very early the next morning, Nelly set off on her last trip to Rosita. Billy was standing in his doorway as she passed.

"Hullo, Nelly! Where 's Rob?" he said.

"Rob 's at home with Arthur," she replied. "He didn't want to come. I only came to bid everybody good-by. We 're going day after to-morrow."

"Be yer?" said Billy, slowly. "Be yer glad, Nelly?"

"Why, yes, Billy, I can't help being glad; and for all that, it makes me cry when I think about going away from mamma and papa. Isn't that queer?" said Nelly: "I 'm glad, and yet it makes me cry."

"No, 'tain't queer," said Billy : "'twould be queerer if ye didn't. Ain't Rob goin' to bid anybody good-by?"

" Oh, he 'll have time when we go by, the day we go," said Nelly. " We 're all coming up to Rosita to sleep to-morrow night at the hotel ; and then papa and mamma and Rob and I are going in the stage to Canyon City. There isn't room for any more in Mr. Cook's carriage. Perhaps Rob 'll go in the wagon with Ralph and Thomas. He wants to ; but mamma wants to see all of him she can."

" That 's just the difference between them two children, Luce," said Billy, after Nelly had walked on : " Rob he 's all for himself, without meanin' to be, either ; he jest don't think : but Nelly she 's 's thoughtful 's a woman about everybody."

" I donno why you say 's thoughtful 's a woman, Billy," said Lucinda. " I 've seen plenty of women that was as selfish as any men ever I see."

" Well, I expect that 's so, Luce," said Billy. " You ought to know, bein' a woman."

Nelly went first to Ulrica's. Ulrica listened with wide open mouth and eyes to the news that she would see Nelly no more all winter. At first, her face was very sad ; but in a few moments she said : —

" Bah ! shame me to be sorry. It are goot ! goot ! Ulrica vill be glad. Ven you come back ?"

" Early next summer," replied Nelly. " Mr. Cook always comes to Colorado in June."

Ulrica ran to the big oak-chest, and opening it took out the blue skirt and red bodice she had been making for Nelly.

" See ! it are not done : that goot-for-not'ing Sachs he promise, promise, all de time promise to make buttons."

"What is it, Ulrica?" asked Nelly.

"Oh, you not know? It are gown, — Swede gown for you: like mine child." And she ran for the picture-book of costumes, and pointed to one like it.

Nelly was much pleased.

"Oh! how good of you, Ulrica!" she said. "Mrs. Cook would love to see me put that dress on, I am sure. I will wear it sometimes in the house, when I am in New York, to remind me of you."

"I get buttons to-day!" said Ulrica, fiercely. "I stay by dat Sachs till he cut dem. It are not work: he do it in five minnit. You come again to-night: it are done."

Mrs. Clapp and Mr. Kleesman were both very much pleased to hear that Nelly was going away with Mr. and Mrs. Cook. Mrs. Clapp kissed her, and said: —

"Good-by, dear! You are a brave little girl, and deserve to have a nice, long play-spell; and I am glad you are going to have one. Wait a minute, and I will give you something to wear on your journey." Then she ran upstairs, and brought down a nice leather belt with a pretty little leather bag hanging from it, just big enough to hold a purse. "There, that is to keep your purse in, and your railroad ticket," she said, and fastened it around Nelly's waist.

Mr. Kleesman also kissed Nelly, and said he was glad she was going.

"You haf earn that you haf playtime," he said. "You haf vork all summer like von voman more as von little girl."

"I wonder why they all say such things to me," thought Nelly. "I am sure I don't know what I have done. If they mean selling the eggs, that was only fun."

"Do you mean selling the eggs, sir?" asked honest Nelly. "That was not work: it was just fun. Rob and I never had such a good time before. We would have liked to come every day."

Mr. Kleesman nodded.

"I know! I know!" he said. "You are not like American childs." Then he asked: —

"And vat do become of the Goot Luck mine? I not hear not'ing since."

"Oh!" said Nelly, "we have almost forgotten about the old mine. It wasn't 'good luck:' was it? But Mr. Scholfield keeps on working at it now. He will not give up that it is not good for any thing."

"I say not, it are wort not'ing," replied Mr. Kleesman: "I say it not pay to work it. It cost too much for so little silver as come out."

"Yes, sir; papa understood that," said Nelly; "and he was very much obliged to you indeed; and so we all were."

Then Mr. Kleesman said: —

"Come in! come in! Can you to vait von little? I make for you silver rose, that you carry viz you."

"Oh, thank you!" said Nelly; and followed him in, wondering much what he meant by a silver rose.

Then he took out of the glass box, where the brass scales were, a little saucer, full of tiny silver beads like pin-heads. These he folded up in a bit of paper, shaped like a little cocked hat. This he put into one of the little clay cups, and set it in the glowing red-hot oven. Pretty soon Nelly looked in. The silver was boiling and bubbling in the little cup; the bubbles looked like shining silver eyes on the red; then there came beautiful rainbow colors all over it.

"See you it haf colors like rainbow?" said Mr. Kleesman: "ven dey come it are almost done."

In a second more he took out the cup: set it on the iron anvil: there was a fiery line of red around the silver button: the button was about the size of a three-cent piece.

"Vatch! vatch!" cried Mr. Kleesman: "in one second it burst."

Sure enough, in one second the round button burst in the middle, and the hot silver gushed up like a little fairy fountain of water, not more than quarter of an inch high: in the same instant it fell, cooled, and there was a sort of flower, not unlike a rose, of frosted silver.

"Dere! ven you are in New York, you can take dis to jeweller, and he put pin on it; and you shall vear it, and tell to all peoples you haf seen it ven it vas made by old man in de Colorado mountains."

Nelly took the pretty thing in her hands and looked at it with delight. She had never had any thing so pretty, she thought; and she thanked Mr. Kleesman again and again, as she bade him good-by.

"Oh, I see you again: I see you ven you go in stage. I not say good-by to-day," he said, and looked after her lovingly as she ran down the steps.

Ulrica had a stormy time of it with Sachs, the tin-man, before she could get him to cut out the make-believe buttons for Nelly's gown. He was at work on a big boiler, and he did not want to stop. Ulrica's broken English grew so much more broken when she was angry, that hardly any one could understand her; and Wilhelm Sachs, who was a German, knew English very little better than Ulrica: so between them they made sad work of it.

"I stamp my foot at him," said Ulrica, telling Nelly the tale: "I stamp at him my foot, and I take out of his hand his big hammer vat he pound, pound viz all time dat I am speak, so dat he not hear my speak. I take out his hand, and I frow down on floor; and I say, 'I not stir till you my buttons haf cut for mine child;' and ven he see I not stir, he take tools and he cut, cut, cut, and all the time he swear at my; he call my 'tam Swede woman;' but I not care. And here are gown: now you come in and put on."

So Nelly went in, and Ulrica helped her to undress. When she saw Nelly's white neck, she stooped down and kissed her, and said: —

"Mine child haf white skin: like your skin."

The red bodice fitted Nelly very well; and she looked lovely in it. It had a low collar, all covered with the shining tin buttons; and in the front there was a square space of white muslin, and the tin buttons were sewed on all round this. The blue petticoat was too long: it lay on the ground two inches or more. Ulrica looked at it dismayed.

"Ach!" she said: "ach! you haf not so tall I tink. I make him now in von little more as short." And down on the floor she sat, and hemmed up the skirt in a wonderfully quick time.

"Ach! if you vait till Jan see you in dis," she said, looking imploringly at Nelly, with tears running down her face. "You are mine child, mine child!"

But Nelly knew that Jan would not be at home till six o'clock, and she could not stay so long. So she took off the pretty costume, and kissed Ulrica, and thanked her many times over; and set off for home with all her presents safe-packed in her basket.

When Rob saw the presents, he said : —

"Oh, my! I wonder if they'd all have given me things too, if I'd gone up. Did they say any thing about me?"

"They asked why you didn't come," replied Nelly; "and I told them you meant to bid them good-by to-morrow, when we started on the journey."

"All right!" said Rob: "if they've got any thing for me they can give it to me then."

"I never thought of their giving me any thing," said Nelly: "I wonder what made them."

"Because they all know that you love them, Nelly," said her father: "don't you?"

"Yes, I think so," said Nelly, hesitatingly: "almost love them, — not quite, I guess: except Ulrica. I love her dearly."

"And Lucinda and Billy," added Rob. "I love them best of all. I don't love any of the rest. You can't love everybody."

At sunset the next night, the March house was shut up; the tents were all gone; the whole place looked deserted and silent. Everybody had gone: Mr. and Mrs. Cook and Flora and Arthur in the carriage; Ralph and Thomas and Rob in the white-topped wag-on; and Mr. and Mrs. March and Nelly in Mr. Schol-field's buggy, which he had lent them. They drove up to Rosita in time to see the sunset from the top of the hill. Nelly looked at the mountains as they changed from blue to purple and from purple to dusky gray: she did not speak. At last her mother said:—

"You won't forget how the mountains look: will you, Nelly?"

"Not a bit more than I'll forget how you and papa look!" said Nelly: "not a bit!"

After tea, Rob went to bid Mrs. Clapp and Mr. Kleesman and Ulrica and Jan good-by. Everybody spoke very cordially to him, and hoped he would have a good time; but nobody gave him any thing, and Rob was a good deal disappointed. He said nothing about it when he came home: he was ashamed to. But Nelly knew how he felt, just as well as if he had told her; and in her good little heart she was very sorry for him.

"Mamma," she said, "isn't it too bad that none of them gave Rob any thing, when they gave me all those nice things?"

"Yes, I'm sorry," said Mrs. March; "but he has not been here so much as you have,—that is the reason: and he is so happy in the prospect of his journey, he will not mind it."

The stage from Rosita to Canyon City set off at seven o'clock in the morning. When it drove up to the hotel door, Mr. and Mrs. March and Rob and Nelly were all ready, sitting on the piazza. While they were getting in, Mr. Kleesman's door opened, and he came running up, with his red cotton cap still on his head: in his hurry he had forgotten to take it off. He looked so droll that even Nelly laughed; and this reminded him of his night-cap.

"Ach!" he said, and snatched it off and crammed it into his pocket.

In a moment more, who should come hurrying up the hill but Jan and **Ulrica;** and, behind them, Billy and **Lucinda.** Billy and Lucinda had come up to town the night before, and slept at Lucinda's father's house, so **as to be on hand to see** Nelly and Rob off.

None of the Cook family were **up.** Their horses **would go so much faster** than the stage horses, they were **not** going **to set out until noon.** Ralph and Thomas had started with **the** heavy wagon **at** daylight.

There **were no other** passengers to **go in** the stage **except the Marches:** so the driver did not hurry them; and, after **they had** taken their seats, Jan **and** Ulrica **and Billy and** Lucinda all crowded around, saying last words.

Ulrica had brought two great bouquets of purple and white asters and golden-rod, the **only** flowers that were then in bloom.

"Dese are for you," she **said to the children;** but, **when** they reached out their **hands to** take them, she shook her head, and said: **"No, I frow dem:** it haf **luck to frow dem."**

Lucinda had brought a little parcel in which **were two** knit scarfs, which **she had** knit herself: one white **and one red.** The red one was for Rob and the white **one for Nelly, she said.** They were very pretty. Billy brought a knife for Rob: a capital knife, one with **four** blades. Rob's face **flushed with pleasure.**

"Why, Billy," he said, "how 'd you know I 'd lost my knife?"

"Oh, I found out," said Billy. The truth was, that Billy had walked all the way down to the tents, a few days before, and asked Ralph and Flora if they knew of any thing Rob wanted; and Flora told him how Rob had lost his knife that very day, — had dropped it in the creek, while he was cutting willows to make whistles of. After Billy had given Rob the knife, he pulled out of his pocket a little parcel done up in white paper, and handed it to Nelly, saying: —

"I donno 's it 'll be of any kind o' use to yer; but I thought 'twas kind o' putty."

Nelly opened the paper. It held a queer little scarlet velvet pincushion, in a white ivory frame, which was made so that it could screw on a table.

"Oh, how pretty!" said Nelly. "Thank you, Billy. I 'll keep it on my table all winter."

Mr. Kleesman stood behind the others. He smiled and bowed, and said to Mr. March: —

"You haf goot day. The sun shine on your journey."

"Yes," said Mr. March. "I 'm afraid it will not shine so bright when we come back without these little people."

"No, dat it vill not," said Mr. Kleesman. "Dat it vill not."

"Well," said the driver, gathering up the reins in his left hand, and lifting his whip, "I guess we 'll have to be movin' along, if you 're ready, sir."

"All ready," said Mr. March.

The driver cracked his whip, and the horses started off on a run, up the hill.

"Good-by! good-by!" shouted Rob and Nelly, leaning out.

"Goot-by!" cried Ulrica, and flung both her bouquets into the stage, into Mrs. March's lap, and Nelly's.

"Good-by! good-by!" cried Billy and Lucinda.

"Goot-by!" cried Mr. Kleesman; "and goot luck go with you."

"That's jest what will go with that Nelly wherever she goes," said Billy, turning to Mr. Kleesman.

"You haf known the child?" asked Mr. Kleesman.

"Well, yes," said Billy, leisurely, "I may say I know her. I brought 'em here, three years ago last spring; an' me 'n' my wife we lived with 'em goin' on a year. Yes, I know 'em. There ain't any nicer folks in this world; but Nelly she's the pick o' the hull on 'em. She ain't no common child; she ain't, now. She hain't minded no more about that mine o' hern, — that mine she found, — I suppose you 've heered all about it —"

"Yes, I know," said Mr. Kleesman.

"Well," continued Billy, "nobody but me knows how that little gal's heart was set on to thet mine. She 'd come an' stand by the hour an' see me work in it. I worked there long o' Scholfield some six weeks: we was all took in putty bad. She 'd come an' stand an' look an' look, and talk about what her father·'n' mother could do with the money: never so much 's a word about any thing she 'd like herself; an yet I could see her hull heart was jest set on it. And yet 's soon 's 'twas clear an' sartin that the mine wan't good for any thing, she jest give it all up; and there hain't never come a com-plainin' or a disapp'inted word out o' her mouth. 'Twas her own mine too, — and after her namin' it and all. I 've seen many a man in this country broken all up by no worse a disappointment than that child had. She 's been jest a lesson to me: she has. I declare I never go by the pesky mine without thinking o' the day when

she danced up and sez she, ' I 'll name it!   I 'll name it
" The Good Luck!" ' "

" Ach, vell!" said Mr. Kleesman, " she haf better
than any silver mine in her own self. She haf such
goot-vill, such patient, such true, she haf always ' goot
luck.' She are ' Goot Luck mine' her own self."

Cambridge: Press of John Wilson & Son.